THE BLIGHT ON THE DEEP WOODS

A KELLAN OAKES NOVEL

DALE W GLASER

Lycan Valley Press Publications
1002 N Meridian STE 100-153
Puyallup, Washington 98371
United States of America

First Edition

ISBN-13: 978-1-64562-036-5

This book is dedicated to all the kids who played in the woods, eating wild mint, talking to ladybugs, looking for tunnels to fairyland under the roots of trees.
I hope there are always green places out there for kids of all ages, for exploration and inspirations.

The Blight on the Deep Woods

CHAPTER ONE: A DAY'S WORK

I DUG DEEP into my pocket, pulled out the contents, and poked them around my palm. One small screw I had found on the floor of my office a few days earlier and still hadn't managed to identify the origin of, one ring of iron an inch wide with nine strands of red thread crisscrossing its interior which I hoped I wouldn't need any time soon, one crumpled gum wrapper, and one quarter. I read the parking meter:

MAX TWO HOUR PARKING

15 MIN PER 25 CENTS.

Fifteen minutes it would have to be, then. I dropped my quarter in the slot, pushed the screw and the sprite trap back into my pocket, and rolled the gum wrapper into a tiny ball as I climbed the steps of the courthouse.

I knew the way to Irina's office by heart, and her door was open. I poked my head through her door and said, "Excuse me, who do I need to see about legally changing my name to Doctor Funkenstein?"

"Impersonating a doctor is a misdemeanor punishable by up to twelve months in jail," Irina said without looking away from her monitor.

"It's an honorary doctorate," I said. "From the school of fools too cool for school."

Irina finally looked at me, if only so that I could appreciate the full effect of her well-rehearsed eyeroll. "What's going on, Kellan?"

"There's a hearing scheduled for next Thursday," I said, tossing the gum wrapper over her desk and into her garbage can. "Judge Porter, insurance claim on arson? You gotta reschedule it."

"Why?"

"Because I'm supposed to be there to testify, but I'm going to be indisposed."

"Oh?" she arched an eyebrow above the frames of her glasses. "Going to a big wolfman convention? Or is an alien mothership going to touch down somewhere?"

Irina had once asked me how I had managed to solve a case that the police were ready to bury, and I had answered that a little bird told me, which was the absolute truth. Sometimes it's helpful for a private investigator to be able to draw on the fact that his mother is a druid priestess, one who taught him how to speak basic arboreal and one whose reputation amongst the forest folk earns her son the occasional favor by association. Sometimes it's equally helpful for the private eye to be on the best possible terms with the county court clerk, and I had hoped the honesty would facilitate the rapport I was trying to build with Irina. She was skeptical, so I had doubled down and told her a few other stories about gnomes and sylphs and woodwoses, which only compounded my initial mistake. Irina came away thinking I was a delusional weirdo who believed in fairies and monsters and stealth invasions from intergalactic civilizations, basically everything rational common sense denies the existence of, right or wrong. The jury is still out on alien intelligence, because while I think it's a longshot we're the only life in the universe, I don't have any firsthand experience with any creatures that didn't originate on earth. Hollywood werewolves aren't real either, but I know which parts of the lore trace their origins to legit forest folk. And fae constitute some of my most profitable clientele; just the month before I had helped track down a runaway buggane for an old knacker, and even factoring in the extra time required to find a discrete dealer willing to exchange the empyreal gold the knacker paid me with for cash, and the processing fee, I still came away feeling well compensated.

I was long past the point of splitting hairs with Irina about the differences between supernatural fantasies and natural realities that the modern world has turned a blind eye to. "It's alien wolfmen. Don't tell anyone, I don't want to start a panic. But you can see how I'm in a bind and can't reschedule my thing, so I need you to reschedule the Judge Porter thing. Come on, I'll owe you one."

Irina exhaled slowly through her nose. She was

probably five years younger than me but could summon up long-suffering matriarchal disapproval and disappointment in a blink. If she hadn't gone into civil service, she would have made a fantastic life coach for people with too much self-esteem who needed to be reminded how insignificant they really were. "You already owe me one for pulling those records for you a couple of months ago."

"All right, so I'll owe you two." I probably owed her six or seven, including a major organ and possibly my hypothetical firstborn child. Part of me wanted Irina to hurry up and start calling in favors so that our professional relationship might start to have a bit more quid pro quo to build on. But people generally come to me for help when they're already in trouble and out of good options, and I honestly didn't want to wish that kind of strife on her. I never wished it on anybody, come to that.

She turned back to her computer. For a second I thought she was ignoring me and I would have to find a new angle of attack, but she opened a calendar window and asked "How far off did you want to reschedule?"

"I just need a week," I said. "The 28th or any time after will work."

She nodded as she manipulated the schedule with her mouse. "I can move it to the 29th but it's going to have to be at… seven in the morning."

I winced on the inside but refused to let it show. "Right. Seven a.m. the 29th. Perfect. I'll bring coffee."

"I prefer lattes," she said, then looked sidelong at me. "But don't think a three dollar drink counts against what you owe me."

"Fair enough, just consider it a thank you," I said. For all I knew, she was planning on hoarding up a dozen markers of credit with me and cashing them in one fell swoop. I'd deal with that when it came time to deal with it.

"Have fun on your thing. Tell the were-aliens I said hello," she said. I declined to tell her that those would be aliens that could change into adult human males, not wolves. Instead, I let myself out of her office.

In the hallway, a typical mix of people were standing and talking or walking from one location to another, lawyers and litigants, permit applicants and paper pushers. At the far end of the hall, a swatch of bright correctional facility orange caught my eye, a bald prisoner flanked by police escorts on either side. It wasn't just the color that drew my attention, it was the sudden movement, as the inmate chose that exact moment to make a break for it. One second the prisoner was walking between the cops, the next he had dropped his center of gravity and thrown all his weight into the officer to his left, who happened to be female and the smaller of the two guards. I thought her name was Alvarez, recognizing her from a case I had worked a couple years ago. The inmate drove Alvarez sideways into the beige brick wall, and caught off-balance Alvarez wasn't able to stop her head from snapping sideways and hammering the surface. Highly unlikely, a lucky shot for the perp in orange, but one he was more than ready to capitalize on. Alvarez's knees buckled and as she went down her male partner's instinctive reaction was to look to her to make sure she was all right. The prisoner took advantage of that distraction and headbutted the male cop on the bridge of his nose. That looked more like a practiced move, one no doubt perfected in countless brawls. Blood exploded from the cop's nose as he reeled backwards, and the inmate turned and ran. Right toward me.

I didn't become a private investigator because I harbored unfulfilled dreams of being an officer of the law. If anything, I have enough problems with the way laws are enforced, or not as the case may be, that I thought I could do some good as an alternative people could turn to aside from the police. And that's not even getting into the fact that a ton of what police do today is bust people on dealing and possession charges, and my stance on the war on drugs is about what you'd expect it to be from someone raised by a druid priestess who gave him his first hallucinogens before he turned ten. That doesn't mean I like seeing the police getting roughed, but I generally wouldn't get involved, either, particularly when something intruded on my day with no context, with no way of knowing if the human being in the dehumanizing orange jumpsuit was Hannibal Lecter or Jean Valjean.

I did get a good look at said human being as he barreled down the courthouse hallway, though, and I saw two things. One was the look in the man's eyes. It may sound like the worst kind of New Age-y aura-huffing twaddle, but there's more than a grain of truth in the metaphor about windows to the soul. The prisoner's gaze wasn't wracked with guilt or blazing with the outrage of a miscarriage of justice. It was pure rage, indiscriminate and barely sentient, the effect only heightened by the surrounding flecks of scarlet drawn from the cop's smashed nose.

The other thing I saw was the inmate's prominent neck tattoo, or rather the portion of a tattoo which curved up across his neck and probably took up his entire chest. It was the Black Sun, zigzag rays inside a thick inked circle, a piece of iconography heavily favored by neo-Nazis. I can see both sides of everything from boosting car stereos to selling smack, but I've got no patience for white supremacist wannabes.

I didn't want to draw attention to myself, which wasn't hard given that most people were staring at the charging prisoner or looking for their best path out of the way. Still, I put on a show of looking like I was paralyzed by fear and indecision, not sure which way I should move to avoid the imminent collision. I made it look like I hesitated a half-second too long and got clipped by the skinhead, and as I spun to the side I kicked out at the side of the prisoner's knee. I heard a crack as he sprawled to the floor, unable to stop himself since his wrists were still handcuffed.

Alvarez and her partner had recovered by then, and other cops had materialized in the hallway, summoned by the noise and commotion, so the prisoner was surrounded by the time he got dragged to his feet. He cursed furiously as he limped along in the center of six police officers. While the entourage moved toward the courtroom once again, I looked around, hoping that maybe the commotion would have gotten Irina's attention and drawn her out of her office. If she had seen my act of selfless valor, she might be more favorably inclined to help me out in the future. But of course she was nowhere to be seen, presumably considering the low-level bedlam nothing more than background noise. I made an unobtrusive exit.

Somehow I still managed to make it back to the curb with five minutes left on the parking meter. I got into my battered gray Corolla and left the courthouse behind, one morning task complete, one to go.

I had arrived at the courthouse early, hoping to catch Irina while she was fresh and even-keeled, before the daily grind made her less disposed to do me any favors. The real reason I had needed to reschedule my arson case testimony was so prosaic I had no reason at all to hide it from Irina, except in the interest of maintaining my crackpot mystique in her eyes. My calendar was booked because my old friend Juvenal Braga was coming to visit for a week.

Juvie and I went back all the way to freshman orientation at Central Oregon College, or at least that's when we had met, living on the same dormitory hall. It takes a while for eighteen year old males acclimating to the whole campus lifestyle to forge friendships, and that goes double for someone like me who had been homeschooled until age twelve and barely had the hang of passing for normal by the time he graduated from high school. Juvie was a genuinely good guy, though, and we bonded over the course of first year thanks to common interests, surprisingly similar family backgrounds (extremely condensed version: his grandmother was a witch, or at least someone who believed in witchcraft), and the first of several shared experiences with the deeply weird (story for another time as there really is no way to condense it). We were roommates for the following three years and by graduation Juvie was my best friend. But he went home to the Philippines while I came back here, and then he relocated to California, and we kept in touch thanks to the internet but didn't see much of each other. Said we should and totally would when circumstances permitted, like people do, but nothing had ever come of those vague, well-intentioned pronouncements. Until Juvie had called me to broach the idea of visiting for a week. I agreed immediately, and only afterwards realized how much I'd have to do to clear the decks for a solid week of entertaining a houseguest. All right, apartmentguest, but at least my loft was bigger than our shared dorm rooms had been. A bit.

And in true Kellan Oakes style, thanks to the same procrastination and laziness that had led me to become a self-employed private investigator rather than taking any other kind of respectable grownup job or following my mother's grass-stained footsteps on the ancient druidic paths, I had left the deck clearing until the day before Juvie was due to arrive. I had a plan to get everything done, at least. Even better, I had an assistant waiting at my office.

I navigated the Friday morning traffic more or less on autopilot. I'd made the roundtrip between my place of self-employment and the courthouse countless times, and traveled all the other streets of the city enough to have the map permanently encoded in my neurons. I love my city, I really do. I love the eclectic mix of people, I love the constant activity and the unceasing progress. The distance and the buffer between myself and my mother wasn't the only reason why I came to live here. I find it genuinely satisfying to see a new restaurant open up, or the groundbreaking on a new building, cranes against the sky raising a blueprint one steel beam at a time. A city is a collection of dreams and desires brought into physical existence by people. Human beings live seventy or eighty years and a mind boggling number of them manage to create something lasting, something new that wasn't there before. Trees live hundreds of years, sometimes thousands, and the wilderness remains constant. I made my choice.

I parked the Corolla down the street and walked to the brick building that housed my office on the third floor. I rode the building's ancient elevator up and approached my office door, a classic entrance with frosted glass and KELLAN OAKES INVESTIGATIONS in gold foil lettering, and was not at all surprised to see my receptionist Phoebe sitting at her desk in the main waiting area. The complete lack of any clientele reposing on the chairs lining the perimeter came as a further relief. "Morning, Phoebe," I said.

"Good morning," she said without looking up from her computer.

"Ready to run down the open cases for me?"

"Oh, I'm ready," she said. "Not sure you are."

"What are you talking about? I'm here, aren't I?" I frowned. "What is it? Something bad? It's something bad."

"Not bad," Phoebe said. "Just… how do you want to do this? Easy or hard first?"

I walked over to the coffee maker. "Easy first," I said, pouring myself a mug of dark roast.

"All right. You have five open cases right now. There's the Boothby case…"

"Nothing I need to do for that one this week," I finished for her.

"Correct," Phoebe said. "Do you want to do the rest yourself, too? Do I need to be a part of this conversation?"

"Sorry, sorry," I said. "Please continue." I took a sip of coffee.

"Then there's the Eglan case. If anyone calls in a Maia Eglan sighting, I'll log it. If I think it's something you can follow up quickly and painlessly, I'll call you."

"Perfect," I nodded.

"All right, let's see, of the next two I suppose the strix case is the easier one. Assuming you actually came up with an answer for them." She looked away from her screen and turned to me, expectantly.

"I think I did," I said. "I'm going to make them understand they only have two options, which both seem bad, but that one is significantly less bad than the other, which makes it the only reasonable choice."

"Reasonable?" Phoebe repeated. "Strix aren't exactly known for their powers of reason."

"Don't I know it," I said. "But they did come to me. On some level I think they already know they don't have any good options, and if not I'll walk them through it. I just have to convince them that if they ignore me and try some crazy third option, it will come down to the same thing as the worse of my two options anyway."

"I was wrong," Phoebe said. "That does not sound easy."

"No, no, you were right," I corrected her. "It's easy this week. All I have to do this week is tell them the plan. After that, implementing it, making them understand it while they do their part, course correcting for them, that is going to be a gigantic pain in my ass. But that all comes later." I took another sip of coffee while Phoebe made some notes in her files, then said. "Did you say five open cases? The only other one I can think of is the Haldeman case."

"Yes, the Haldeman case is one," Phoebe said. "They are expecting the results in the coming week."

"Results which I don't have. Yet," I added, as my mind raced through several options. "I have some irons in the fire, but nothing concrete. Some of those might start paying off soon, but they might not, and it's extremely unlikely they'll give me anything to work with today."

Phoebe watched me but said nothing.

"All right, how about this," I said. "I'm just going to give them what I have right now. It's not what they want, but it's all I've got. If I pull all of my notes together and punch them up to sound as impressive as possible, can you spiff them up? Official Kellan Oakes Investigations letterhead, all that fancy razzle dazzle?"

"I can," Phoebe nodded. "Seems like a lot of effort for both of us to polish a turd."

I shrugged. "If I do nothing, and give them nothing, Haldeman will in all likelihood just walk away. I don't get paid for any of the work I've already done and I lose out on potential future work, too. If I give them something, even if it's all flash and minimal substance, at least there's a chance Haldeman will appreciate the appearance of effort. That's mostly what people want, especially people like Haldeman, that feeling that people are bending over backwards for them. The outcome itself is secondary." I finished my coffee. "But he will get his answers, eventually. I'll chase them down week after next, I just need to buy some time."

"If you say so," Phoebe said. "You're the boss. If you say a bunch of busywork up front is worth it so you can have your week off to yourself, so be it."

"You still sound skeptical," I observed.

"It just doesn't seem like you," Phoebe said.

"Why, because in all the years you've worked for me I've never taken a vacation?" I asked. "Number one, that's a reason in and of itself why this is so important. I'm overdue for the downtime. And number two…" I trailed off into a sighing chuckle.

"What?" Phoebe asked.

"Have you ever heard the expression, the older you get, the more important it is to stay connected to the people who knew you when you were young?" I asked.

"No," Phoebe said, and I believed her. It was a human saying, a very human notion, and Phoebe was not human, not entirely. She was a hamadryad, a creature of the Deep Woods. Sometimes she treated me like I was her clueless little brother and she was the put-upon, older and wiser and infinitely more responsible sibling. To be fair, she had known me since I was a baby, and she was older. A couple centuries older, which was still pretty young as hamadryads go. Her dryad mother was ancient, and a longtime friend of my mother's, so when Phoebe had become restless within the Deep Woods and curious about the human world outside it our mothers had decided that it made perfect sense for Phoebe to come work for me while she got her bearings. All in all, it had worked out well for both of us; Phoebe was a fast learner and an amazing receptionist, and overbearing quasi-family dynamics aside I considered her a good friend, too.

"Well now you have," I said. "Juvie knew me back in the day, and I haven't seen him for a while, and I'm looking forward to it and it's important. Important enough to make work for myself I wouldn't otherwise bother with. So, nothing for Boothby, see what happens with Eglan, convey the plan to the strix, and put together a little song and dance for Haldeman. I swear that's everything. What fifth case?"

Phoebe took a deep breath. "Masterson."

"There's no Masterson…" I started, then cut myself off. "No."

"Yes."

"No!"

"Yes."

I groaned. "When did he call?"

Phoebe's eyes flicked to the clock in the corner of her computer screen. "Twenty minutes ago."

"And there's a genuine marker to call in?" I pressed. "Or did you not ask?"

Phoebe looked hurt. "Of course I asked. And yes, it's genuine. I explained you weren't in yet and I'd have to get back to him. He said the sooner the better."

"Of course he did." I rubbed my eyes. "Okay. All right. I mean, there's really nothing for it. Can you call him back and set something up for tonight? I'll meet him anywhere within an hour of here."

"When tonight?"

"Doesn't matter. The later the better, but whenever."

"Will do."

I poured myself a second cup of coffee. "Thanks, Phoebe." I headed into my private office, to start another glamorous day of the P.I. life: sorting through the notes I needed to turn into a dazzling write-up for Haldeman, outlining and mentally pressure-testing the argument I was going to make to the strix, and generally preparing my soul for my latest tete-a-tete with an unscrupulous warlock who had me over a barrel. All right, maybe those last two were only part of the P.I. life when the P.I. was also the son of a druid who couldn't get away from the intrigues of the Deep Woods and had stopped trying. But that was my lot.

I emailed the Haldeman files to Phoebe by 11:00 a.m. and was feeling confident about the strix agreement by noon, when I emerged from my office. "Any luck with Masterson?" I asked.

Phoebe nodded. "He said he can meet you at Fountainview Park at 9:00 p.m."

"Good."

"Good?"

"Well I'm not looking forward to it," I acknowledged. "But I had half-expected Masterson to randomly pick the most inconvenient time in the middle of the day. So good job steering him later in the evening."

"I didn't steer anything," Phoebe said, honest to a fault as always.

"Good. Job," I repeated much more loudly. "Take the rest of the day off. I'm going to."

"Not yet," Phoebe said. "But I might lock up early, in a bit. Thank you."

"Don't work too hard," I admonished on my way out the door.

I drove to the grocery store. I expected Juvie and I would wind up eating out a lot, but stocked up all the same on things I thought would be in demand over the coming week: coffee, beer, bagels, toilet paper. I took everything home, put it away, and cleaned my apartment. By the time I felt like it was presentable, it was late in the afternoon and I realized I had skipped breakfast and lunch. I headed out for an early dinner, which turned out to be a sausage and peppers sub from Narducci's.

I got the sandwich to go and, once I was back in the Corolla, I checked the weather app on my phone. Sunset was thirty-seven minutes away, which I reckoned was about enough time for me to drive out to the woods, park, and eat, if I made good time. Which I did.

I savored the sausage and peppers as the sky deepened to indigo overhead. The clouds in the west went rosy and I got out of the car. I walked into the woods, mostly to get away from the car, which tends to spook the woodlanders. About a hundred yards in, I gave a cry that would have sounded to a random passerby like a giant chicken choking down an angry bobcat.

I heard the strix answering my call before I saw it. The monster alighted on a bough ten feet above the ground and stared at me with huge yellow eyes peering down a long, thin, curved beak. Its body was about the size of a chimpanzee, with short legs and a longer torso, but more skeletal, barely any meat on it at all. Its arms were batlike, ending in elongated, webbed fingers. Except for that webbing, and its eyes and beak, it was covered in dark rust-colored feathers, including two long vanes extending up above its eyes like antennae, or devil horns. I made another guttural caw, then spoke in arboreal to say "Greetings, Stagbane." That was not exactly its name. Strix, like most beasts, even intelligent ones, don't have the same need for proper names we do. It was somewhere between a plain description and an honorific, translated from arboreal into English. Just go with me on this.

Stagbane skipped the formalities. "What answer do you bring from the larth?"

"Only a refusal to answer," I said. Stagbane

flexed the massive black talons it was using to grip its perch, and growled menacingly. I held my hands up and added, "But I do not come to you with nothing."

Stagbane flapped its wings once, and I felt the air rush past me, smelling vaguely of rotten meat. Then it settled and fixed its gaze on me intently.

"I come with a choice," I went on, "not as offered by the larth, but offered to you nonetheless."

The strix case, such as it was, boiled down to a territorial dispute. An entire flock of strix hunted through a section of the woods that had recently come under the protection of another woodland spirit, a larth. Larth are generally benevolent and this one was no exception, though apparently she had decided to step up her game considerably. Some random human must have done the larth some service, knowingly or otherwise, which led the larth to swear no harm would come to him or her or any of their kin in the area. Larth are powerful enough to keep their word on something like that, too. But what would set up a happily ever after for a peaceful and prosperous little village in a fairy tale a thousand years ago creates some logistical nightmares in the here and now. A flock of flesh-eating, blood-drinking strix, for example, suddenly finds itself suffering the wrath of the overprotective larth whenever they try to feed. Present-day wildernesses are so small, and human spaces so sprawling, that the larth's vow covers the entire strix hunting grounds, and there's nowhere else for the strix to go.

Faced with the insolvable dilemma of either

starving to death or being harried to death by the larth, the strix turned to me, Foltchain's son, everyone's favorite troubleshooting mediator for modern mythic squabbles. Unfortunately, I didn't have a shred of leverage over the larth, nor was I able to gin any up. I managed to meet with the spirit and found her to be decent and reasonable in almost all respects but completely obstinate in defending her newly established protective vow. The strix wanted to know what they were supposed to do, how they were supposed to survive, and the larth simply did not care.

Normally I wouldn't have cared, either. Don't get me wrong, strix are monsters. They'd just as soon disembowel a pack of cub scouts as anything. I don't know why I always take these impossible woodlander disputes, but I do, and once I do it's my reputation on the line. So I had to throw my hail mary and hope that Stagbane would catch it rather than express its displeasure by slowly and painfully gutting me.

"The larth is terrible when roused to anger," I said. "You must choose whether to risk that anger, or not."

Stagbane cawed derisively. "Risk the anger or starve."

"Risk the anger by hunting as you always have," I said, "or choose to change."

Stagbane shifted uncomfortably on its talons, but said nothing.

"Your kind are wanton," I said, which earned me another angry flap of Stagbane's rank-smelling wings, but I forged ahead. "You hunt almost as much for sport as for food. You bathe in entrails and leave them to rot on the forest floor. You gorge on flesh while it is warm and abandon it as it begins to cool. You kill more than you need to survive. You are wasteful."

"Is this what offends the larth?" Stagbane demanded. "Waste?"

"No," I shook my head. "It merely draws her attention. The larth proclaims herself steward of all creatures in her demesne, particularly the humans, now. The larth is powerful, but not all-powerful. Even she knows she cannot prevent all harm, and she cannot stave off death forever. Other animals prey upon each other by her leave. You must not stand apart from these others. Claim the life of a single creature, devour it entire, crack its bones, and the larth will be unmoved. Slaughter them by the herd or the flock and leave a bloody trail in your wake and the larth will surely follow it."

"And if we so choose to waste not," Stagbane grumbled, "the larth will forswear any violence against us?"

"I can't promise you that," I admitted. "The less she feels provoked by you, the less likely she will devote herself to rooting you out. But given your history, and your reputation, any moment when your paths cross hers will be fraught."

"You ask us to give up what we are, and gain no certain recompense in the bargain?" Stagbane screeched. Before I could answer, the strix launched itself from the bough and dove for me. The eye-watering reek assaulted me a moment before the talons crashed into my chest and the hooked beak stabbed at my throat.

I had figured the conversation stood a good chance of devolving into violence, so I wasn't caught completely off guard. I bent my right arm and raised it to shield my neck. With my left hand I grabbed Stagbane's wing and squeezed membrane, bone and feathers in my fingers. Not enough to do permanent damage, but it's a sensitive part of the strix anatomy and Stagbane left off trying to chew through my carotid, screaming in pain instead. I shifted my stance and threw Stagbane to the ground, not letting go of the wing. I knelt and put most of my weight on the humerus bone, which hurt my knee more than it hurt the strix, but at least succeeded in pinning Stagbane on the turf. I drew my SIG Pro from my shoulder holster - another sensible precaution taken before heading into a meeting with a bloodthirsty forest dweller - and aimed it at Stagbane's head.

"You know what this is?" I asked, rotating the gun a bit in Stagbane's view before returning it to sight between the strix's eyes. It doesn't hurt to check with the wild ones, who are often completely unfamiliar with modern tools and weapons. A gun loses pretty much all of its psychological negotiation weight if the entity at the other end of the barrel is ignorant of what it can do.

Stagbane growled murderously, slowly forming the noise into an approximation of "Yes."

"Good," I said. "Now listen. You asked me to intercede with the larth. I said I would try. I did try, but the larth was immovable. I could have merely relayed that to you and fulfilled my duty. Instead, I freely offered you counsel. Do with it what you will, but do not fault me for your fate."

The entire time I spoke, Stagbane had stared into my eyes, without interruption and without a single side eye for the gun. I kept it trained on him for a few seconds of silence, then slowly stood up and shoved it back in the holster.

Stagbane hopped upright, wings outstretched, and gave a few experimental flaps of the limb I had treated so roughly. "Do not fault me," the strix said, "for your fate." He flew upward and away, disappearing into the gathering shadows of the canopy.

"Quit copying me," I muttered in English. I turned to walk out of the woods and back to my car, not entirely sure if the angry warbles I heard following me were the strix getting in the last word, or just my imagination.

Ajax Masterson had wanted oh so badly to become a warlock for a very long time. From his perspective, he already was a warlock, and was continually adding to his arcane prowess. This unshakable belief in his own thaumaturgic potency was what had led him, years earlier, to legally change his name from Alan Meyrowicz to Ajax Masterson, a name more befitting a figure who had pierced the supernatural veil - and what led him to casually throw words like 'thaumaturgic potency' and 'supernatural veil' around in conversation. His ongoing goal, again from his point of view, was to become the mightiest warlock the world had ever seen.

I would never call Masterson a warlock. Not because magic isn't real or warlocks don't exist; it is and they do. It's just a gross overstatement in Masterson's case. I would call Masterson a definitive example of the truism that a little knowledge is indeed a dangerous thing, but that's not a very succinct label. 'Wannabe warlock' might be the best possible compromise on the matter.

In any case, Masterson and I had met a couple of years ago when he had made an appointment, come to my office, and proceeded to outline his intent to blackmail me. Specifically, he threatened to reveal my connections to the supernatural world unless I provided him with material assistance towards the end of increasing Masterson's magical dominance.

I run Kellan Oakes Investigations as a no frills, no nonsense operation, exactly as I always intended it to be from the beginning. I don't advertise as anything other than a mundane provider of services, including surveillance, research, process serving and other negotiable tasks. I don't go seeking out weird stuff. Instead, weird stuff always manages to find me. It started out with the nature spirits and denizens of the Deep Woods who knew my mother, personally or by reputation, and then heard that Foltchain's son was a man for hire fully immersed in the modern urban world. They concluded, not altogether unfairly I admit, that I might be their best hope for navigating the unnatural kingdom that had grown up like metal weeds and glass thorns all around them, and I couldn't turn them all away. So I took on strange cases for faeries and monsters and intelligent animals right alongside humdrum jobs for people who had no reason to believe faeries, monsters or intelligent animals had ever existed outside of myths. At some point it started to bleed together a bit. Normal people started bringing me their non-normal problems, either because the universe has a sense of humor and dumped them in my lap, or because they had heard, through vague rumors, that I was the P.I. of last resort when a case was too weird for anyone else to crack.

And honestly, as long as they pay my fees, I don't care whether I'm working for a normal person with normal problems, a normal person with non-normal problems, or an entity that isn't supposed to exist with crazy problems. But all of those non-normal elements are between me and my clients, kept in unspoken confidence. I don't need anyone broadcasting my connections to the other side.

So Masterson had me in a bad spot, and we struck a deal. I would, from time to time, provide his requested assistance. Empowered artifacts, rare spell components, long-lost arcane knowledge - these were all things I was supposed to keep an eye out for. Masterson was sure I ran across them all the time, and had a treasure trove of glowing, pulsating objects of sorcerous power just hoarded away in my basement or something. From time to time, I was required to hand one of these relics over to him or suffer the consequences.

I arrived at Fountainview Park a few minutes before our 9:00 p.m. rendezvous. I strolled through the park, following the stepping stone paths that some urban developer had chosen for the public green space. Fountainview was cultivated and landscaped far beyond any trace of primordial wilderness but it was still a vital little plot of land, and walking through it was, I had to admit, soothing. Until I heard an attention-seeking hiss from the shadows near a wooden stand closed up for the night.

I altered my course toward the stand without making it look like I was heeding a summons. As I drew close to the side facing away from the nearest lamppost I was greeted with "Well met, Son of Foltchain."

That was Masterson, speaking English. Not speaking arboreal, which has a tendency to sound stilted and archaic when translated into English. Just Masterson being pompous on purpose, doing his best impression of Saruman, as usual. "Sup, Ajax," I hailed him in return.

"Have you brought my tribute?".

This guy. "Are you calling in a true marker?" I asked. Yeah, I had already asked Phoebe if she'd verified it, but Masterson didn't know that, and I saw absolutely no upside in letting him roll right over me.

"Indeed," Masterson chuckled. He sounded smug. "You were recently entreated by an aonbarr to grant it safe passage back to the Otherworld. Of course, for one of your lineage and power, this was trivial. But you did not cover your tracks as well as you might have thought."

My lineage is the decidedly mixed bag of being

the only child of Foltchain of the Oak. She bore me, she raised me, and she taught me a fraction of what she knows. Her druid priestess knowledge was amassed over centuries and centuries; nobody knows how many, because nobody knows exactly how old she is. I picked up a tiny sliver of her overall knowledge because I have only been alive for three decades and change. And Foltchain was only actively trying to teach me for the first two decades. And I was only really paying attention for the first twelve years. Maybe less. That's it. My power amounts to an incomplete druid education and my naturally charming personality. I'm not immortal, as far as I know, based on how close I've come to definitively disproving that notion. I don't have any supernatural abilities. I don't practice any kind of magic. I'm not special.

Masterson didn't believe any of that, of course. He was zealous in his convictions that the modern world was positively teeming with mystical energies swirling just below the surface. There's more at play than most people are aware of, sure, but Masterson grossly overestimated just how much, including his insistence that I was some kind of verdant wizard. Further tightening his blinders was his innate sense of entitlement, that these arcane mysteries always just out of reach and just beyond perception were being denied him in a cosmic miscarriage of justice. Telling someone that the thing they most desperately covet actually isn't that great doesn't go over well. I'd tried, many times, but at a certain point it just became easier to play Masterson's game.

The rules of the game were these: I refused to let him continuously blackmail me over the same piece of information he confronted me with on the day we met. There was a little boy who had gone missing and I had found him. He'd fallen down an old well on a condemned property, and nobody ever heard him calling for help because the rusalka living at the bottom of the well had decided she would keep him as a surrogate child. I talked the rusalka into letting him go, not realizing at the time the whole exchange was witnessed by Masterson, who'd been collecting plants by the full moon on the same property, of all the luck. I bought Masterson's silence with a sprig-of-rue charm and I could tell by the look in his eyes that he thought he'd hit upon a magical gravy train, so I warned him: consider the debt paid or prepare for a punishing feud. He'd agreed that he would never tell anyone about my parley with the rusalka, but quickly added that he was bound to observe me in supernatural circumstances again, sooner or later, and his continued silence would have to be negotiated anew.

So Masterson calling in a marker meant that he had seen or heard something connecting me to outlandish and unreal happenings once again. The vast majority of the time Masterson managed to completely misinterpret what had happened, but I played along. As long as he felt in control he was like a snake in a glass tank, slightly dangerous but contained. I fed him the magical artifact equivalents of baby mice and the world kept on turning.

"Do you deny it?" Masterson asked.

And even though it had been a sihuanaba, not an

aonbarr, although both have horselike characteristics I suppose, and even though it hadn't been remotely about safe passage to Otherworld, which is not even a real place, but rather about witnessing a contract between the sihuanaba and a human woman, pretty dry stuff honestly, I conceded the point. "No, no denial. Just following the protocols, you understand."

Masterson held out his hand. I shoved my hands into my pockets, trying to think of a plausible piece of arcana I could spout off to satisfy him. He preferred physical objects, but every once in a while he'd be mollified by a bit of esoteric lore, or a bit of complete and total malarkey that I assured him was true. The hardest part sometimes was keeping a straight face while he nodded and reveled in the secret knowledge that, say, the most spectacular way to kill any non-corporeal was with potassium dichromate. I liked the idea of him pestering industrial chemical suppliers and getting the runaround from them for a while. Unfortunately, I had already used that particular one on Masterson not too long ago.

Then my fingers brushed thread and iron, and I pulled out the sprite trap. I nonchalantly dropped the ring on Masterson's palm. He drew his hand back and scrutinized it. "What is this?" he asked.

"You don't know?" I asked, trying to sound a little surprised and not completely mocking.

"I am not familiar with this... particular... configuration," Masterson said. The look on his face told me that he could feel something ethereal clinging to the trap. Like I said, Masterson knows just enough to be a volatile pain in the ass, and he was reasonably well attuned to sensing supernatural energies when they were close enough to bite him on the nose. He was buying that it was magical, even though he had no idea what I had handed him.

For my part, I wasn't about to tell him what it was, because the last thing anybody needed was for Masterson to think it was open season for capturing woodland folk. I rolled with the first thing I could think of. "It's a curse attractor. Like a lightning rod, but for malevolent magics. Put it somewhere safe, somewhere indoors, and if anyone tries to strike out at you with a dark spell, the effects will be drawn into this instead."

Masterson looked up at me and said, "You must think I have powerful enemies, to consider this a fitting tribute to me."

I shrugged. "At the rate you're going, if you don't already, you will soon." More stroking for his ego, and Masterson ate it up. He nodded, slipped the sprite trap into his own pocket, and patted it possessively. He seemed about to say something, held back by uncharacteristic uncertainty. "Something wrong?" I asked.

He shook his head, then threw his shoulders back, resolute. "I was not expecting such a remarkable tribute. It more than settles the current marker. So much so that I fear I am now in your debt until I can make restitution."

I waved him off, "No, really, it's…"

He reached for his chest and unfastened his tiepin, handing it to me. "Take this," he said.

"Ajax, seriously…"

"Take it," he repeated, turning the request into a command.

I held out my hand and he dropped the pin. The head was a sphere, smaller than a marble, made of some kind of dark metal with a faint bluish iridescence in the electric light of the lamppost. "Thank you," I said.

"I assume you recognize the starstuff," Masterson said, "but know that this was collected from a meteorite which fell through the aurora borealis and was embedded in the ice of the Arctic for millennia. You may find its elemental control over cold and wind… intriguing."

Probably not remotely true, but Masterson clearly believed every word. "Are you sure you want to part with it?" I asked.

"I insist," he said. And, I reminded myself, he was blackmailing me for magic trinkets, so I couldn't feel too bad about him handing over what was most likely a souvenir from some Alaskan village that catered to AARP cruises. "Until we meet again, Son of Foltchain," Masterson said, and bowed slightly.

It wasn't as hard to resist the urge to laugh at his ostentatious ridiculousness as it might have been, since he had at least tried to end on a noble and magnanimous note. "Til then," I said.

Back in my car, I checked my cell phone. One email notification awaited: Phoebe copying me on the progress report she had sent to Haldeman. The timestamp was later than I had wanted her to stay at the office, but I was thankful the to-do item had been crossed out all the same.

It had been a long day and I was more than ready for it to be over. All in all I was proud of my productivity, between begging a favor from Irina and compiling the report for Haldeman - with Phoebe's indispensable help, of course - and delivering my longshot proposal to the strix and resetting the clock on Masterson's game. Plus I had shopped and cleaned like a normal grown up, to boot. I had earned a week's vacation, at least.

As I pulled into the alley behind my apartment, I was already thinking about Juvie's arrival the next day. One bright side of my encounter with Masterson was that I could relate it to Juvie, and I expected he'd get a big kick out of it. Masterson was a bit like a guy we had both known back in college, Fred Wolpert. He actually went by Frederick and insisted that everyone call him that and corrected people when they called him Fred, so of course Juvie and I called him Fred as a matter of principle, or Freddy if we were really intent on aggravating him. On top of the name thing, Fred was a vegan and could not have been more smug about it. I respect anyone who commits to that decision, for whatever reason from ethical to environmental, so long as they acknowledge that what they eat is their personal decision and what I eat is mine. Fred was the kind of person who would wander out of his room and into the dorm lounge if anyone had the gall to open a pepperoni pizza box or a kung pao chicken carton in that communal space, swearing he could smell the offending animal flesh from down the hall and that it was turning his stomach. Then he would launch into a lecture which highlighted not only his moral superiority but also threw in more than a dash of conspiracy theory about how commercially farmed meat was dosed with so many hormones and antibiotics in order to make us all docile and weak with infirmity to pave the way for the looming One World Government takeover. I had a particularly hard time ignoring Fred because, in addition to only being nineteen years old and lacking some of the patience I would develop as an adult, I was someone he would single out for failing to know better, owing to the fact that I was a forestry major and should understand unsustainable land usage and whatnot. So Fred was my nemesis, and Juvie's, simply because Juvie always had my back. He'd helped me torment Fred, and although a time or two he'd talked me down from retaliating too disproportionately, he had definitely been my willing accomplice the time that we delayed our departure at the beginning of spring break just long enough to see Freddy take his leave, after which we jimmied the lock on Freddy's door, snuck into his room, and dumped a bottle of bacon bits down the vent grate of his PTAC.

Maybe, I thought as I came out of the building stairwell into the third floor hallway, Juvie could help me come up with some more gratifying ways to mess with Ajax Masterson. At the very least he'd be sympathetic to the indignities I had to suffer, and we could have some laughs over the absurdity of it all.

I reached my apartment door, unlocked it, and pushed through. In a mindlessly automatic motion, one hand pushed the door shut behind me and twisted the deadbolt, while the other found the lightswitch on the wall. A tiny tiffany lamp on the entryway table came on, shedding just enough of a glow for me to see where I set down my keys. I turned the corner into the dark of the living room, suddenly feeling the exhaustion of the day physically as well as mentally, and paused for a moment mid-step. I could turn on more lights and go through the motions of unwinding, or I could turn around, flip off the tiffany, navigate the apartment in shadows and collapse directly into bed. Both options were tempting enough that I stayed in place for a few heartbeats.

In the quiet darkness, I didn't see anything out of place or hear anything unusual, but I felt something off in the air. A wave rippled over me, not heat or cold, not vibration exactly, some kind of tactile potency that raised goosebumps all over me. Before I felt it I had been absolutely certain I was alone in the apartment. Now I felt a presence, intelligent but not recognizably human. I'd been around countless woodland spirits, wild animals, and more than a few sentient plants, but it was nothing like any of those, either. I couldn't get a bead on what it was or what it wanted, which was more unsettling than if it had been more traditionally predatory or hostile.

Whatever it was, it put all speculations to rest when it attacked me. It leapt from somewhere out of the blackness behind me and clawed at my shoulders. I dropped to the floor defensively, pinning the assailant between my back and the carpet. I regretted it instantly. The thing was all sharp edges and points, and uncomfortably hot, digging into my flesh like a jumble of burning sawblades.

I rolled to my side, throwing an elbow where I assumed the thing's head was as I moved. I connected with a satisfying crunch, almost too satisfying as my elbow shattered a substance that felt less like a skull and more like an ostrich egg, a brittle outer layer cracking into shards that were nonetheless held together by a tough membrane underneath. I tried not to dwell on it too much as I kept rolling away and, once I had created a few feet of separation, pushed myself to my feet.

I tried to see the thing amid the shadows but it was faster than I expected, already launching itself at me, its ferocity unaffected by having its head partially caved in. Its lower limbs hooked onto my hips while its foreclaws pierced the sides of my throat. The heat and keen biting multiplied the agony, making it difficult to breathe, and some part of my mind realized I would probably pass out soon if I didn't get the thing off me.

I staggered backwards until I struck the edge of my dining table. I reached behind for the heavy glass bowl that sat in the middle, the receptacle for mail I hadn't yet sorted and other odds and ends. I swung the bowl around, scattering envelopes and flyers like oversized confetti, and slammed it into the thing's head, once again meeting very little resistance and doing enough damage to kill any normal creature.

The thing let go of my neck and arched away from me, though its legs remained locked in place. Not entirely locked in, though. Through my clothes

I could feel the thing's lower limbs shifting, not just in position but in shape, bending in different ways and extruding new jagged configurations. The thing was hanging off me inverted one moment, then bracing itself with its upside down arms and throwing me with its upside down legs the next. I would have marveled at the improbability of it all if I hadn't been busy cracking plaster as my spine collided violently with the bookcase against the far wall.

I fell to the floor, shooting stars whirling madly behind my eyes, limbs failing spectacularly to respond to my brain's urgent orders to crawl to safety, somewhere, anywhere else but here. The most I could manage was to flop onto my back and force a deep breath. Good news, I didn't feel anything like a broken rib. Bad news, I was about to be bludgeoned to death by something that was itself impervious to bludgeoning, some savage, spiky, superheated…

I slowly worked my hand towards my pocket and slid my fingers in. The thing was probably waiting for me to make a move it could react to, which was fine by me. I drew out my hand and balled it into a fist, then sprang to my feet. I intended to spring, at any rate, though the actual motion was a herky-jerky collapse in reverse. I steadied myself and braced for impact, fully aware that I was unlikely to see the next attack coming.

The thing that had invaded my apartment, unfazed by two grievous blows to the head, had no difficulty orienting on me or closing the distance between us. I thrust my fist forward to meet it as it flew at me, with the meteorite stone of Ajax Masterson's tiepin protruding from between my middle and ring fingers. If Masterson had been right, and it really was magic starstuff with powers over cold, maybe it would have more effect on the heat-radiating monster than punches and weighty glassware did. And if Masterson was wrong, well, I'd already acknowledged the likelihood that I would be mauled to death in the middle of my living room in short order anyway.

As usual, Masterson proved to be wrong, but also as usual there was a dangerous grain of truth buried under his bluster. As the meteorite touched the thing in mid-leap it did not unleash a blast of galeforce arctic wind, nor did it encase the thing in glacial ice. It did, however, toll like a bell, one about a thousand times the size of the stone at the end of the tiepin. Everything in the apartment rattled as the rumbling peal detonated, accompanied by a brief flash of cobalt glare. That gave me a glimpse of the thing, not that I could make much sense of it, all irregular serrated planes in the approximate shape of head and torso, outstretched limbs and splayed claws. The light faded quickly, the noise much more slowly, and through it all I remained unmurdered. I couldn't sense the presence of the invader any longer.

I edged towards the switch on the wall for the overhead light. Once it came on I could see books that had toppled from the bookcase, scattered junk mail and other debris from the glass bowl, but no physical remains of the thing that had been so intent on putting me down. As grateful as I was to still be breathing, I was deeply disturbed by the fact that I had no idea what the thing had been or why it had been in my apartment. It didn't seem to have anything to do with the strix, or any other cases where I'd made enemies. It was an odd anomaly.

Odd anomalies wander into my life now and then, probably more of a frequent occurrence for me than for most other people. And my usual approach for something completely baffling was to speak to my mother about it. If that sounds like some form of failure-to-launch codependence, consider the baseline human tendency to consider parental figures as knowledgeable authorities throughout our lives, and then add on top of that my mother's centuries of lived experience and deep vocational focus on all things traditionally considered supernatural, and finally tell me who you think would be a better candidate to appeal to for answers to "what the hell?" kind of questions than the druid priestess who raised me.

Unfortunately, the only way to talk to my mother was face to face, since she lived outside of town in a cottage in the woods with neither telephone service nor internet nor simple electricity. It was late and I was roughed up and in no condition to go anywhere except the bathroom. I stripped, checked my wounds in the mirror and saw nothing serious, jumped in the shower to wash off the blood, and was in bed ten minutes later. Maybe things would make more sense in the morning.

CHAPTER TWO: DEPARTURES

MY MOTHER WASN'T home. By which I mean, she was nowhere on the property to which the local authorities would have recognized her legal claim. As I rolled up her rutted dirt lane, the early morning sunlight splashing through the green and yellow leaves of the trees on either side, I didn't see her anywhere amidst the blue-purple scatters of ironweed and coneflower and flax in the meadow that comprised her front yard. I got out of the car, walked around her cottage and looked into the back yard, where there was similarly no sign of her. I crossed the grassy expanse to the small herbarium and poked my head in, confirming that she was not inside mortaring roots or drying seeds. Finally I backtracked to the cottage itself, let myself in, and moved through the few spartan rooms, verifying her absence from each one.

So she wasn't in her house, her herbarium, or the immediate vicinity. But Foltchain of the Oak considered the whole, wide natural world to be her home, and notions such as permanent residences and real estate parcels never constrained her. She understood them, certainly, since she wasn't a naif visiting from another time and place; she had lived through the ongoing development of modern human society and was fully aware of it from her self-imposed outsider's perspective. Her general rejection of boundaries was entirely conscious and willful, and her periodic, unannounced walkabouts were neither surprising nor unusual.

I walked through her cottage again, this time looking not for my mother in the flesh but for any clue as to where she might have gone, or more to the point when she might be back. But nothing obvious presented itself. Sometimes I would find a half-prepared stargazy pie on her kitchen counter and conclude that she had just stepped out to gather some fresh wild scallions and mushrooms from the woods. Other times I would find a book about mandragora mating rituals splayed open on the table beside her reading chair, offering a hint that she had been inspired to undertake some druid field research of her own. This particular morning there was not a thing out of place in her cottage, no obvious unfinished tasks. Again, neither surprising nor unusual. Foltchain of the Oak was capable of embarking on the spur of the moment on any kind of errand, large or small, near or distant, with the slightest provocation. But she was also capable of making deliberate plans and preparations, and it was perfectly in character for her to tidy the cottage, go to bed for the night, and leave the following dawn to pursue her predetermined agenda. It was annoying, because I wanted to talk to her, had no way of reaching her, and no means of determining when she might be available again, but dealing with my mother had always been arduous.

Still, since I had come all this way, I decided to make the best of it. The longest wall in my mother's dining room was completely covered by a rustic floor-to-ceiling bookcase containing her personal library. Commercially available books published in the last twenty years sat side by side with relics which might be the only extant copies of their kind and numerous leather-bound notebooks of Foltchain of the Oak's own writings. I had spent a lot of time as a kid poring over the contents, partly at my mother's behest when she was homeschooling me, partly because, even once I entered public school, so long as there was no electricity at home, no television or video games or stereo, there wasn't a lot else to do besides read. Did I accumulate a ton of esoteric knowledge which to this day serves me pretty well? Yes. Did I once complete a seventh-grade assignment to write a biographical report on "any American hero" by lauding Norman Borlaug, baffling my classmates and even my teacher? Yes again.

Norman Borlaug was an agronomist and a leading figure in the Green Revolution. He won the Nobel Peace Prize.

At any rate, I pulled a few of the bestiaries and compendia off the shelves and sat down at the trestle table. I flipped through the volumes looking for anything resembling the jagged little nightmare that had attacked me the night before, but nothing came close, even accounting for the extreme liberties medieval illuminated manuscripts tended to take with trifles like anatomy and perspective.

My phone buzzed in my pocket. I thumbed the screen and saw the entirety of a text message from Juvie in the preview: GPS ETA 30 min. That settled that, then. I reshelved my mother's books, resigning myself to an indeterminate wait before the chance to speak to her arrived.

I drove back home, stowing the Corolla down the street a ways from my apartment building so that Juvie could park in my spot in the back alley. I took up casual lean against the railing of my building's front steps and watched the traffic. Right on schedule, Juvie came rolling up the street. I might not have known it was him, since the morning sun was bouncing off windshields in a way that made it hard to identify any occupants, and I hadn't even thought to ask Juvie what kind of car he was driving these days - a Lexus IS 300, as it turned out. But Juvie conveniently announced his presence, honking his horn, rolling down his window and thrusting out a bronzed arm to hail me. In the span of a few seconds he had pointed at me, raised a fist triumphantly, thrown up the horns, and pointed at me again.

I waved back and chuckled. Same old Juvie, exuberant as ever. I gestured toward the corner to indicate he should keep driving that way, and he obliged. I walked to the alley entrance and showed him where to park, and then Juvie was out of the car with his arms spread wide. His black hair was stylishly messy, but only on the top, sides much more neatly trimmed than the overall shag he had sported back in college. He wore a button down printed in muted geometrics with a much bolder patterned lining, visible at his rolled up cuffs and open collar. His jeans were dark, and both the shirt and pants seemed tailored to his stocky, muscular frame. I noticed his freshly shined shoes and momentarily felt underdressed myself. "Kellan!" he crowed.

"Hey, man," I said as I accepted a fierce hug. "How was your drive?"

"It was all right. Parts of it were bullshit. Doesn't matter, I'm here now. How you doing, man?"

"Good, good," I said. Mere seconds in Juvie's presence had actually bolstered my mood quite a bit, and it was almost embarrassingly gratifying to see Juvie's deep brown eyes brighten with pleasure just hearing that I was doing good, which pumped me up a little more and threatened to spiral out of control into over-emotional affirmation if I didn't redirect. "You hungry or anything?"

"I could eat. Been cooped up in the car long enough, got any good neighborhood places within walking distance?"

I did, and a few minutes later we were sitting across from one another in basket chairs at a wobbly table with orders for breakfast underway. "So then she says, 'I don't know, a Klondike bar?' And I swear to God I just stared at her, mind blank, until it got super awkward."

I shook my head and picked up my coffee. "No. No. Did not happen," I said before taking a sip.

Juvie sighed. "All right, fine, my mind wasn't totally blank. I was thinking about how hard it is to get melted chocolate stains out of bedsheets. But I couldn't say that to her, right? Anyway, point is, the rest of the night did not go as well as had been hoped."

"Did it go anywhere after that?"

"Not really. She went to the bathroom. I put my drawers back on, because I figured when she came out she was going to get dressed and leave. Which she did," Juvie recounted.

"So your instincts aren't totally worthless," I observed.

Juvie drained off his coffee, and smiled crookedly as he set the mug back down. "Pretty worthless at picking up on what the lady wants, but dead accurate on whether or not she's ready to bail."

"Her loss," I said. "At least if your instincts ever prove right before things blow up in your face, you'll have a pretty good idea she's a keeper. You'll find the right girl, sooner or later."

"Your lips to God's ears," Juvie nodded. Our waitress approached the table with a pot of coffee and a raised eyebrow. Juvie pushed his mug across the table for her and I did the same. "Thank you, Viola," Juvie said. "Viola, can I ask you a question?"

"Juvie…" I said warningly.

"Sure thing, sugar," Viola said, allowing Juvie to conveniently ignore me.

"Okay," Juvie said. "So, what do you think is the

best way for a guy like me to make the first move? Say something, or just do something?"

Viola put a hand on her hip as she considered Juvie. "If you don't know the answer to that, maybe you need to go after the women who'll make the first move for you."

Juvie raised his newly refilled coffee mug in salute to the sage advice, even though Viola was already turning around and sauntering away. I couldn't quite tell if Viola had been offering an honest opinion or throwing shade, or possibly both, but as usual Juvie was wholly immune to any embarrassment.

"So, anyway, enough about me," Juvie said. "What's your latest and greatest?"

"Latest case?" I asked. "Have I ever told you about this guy, Ajax Masterson…?"

Juvie's mouth was full of hashbrowns, but he waved his fork negatingly at me as he chewed and swallowed. "Nah, nah, not talking shop, man. What's up in your personal life?"

"Not much," I answered, which was neither false humility nor unwillingness to open up. My personal life had been taking a back seat to work for a good long while. The perks of being sole proprietor of Kellan Oakes Investigations included not having a boss or a fixed schedule or any other arbitrary outside forces to answer to. The flip side to it was that if I didn't get things done no one else would pick up the slack, and no one ever hounded me to stop racking up overtime. I worked when I felt like it, but that tended to be most of the time, when I wasn't dealing with absolute necessities like eating and sleeping and occasionally decompressing. I didn't have any hobbies, and the last time I had been on a date had been an internet match meetup about a year ago.

"How's your mom?" Juvie asked, smoothly pivoting to what I'm sure he assumed was safer territory.

"Good question," I said.

"You two beefing again?"

I laughed, partly because it reminded me of late night shenanigans back at school, when Juvie had been a sympathetic witness to an array of my personal firsts: first time getting drunk, specifically wasted on Mr. Boston rum mixed with Fanta orange soda, neither of which I can stomach to this day; first time really giving voice to all the conflicts and misunderstandings and mismatched expectations between Foltchain and I, which I'd been swallowing and suppressing for years; first time barely dodging the bullet of disciplinary action when the R.A. found me in the bathroom in the middle of the night after multiple complaints of 'aggressively loud vomiting noises' from hallmates, with Juvie fast-talking our way out of it, barely, with a warning and a promise it wouldn't happen again. "We're not, actually," I said. "It's kind of hard to beef when we don't even see each other very often. Because we're both busy, not because we're avoiding each other."

My phone buzzed, and for half a second I thought my mother's ears must have been burning. But the caller ID showed Phoebe on our main office line.

"One sec," I told Juvie. He made a nonchalant

go-ahead gesture and returned his attention to the frittata on his plate. "Hey, Phoebe," I answered the call, trying to exude confidence that this would be a quick check-in formality.

"Kellan, where is your mother?" Phoebe asked, sounding unreasonably irritated.

"I have no idea," I answered, slightly unsettled by the eerie timing of the call.

"She was supposed to meet me at the office this morning," Phoebe went on. "I came in fifteen minutes early so we could see each other before I opened for the day. She never arrived."

"She must have forgotten, or something else came up," I said. It had been known to happen.

"It wasn't just some casual plan," Phoebe said. "She was going to give me a new batch of tea."

Phoebe was trying to give me pause, and it worked. 'Tea' was shorthand for the various herbal concoctions that my mother had made for Phoebe over the years which allowed her to live a normal life in human society, suppressing the more treelike aspects of her hamadryad nature while also maintaining her overall health. My mother had never failed to come through for Phoebe, year in and year out, and if they had been discussing some new formulation and set a specific time and place to deliver it, that was an appointment Foltchain of the Oak would keep. If she had been seized by sudden curiosity or wanderlust, she would have kept it in check until after she had put the goods in Phoebe's waiting hands.

"Kellan?" Phoebe asked.

"Still here," I confirmed. "Though maybe I

should be there. Sit tight, I'll see you in a few minutes."

Juvie raised an eyebrow as I hung up. "Everything cool?"

"Remains to be seen," I said. I reached for my wallet. "If I settle the check, can you hang out on your own a bit? Here, I'll give you the key to my apartment, too…"

Juvie held up his hands. "Whoa, whoa, whoa. Relax, man. Why don't I just come with you?"

"No, really…"

"Come on, you're going to your office, right? I wanna check that out, I was gonna make you give me the tour at some point, might as well be now if you've got some business to take care of," Juvie said.

"You don't have to…"

"Yeah, no shit," Juvie grinned. "Come on, Kell, when have you ever known me to do something I didn't want to do just because someone said I had to?"

He had a point. I stopped fumbling with my keyring and went for my wallet again.

"And put that away," Juvie said. "I got breakfast. You're putting me up for a week." He shoved a couple more forkfuls into his mouth as he stood up, then chased them with the remains of his coffee. He stood there, chewing and swallowing with his cheeks bulging, a small dribble escaping the corner of his mouth. I remembered how Juvie ate like he didn't know when he would see food next, and hated to leave anything on the table. Finally he wiped a napkin across his face and then belched appreciatively. "Let's go."

I threw the deadbolt on the front door of the office after Juvie and I had entered. Phoebe was at her station behind the reception desk but looked to me immediately as we walked in; whatever she had been doing on the computer just before we arrived had been nothing but killing time. I saw her eyes skip over to Juvie questioningly for a beat before settling insistently back on me. "Phoebe, Juvenal," I introduced them perfunctorily.

Juvie stepped up and held his hand out to Phoebe. "Pleasure," he beamed. "Kellan's told me about you. Says you're the secret sauce that holds this place together, the whole operation would fall apart without you."

I had said no such thing. There was more than a little truth to it, I'd be the first to admit, but I honestly couldn't recall if I had ever mentioned Phoebe to Juvie in any context at all. It seemed doubtful. Phoebe reciprocated the handshake out of obligation but said nothing, her eyes narrowing slightly, her characteristic tell that she was caught off-guard by another person's bombast. It happened sometimes with clients who were willing to hire a private investigator because they were accustomed to getting their way more often than not. With Juvie, it was more a case of him either messing with me or trying to charm Phoebe, or probably both. I'd explain it all to Phoebe later.

"When's the last time you talked to my mother?" I asked Phoebe.

"Eight days ago," she answered immediately, as

if she'd basically been ready for me to jump right into this line of questioning.

"Where?"

"At her house," Phoebe said.

"Anything unusual about the visit, or about her, that you remember?"

"No, no, it was all normal. I stopped by after work and she was in the herbarium. We chatted a bit while she finished some repottings and she invited me inside. Talked some more, she asked when would be good to drop off the tea, we agreed on today and I left."

"Were you there to ask for tea specifically, or just visiting?"

"I… yes, the tea was the reason I was there."

I stared at Phoebe silently, giving her a moment to elaborate. She chose not to. I wondered briefly if she was playing her cards close because Juvie was there, though he had done his best to hang back and not intrude on our conversation, or if she would have been just as tight-lipped if the two of us were alone. I let it slide. "You said she was bringing you a new batch, as in… new formulation? Different from the usual?"

"Yes."

"Did she say anything about the new formulation needing ingredients that were hard to come by?"

"No."

"Did she say she'd definitely have it for you today, or that she hopefully would?"

"I get where you're going with this, but no, nothing like that," Phoebe shook her head.

"And that was it, no word from her since last

Wednesday?"

"Right… well, no. Last Wednesday was the last time I saw her. But I heard from her the day before yesterday. Indirectly."

"From whom?"

"You know how she sends messages sometimes via dragonflies?"

I said, "Okay," as noncommittally as I could. Phoebe had the very sisterly habit of behaving as though her relationship with my mother was exactly like my relationship with my mother, which we both knew was not true, in order to passive-aggressively demonstrate to me the very real differences in our respective relationships, which always tilted in the direction of Phoebe knowing things about my mother which I did not and which Phoebe apparently thought I should. It was neither the time nor the place to get into how Foltchain doubtless knew that random messenger dragonflies showing up when I was not expecting them would be annoying and ultimately counterproductive.

"She sent one to remind me that we'd see each other this morning."

"Even though you had no reason to think otherwise based on the way you left things last Wednesday."

Phoebe gave an almost imperceptible shrug. "Maybe she was just being polite. That was less than forty-eight hours ago, though, and since then, nothing."

"Hang on a second," Juvie said, unable to keep out of it any longer. "Kellan, is your mother missing?"

"Nobody said that," I said.

"I'll say it," Phoebe said. "Your mother is missing."

I closed my eyes, unable to decisively contradict Phoebe. I suspected she was right. I was growing more and more certain that she was right. I didn't want her to be right, of course, I wanted to argue with her, at the very least to play devil's advocate for why we shouldn't freak out and panic, but it was hard enough to convince myself of that, let alone Phoebe. I needed a moment to focus and gather my thinking into rational, productive directions. And while I was standing there, in the reception area of my office, knowing that both Phoebe and Juvie were staring at me expectantly, not knowing where in all creation my mother had gone and not liking the not knowing one bit, I felt an unnervingly familiar sensation. Something like a phantom memory of pain, like a jellyfish sting that sizzled across every inch of my skin in a split second, like the instant after waking up from a nightmare and knowing in my bones that whatever had been chasing me in my sleep had followed me into the waking world and was right behind me. I recognized the feeling from the night before, from the thing that had attacked me in my apartment.

I dropped into a hunched half-crouch out of sheer reflex an instant before the thing barrelled into me from behind. I heard Juvie and Phoebe both scream, and I had every intention of screaming at both of them to get the hell out, but the weight of the thing drove me forward and down into the floor, smashing my face into polyurethane before I could say a word.

The thing was still on my back, talons digging into my shoulders like it was trying to root out my spine. I felt its mass shift at the same time I heard Juvie cry out, not in surprise but pain this time. Part of my gray matter was processing the fact that Juvie had probably tried to tackle the thing and regretted it instantly, while the rest of my brain, the part dedicated to prolonging my own survival, realized that I had a split second to get out from underneath the thing while its attention was otherwise occupied. I wriggled across the reception area, propelling myself away from the thing while also rolling from my stomach to my back and blinking away the blurred vision left in the wake of being plowed into the floorboards. I was crab-walking backwards and half sitting up when my shoulders collided with the far wall, fresh pain flaring from the claw marks.

Squinting and hissing, I pushed myself to my feet while Phoebe took a swing at the thing. In the light of day the thing was somehow even weirder than the fleeting impressions I had gotten in my dark apartment the night before. The surface was broken into irregular facets, each individual plane either expanding or contracting constantly, like watching water boil into cloudy, angular bubbles. The limbs went thicker and thinner, longer and shorter at will. All the same, even with a target which was not so much moving as constantly reconstituting, Phoebe was deliberate and precise. She dropped her weight and swung a knifehand strike at the thing's knee.

I knew what would happen, I had seen it before. The thing's leg buckled like a snapped piece of balsa, albeit sheathed in something elastic and unbreakable. For a moment the thing lost its balance and toppled to the side, but the matter composing its body rearranged so that what should have been catching itself on its hands became landing gracefully on its feet. The fractured leg, now an arm, straightened itself, while the opposite limb reared back to swipe at Phoebe.

Juvie came barreling across the reception area. He had pulled one of the cushions off the couch and held it in front of himself like a shield as he rammed into the jagged thing. Juvie had wrestled in junior high school and lettered in high school. When he got to Central Oregon he wound up playing on an intramural rugby team just for fun. He was athletic and he knew hits and takedowns. His momentum carried the thing toward the wall, even as its limbs flailed and split and extended, all the way to the window.

I'd been meaning to speak to the landlord about replacing the office windows for a while. They were original to the building, old wooden sash and case features with thin panes of glass, never terribly energy efficient and downright drafty on cold and windy days. I would have been happy to pay some or all of the costs of the renovation, or work it into my lease somehow. I just hadn't gotten around to reaching out to Mr. Marks. If I hadn't been such a lazy procrastinator, maybe Juvie would have slammed the thing into a set of triple-glazed panes set into composite aluminum vinyl frames and bounced directly off them. Instead, the sash splintered, glass cracked, and the thing and the couch cushion went sailing out the window. Juvie caught himself on the windowsill and halted before following them to the ground three floors down.

Staring wide-eyed through the broken window, gasping for breath, Juvie asked, "What the holy fuck was that?"

"Don't ask me," Phoebe said. "I've never seen anything like that in my life."

"We need to get out of here," I barked. Phoebe recognized the uncharacteristic urgency, bordering on panic, in my voice, and started for the door immediately. Juvie was still in shock, and I had to go to him and pull on his shoulder to turn him around. He looked to me for an explanation but I knew that could wait. I shepherded him out the door.

The three of us ran down the stairwell and out the front door of the building. On the sidewalk, Phoebe asked, "Kellan, is someone after you?"

"I don't know," I said. I could see both Juvie and Phoebe winding themselves up to argue with what they deemed an insufficient answer, so I held up my hands. "I don't know what exactly is going on and I don't want to jump to any conclusions but yes, it makes sense for the moment to err on the side of caution and assume someone or something is after me, while at the same time trying to figure out the real deal."

"So what does that mean, exactly?" Juvie asked, coming back to himself.

"For starters it means we need to get out of here," I said. "Obviously they know where I live and they know where I work. We need to regroup in neutral territory."

"Just tell me where to drive," Juvie said, jangling his keys. He smiled at Phoebe and added, "Lady gets shotgun."

Chapter Three: Off the Grid

Chumley's was the first place that popped into my head when I tried to pin down the idea of 'neutral territory', a specific destination for which I had no personal affinity. A couple of years ago I had been working a pre-split case, tailing a husband suspected by his wife of being unfaithful. If I could produce solid evidence that he was in fact cheating on her, she would file for divorce and demand obscene amounts of alimony. We didn't talk about what would happen if I came up short of irrefutable proof, or somehow disproved her suspicions. By the time they come to secure my services, it's rarely necessary.

It was a depressing case, but one that would pay to keep the lights on that month, and Chumley's Tavern and Grill was emblematic of the whole grimy, sordid thing. On the outside, a squat cigar box building with dark brown wood siding, peeling tarpaper along the foundation, and chicken wire windows displaying neon signs for long-defunct brands of beer. It sat back from the road at the edge of a dull gravel parking lot, flanked on one side by an overflowing dumpster inside a fence missing its gate, and on the other side by a rusting propane tank tagged with sophomoric graffiti. On the inside, a row of booths along one wall, a scattering of tables in the middle of the floor, and a bar running the length of the other wall. The chairs and the barstools were all mismatched. The back wall was divided by three doors: men's room, ladies' room and kitchen. Other than an ancient coat of dark green paint and the accumulated stains of spilled beer and cigarette smoke and the vapors of frying grease, the interior vertical surfaces were undecorated. No television, no jukebox, just an old battery-powered radio behind the bar that played whatever the bartender felt like listening to.

When I followed James Dalrymple to Chumley's, I passed by the entrance - a hump of loose stones and dirt crossing over a battered pipe in a drainage ditch - as he turned in. There were only three other cars in the lot and I was trying to be inconspicuous. I drove aimlessly for a few minutes and saw nothing but overgrown fields and scrub pines. Chumley's was out in the middle of nowhere, which I supposed was part of the appeal. Dalrymple's SUV was still there when I returned, with no other new arrivals. I headed into Chumley's to wait and see if Dalrymple would be joined by the theoretical girlfriend, or boyfriend, as the case might be.

Dalrymple had taken a seat at the bar, I noted, as I scanned the beers on tap, which numbered exactly two, Miller High Life and Miller Lite. Strictly rail quality liquor, too, as far as I could tell from the absence of high end bottles lined up behind the bar. I took a seat at an empty table and picked up a menu, the corners of the lamination curled and ratty. The grill offerings were on par with the tavern aspect, consisting in their entirety of nachos, burgers, hot dogs, reuben sandwiches and french fries. If I hadn't seen the propane hookup outside I'd suspect that the kitchen held little more than a refrigerator, a microwave oven and a tub of congealing dishwater.

Other than Dalrymple, whose boyish face and moussed chestnut curls I recognized from a picture his wife had provided, and myself, the bar had four patrons. A man and woman sat together at the opposite end of the bar from Dalrymple. They both looked fifty- or sixty-something, some missing teeth, thinning and graying hair, loose neck flaps, but maybe they were younger and had just done some hard living. They chainsmoked Pall Malls and nursed Miller Lites and laughed at almost everything each other said. At a table sat a man with a highball glass in front of him and a faraway look in his eyes. And in one of the booths sat a young woman attacking a reuben and fries with a relentlessness that suggested if she stopped biting and chewing for a second the sandwich might start to fight back. Part of me wanted to figure her out; maybe she was a vegetarian lifestyle guru who could never allow the world to know about her cravings for corned beef. But I reminded myself I was on the clock. All in all Chumley's was a perfect place to go and feel sorry for yourself and wallow in whatever form of self-loathing excess felt right, with a modicum of solitude but also the ability to witness other people doing their version of the same thing. Sometimes people needed a place like that, and I found myself hoping that was all it was for James Dalrymple.

The bartender was barely five and a half feet tall, with ash blond hair combed into a severe, old-fashioned side part and a close-cropped mustache. His skinny, tattooed arms poked out of frayed holes where the sleeves had been cut-off a checked shirt. He yelled "Getcha anything?" in my general direction and I realized he expected me to shout my order back. I kept it simple, asked for a High Life, and he grabbed a mug from under the bartop. I expected him to simply set it next to the tap for me to pick up, but he walked out from behind the bar and carried the beer to my table. I breathed in as I raised the mug to my lips and was relieved that I couldn't smell any evidence of funk growing in the tap lines, at least.

A woman walked in, unremarkable in almost every way. Dark brown hair pulled back in a ponytail, no makeup. Indeterminate body type hidden by a thick sweatshirt and baggy jeans. She made a beeline for Dalrymple, then sat down next to him without any greeting. I watched them out of the corner of my eye. Despite projecting virtually no sex appeal, the woman still might be Dalrymple's side action. I'd learned pretty quickly that a man doesn't cheat on his spouse because he meets someone objectively hotter, or because he's seduced by someone possessed of noteworthy come-hither sensuality. They cheat because on some level they just feel the need to cheat. It often helps if the new object of their attention is younger, to trigger those primitive alpha male endorphins I guess, and the woman sitting next to Dalrymple looked five or ten years his junior. Maybe she was also cheating on someone back home, and left the house dressed all the way down to keep from seeming suspicious. Maybe that was just the way she always dressed and Dalrymple didn't care.

She got a tequila sunrise from the bartender, and she and Dalrymple exchanged a few words, barely looking at each other. He reached into his pocket, pulled out a bill, and put it on the bar between them. She drew a baggie from the pouch of her sweatshirt and passed it to him low under the bar; it disappeared into his pocket. She finished her drink, palmed the money he'd laid down as she rose from her stool, and left Chumley's without a backwards glance.

I tried to decide if informing Mrs. Dalrymple that her husband was not cheating on her but, instead, was hiding a drug habit from her qualified as good news or bad news. She'd probably take it as good news, initially at least. She wanted a divorce and she wanted it to be his fault, and now her bargaining chip was not mere infidelity but activities which cops might actually do something about. I could only hope that she'd settle her accounts with me before she found out how deep an impact her husband's habit had made on the family finances she was girding herself to battle over.

Dalrymple settled his tab, his eagerness to get to his drugs making his exit a bit suspiciously hasty, but no one seemed to notice or care. Presumably Chumley's had something of a don't ask, don't tell policy on drug deals transacted on the premises, or any other inherently unsavory conduct. It was that kind of place, a hole to crawl into to blot out or tamp down your problems, the overriding rule being that you weren't to make your problems anyone else's problem.

I did my best not to judge, to stay focused on the job I was there to do. Not that there was much left to do after Dalrymple hustled off to get his fix. I doubted that Dalrymple would be even marginally aware of me if I tailed him out of Chumley's, but I put another beer between our respective departures all the same. By the time I hit the parking lot again, Dalrymple's SUV was long gone.

I had no desire to set foot in that dive again. I followed Dalrymple back there again a week later, but I parked my car on the shoulder a quarter mile down the road. Armed with my camera and its telezoom lens, I hung out in the tall grass beside the gravel lot, watched the dealer arrive, watched her leave again, and watched Dalrymple exit the tavern and climb into his SUV. I had guessed that he would do a bump from the bag right there behind the wheel, and he did not disappoint me. I took several photos of him partaking, to be delivered to his wife with my condolences and my invoice, after which I intended never to lay eyes on Chumley's Tavern &

Grill again.

And yet, here we sat, Juvie, Phoebe and I, occupying the booth farthest from the front door, the very same one where I had seen a woman show a sandwich no mercy some time ago. It was early afternoon and the only other people in the place were the same bartender as last time and a lone barfly, a man with thinning hair greased back against his scalp and moles dotting the back of his neck, wearing coveralls of dull blue-gray. "So, what's good here?" Juvie asked, feigning obliviousness.

"Nothing," Phoebe said.

"The expectation of privacy," I said. "Paying customers can keep to themselves and not be bothered."

"I'll get the first round, then," Juvie said, sliding off the bench. "Any requests?"

"Whatever you're having," I said.

Phoebe gave an acquiescent nod and, as Juvie wove between tables to cross the floor, she asked, "Are we really going to get much out of comparing notes here? None of us has the first clue what is going on."

"True," I said, "but we need a plan, too, even if it's just to figure out how to go about figuring it all out. I'd rather do that with a moment to sit and think than on the fly."

"I suppose," Phoebe said begrudgingly. Her eyes went unfocused, and I could tell she was grappling, not altogether successfully, with the memories of the thing in the office. "I meant it when I said I had never seen anything like that before. Not whatever that thing was, and not anything even remotely close."

"I know," I told her.

"But… I still have this feeling like I should know it, somehow. That I do know it but I can't quite place it. Do you know what I mean?"

"I understand what you're saying," I said, "but I can't relate. There's nothing familiar about those things."

Phoebe's eyes snapped to me. "Things?"

"The thing in the office, and the other thing that showed up in my apartment last night."

"Kellan!" Phoebe gasped, splitting the difference between concern for my well-being and irritation that this was the first I was bringing up the prior assault.

I rubbed my eyes. "Can we put this on pause until Juvie gets back, so I only have to tell the story once?"

Phoebe crossed her arms stiffly over her chest. I pretended to study the menu, unsurprised that the grill had not expanded its offerings since my last visit. Juvie returned to the booth with three pint glasses, one a slightly different height and tapering angle than the others but all filled with cloudy liquid and ice. As he lowered himself onto the bench beside me and slid drinks in front of Phoebe and me, I asked, "Are these… lemonades?"

Juvie was already gulping from his glass, but shook his head as he lowered his drink. "Tom Collins."

"Seriously? Isn't it a little early for the hard stuff?"

"One, I've been on a mission for a few years now to sample a thousand Tom Collinses from a thousand different bars before I die," Juvie said. "I was gonna start a YouTube channel but I never got around to it, but then I had been committed to the premise for so long that I couldn't give up on it. And two, any time after a narrow escape from a freaky life-or-death situation is plenty late enough for booze. So three, you go to hell, lightweight."

I took a tentative sip and felt the wallop of the gin immediately. "A double?" I asked.

"Again I refer you to the aforementioned points two and three," Juvie said.

"This is actually really good," Phoebe said.

Juvie raised his glass in appreciative salute. Turning to me he said, "If you don't want to drink with us, fine. Talk. What is going on?"

I told Juvie and Phoebe about the incident in my apartment the night before. When I finished, Juvie said, "So the obvious question seems to be, is there some connection between these things attacking you and your mother going missing?"

"And the obvious answer seems to be, there has to be," I said. "It's too big of a coincidence otherwise."

"Unfortunately, the two being related doesn't make either one any more comprehensible," Phoebe said.

"True," I said, "but it still helps. Anything we can figure out about one side of things might help illuminate the other."

"So where do we start?" Juvie asked.

I took a deep breath and let it out slowly. "The

Deep Woods."

Phoebe set her drink down, and Juvie looked back and forth between her and me trying to catch a hint as to what he'd missed. "You mean, like, just go hiking around in the forest and hope you bump into your mom?" he asked.

"Not exactly," I said. "Actually, not at all. Not the forest in the way that you mean, and not searching for her per se, either."

"I'm lost," Juvie admitted.

"You're thinking about The Oak," Phoebe said.

I nodded.

"The Oak what?" Juvie asked. "Oak furniture? Oak barrel whiskey? Tie a yellow ribbon round the old oak tree?"

"Just The Oak," I said. "The one in my mother's name, Foltchain of the Oak."

"She's named after a tree?" Juvie asked.

"Yes and no," I said. "She belongs to the trees, and the oak trees in particular, and one Oak very much in particular."

"One oak tree out of… what, hundreds and thousands in the forest?" Juvie asked.

"Not the forest," Phoebe said. "The Deep Woods."

Juvie turned a skeptical eye on her. "You say that like there's a big difference and I should already know what it is."

"There's definitely a difference," Phoebe said. "Whether you know it or not."

"Care to enlighten me?" Juvie asked.

Phoebe rolled her eyes, so I stepped in again. "Some parts of the forest are harder to get to than others. Some are so remote that you would never, ever accidentally stumble into them, no matter how hard you tried or how wildly lost you were. Some can only be reached by people who know how to find the way, and that's what we mean by the Deep Woods. And in the heart of the Deep Woods is The Oak, an ancient tree with a connection to my mother. If there's any place I can go to get a bead on where she is and how she's doing, that's it."

"All right," Juvie nodded. "I assume there's more to it, but you can explain as we go."

"Or I can explain when I get back," I said, causing Juvie and Phoebe to both immediately protest, clamoring over each other to object until I held both my hands up to plead for quiet. "Look, Juvie, I'm sorry this all blew up right when we were supposed to hang out, but I'll have to take a raincheck. I'll make it up to you. And Phoebe, I need you to hold down the fort while I'm gone, especially in case my mother spontaneously reappears on her own, so you can tell her to stay put until I get back. All right?"

"Absolutely not," Phoebe said.

"What she said," Juvie nodded.

"Are you actually going to make me say it?" I asked.

Phoebe stared me down. "Say what?" Juvie asked.

"These things know where I live and know where I work," I said. "They don't look like anything out of the Deep Woods, so it's possible they don't know about that. Maybe while I'm in the Deep Woods they won't be able to locate me. But if they do, at least they'll only come after me. I'll have drawn them away from populated areas, and… people I care about."

"What about the flip side of that?" Phoebe asked. "What if they can't find their way into the Deep Woods, and they can't figure out where you've gone, so they just start randomly attacking to try to flush you out?"

"That's not an argument for you to come with me, that's an argument for me not to go at all," I said. "In fact, that's also an argument for you to stay here. If we're both in the Deep Woods and these things start just firebombing the block I live on or whatever, we wouldn't know, we wouldn't be able to respond. If you're here and see that happening, maybe you can get word to me. Send dragonflies or something."

"That's your mother's system, not mine," Phoebe said. "I don't have a system, and I'm not going to sit around waiting for you to get back before something terrible happens. Which, by the way, might happen to me, did you think about that?"

"What?" I blinked.

"Trees above, Kellan!" Phoebe said, a shout she barely restrained through clenched teeth. She slammed her Tom Collins down on the table and, I admit it, I flinched. "You think you're the only one with any connection to Foltchain? Why, because of… of… of blood? Could you be more… human?"

"No," I said quietly, deliberately refusing to match her intensity, "I'm about maxed out on being human, I think. That's all I've got to work with."

"And you think that's going to serve you well in

the Deep Woods? Really?" She picked up her glass, took a dramatic sip from the straw. "Really?"

"It's all I've got," I repeated.

"No, it's not," Phoebe said. "Are you listening? They've come after you, in your home, at your work. It's my work, too. Foltchain is part of my life, too. They might come after me, too. If you can hide from them in the Deep Woods, I can hide, too. You want to go to the Oak? I do too."

"Phoebe…"

"What?"

"I don't…" I didn't want her to come. But I didn't know what else to say. She was right, she knew far more about the Deep Woods than I did. She was born there, raised there. I could have learned more about it, but I had given up on that path. And she was right about everything else, too. If someone or something was trying to stop people from coming after my mother, from coming after them for taking my mother, they'd have to stop Phoebe just as surely as they'd have to stop me.

"You don't what?"

"Nothing," I shook my head. "Fine. You can come."

"All right," Juvie said. "That's settled. When do we leave?"

"Exactly which part of the argument she was making on her own behalf did you think applied to you?" I asked.

Juvie shrugged, but also gave the question some thought. "Well, there was the part where apparently no one can get in touch with you while you're in the Dark Woods…"

"Deep Woods," Phoebe corrected him.

"Right. So if I can't contact you, I can't help you. But you're my boy, so I'm gonna have your back."

"Juvie," I said, "I appreciate the sentiment, but I don't need your help."

"She made it sound like you need all the help you can get," Juvie pointed out.

I covered my eyes with one hand and pulled it down the length of my face. I was exhausted and this conversation would have been draining on a good day. "Be that as it may…"

"Whatever help you might offer," Phoebe interjected, "it would probably be offset by the effort Kellan and I would have to put forth keeping you safe from harm."

"Now that is just ridiculous," Juvie said. "I can take care of myself fine. I once spent a month in Australia and lived to tell about it."

"Really not the same thing," I said.

"Australia is widely recognized as the foremost place where everything is trying to kill you."

"Foremost place on Earth," Phoebe muttered.

"As opposed to?" Juvie asked.

Phoebe shook her head and rattled the ice in her empty glass. "I'm going to get another round," she announced, sliding off the bench. "You two?"

Juvie said, "Count me in." I shook my head. Phoebe crossed to the bar.

"Juvie," I started, "Look… how do I explain this? Granted, Australia has poisonous snakes and spiders, and crocodiles and drop bears and all that, but those are wild animals. Dangerous, but avoidable, and still subject to all the old more-afraid-of-you-than-you-are-of-them rules. Don't seek them out, don't provoke them, don't accidentally stomp on their nests, and you'll be okay. Australia's not actively hostile. It's not as if the continent of Australia has its own volition and wants to punish any and all intruders."

"I'm with you," Juvie said.

"So that's the difference," I said.

"The Deep Woods are going to actively try to kill you?"

"Parts of it, yes. Maybe. Probably."

"Well that's…" Juvie trailed off. He was looking toward the bar, and I turned my attention that way. Phoebe was standing at one corner and the only other of Chumley's patrons, the man in coveralls, was leaning toward her and talking animatedly, a development Phoebe did not look happy about. "Scuse me," Juvie said.

I reached for his arm, but he was already out of the booth. I followed him to the bar, picking up more of the old barfly's running commentary as we drew nearer. "I'm just sayin', we're both here, we're both drinkin', we might as well drink together, right? Just one shot, right? I'm buyin'."

Phoebe was doing what she usually did when someone got unpleasant with her: nothing. It was an asset in our workplace, as no matter how upset a client got, over the phone or in person in the reception area, screaming and cursing or sobbing or whatever flavor of freaking out, Phoebe remained cool and professional in her interactions, getting the necessary information, waiting patiently for however long the emotional outburst took to run its course, unflinching in the face of any and all invective. But it wasn't something I had taught her or something she picked up on the job, it was part of her nature. If anyone became antagonistic with her and there was no occupational reason for her to overcome the antipathy and interact with them, she just went blank. Her face became a wooden mask, not literally, although on some level, actually, yes, literally. She was wearing the mask now, her expression neutral with the slightest hint of annoyance in her eyes. She stared at the bartender, who hadn't aged a day since last time I had been here, but had at least changed his top to an olive green and brown bowling shirt, ragged where the sleeves were missing. I wondered idly if he ever allowed cloth to touch his biceps. Phoebe's eyes bored holes into him, while she ignored the relentless offers to buy her a drink.

The bartender, for his part, was holding a shot glass at waist level and wiping it with a threadbare towel. He scrutinized the glass, spinning and stroking it like he was polishing a crown jewel for ceremonial perfection. The corners of his mouth puckered and trembled as if he were fighting the urge to laugh, deeply amused by the unwanted attention one of his regulars was lavishing on the newcomer. So he would be no help at all.

The barfly was still haranguing Phoebe, crowding in on her personal space in a way that made it impossible for her silence and her averted eyes to be anything other than a deliberate snub. "You gonna answer me? I'm just tryin' to be friendly, you know, hospitable," the barfly said, with particular emphasis on the 'spit' syllable. "You too good to do a shot with me, that it? You gonna tell me no, you better tell me why."

"She doesn't have to tell you anything, buddy," Juvie said. He tried to step between the barfly and Phoebe, probably expecting to catch the belligerent drunk by surprise and make him retreat. But the barfly was in high dudgeon and didn't step back at all, leaving himself, Juvie and Phoebe in an awkwardly crowded cluster at the bar.

"I ain't talkin' to you," the barfly sneered.

"Yeah, no shit," Juvie said. "You're talking to her, but she's not into it. Take a hint and back off."

I stared daggers at the bartender, wishing he would realize that whatever had made the situation such a big joke to him had lost all of its potential humor. No bartender wants a fight to break out under his roof, no matter how bad any of the drunks are spoiling for one. The bartender glanced up, maybe a little guiltily, but didn't make any attempt to referee.

"Why don't you back off?" the barfly echoed. "Why don't you let the chickie answer for herself? Why you lettin' her get away with pretending I don't even exist?"

Juvie turned his back on the barfly, one elbow nudging Phoebe while the other levered none too gently against the drunk. Now Juvie was pretending the barfly didn't exist, as well. "Why don't you head back to the booth?" Juvie suggested to Phoebe in a low voice. "I'll get the drinks."

Phoebe said nothing, didn't even shift her eyes to

Juvie. Juvie would have waited patiently for her to acknowledge him pretty near indefinitely, I imagine, but the offended regular had burned his fuse down to its end. He reached for the small of his back with his right hand.

I know what it looks like when someone goes for a weapon, especially when they're making no particular effort to disguise the action. I didn't know whether this guy had a knife or a gun, but either way I wasn't going to give him a chance to use it. I moved, quick but controlled, closing the distance between us and seizing his right wrist. I had his arm pinned against his back in half a second, with just enough pressure on it to make it feel like it was a twitch away from a painfully dislocated shoulder. The barfly wailed, a sound that conveyed pain and protest but was far from resembling any actual words in English, but by then I was frog-marching him to the opposite end of the bar.

I guided the barfly onto a stool and released his arm. He cradled it in his lap, hunched over it defensively. I looked to the bartender, who was staring at me wide-eyed. "Why don't you give this fellow a shot of whatever he likes," I said, pulling out my wallet and transferring a twenty to the surface of the bar. "Provided he stays right here in this seat."

"Hey what about our drinks?" Juvie asked.

I tilted my head towards Juvie and Phoebe, and the bartender with visible effort tore his gaze from me and directed it to their end of the bar. Phoebe took a deep breath and said, clearly and serenely, "Three Tom Collinses, please."

"I told you I'm good, Phoebe," I reminded her.

"I know," she nodded. "One for Juvie, two for me."

The bartender looked to me as if he needed my permission. I made a little shoo-shoo motion with my fingers, indicating he should get busy, and he did. I squeezed the barfly's shoulder and retreated back to the booth, followed a minute later by Juvie and Phoebe.

"So where were we?" Juvie asked with an easy smile, as if the entire day so far had been a lark.

"We were at the point where I give up trying to argue with either of you about anything," I said.

"That's progress," Phoebe said.

"So we're all going to the Deep Woods?" Juvie asked.

"Looks that way," I said. "In the morning. And I'm not entirely ruling out the possibility that after I sleep on it, I might change my mind."

Phoebe, sucking down Tom Collins, shook her head. Whether she was saying I shouldn't change my mind, or simply that I wouldn't, I didn't know.

"Where to sleep is an open question, though," I went on. "If Phoebe's right, and she's a likely target because of her relationship with my mother, then her place isn't any safer than mine. We should probably avoid places where we'd be expected to be found."

"So a hotel then?" Juvie asked.

I nodded. "Sorry, I know you were expecting me to put you up this week…"

He held up a hand to cut me off. "Nah, it's a good call." He pulled out his cell phone. "I'll make the arrangements."

"You don't have to do that," I protested, but he was already deep into the reservation process and didn't even look up from his screen.

Juvie and Phoebe finished their second round without incident and we left Chumley's. The sobering barfly glowered at us over the untouched drink my money had paid for as we headed for the door, but he held his tongue. If I had my way, I wouldn't set foot in Chumley's again for a long time, if ever, but then again, that was what I had thought last time.

Juvie had reserved us three rooms at a mid-priced hotel a few exits down the highway. He checked us in and put all the rooms on his credit card, after insisting that he should be the only one creating a paper trail given he wasn't part of Foltchain's inner circle like Phoebe and I were. I was fairly certain that the things that had attacked me were not familiar with modern methods of tracking individuals by financial transactions. They struck me as operating on a much more primal level. But I stayed out of Juvie's way all the same.

We took our keys to our rooms and checked them, one by one, all three of us entered together and verified nothing jagged and faceless was hiding in a closet or bathtub or mini-fridge. Once that was done I suggested we get an early dinner, get to bed early, and set out before dawn the next day.

We ordered a couple of pizzas, by which I mean once again Juvie made the order on his cell phone with his credit card under his name, with all of us gathered in his room. When he hung up, I asked him, "Did the front desk make you give names for the two other guests?"

"Sure," Juvie shrugged.

"And what names did you give?" I asked.

Juvie grinned. "Desiree Wilder and Bootsy Hemlock."

I vaguely recognized the names, from some raucous conversation back at one of our college watering holes, something about fake IDs or porn star aliases. Phoebe rolled her eyes, disdaining what she correctly assumed was an inside joke.

We flipped around on the television for a bit and then the room phone rang, the front desk announcing the pizza delivery person was downstairs. Juvie left to retrieve dinner. As the door closed behind him Phoebe flopped back on the bed and said, "So how are we going to ditch him in the morning?"

"I don't think we can," I sighed.

She sat bolt upright. "You were serious about him coming with us?"

"Yeah," I admitted. "He wasn't going to take no for an answer. And maybe he'll be able to help."

"That is exceedingly unlikely," Phoebe said. "He's only going to slow us down and make things more difficult, if he doesn't just get himself killed outright. Or get us all killed."

"He's one of my oldest friends," I said. "I trust him to listen to us, follow our lead, and not get himself or any of us killed. Maybe he will slow us down, maybe he won't do us a lick of good, but…"

"But what?"

"You have to admit, whoever or whatever we're up against here, they wouldn't expect us to bring someone like Juvie into the Deep Woods. We're making unexpected moves. That's got to count for something."

Phoebe laughed, a scoff of pure disbelief. But she dropped the subject. Juvie was back with the pizzas shortly after that, and we ate in companionable silence. Phoebe excused herself first, and I headed to my own room not much later.

I stripped out of my clothes, took a shower, and got into the bed. I stared at the ceiling for a long, long time. My mother was missing. I was being targeted, and the closest thing in the world I had to a sister was very likely in similar danger. The closest thing I had to a brother was willing to put himself in harm's way to help me, but I didn't even know what help I needed, beyond my vague plan to visit my mother's namesake oak and hope for a miracle along the way.

Sleep wouldn't come, even as the room darkened to blackness. Eventually I got up and went to the window, looked out at the night sky. I wouldn't see stars for a while once tomorrow came; the canopy of the Deep Woods was too thick for that. Motion in the parking lot below caught my eye, and I looked down. Juvie was pacing the asphalt, smoking a cigarette.

I threw my clothes back on and took the elevator to the lobby. As I crossed the parking lot, Juvie was exhaling smoke from his nostrils in a slow, steady stream as he stared at the ground contemplatively.

Without looking up, he flicked the butt toward the grassy slope beside some empty parking spaces, where it was swallowed in a patch of clover. "You know it takes about eight years for one of those to biodegrade," I said.

Juvie's head snapped up, a startled look on his face, but he relaxed as soon as he saw that it was me. "Yeah, I know," he agreed. "That's why I figured I better have one tonight. I'm guessing there's no garbage cans in the Deep Woods."

"Not that I've ever seen," I said.

"And littering in the Deep Woods, that's probably, like, some seriously bad karma we don't need," Juvie went on.

"Bad karma anywhere," I said. "It's all connected, one big biosphere."

Juvie nodded slowly, a somewhat pleased expression on his face, as if he were grateful for a new piece of information to assimilate into his worldview. Then he turned away from me and ambled toward the grassy slope. "Juvie, you don't have to do that," I called after him.

He ignored me, bending over and combing his fingertips through the clover until he came up with the discarded butt. He rolled it back and forth in his palm as he walked back to me. "Bad karma we don't need," he repeated.

"No argument," I said. "But I was gonna say, I could pick it up. Least I could do after you sprang for dinner on top of the rooms."

Juvie rolled his eyes. "Think you got that backwards. Picking up the tab in the real world is the least I can do, before we take off."

"I told you, the Deep Woods is part of the real world…" I began.

"Yeah, but it's a part where money won't do us much good," Juvie countered, and he had a point. "A part where I won't do much good. If hiding out here and getting food in our bellies helps, I'm all for it. I might as well be the one to foot the bill, instead of being useless the entire way. I'll do whatever I can to help you."

"I appreciate that, man. Really." I paused a moment before I added, "Phoebe appreciates it, too."

His eyes flicked to mine for an instant, then sought out the cigarette butt he was jittering around in his palm, as if it were an object of tremendous fascination. But the look he had given me was enough, and if it hadn't been, the refusal to maintain eye contact did the rest. I had known Juvie for a long time, and had spent copious amounts of time with him back in college, so I knew his tells. I knew he was equal parts hedonist and hopeless romantic, Don Juan taking his idle pleasure with Dona Ana one day and Don Quixote pining for his idealized Dulcinea the next, and I had always been able to tell just by dropping a feminine name whether Juvie was into her or not, and whether it was fleeting lust or full-blown infatuation. I had suspected that Juvie was infatuated with Phoebe. I'd suspected it, mostly subconsciously, when I'd introduced them that morning and recognized it for what it was when he'd come to her defense at Chumley's. It was the reason I had finally stopped arguing with Juvie about staying away from the

Deep Woods, realizing he was just as concerned with watching Phoebe's back as mine. Mentioning her now had effectively confirmed what I'd been assuming. There was no separating Juvie from Phoebe now, not until the danger had passed.

I cleared my throat. "Can you get a wakeup call for 5:00 a.m.?"

Juvie looked to me and smiled. "Already did, man, before I came out here."

"All right, then. Bang on my door after you're up, and we'll roll."

Chapter Four: The Trailhead

Part of me had hoped that, twenty-four hours later, my mother's cottage would look different. Not so much due to the passage of time, but the manner in which everything had been reframed in a new context during the intervening day. The day before I had been looking for some indication of where my mother might have gone of her own volition, but now I was aware of the possibility, or very high probability, that she had been abducted.

Unfortunately, that new information did nothing to transform the blank ordinariness of my mother's home. There were no signs of forced entry or struggle, which was really no surprise. If there had been, I would have noticed them yesterday, challenging my assumption that my mother had simply gone on a spontaneous walkabout. Once again I poked curiously into every corner of the cottage, while Juvie and Phoebe did the same, but when we had reconvened at the dining room table none of us had discovered anything of interest.

"All right, no point hanging out here any longer than we have to," I announced. We had come directly from the hotel, bypassing my apartment and Phoebe's to avoid anywhere that might be an easy target for the things to attack again. We were all wearing the same clothes from the day before, so I turned to Juvie and said, "Come here, follow me."

Juvie obliged and I led him back to my mother's bedroom. He paused a few feet past the threshold, maintaining a respectful distance from any and all of my mother's personal effects. I went straight for her closet and started rummaging through the clothing hanging at the far end. "You need help looking for something?" Juvie asked.

"Nah," I said. I turned away from the closet with an armful of clothes and dumped them on the bed. I went back for a large canvas bag on the floor of the closet and hefted it onto the bedspread.

"What's all this?" Juvie asked.

"Hiking gear," I said. "Go ahead, find some stuff that fits you and get changed."

"I thought you said your mom lived alone?"

"She does."

"So is she…?" Juvie pantomimed projecting the height and shape of his body outward from his shoulders.

I shook my head. "No, these aren't her clothes. They're extras." Juvie raised an eyebrow at that and I went on, "Short version, sometimes people contact my mom for help connecting with nature, and sometimes she invites them here so she can take them into the woods…"

"The Deep Woods?"

"Not usually. In exceptional cases, maybe the very outermost fringes. But anyway, in other cases a person shows up not realizing they've signed up to go tromping through the forest, not really dressed for it. So my mother started keeping spare clothes on hand." I waved at the pile of clothes to encourage Juvie to get started, then grabbed the canvas bag and upended it. A half dozen pairs of heavy boots tumbled out.

Juvie divested himself of his stylish attire and put on expedition pants and a heavy button-down shirt, army surplus stuff. He pawed through the boots and found a pair that were his size, or close enough. He slipped off his shoes and started to lace up the boots. "You gonna change, too?" he asked.

"Yeah, just giving you first dibs," I said. Truthfully I had been entirely concerned with putting Juvie in practical gear just to slightly increase his chances of surviving the Deep Woods. I had a bit more faith in my own ability to navigate them safely. If I had to, I could do it barefoot in a Speedo. But I couldn't see any advantage in rubbing Juvie's face in the vast gulf between our respective preparedness. I swapped my outfit for some of my mother's guest wardrobe.

I took my cellphone and car keys out of the pocket of the pants I had been wearing and set them atop the chest at the foot of my mother's bed. The cellphone was already semi-useless, barely able to pick up any tower signal on my mother's isolated property, and neither the phone nor the keys would do me any good in the Deep Woods. "Don't bring anything you wouldn't be okay with losing forever," I told Juvie, and he took my point and laid his own phone next to mine. I undid my shoulder holster, laid it on the chest, and changed into hiking attire. As I strapped my SIG Pro back in its place, I led Juvie to the dining room.

Phoebe was leafing through one of my mother's books, and looked up at us as we emerged from the hall. "Good idea," she nodded approvingly. "Be right back, less than a minute."

She departed and I stole a glance at Juvie. I could see him trying very hard not to think about Phoebe undressing a few yards away. "You remember that Burnsie concert we went to sophomore year?" I asked.

"What?" Juvie looked to me, startled from his reverie.

"Right after we got back from fall break," I went on, "there was a concert in the football stadium parking lot. The opening act was... oh what were they called, the artsy drama majors channeling Mountain Goats and Tori Amos..."

"Runcible Spoon," Juvie said.

"Of course," I smiled. "Runcible Spoon. They set up risers and amps they borrowed from the music building and just took over the parking lot on a random Monday night, and nobody knew if it was a student activities fund thing or a frat thing or a club thing or what, and then Burnsie came out and did a set and people lost their minds."

"Yeah that was pretty crazy," Juvie agreed. "Was

that the show where you made me run back to our room for a bottle of Rumple Minze?"

"You offered," I said. "And you weren't even offering to me, you were offering to those two girls who wound up standing next to us."

"And we never saw them again, the little schnapps stealing minxes," Juvie said. "Why do you ask? Some deeper meaning, some analogy to keep in mind that's going to be strategically important in the Deep Woods?"

"Not that I can think of," I said.

"Priming me with happy thoughts so I can mentally fight off the terrors awaiting us?" Juvie pressed.

"Nah," I shrugged. "Just crossed my mind is all. The most important thing about the Deep Woods is that you need to stay behind me and Phoebe, only go where we go, don't touch anything and do whatever we say without question."

"I hear you," Juvie said.

"Do that and we'll be in and out," I said, "and when we get back I'll dig out my old Burnsie CDs and a bottle of whatever you want." I didn't really believe it was going to be that easy, but we were at the edge of the precipice now. Nothing for it but brazen, unearned confidence.

Phoebe returned, dressed in similar style as Juvie and me. We looked like a three-man paramilitary squad, though I was the only one armed. Juvie looked back and forth between Phoebe and me and must have developed a similar thought. "Is this it? Any other supplies we need?"

Phoebe shook her head. "We should travel light,"

she said.

"Less is more, as far as what we carry in," I agreed.

"What, like, the trees will provide?" Juvie asked. "Seriously? I mean, dude, we are in your mother's house. She must have some stuff lying around here that might come in handy, right?

"Maybe she does," I said. "She doesn't exactly stockpile stuff like that, though. She makes what she needs when she needs it."

"For real?" Juvie raised an eyebrow.

"If she kept preparations lying around, don't you think I would have checked for my tea already?" Phoebe challenged him.

Juvie shrugged. "Still worth a look, though, right?"

I stepped into the kitchen and rummaged through my mother's cupboards. A couple of clay jars and a small glass flask yielded up a few items I was able to identify as useful. I set them on the countertop, then on impulse checked the icebox, and discovered an untouched loaf of my mother's homemade protein bars. She didn't call them that, of course, I think 'pan of provision' was her name for them, but protein bars was basically what they were: rolled oats, whey, honey, almond butter, and cinnamon mashed and mixed together and solidified. I cut a few slices, wrapped them in wax paper, and slid them into one of the nylon-lined pockets in my expedition pants. I scooped up the cuttings and the vial and came back into the hall, showing Juvie and Phoebe a scatter of downy leaves, a jumble of seeds, and the tiny bottle. "Hagwick, four thieves vinegar, and fennel. That was all I could find," I explained.

"Better than nothing," Juvie said.

"Chances are it just guarantees that we won't even cross paths with any witches, plague rats, or evil spirits," I said, shoving the materials into the pocket opposite the protein bars. "But sure, I guess even that is something. Let's go."

The woods behind my mother's cottage were cool and fragrant as our trio passed under the outermost edges of the canopy. We automatically took up positions in a single file line, Phoebe at the front, me in the middle, Juvie bringing up the rear. We picked our way among the brush on the forest floor, following Phoebe's meandering path wending through the trees. The three of us were silent, surrounded by chirping birds and bugs, small animals scurrying out of sight, and the whisper of wind in the leaves.

"I thought you said there was a path to the Deep Woods that started at your mom's place," Juvie said after we had been walking for about five minutes.

"Right," I said.

"So where is it?"

"It's not a path like a marked trail, like a walking course in a park," I explained. "It's just… a way."

"But not the easy way," Juvie said, focusing on climbing over a fallen tree covered in thorny vines without getting snagged or slashed.

"Depends," I answered.

Juvie let me slide on that extremely vague note,

and we continued on our way. Phoebe kept us moving at a good pace, and I could hear Juvie's breathing, the steady in and out of moderate exertion with the occasional stop as he held his breath, presumably to bite back a curse or complaint, then let it out in a rush. After we had plowed through a wide, sucking mudhole dotted with milkweed, Juvie asked, "Is this just going to keep getting harder and harder?"

It was tough to be certain if he were asking me, or just venting aloud, but I chose to engage. "A little harder. Then it gets easier. Well, easier walking at any rate."

"For real?" Juvie asked hopefully.

"Yeah," I said. "The Deep Woods aren't that hard to get around in. It's the transition to it from the normal world that's tough."

"So how do we make the jump?" Juvie asked. "Do we go into some cave, or crawl into a giant tree and down the rabbit hole, or what?"

"It's not a doorway," I said. I thought about my mother, the timeless walks we had taken together in the forest and, occasionally, the Deep Woods when I was growing up. When I was very young she did almost all of the talking, prodding me every now and then to name something or demonstrate that I understood how things worked. As I got older she still did most of the talking, me asking questions and her patiently illustrating the principles that would allow me to understand. It did something strange to my emotional equilibrium to feel the positions reversed, leading someone else through the green wilderness, trying to give not just information but perception and appreciation.

"What is it then?" Juvie brought me back from my musings.

"It's something more gradual," I said. "It's like… all right, have you ever read a book about general relativity?"

Juvie laughed. "You do recall I was a business major with a minor in sociology, right?"

"Sure," I said, "but you took electives. And some people read books just for fun. I know I'm just a homeschooled weirdo but my understanding is that some kids do book reports on reading-level appropriate biographies of Albert Einstein in third grade."

"Fair point," Juvie said. "All right, assume I have a third grader's understanding of Einstein's theories."

"You know the pictures that they use to illustrate the concept of massive objects like stars distorting spacetime?

"I think so," Juvie said. "Where space is this grid sheet and the star is a heavy ball and it sinks into the middle of the sheet?"

"Exactly," I said. "So, on the one hand, the Deep Woods is kind of like that. Sometimes they show stars of different sizes and obviously the bigger something is, the deeper it sinks, the bigger gravity well it creates, right? The Deep Woods is at the bottom of a very long well, not a gravity well but a reality well. They're so far down that if from the outside of it you would never even see it. Standing on the sheet, it just looks flat all around you."

"Until you get right on top of the hole, or fall in

it," Juvie said. "But Phoebe said it was impossible to stumble into the Deep Woods."

"Right, so on the other hand, it's the opposite of the spacetime diagram," I went on, "because gravity draws smaller objects toward bigger objects. The diagram makes sense to our brains because things roll downhill, and the diagram depicts gravity wells as big sloping funnels. But spacetime isn't a two-dimensional sheet, it's three-dimensional, or four-dimensional, I guess, I never quite got that aspect of the model."

"Same here," Juvie said.

"Anyway, gravity is about in and out, not up and down, right? Objects don't fall down gravity wells, they fall into them, from any direction."

"All right."

"So the Deep Woods is so densely its own reality that it bends the places where it connects to the normal world. It's an in-and-out bend, not an up-and-down bend. But if it helps you visualize it, think of it as the opposite of the gravity wells. It's an uphill bend. It's harder to enter the Deep Woods than not to."

"Except… say someone got lost in the regular woods. What if they chose going uphill, even though it's harder. It makes logical sense to try to find higher ground to get your bearings, doesn't it? Wouldn't those people at least have a chance of stumbling into the Deep Woods?"

"Fair point, but 'uphill' in this case is an analogy. It's not about actual physical elevation. The entry points to the Deep Woods aren't literally at the tops of mountains. It's just mentally harder to get there, I guess you'd say. There's some kind of… interference that turns people away from the Deep Woods' density. If you know how to navigate the interference, you can get there, but if you don't, there's just no way it won't get the better of you, whatever your conscious plan, and steer you aside."

"That's pretty crazy," Juvie said, then quickly added, "No offense."

"None taken."

"So is that how I'll know we're getting close, the interference? What's it going to feel like?"

"You wouldn't feel it," I assured him. "One trick is to follow someone who knows how to get there, which is what we've been doing." I gestured ahead at Phoebe's back.

"When will we get there, then?"

"A couple minutes ago," I said. "Take a look around."

Walking through the forest behind my mother's cottage, we had at first been on relatively flat and clear ground, covered with the usual assortment of dead leaves and twigs, the trees spaced in such a way that we could see dozens of yards away along various sightlines. As we'd progressed, the trees had become taller, thicker, closer together. Boles no wider than telephone poles had been replaced by massive trunks five or ten feet or more in diameter. We were no longer crossing a room with occasional columns but navigating a maze among colossal pillars supporting tapestries of moss and lichen, mounted atop wild, gnarled roots. The quality of the light had changed, from golden sunshine to a more muted blue-green. I watched Juvie realize the shift: he looked up, where there was no longer even a sliver of open sky visible. The canopy of the Deep Woods was dizzyingly distant, lush and impenetrable. "Whoa," Juvie said.

"Yeah," I agreed. "Here we are. Don't go wandering off."

"Don't worry," Juvie said.

We passed through a labyrinth of ancient trees, between the forks of a huge V-shaped rowan and under the intertwined boughs of a pair of stately elms, skirting around a crooked juniper and up and over a felled and partially decomposed trunk that was unidentifiable beneath all the brackets of turkey tail fungus, horizontal fans scalloped in gray and brown and green stripes. Phoebe paused and held up a hand; I stopped and put an arm out to halt Juvie as well.

A monstrous bear trundled by, maybe thirty yards ahead of us. It was, without exaggeration, the size of a city bus, covered in shaggy brown fur. Every time it lifted a paw to step forward, the tips of its claws were momentarily visible, each one as big and as sharp as the steel teeth on an excavator bucket. The bear's head was down, its massive snout rooting through the brush. It paid no attention to us whatsoever and continued on its way.

I heard Juvie release his breath and turned back to look at him. He looked a little shaken, but not as bad as I might have feared. "You don't mess with them, they don't mess with you," I reminded him.

"Got it," he nodded.

Phoebe was on the move again, and we fell in behind her. We came to a deadfall, several collapsed trees in a haphazard pyramid of snapped limbs, half-hollowed trunks and the various smaller plants and fungi that had colonized the agglomeration for structural support or sustenance. Phoebe stood at the apex, looking down at Juvie and me. "You boys keeping up?"

"We're fine," I called back.

"Wouldn't mind taking a breather," Juvie added. "If you want."

"I'll see you down the other side," Phoebe announced, not really addressing Juvie's suggestion and disappearing from sight with quick grace. We set to the task of climbing the deadfall. I felt a little out of practice, but remembered enough to help Juvie find his footing on the ascent, not to mention steer him away from a nasty angelwhip that had taken root halfway up one of the lifeless trunks. The pale green tendrils were only as wide as spaghetti, and covered in layers of fine hairs translucent as halos. The hairs were sharp enough to pierce the skin and were coated with toxins that would give a person head-splitting migraines for a week and night terrors for a month.

At the top of the deadfall, at least fifty feet up, we could see a small clearing of sorts. It was a minuscule pocket of space in the otherwise dense forest, but not entirely empty. The enormous stumps of three trees were still rooted in the earth, jagged crowns only a few feet above the ground. Much of the mass of the deadfall must have come from those three trees being knocked down.

Juvie looked from the stumps to the deadfall, back to the stumps again. "What do you think did that?" he asked. "Something like that giant bear?"

"Could've been any of a surprisingly large number of things," I said. "I could probably figure it out if we spent some time here but it's not exactly relevant at the moment."

Juvie nodded, then frowned. "Where's Phoebe?"

I couldn't see her either, but shrugged it off. She could be ten feet away, but completely hidden by the intervening trees. "Let's get down, and then we can look for her, if she hasn't made it obvious which way she went."

Juvie acquiesced, not that he had much choice. We worked our way down the deadfall, and no sooner had our surplus boots hit the ground than Phoebe emerged from behind a nearby tree. "Scouting ahead?" I asked. "Everything all right?"

"Everything's fine," Phoebe said. "Here, Juvie." She held out a piece of hazel, about five feet long and thick as an axe handle.

"Uh, thanks?" Juvie floundered as he took the length of wood and ran his hand over the crackled, gray-brown bark.

"It's a walking stick," Phoebe said. "We don't really have time to take a breather, but this should help you keep up with us."

"Oh, okay, cool," Juvie said. He planted one end of the walking stick in the ground and adjusted his grip near the head. "Lead on."

Phoebe turned Dand strode through the trees, and Juvie followed. I'd half-expected him to protest, to insist that he didn't need any help and he'd be fine, but he was apparently willing to defer to Phoebe's expertise without worrying about his own ego. So far, at least.

We trekked through the trees for a couple of hours, give or take. Time was a bit funny in the Deep Woods, not least because it was impossible to see the position of the sun. Eventually we came to a grassy trail through the forest, more than wide enough for the three of us to walk abreast.

"I thought you said there weren't any paths here," Juvie said.

"There aren't any paths leading to the Deep Woods from… our neck of the woods," I said.

Juvie gave me side-eye. "How long have you been waiting to use that one?"

"Just came to me," I said. "Anyway, parts of the Deep Woods are easier to navigate than others. Parts are downright well-traveled. The outer edges are more defensive, with that whole keeping people deflected away thing. But we're far enough in now that we can find some of the thoroughfares the denizens use."

"Thoroughfares? Denizens?" Juvie echoed.

"You sound like your mother," Phoebe smirked.

"In any case," I said, ignoring both of them, "there are paths, this is one of them, and it's all good. Right, Phoebe?"

She considered the question seriously. "We'll make better time if we follow the path, sure," she said. "But it's exposed. It's the first place someone would look for us, and see us coming from a ways off. If we keep to the denser parts of the forest we'll be more protected."

"I'll take speed over cover at this point," I said. "We can protect ourselves." I patted my SIG Pro under my arm.

Phoebe nodded, and started along the path. For a little while we moved as a trio, with Juvie between Phoebe and me, but Phoebe's natural stride pulled her ahead of us, and I let her take the lead while matching my pace to Juvie's. He made good use of the hazel staff, automatically matching its rhythmic swing to his footfalls.

"You doing all right?" I asked.

"Physically? I'm fine," he said. "Gonna sleep like a rock tonight, probably be a little sore in the morning, but I'm not complaining."

"Everything non-physically all right?"

Juvie gave a little snort of a laugh. "More or less. Just feels… I mean, it makes no sense to say this. We're literally in the great outdoors. I've got grass under my feet, a breeze in my face, we're making forward progress, but it's… kind of claustrophobic. Crazy, right?"

"Not completely," I said. The Deep Woods had never felt oppressive or confining to me, even as a child, but there was something about how vast it all was and how it completely surrounded us, the impenetrable green canopy overhead blotting out the sky, the concretion of individual tree trunks into an encircling wall of forest. And whether Juvie knew it or not, whether he had divined as much from our earlier conversation about how difficult it was to find a way into the Deep Woods, we were on the other side now. It would be just as hard to get out as it had been to get in, if not harder. If anything happened to me and Phoebe, and somehow Juvie was spared, he'd still be far more likely to spend the rest of his life wandering the Deep Woods than to return to what he thought of as the normal world.

"It's kind of like, how it would feel to be a mouse in a maze, you know?" Juvie went on. "Like, not trapped in a box, free to scurry all around, but still not completely free."

"So being on a relatively straight, flat path like this doesn't really help, I guess."

"Right," Juvie said. "If anything it adds to the feeling that something is trying to control where we go. Something massively bigger than us, with its own agenda."

Juvie understood the need to keep his guard up well enough, I figured. I had a hard time deciding if that should make me feel less guilty for letting him tag along, or more. "You may not believe this, but it's not quite as bad as that," I said. "The only agenda the Deep Woods has is to protect itself, not guide us through from any point A to a particular point B."

"If you say so," Juvie shrugged.

"Just remember that when we get to the holloways," I said.

"The what?" Juvie asked.

I didn't answer, as I noticed that Phoebe had stopped ahead of us. As we drew even with her, she put a finger to her lips. Neither Juvie nor I spoke a word or moved a muscle. A bird called from far overhead. Along the left side of the path stood a huge umbrella plant between two mahogany trees. The veiny, dark green leaves, each one three feet wide and edged in coarse teeth, rippled with more force than the breeze Juvie had mentioned should have caused. Two of the leaves dipped away from each other and toward the path, stalks parting as a leg emerged from the innermost shadows of the umbrella plant.

The leg was thickset with smooth skin mottled in shades of light and dark brown, all the way down to where three slender white toes splayed. An identical leg stretched out beside the first, both legs bowed, and in a rushing burst that rattled every broad leaf of the umbrella plant it had been hiding within, the creature hopped to the middle of the path, facing the three of us.

It was recognizably a bullfrog, which I imagined would be comforting to Juvie. Bulbous eyes of amber inset with black opal sat atop a wide head. Its body was a bright, limpid green with patterns of brown splotches, except just behind the eyes, where eardrums of unmarred chartreuse rose from the dark rings of their sockets. The green faded down the neckless shoulders until the back was the same brownish meld as the legs, while the white throat and belly matched the toes. All perfectly familiar, except for the fact that the bullfrog was the size of a large dog, easily weighing a couple hundred pounds. But that aside it didn't look dangerous, no extraneous claws or fangs, nothing threatening other than its freakish size. Not that it was freakishly large for the Deep Woods, a point which Juvie's continued silence conveyed was impressing itself well enough.

The figure seated on the back of the bullfrog, on the other hand, was a different matter. While the bullfrog was giant, its rider was miniature, about a foot and a half tall. A hairless, androgynous face stared at us from within a conical helmet carved from a large brown bur, covered in wicked barbed hooks. A poncho woven from green grass draped the rider's body and one arm, presumably steadying the mount with a touch at the base of the bullfrog's skull. The legs straddling the frog's back were clad in grass-weave leggings, the feet in boots that resembled the knobby cap of an acorn. One bare arm, its flesh the yellow hue of wet straw, extended to the side, banded with a ring of toothy bur. The delicate hand held a spear tipped with a curved bronze blade. The weapon was pointed away from our trio, but could swing toward any of us in an instant.

"Kellan of the Derryth," the rider said, in a voice high and clear and every bit as otherworldly as the facial features of the speaker, "I am Mabonnyn, harrier of the Floret folk. I come to offer you aid and escort."

Out of the corner of my eye, I saw Phoebe relax, and realized I was doing the same thing, letting out the breath I'd been holding. The denizens of the Deep Woods who deigned to speak with travelers from the other side tended to fall in two groups: those who dealt fairly and honestly, returning the same respect given to them, and those whose sole capricious reason for existing seemed to be to cause mischief or misery in anyone they encountered. Every troublemaker had his, her or its preferred brand of trouble, but name games were common, and volunteering a standard introduction was unheard of for them. By greeting me by name and offering a name as well, Mabonnyn had vouchsafed that we weren't about to be waylaid or worse. "Did my mother send you?" I asked.

Mabonnyn's head cocked to the side. "Foltchain of the Derryth has not been seen in some time. She is overdue."

"Tell me about it," Phoebe muttered.

"Have you looked for her?" Juvie asked Mabonnyn.

Mabonnyn turned skeptical, narrowed eyes on Juvie, but answered, "Many of the Floret folk have searched the woods, and many messages have been sent to the other folk and the beasts who are friendly to us. No sign of Foltchain has been found."

"So how did you know I'd be coming this way?" I asked.

"I was tasked with finding you," Mabonnyn said. "The clere of the Floret folk knew you would come, if not which weg you would tread. But that the Derryth would be your aim was known. And now that I have found you, I would accompany you thence, if you will have me."

I felt a little paranoid, and wondered if knowing I would come meant genuine metaphysical foresight, or just assuming that families stick together and sons lead the search when mothers go missing. I'd have to get Mabonnyn to clarify after we spent a bit more time together. For now, I didn't see the harm in trusting the harrier. "Any objections?" I asked my companions.

Phoebe shook her head. Juvie shrugged and said, "Lots of questions, but no objections, I guess."

I bowed slightly toward Mabonnyn. "We thank you," I said.

Mabonnyn made as much of a bow as possible from the back of a bullfrog, tucked spear beneath shoulder, and prodded the steed with it, saying, "Hyah, Gern!" Gern waddled in a circle, turning away from us, and hopped a few feet ahead. Phoebe, Juvie and I followed, Juvie shivering as we got underway.

"You all right?" I asked.

"I just realized there must be some giant insects in these woods for a frog that size to eat," Juvie answered. "So that's my nightmare fuel for tonight." He paused a moment, then added, "He does just eat insects, right?"

"She," I corrected. "And she'll eat whatever she can fit in her mouth and swallow, bugs, worms, mice, smaller frogs. You'll probably be safe."

"How do you know it's a she?" Juvie asked.

"Sexual dimorphism," I said. Juvie gave me an annoyed look, so I elaborated: "Male bullfrogs have darker throats, and eardrums bigger than their eyes."

Juvie shook his head. "So this is what you were doing as a kid while I was watching cartoons after school? Learning to differentiate male and female giant frogs on sight?"

"Among other things," I agreed. I was waiting for Juvie to bring up Mabonnyn, as I imagined he'd have a lot more questions about the Floret folk than about Gern, fascinating as a mega-ranid might be, but no follow-up questions came. I didn't know if he was being polite because Mabonnyn was in earshot, or if he was still wrapping his head around the alienness of a true Deep Woodlander. Either way, he kept his thoughts to himself.

Mabonnyn rode Gern ahead of us as the path rose and fell, curved and banked along a corridor formed by looming hawthorns, teak, beech, and cypress. We didn't see any other denizens of the Deep Woods, no remarkably large animals or mythical creatures, but I was convinced that, if I concentrated and listened, I could hear them moving through the depths of the trees. When Phoebe, Juvie and I had been making our own way through the Deep Woods, the native woodlanders, folk and fauna alike, had either given us the widest possible berth or remained still and silent as we passed. Now that Mabonnyn was our escort, there seemed to be a collective relaxation upon the forest, a return to normal routines, treating us as if whatever we were doing fell within the natural order of things.

Eventually Gern hopped off the path and into the forest. Mabonnyn looked back, and waved the spearhead beckoningly to make sure we understood we were to follow. So we did. After a few hundred yards of clambering through dense snarls of brush, we came to the edge of a large basin filled with dark water, fringed with swaying reeds and cattails. Out in the middle of the water, darkly lustrous ellipsoid shapes moved around on the surface in randomly spiraling patterns, whirligig beetles on the hunt. An aging stone arch bridge spanned the water.

Mabonnyn and Gern crossed the bridge without stopping, but at the midpoint Phoebe motioned for Juvie and I to stop. She peered over the edge, to the surface of the water below. "Juvie, take a look."

Juvie looked to me reflexively but I could only give a tilt of my head. I had no idea what Phoebe was on about. Juvie moved to the waist-high parapets beside Phoebe, and I sidled over there as well.

Movement among the water lilies drew our attention, a shimmering, argentine dart among the rose-gold crowns on their green velvet cushions. The ghostly blur below the surface made its way to the pier beneath us and rose up out of the water. It was a little bigger than Mabonnyn, with a similarly humanoid shape but very little else in common with our escort. It was naked, covered in glistening silver fish scales, with a crested fin running from the top of its head down to the base of its spine. It climbed a few feet up the spandrel wall of the bridge, moving its arms and legs as stiffly as the limbs of a crayfish. It surveyed the watery surroundings, then suddenly looked up at us, as if it could feel our gazes. Its eyes were glassy and black, and they shrank to slits as it opened its mouth and hissed furiously, revealing most of its teeth, pointed as the tips of carving knives.

"Jesus," Juvie gasped, taking a step back reflexively as the thing dove underwater and disappeared before the splash had settled. "What was that?"

"Nicor," Phoebe said.

"Any particular reason you felt compelled to

point that out to us?" Juvie asked.

"So you wouldn't forget the rules," Phoebe said. "Just in case you were thinking the big bear didn't take any notice of us and looked basically harmless, and Mabonnyn of the Floret folk sure seems nice, and maybe it's not nearly as bad here in the Deep Woods as Kellan and Phoebe said. But we were lucky the bear didn't smell us, and you need to know that Mabonnyn's the exception. Most of the locals would just as soon gut you for looking at them funny."

"Duly noted," Juvie said. Phoebe turned away from us and continued across the bridge. To me, Juvie said, "Dude, what does she think you and I have been talking about this whole time?"

"Whatever it is, I'm sure she thinks I'm being too nice about it, sugarcoating the scary stuff and telling you everything's copacetic," I said.

"Is she always like this?" he asked.

"More or less," I said. "Actually, usually less. She's on edge. Worried."

"Yeah, all right, I get it," Juvie nodded.

We needled our way through the crowded trees on the other side of the bridge for close to a quarter of an hour, and then Mabonnyn and Gern dropped out of sight. I kept my eyes fixed on the last place I had been able to see them, and soon reached a steep embankment that fell four or five feet to a clear pathway just wide enough for two to walk abreast, with another embankment rising on the opposite side. I could see Mabonnyn and Gern off to our left, following the sunken lane as it cut through the floor of the Deep Woods. Phoebe jumped down lightly to the middle of the thoroughfare and followed our mounted guide, and Juvie and I skidded down the embankment as well.

The walls on either side of us were tightly packed earth, with colossal tree roots visible amongst slender sprays of ferns and broad pigsqueak leaves spilling over the edges above. I was about to remind Juvie that I had warned him about this when he spoke up, "Holloways, huh?"

"You got it," I said. "Definitely normal to feel like a mouse in a maze at this point."

"Right," Juvie nodded. "Although, this is a seriously old track, am I right?"

"Totally," I confirmed. "Commonly used routes, worn down over centuries. Maybe millennia."

"So that means it looked like this before we were even born," he said. "Which makes it hard to feel too paranoid that someone dug it on purpose just to funnel us into their clutches."

I wasn't inclined to argue with that. We walked along the deep groove, and gradually the roots and rhizomes flanking us became more sparse, and the striated topsoil and subsoil became a channel worn through weathered limestone. After a while the pale rock gave way to plants and compacted earth once more. We followed the ancient road until the light failed enough to slow our progress, and then Mabonnyn urged Gern to hop out of the shadowy half-tunnel to find a likely site to make camp.

The site was in a small clearing not far from the holloway. As we approached, it looked like another deadfall, with enormous tree trunks stacked horizontally five high. Mabonnyn led us around the end of the boles, where it was revealed that the trunks were all hollow and open on the side facing away from the old sunken road. Each felled tree served as a private bunk, lined with purple forkmoss, providing shelter and camouflage for the night.

Gern hopped up the deadfall, carrying Mabonnyn to the topmost level of the structure. "I will stand watch through the night while you rest," the harrier called down to us.

Juvie looked at me and I shrugged. The Floret folk didn't need sleep in the same way we mere mortals did, so if Mabonnyn was volunteering to play lookout all through the night - or, more likely, considered it an honorbound duty as per the task set forth by the clere - then I wasn't about to argue.

"I'm going to have a look around myself," Phoebe said. "Don't wait up."

"You okay?" I asked. I had spent most of the day keeping an eye on Juvie, and letting Phoebe look out for herself. But I took a moment now to really consider her. The day was growing dimmer by the minute, deep green darkness pooling all around us, and Phoebe refused to look directly at me. Her voice had its usual timbre, nothing in particular about the way she held her body or anything else gave me specific cause for alarm. It was just a hunch, and playing out hunches was allegedly my day job, so I tended to give them more than passing attention.

"I'm fine," Phoebe said gand, without waiting to see if I believed her or not, she pushed between two dense broom shrubs like passing through a curtain and disappeared into the gloaming.

"You mind if I take the bottom bed?" Juvie

asked. "Because I don't think I have the energy to climb anywhere." He collapsed theatrically to the ground and crawled toward the bottommost tree, dragging his hazel staff beside him.

"Sure, be my guest," I said, even though he was already rolling himself into the bunk. I suspected that his willingness to own up to his exhaustion had a lot to do with Phoebe's absence, not that he had anything to be ashamed of. I reckoned we had covered fifteen miles, maybe more, over uneven terrain at best, climbing significant obstacles every so often. It was a killer pace, and Juvie hadn't complained once.

"Oh my god, this moss is so soft," Juvie groaned as he settled on his back, laying the staff alongside his body within the curved tube of aged bark. "I'm gonna sleep like a baby tonight. Like the dead. Like a dead baby. Like a dump truck full of bowling balls."

"You go right ahead and do that," I said, stepping up to the bunk directly above him. "It's another long day tomorrow."

I thought that might be the end of our conversation, and that I'd hear Juvie snoring soon enough. I got myself comfortable along the velvety interior of the giant log, closed my eyes and listened to the ambient noises of the Deep Woods: bird calls, frogs, crickets, twigs and dried leaves crunching under padding paws. And then, cutting through it all, Juvie's voice: "Whoa."

I opened my eyes. The fireflies had come out and the woods ringing the clearing were aglow with dots of yellow-green bioluminescence that flared and faded, disappearing and reappearing in dizzying patterns. Night had fallen and the Deep Woods were dark, a black sable backdrop for the pulses of hovering light. The columns of beetles rose as high as the trees themselves, hundreds and hundreds of feet above our heads. If you've ever been camping someplace wild and remote, and seen swarms of fireflies signaling to one another after sunset, and if you can take that memory and multiply it a hundredfold, you might be able to visualize the awe of the moment.

"It's pretty cool," I agreed, loudly enough for Juvie to hear me.

"Gorgeous," Juvie responded. "I get where Phoebe was coming from, you too, for that matter. I get that we're way the hell off the map here and there's no shortage of hostility all around us, but damn. It's all I can do to repeat all that to myself and believe it when I see something like this."

"It's gonna get weirder," I promised. "It's just a matter of time, no matter how carefully we pick our way through. Sooner or later something hungry, ugly and short-tempered will cross our path. Enjoy the tranquility while it lasts."

Juvie didn't answer. A few minutes passed, as the fireflies continued their coruscating dance, and then a moth fluttered into the clearing. It was a Deep Woods specimen, its furry body a foot long and wingspan double that. The horn on its tail made me think it was a Sphinx moth, though there wasn't enough light to make out the telltale pink stripe across its hindwings that would have confirmed it. The moth bobbed along through the air and then disappeared in an upward blur, looking for a split second like it had been speared with a harpoon on a line and reeled in with one yank. It must have been Gern, availing herself of the late-night snack presenting itself.

I hung my head down past the lip of my bunk, to ask Juvie if he had seen the predation. Juvie was sound asleep. I drew back into my log to attempt forty winks of my own.

INTERLUDE I

Foltchain of the Oak breathed in through her
nose and out through her slightly parted lips. Every
inhalation was slightly unpleasant, the air dry and
hot and completely devoid of any familiar scents.
Yet the druid priestess was disciplined enough to
control her breathing all the same, to draw air in
and allow it to escape again, over and over. It was
the simplest of the sacred traditions, honoring the
fundamental respiratory mode of life. Normally she
would slow her breaths mindfully at first, then
gradually allow herself to become attuned and
aligned with the natural rhythms all around her.
Here and now, she was cut off from those cycles and
systems which had always been vibrant extensions
of her body, mind and spirit. Here and now, she
could only seek harmony with herself. So she
breathed in, and breathed out, at her own pace,

according to her own inner congruity.

After a time, Foltchain opened her eyes. Her surroundings had not changed, nor had she expected them to. She sat in the middle of an irregularly shaped chamber, a hollow asymmetric sphere ten feet in diameter. The surface beneath her crossed legs, which curved up around her on all sides and continued to curve into a dome above her, was composed of a myriad of multi-sided, uneven facets. Bulges interrupted the surface haphazardly, appearing for an interval and then receding, with no discernable pattern. The entire compartment was a cloudy colorless substance which appeared white in her peripheral vision but was disorienting if stared at for too long. The space had neither windows nor doors, yet Foltchain knew intuitively that it was more than a featureless barrier which separated her from her birthright of living things, sun and wind and rain. Whatever was on the other side of the pallid stuff encircling her, it was unimaginably distant from anyplace she would recognize as home.

A line of facets along the surface opposite her began to shrink, drawing inwards and separating, creating a lacuna in the concave wall. An entity entered the room, near enough to the shape of a man but made of the same material as her prison. The facets along its exterior surface were smaller than those of the chamber, but the front of its head lacked distinct features just as the room lacked true furnishings. One of the entity's claw-like appendages was significantly larger than the other.

"Have you had sufficient time to reconsider?" The voice came not from the creature standing before her but from somewhere just outside her cell, though Foltchain could not see the speaker. Through the lacuna, only darkness was visible.

"No matter how long you keep me here," Foltchain said, "I will not change my mind. I have no shortage of patience."

"Nor do we," the inhuman voice answered. "We have waited far longer than the brief instant of time you have called a life."

Foltchain of the Oak was supernaturally ancient by human measure, but she did not doubt the words of her captor. "You'll wait longer still," she said.

"We have other possibilities to consider," the voice said.

"Such as?"

"Death."

"Death is a part of every life, and mine is no exception," she said. It was as true as any other druid tenet, and she meant every word, speaking them without fear. Even so, she suspected her captor was not eager to end her existence. She had been taken for a reason, an end which her death would not serve.

"Death holds no sway over you, then," the voice mused.

"None."

Silence followed. The creature in the chamber with her wavered in place, its outline shifting like the patterns of light on open water. It raised its oversized fist, holding it toward the priestess's head as if lining up an executioner's axe for the fell blow. The appendage split open and foodstuffs tumbled from within, exotic fruits and leafy greens and strange eggs and an unrecognizable blob of raw meat. Foltchain reached out and caught the egg, letting the rest of the food fall to the cell floor.

"Our kind could learn much from you," the voice beyond the cell said. "Refuse us, and you will force us to learn what might persuade you, if death cannot."

The creature shuffled out, and Foltchain felt the voice withdraw as well. The lacuna erased itself, polygonal planes expanding and fusing until the entire surface was a single membrane once more. Foltchain spread out the foodstuffs before her. She tore the greens into strips, and split open the fruit, removing the seeds which were smaller than grains of rice. She set the seeds aside and cracked the egg near its narrow end, patiently working the shell until she could remove a small cap. The egg smelled slightly reptilian, even with the sweetness of the fruit's aroma mingling with it. Foltchain set the egg down, balancing it on its rounded bottom. She pinched several bits of fruit flesh, and dropped them to the side. Perhaps all of her handling of the food would convince her captors that she had eaten some of it, though she had no intention of doing so. She could go without eating for a very long time.

Foltchain closed her eyes. She had no idea where she was, when she would return home, or how to take control of the situation. She breathed in through her nose and out through her lips. Mere air and inner calm were enough for now, and the rest would come in due course.

Chapter Five:
Root and Branch

I WOKE UP second to last in the morning. Mabonnyn was already mounted on Gern in the middle of the clearing floor, and Phoebe was engaged in what looked like a serious discussion with our escort, standing beside the giant bullfrog. I descended from my log bunk and nudged Juvie's hip with my foot; he responded by groaning and stretching. That brought back a flood of memories from our college roommate days which I didn't have time to indulge in at the moment.

Mabonnyn looked to me and nodded as I approached them. Phoebe reached into her pocket and said, "Here, thought you might need some of these." She pulled her fist back out of her pocket and held it toward me expectantly. I opened my palm and she dumped a small pile of purple berries with longitudinal seams into my waiting hand.

Juvie appeared at my shoulder. "What's that?" he asked.

"Breakfast," Phoebe said. She reached into her pocket for another handful and offered them to Juvie.

"Is this what you were scrounging around for in the woods last night?" Juvie asked, poking the little lobed balls with his fingertip.

"Yes," Phoebe said flatly. "Shall we get going?"

Mabonnyn answered with a strident "Hyah, Gern," and the bullfrog hopped into the woods, back toward the holloway. Phoebe passed between the trees behind him, leaving Juvie and I to bring up the rear once more.

Juvie was still sniffing his berries as we pushed through the brush, so I tossed a few into my mouth and chewed them. The flavor of the fruit was subtly sweet, and undercut by the bitterness of the seeds mashed between my teeth.

Juvie popped one berry onto the tip of his tongue, rolled it back and forth, and finally bit into it. "Did yours have pits?" he asked through clenched teeth and pursed lips.

"Yeah," I confirmed. "That's where the stimulants are. It's like eating coffee beans, but about double the kick."

"Oh, okay," Juvie said. He chewed contemplatively, then made a low sound in the back of his throat. "Hey, that's not bad. Not bad at all. What do you call these things?"

I shook my head. "I don't think they have a name. Not one I ever learned, anyway. I remember my mom showing them to me once when she took me walking. She made me try them, said they were good for energy. I think the idea was if I were ever in the Deep Woods on my own, I'd recognize them and know they were safe to eat. It wasn't like I was going to go to a store and ask for some."

"I guess not," Juvie said. He poked the ground ahead of him with his hazel staff, swept aside some thorny brambles, and said, "Your childhood must have been so bizarre."

"Not that I noticed," I said. "It was when I tried to assimilate into the world full of normals like you that things got weird. But, everybody's adolescence is bizarre and makes them feel like the first visitor to a weird, weird world. I didn't think too much about how I came to be so unprepared for what crunch berries would taste like in the context of Cap'n Crunch."

"Dude, I love Cap'n Crunch," Juvie said.

We had reached the lip of the holloway by then, and the conversation lapsed as we clambered down the embankment, then tried to match our strides to Phoebe's surefooted gait and Gern's leaps ahead of us. The forest around us murmured and rustled, keeping its own counsel. Occasionally we could hear something distinctive and recognizable, the percussive chiseling of a woodpecker's beak or the high-pitched yip of a fox, but nothing emerged from the trees to descend across our path.

Once early morning gave way to late morning, it became more difficult to gauge time. The canopy still blocked the entire sky, rendering the position of the sun unknowable. There were no long shadows to judge by, either, just a chlorophyll-filtered lambency that was neither bright nor dim. The hours passed, relentlessly undifferentiated, with every mile we hiked.

Then the embankments shrank as the lane sloped upward, and the light sharpened as if a curtain had been drawn back. The forest stopped as the holloway's incline reached ground level, and Mabonnyn and Gern, Phoebe, Juvie and I stepped forward to the edge of a sharp drop. A rocky cliff fell before us, one wall of a wide chasm where stunted bushes clung to knobby outcroppings but the majestic, sentinel trees could gain no purchase. The cliff descended hundreds and hundreds of feet, the bottom swallowed by dark shadows. On the far side of the gap the terrain leveled out again and the impenetrable phalanx of towering trees resumed, albeit at an elevation something like fifty feet lower than the spot where we stood. Over our heads, the blue midday sky was visible through the slash separating one side of the Deep Woods from the other.

A wooden staircase connected the path across the chasm, obviously the work of ancient denizens of the Deep Woods. It was supported by straight, slender poles mottled with lichen the pale blue color of oxidized copper. The steps and rails were finely wrought, at least as far as I could see through the various creeping vines and clumps of wild grasses and weeds that had taken root all along the structure. Impressive as the workmanship was, though, the staircase was not impervious to harm. Something at some point had taken a chunk out of the stairs about two-thirds of the way down, leaving a ragged bitemark behind. It could have been a convenient target for a bored troll heaving boulders, it could have been collateral damage in a midair fight between two giant kestrels, it could have been nothing more than the ravages of time and the elements. Whatever the cause, it left our way forward looking precarious and uncertain.

Mabonnyn dismounted and addressed the rest of us. "I will examine the stairway and ascertain whether or not it is safe for the rest of you to cross."

"Or we could just find another way?" Juvie suggested.

"We may yet need to," Mabonnyn admitted. "But it would cost us precious time. I would prefer this route if it is at all practicable."

Juvie said nothing more, and Mabonnyn stepped lightly onto the first stair. Phoebe stepped closer to me and said, "Does this feel like a setup to you?"

I didn't even consider my answer before speaking. "Not really, honestly. It's too little damage to be an overt attempt to slow us down, and too much to be a trap that we might not notice. Just bad luck, is all."

"Or that's just what someone wants us to think," Phoebe said. "Someone who realized that splitting the difference between an obvious waylay and an insidious snare would be the perfect way to catch us off guard."

"It must be utterly exhausting to be so paranoid," I said. Phoebe huffed, and I caught a whiff of her breath, smelling sour. I was sure after a couple of days on the hike my mouth was unpleasantly fragrant, too, but Phoebe's had a tinge of rot to it, like a dumpster in high summer during a garbage strike. There was really nothing to be gained by digressing into oral hygiene critiques, so I added, "Mabonnyn is scoping it for us. If it's anything worse than random entropy, I'm sure he'll suss it out."

"I hope you're right," she said.

"I gotta go water the wildflowers," Juvie said. Phoebe ignored him, and I made a sideways gesture with my head to give him a greenlight. Out of the corner of my eye I watched Juvie walk several yards along the cliff's edge to a semi-private stand of ferns. Most of my attention, and all of Phoebe's, was fixed on Mabonnyn's cautious descent.

Step by step, spear held at the ready, the harrier moved out along the staircase. The structure gave no signs of distress or hints of imminent collapse, even as Mabonnyn approached the damaged area. Most of the staircase was wide enough for two human adults to walk side by side, but the ravaged section had been reduced to a narrow sawtooth only a few inches across, fringed with dried tendrils of grass. Mabonnyn jabbed at the thin remnants of several steps with the spear's tip, but nothing moved. The harrier edged out along the damaged planks, testing the support, then turned around and whistled sharply.

Gern hopped to the top of the staircase, then waddled down toward Mabonnyn. I felt my shoulders relax. If the steps could bear the giant bullfrog's weight, we'd all be on our way again soon enough. I looked down the length of the chasm and spotted Juvie walking back to us. His hands were cupped chest-high.

"Okay at some point you seriously gotta explain to me how the rules of dwarfism and gigantism work here," Juvie said, sounding both confused and delighted.

"Juvie, what have you got in your hands?" I asked, trying not to panic.

"Relax, it's harmless," he said.

"Don't you think you should let us be the judges of that?" Phoebe asked, not at all panicked but moderately annoyed.

"I think I'm pretty secure in my own judgment of how harmless cows are," Juvie said. "And at this size they're, like, beyond harmless." He held out his hands and uncovered what lay in his palm: a black and white Holstein, perfectly formed and proportioned but no bigger than a mouse. It could have been a figurine out of a nativity set, except for the serene way it opened and closed its dark eyes and the swell and fall of its rounded flanks. "This thing is too freaking cute, but I don't get how teeny tiny cattle go with gargantuan trees and frogs and…"

"Fuck," Phoebe growled.

It did not take years of investigative training, or even my personal brand of lackadaisical on-the-job experience, to see Juvie physically startled by the obscenity. He blinked, his facial expression not far from bovine. "Excuse me?"

I drew my SIG Pro. "It's not a Deep Woods dwarf cow, Juvie, it's a regular cow from our regular world. Somewhere there's a regular farmer wondering how one of his herd got loose and ran off without a trace, because it would never occur to the farmer that a cow would be magically shrunken and stolen away."

"Shrunken? Stolen?" Juvie asked. "By who? Or what?" He looked again at the miniature Holstein and squatted down, gently setting the beast on the grass.

"Probably too late for that," Phoebe noted, turning in place, her eyes scanning the area.

A bellowing roar sounded from somewhere unsettlingly closeby. "Definitely too late," I said.

A large and hairy arm reached up from the chasm, maybe another dozen yards farther down its length than the spot Juvie had chosen to answer the call of nature. It was large not in the sense of belonging to a muscular athletic body type but in being about eight feet long from shoulder to wrist and as thick as a truck tire, and hairy not in the sense of normal human body hair but something more ape-like, with wild strands of bracken-green that cascaded like Spanish moss. Still, the overall anatomy was human-adjacent, at least. Its massive hand slammed into the ground beside the chasm, gnarled fingers sinking like the points of an anchor into the soil, and the creature pulled itself up.

The face that rose from the depths was so misshapen it looked like Humpty Dumpty from Hell. Disproportionately large even for the gigantic frame supporting it, and egg shaped with the narrow end up, topped with an unruly tuft of dark hair. Its small round eyes were yellow but bloodshot, set on either side of a hooked nose, which bisected a mouth full of uneven teeth and two tusks protruding up from the lower jaw. It had huge triangular pig's ears, one which folded over itself lazily and one which looked to have been half torn off long ago. It cast its bleary gaze around, saw us, and let loose another barbaric roar.

As the huulder climbed the rest of the way out of the chasm, I gestured behind me. "Stairs! Now!"

"Are they safe?" Juvie asked. He was holding his hazel staff in front of his midsection, fingers clenching and unclenching around the wood. "Is the little guy finished…?"

"No time!" Phoebe yelled, grabbing Juvie's shoulder and propelling him toward the topmost stair. I walked backwards in their wake, keeping my sights set on the huulder. It was all the way out of the chasm now, and lumbering toward us, distended belly wobbling back and forth as it stomped along on legs which were just as thick and mossy as its arms but only about half as long. It didn't seem filled with urgency to catch up to us, which gave me a momentary spark of hope. Maybe once we were all on the staircase and obviously headed out of its domain, retreating from whatever boundary Juvie had unwittingly crossed, it would just consider us sufficiently menaced and amble back to its lair full of rodent-sized cattle.

I felt the rail of the staircase poke me in the small of my back. I put my left hand out to grab the rail and walked backwards down several steps, still keeping my gun trained on the huulder. It clumped to the top of the stairs, roared once again, and descended after me. So much for the contrite exit, but I wasn't going to feel any remorse about opening fire once I had a good clean shot.

I flashed back on the altercation with the neo-Nazi clown at the courthouse, impossible as it was to believe it had only been the day before last. The same noxious, sinister force burned in the huulder's eyes as I had seen blasting out at me from the prisoner's eyes. A particularly cruel strain of anger, not just willing but eager to wreak violence on an unsuspecting world. My mother had taught me to recognize that bleak impetus. My mother had taught me to call it what it was: evil.

Whenever she had taken me into the Deep Woods, my mother had avoided conflict as much as possible. Partly it was because she had me in tow, and I was just a kid, and she didn't want to risk the possibility of me seeing something violently and traumatically gory, or of me getting caught up as collateral damage in a fight, or of me getting abandoned in the primordial, reality-adjacent forest if a given altercation happened not to go her way. Or any combination of all of the above. But avoiding conflict as much as possible was her highest intention, even though sometimes circumstances made conflict inevitable. Once when I was only about six or seven we were in the Deep Woods together and a valva attacked us just after sunset. I remember it was the size and shape of a teenage girl, but made entirely of blank blackness, and something in its voidlike dark hungered for my life force. My mother didn't hesitate for an instant. She stabbed the base of its spine with a silver knife she carried on her belt, and the monster dissipated like a drop of ink in a pool of water.

After she'd confirmed that I was unharmed, my mother had laid out another one of her teachable moments. The Deep Woods, she instructed me, were so vast that I could come back to them a thousand times and I would always see some creature I had never seen before. Some I might recognize as being close to something from home, and some might be exotic or alien, but one rule applied unwaveringly: if it looked like a beast, it operated on instinct; but the more it looked like a human, the more it was capable of morality. Animals can't be considered evil, they just protect their territory, their mates and offspring, and they use violence as a last resort. But valva, and trolls, and pixies and all the other folk, they had the true capacity for evil. Killing an animal was one thing, and dispatching evil was another. And recognizing evil was often as simple as looking it in the eye.

Not that it was hard to make a case for huulder being generally evil. They knew stealing cattle was wrong, but they did it anyway, and reveled in the discord it created. And they could keep humans away by various means, but enjoyed all opportunities for intimidation and brutality. So, like I said, no compunction about putting an entire magazine into this one's hairy hide.

The huulder took a swing at me with one of its wreckingball fists. That was the opportunity I had been waiting for, a chance to unload several rounds into the thing when it was already committed to an attack and unable to dodge, duck or otherwise spoil my shot. I leaned back and to the left, pressing hard against the rail, and my finger tightened on the trigger.

The flaw in my brilliant little stratagem was that the huulder failed to cooperate. It looked so gangly and uncoordinated climbing out of the chasm and pursuing us to the stairs, so sluggish. When it threw its haymaker I expected a clumsy sweep of the limb and not much more. But the huulder's instincts were much more lethal than I gave it credit for. It knew how to deal a blow with its entire body, leaning forward, twisting at the waist, snapping its arm like a gargantuan whip with an iron weight at the tip. If I hadn't leaned back while lining up my shot, the huulder would have fractured my skull and broken my neck. As it was, it still connected solidly with my right shoulder.

The SIG Pro went off at the same moment my entire right arm went numb. The gun fell from my insensate fingers, and tumbled into the shade-shrouded depths of the chasm, but I barely registered it, because the sheer force of the blow had knocked me off my feet. And because I had already been leaning back over the rail, momentum carried me up and over. My upper body dropped and my legs kicked up toward the sky. I fell.

My left hand shot out, fingers grasping reflexively, and I caught hold of the wrought wood of the railing. My back slammed against the outer edge of the stairs. The pain was electrifying, but my most primitive brainparts understood that if I let go, I would plummet to a messy death at the bottom of the chasm. I held on, which of course only made me an easy, stationary target for the huulder.

The huulder loomed above me. It would have

been simple enough for it to smash my hand or pry my fingers loose and send me down to dash against the rocks below, but the huulder apparently wasn't interested in doing things the easy way. It bent over the rail and reached down to grab me. Its fingers cinched around my waist while I glared up at it with impotent rage, searching for some kind of weak point I could potentially strike.

A pale blur passed over the huulder's stooping back, and then lashed out at its head, knocking the huulder off balance. It let go of me, and my back slammed against the staircase again, wind driven from my lungs for the second time inside of a minute. My vision started to go worryingly dark at the periphery, but not so much that I couldn't make out Gern and Mabonnyn, now between the huulder and the top of the staircase. Mabonnyn pointed the spear at the huulder and gave a ferocious yell, urging Gern to press the attack.

I willed my right arm to move, but it was still deadened from the huulder's blow. I couldn't pull myself up with just my left arm, and my dangling legs couldn't find any purchase to push against. My left wrist was protesting the weight of the rest of me and felt ready to pop. I was running out of time.

Juvie and Phoebe appeared at the rail. Juvie lowered his hazel staff over the side for me to grab with my free hand. I tried, but my right hand remained uncooperative. Phoebe dropped to her knees and reached through the spindles of the rail, catching my right arm as I flailed it upward. "Get his other arm!" she yelled, and Juvie set his staff down and obeyed, clutching my left forearm.

Together they hauled me up, until my feet could rest on the outside of the step. I hung over the rail like a wet coat, catching my breath for a second.

The huulder staggered backwards under Gern and Mabonnyn's combined assault. The giant bullfrog had its forelegs wrapped around the huulder's neck, while the harrier on her back stabbed at the huulder's face. In another couple of backwards steps, the huulder would either trample Juvie, Phoebe and me or crowd us off the stairs. I got the lower half of my body over the rail and the three of us hustled down the stairs.

We reached the damaged section of the staircase and Phoebe took the lead, edging across the narrow remains. Juvie followed her, a little more tentatively, even though the overall structure seemed to be holding together just fine. Juvie reached the far side of the ragged wound in the stairs and slammed his foot down on the first complete step, directly into a colony of slime mold that had established itself along the neglected surface. His foot shot out from under him and he pitched forward, upper body sprawling down the stairs and legs dangling.

I checked backwards over my shoulder to see how much lead time we had on the huulder. None. The creature was a step away, and had yanked Mabonnyn off Gern, holding the tiny woodlander aloft in one crushing fist. The bullfrog released her grip and clamped her mouth onto the huulder's wrist. No teeth to savage the flesh, but the crushing power of Gern's jaw alone was enough to draw an angry roar from the huulder. It clamped its free hand over Gern's nose to tear the frog away.

I spared a glance at Juvie, who was scrabbling up over the edge of the hole in the stairs. Returning my attention to the huulder, I called out, "Mabonnyn! Spear!"

Mabonnyn lobbed the weapon to me. In my hand it was about as menacing as a pen knife, but since I'd lost my gun, it was better than nothing. I climbed up onto the rail, balancing precariously for all of about two seconds before I had to cheat and lean on the huulder's shoulder. The huulder looked at me with a sneer. I stabbed it in the eye with the harrier's miniature spear.

Black blood spilled down the huulder's jowl and it screamed. I pulled Mabonnyn's spear out of the eye socket, twirling my wrist as I did to inflict as much damage as possible on the exit. The huulder's screams intensified as it finally dropped Mabonnyn. Gern released her lockjaw hold on the huulder's arm and it clapped both massive hands to the newly opened, ichor-weeping cavity in its skull. I half-hopped, half-fell down from the rail to a stair behind the creature, and just for good measure planted my boot on its backside and kicked hard.

The huulder staggered forward blindly and toppled through the empty space where the forcibly removed stairs had been. I smiled, completely mean-spiritedly, as the huulder flailed against gravity, until the knobby fingers of its right hand found Juvie's heel on the way down. One moment, Juvie was on his hands and knees at the edge of the ruined section of staircase, and the next he was being dragged down by the huulder.

Juvie grabbed frantically at the stairs, arresting

his fall with a jolt that shook the huulder loose. The dwindling screams of the plummeting monster barely registered with me; all of my attention was focused on Juvie. I could see his arms trembling with all the effort it was taking just to hang on.

"Don't move!" I called to Juvie, stupidly. I had to cross the gap myself to be able to help him. I tucked Mabonnyn's spear into my waistband against the small of my back and edged along the narrow remnants as quickly as I could without losing my balance, my heart jackhammering in my chest. Juvie slipped a little, and it was all I could do not to lean out and grab him with no leverage and no support. I forced myself to continue on to where the staircase resumed with whole steps, then dropped to my knees and grabbed hold of Juvie's arms.

Juvie was exhausted, more or less dead weight, with nowhere to brace his feet and help me lift him up. I strained awkwardly, but wasn't making any progress.

Gern hopped across the gap in the stairs, Mabonnyn on her back, and alighted just behind me. Slowly, she extended her back leg beside me, stretching it out toward Juvie. "Okay, man," I grunted. "I'm gonna let go of your right arm…"

"Don't," Juvie pleaded in a cracked whisper.

"Shut up and listen. I'm gonna let go of your right arm and grab onto your left arm with both my hands. You're gonna take your right hand and grab onto Gern's leg, or foot, whatever you can hold. Gern can't grab you, but she can help pull you up if you can hold onto her. Got it?"

Juvie made a harsh, desperate sound which I had

to take as assent. I transferred my grip, and he swatted at Gern's hind leg, once, twice, finally getting a decent hold on the third try. I leaned back and pulled, and the bullfrog flexed her leg, dragging Juvie up onto the stairs. I let go once Juvie's hips cleared the edge, and helped haul his feet up and over.

Juvie huddled against Gern's backside, but Mabonnyn wasted little time urging the bullfrog forward down the staircase. I could see Phoebe waiting at the end of the stairs. "Come on, Juvie. Solid ground awaits."

Juvie shuffled to his feet and we crossed the chasm. Once we reached the grass, I held the spear out to return it to Mabonnyn. Juvie looked back and forth between Phoebe and me and said, "Sorry I picked up the cow."

"Live and learn," I shrugged. Phoebe looked less sanguine about it, but also too tired to dispute me. Another holloway through the trees awaited us, and we resumed our trek.

Gern and Mabonnyn led the way at a relentless pace, and no one was inclined to argue with them. For one thing, putting as much distance as possible between our party and the huulder was compelling enough on the level of survival instinct to have us all running to keep up with the bounding bullfrog. For another, even after we had put the chasm a half a mile or more behind us, and even taking into account the fact that the huulder was missing an eye even before tumbling off the stairway and likely much more seriously injured after coming to a sudden stop at the bottom of the rocky gap, and even allowing for the likelihood that the huulder would have second thoughts of its own about leaving its territory to chase us into the forest, we still chose to run because it spared us from having to talk to one another.

Juvie was my friend, arguably the best one I'd ever had, but that only meant I was inclined to forgive him for what had been an utterly avoidable mistake that had nearly gotten some or all of us killed. I knew he felt terrible, and I knew he wouldn't do it again. I also understood how easy it was to latch onto some seemingly harmless outlet after spending a couple days not allowing yourself to deviate even slightly from the prohibition against touching or interacting with anything you saw. I saw both sides, as opposed to Phoebe and Mabonnyn, who were less likely to let bygones be bygones. Phoebe would make an effort, if only to keep the peace between her and me, since we needed each other to make a go of finding my mother. Mabonnyn, dutiful and honor-bound, would execute the task set by the clere of the Floret folk. But all of us single-mindedly, breathlessly charging through the holloway was the optimal scenario under the circumstances.

Until suddenly, it wasn't, because the sunken road dead-ended. A boulder blocked our progress, a bit wider than the lane and pressing into the natural walls of the holloway on either side, and several feet taller than the embankments as well. It wouldn't have been hard at all to climb over the boulder, or scramble up out of the holloway, through the trees, and then jump back down into it on the other side of the obstacle. What gave us all pause was a good-sized fairy ring of mushrooms that sprouted in front of the massive stone, knee-high white stalks topped with convex pink and purple caps, wood blewits. Gern stopped well outside of the circle, and we halted behind the frog and rider.

I looked back and forth between Juvie and Phoebe, and couldn't tell which of them was more gassed. Phoebe spread her legs wide and bent at the waist, bracing her hands on her slightly bent knees. Juvie held his hazel staff in a death grip, the butt end stabbed into the earth and the length of wood propping up his slumped form. Juvie being wiped out didn't surprise me, but Phoebe usually had inexhaustible stamina. It was just as well that they both had an excuse to stop and catch their breath, and while they did, I asked Mabonnyn, "Did we take a wrong turn somewhere?"

Mabonnyn gave a negating head shake as Gern waddled in a circle. "This weg follows another ten leagues and then meets the treadway of the Derryth. This," the woodlander pointed at the fairy ring with the spear, "betokens ill intent, I hazard."

Fairy rings were naturally occurring phenomenon in the Deep Woods, fruiting bodies growing in radial symmetry from an underground mycelium, same as in our world, but these particular blewits were too identical to one another, too perfectly undamaged for their size. This was a namesake fairy ring, and I knew what Mabonnyn was hinting at: someone was trying to send us a message. A warning, or a threat. "We should look for whoever spawned this," I said. "They might still be nearby."

"So let's… get… looking," Phoebe agreed between labored breaths.

"Rest a moment," Mabonnyn said, urging Gern up the embankment. "I will ferret them out, if they tarry near."

"Splitting up… is where things… went wrong… last time," Phoebe said. Somehow she managed not to glance at Juvie.

Juvie remained pointedly silent, leaning on his staff. "I really don't think we have much choice," I offered. Mabonnyn was already dutifully proceeding in any case, not waiting for our approval. I saw the harrier duck under a drooping pine bough, and a moment later the bullfrog was out of sight.

The forest murmured to itself as always, and I listened. The longer we spent in the Deep Woods, the more I remembered my mother's lessons and the more attuned to the undercurrent of activity I became. I could just barely make out the snuffling of a groundhog, nosing its way through a patch of clover. A katydid started to chirp and I automatically counted off the intervals. The katydid's monotone song stopped, too soon, and a heartbeat later Phoebe straightened up and put her finger to her lips. I would have been proud of myself for noticing at the same time as Phoebe if not for the wariness in her eyes, a look that said whatever was coming was not something she wanted to see.

The three of us drew a little closer together,

circling the wagons as much as we could, eyes flicking all around even though the dense trees and undergrowth on either side of the holloway were an opaque curtain of green and gray. We waited, and waited, until a huge spindle bush along the northern embankment rattled furiously. A head poked out of the leaves, followed by another, and another, all three virtually identical. The faces were almost lupine, covered in gray shaggy fur, but where canine noses would have tipped the snouts, hooked black beaks perched instead. The ears were much larger than wolves' as well, fanning out like bat wings with veiny skin visible between needle-like bones. The heads sat on long, serpentine necks covered in the same ash-colored fur, and as the creature continued to emerge from the spindle it became apparent that all three necks were connected to a single body the size of an elephant. The four legs were thick through the furry haunches while the shanks were slender and covered in dark scales, ending in scythe-sized black talons that curved over the edge of the holloway wall.

"Whaaaaaa…" Juvie said in a bare whisper.

"Balaur," Phoebe answered. "Extremely dangerous but not aggressive unless provoked. Don't move. It's probably just passing through."

Everything Phoebe was saying checked out. I had never seen a living balaur up close before, and from her tone, neither had she. It was unsettling, kind of how I imagined it might feel to see a great white shark from the deck of a small boat. In theory, the predator would go about its business without incident, but while waiting it out normal breathing was difficult and time seemed to stand still.

The balaur peered down at us. All three heads shrieked in unison, baring the fangs lining their lower jaws. The balaur charged down the embankment at us.

For a second Phoebe and I were both too shocked to move, and Juvie was still obeying the admonition to hold still. A bolt of cold dread shot through me as it occurred to me that I had lost my gun in the chasm and Mabonnyn, spear in hand, was far off in the forest trying to find whoever had set the wood blewits in our way. The options for battling an enraged balaur were extremely limited, assuming we survived the initial onslaught long enough to fight back. "Move!" I shouted, pushing Juvie and Phoebe toward one embankment before diving to the other.

Interesting thing about multi-headed creatures: while each head possesses a degree of autonomy, it's often limited and imperfect. They are all, ultimately, attached to a single body. While one of the balaur's outer heads lunged and snapped at me, the opposite head went for Phoebe and the central head tried for Juvie. The only thing that prevented any of us from being eviscerated by beak and fangs was the tug of war among the divergent spines and skulls. But since I had gone left and Juvie and Phoebe had gone right, the combined will of two heads won out over the lone third, and the balaur veered after my friends.

I gave myself a total of five seconds to find anything I could use as a weapon before resorting to attacking the beast with my bare hands. An abandoned fairy sword certainly would have done the trick, or a healthy clump of deadly death-sap. What my eyes fell upon was a moss-covered chunk of rock about the size of a football. I picked it up with both hands and ran back down the holloway.

Phoebe and Juvie had scaled the embankment and moved into the dense rows of boles, with the balaur roaring after them. They were running separately, zigzagging from tree to tree and hiding behind each trunk. The balaur took a swipe at a tree and blasted away more than half of the heartwood, then pushed it aside and crawled over it as the crash of the felled tree echoed through the Deep Woods.

"Climb! High as you can!" I bellowed as I neared the balaur. I raised the rock over my head and brought it down on the balaur's tail as it slithered across the sheared stump of the ruined tree. I did more damage to the splintered heartwood than to the balaur's tail, but then again I hadn't really been trying to injure the creature, stun it or slow it down. I just wanted to get its attention, and at that I succeeded spectacularly.

The balaur wheeled around on its rooster legs and all three of its heads trumpeted riotously at me. I turned and ran, mind racing to come up with natural enemies or anathema of the balaur, but only finding blank gaps. In the storybook encounters, a white stallion and a rider with an iron-tipped lance would put an end to a balaur just like any other dragon. The closest thing I had to a knight was one smallish woodlander on a bullfrog, who might eventually hear all the crashing around but would still be overmatched by the monster. On the other hand, even if my mother's attempts to impart her wisdom had gone beyond "let sleeping balaurs lie" it wouldn't do me much good to flash on an inspired recollection about balaurs' natural fear of centipedes or allergies to moonflower. Knowledge is power, but not even my mother has magical abilities to summon animals at will or conjure plant materials out of thin air. I doubted the balaur would give me enough time and space to methodically rustle up its least favorite things.

As if to underscore that very point, the balaur snapped at me as I ran and tore a chunk of cloth and skin from my hip. The flare of pain was intense and I slapped my hand to the wound even as I forced myself to keep running. The laceration was four or five inches long and my entire palm was slick with scarlet within a few strides. I flicked blood down at the ground and was struck by the fact that the balaur hadn't followed up with another strike from behind.

I risked a look back and saw the balaur stopped in its tracks. The head that had bitten me was licking its beak, while the other two heads sniffed greedily at the grass where I had left red spatters in my wake. It was another oddity, in addition to the balaur attacking us out of nowhere when we had been presenting the most passive targets possible. They might even have been related.

The head that had bitten me finished cleaning the tip of its beak and focused its gaze on me. I spotted what I had missed before, the febrile magenta rimming each eyeball, all six of the balaur's ocular cavities overflowing with raw, glistening, infectious-looking pink slime, cerise rivulets oozing down through the gray fur. And before that even had time to sink in, the flesh above the balaur's eyes stretched and split, two horn-like growths emerging, twisted and pale and almost crystalline. They pulsed and twitched like faceted antennae, and the balaur's other two heads, with asymmetrical horns of their own, lost interest in lapping up my blood and stared in my direction.

It was well past time for me to heed the same advice I had shouted at Phoebe and Juvie. I ran for the biggest tree in sight, an ash, grabbed the highest sturdy bough I could reach, and hoisted myself up onto it. From there I jumped to a branch on the neighboring elm, this one ten feet off the ground. I jumped and climbed, climbed and jumped, working my way farther and farther from the path. Below me I could hear the balaur crashing through the woods, and from time to time I felt its weight slamming into whatever tree I was holding onto, the entire trunk shuddering.

I grabbed a handful of leaves and swiped them across my palms to scrape away some of the blood, while the wound in my hip was still weeping. If I didn't stop and bind it up properly soon, I'd likely pass out. I dropped the sticky reddened leaves, letting them flutter to the ground, and heard the balaur snapping at them. I kept going, making a trail for the balaur to follow, bloodleaves in place of breadcrumbs. After a dozen or so handfuls of leaves I doubled back, as quietly and gracefully as I could, then struck out in the direction I had seen Phoebe and Juvie heading last.

I roved through the canopy as fast as I could with the gash down my hip blazing like a hot brand every time I put weight on that leg. I had managed to lure the balaur away by appealing to its unnatural bloodlust, but eventually it would run out of leaves and hunt for me again. And I really didn't have a plan for dealing with that inevitability. Nor did I have any idea exactly how to find Phoebe and Juvie, assuming they had managed to stay together while fleeing the balaur. Plus I was slowly bleeding out, and if I stopped to properly dress the wound I'd be sacrificing the lead I'd built up in evading the balaur, whereas if I kept pushing and lost consciousness the balaur would have a much easier time finding me passed out on the forest floor.

I pushed on anyway, and for the first time in a long time my luck turned good. I felt a change in the air around me, a sensation similar to the harbingers of the balaur's arrival, yet subtly different. It wasn't the tense silence of fear, but the hush of reverence. I was approaching the demesne of one of the name trees, and I made my way toward it, drawn on like a proverbial moth to a flame. Finally I saw it, a colossal aspen tree, the biggest aspen in the Deep Woods: Eadhadh.

I climbed down the spruce I was in, wincing from the pain shooting up and down my leg but buoyed by a vast sense of relief. The Eadhadh was, like all the name trees, a sanctuary, avoided by predators. The balaur wouldn't be able to enter its demesne for violent purposes, not even while it was being controlled by some alien malevolence, as seemed to be the case. Or so I hoped, and if I was wrong, I probably wouldn't be alive long enough to regret my assumption proving false.

The Eadhadh was also the most likely place Phoebe would have headed once she sensed its presence, and sure enough, as I approached I saw her and Juvie sprawled against its gargantuan trunk. The base of the tree was thirty feet across, the white bark rising a hundred feet before the first limbs spread their branches full of dazzling green pinnate leaves. The area around the Eadhadh was cleared for two hundred feet in every direction, anything bigger than a blade of grass maintaining a respectful distance from the name tree. The space formed a clearing that was almost perfectly circular, and as still and hushed as a cathedral.

"Dude," Juvie said as he saw me enter the clearing, not bothering to get up.

"The balaur?" Phoebe asked.

"Still out there," I said. "But don't worry, it won't come here."

"That's what she said," Juvie said, inclining his head toward Phoebe. "You guys gonna tell me how you can both be so sure?"

"Sure, just… gimme a sec," I said as I awkwardly lowered myself to the grass.

Phoebe's eyes widened. "Kellan, what happened to your leg?"

"Balaur," I said.

"How long have you been hemorrhaging?" Phoebe demanded.

I shrugged. "Kind of lost track of time."

Phoebe shook her head as she pushed herself

upright. "I'll get some yarrow."

"You think you can find…?" I started to ask, my question trailing off as Phoebe fixed me with a look of annoyance. "Right," I nodded. "Thanks."

Phoebe closed her eyes and immediately staggered forward as if the ground had tilted forty-five degrees. She caught herself and said, "Whoa."

"You all right?" Juvie asked.

"Fine," she said, followed by a slow, deep breath. "That was intense. But I'll be right back." She strode off into the woods.

"For the record, I am still fine with doing exactly what I'm told and not doing anything else without asking first," Juvie said.

"Good," I said.

"But I have no idea what's going on right now," he added.

I started unbuttoning my shirt. "Where do you want to start?"

"Where did Phoebe go?"

"To get some yarrow."

"Why?"

"It's a natural styptic. She'll pack it into this mess and it will slow the bleeding enough that we can keep moving."

"Why didn't you pick some yourself?"

"I didn't happen to see any. It's not a very big plant, and I was running from an apex predator up until I got here."

"What happens if the apex predator finds Phoebe while she's looking for it, then?"

"She won't be gone long," I said. "She won't have to poke around for it. She's a hamadryad, right? The trees will tell her where to find some."

"Like how moss grows on the north side, that kind of stuff?"

"Not exactly. She can hear what the trees are thinking, what they tell each other and all the plants around them. Kind of, it's more complicated than that and it's not a perfect analogy, but that's the gist." I slipped off my shirt and tugged at the shoulder seam.

"So… here, give it," Juvie said. He took the shirt from me and started working the sleeve. He got a rip started faster than I would have. "So was that what was happening when she looked like she was going to fall down? She was talking to the trees or whatever?"

"Yeah, basically," I said. "Usually it would just be like opening a window to eavesdrop on someone else's conversation nearby, but I think the Eadhadh overwhelmed her for a second, like suddenly the window opened on a monster truck rally where every truck had a heavy metal concert happening on its hood."

"The E-what?"

I pointed at the giant aspen. Juvie looked back at it, and the huge black knotholes all up and down its trunk seemed to regard us as well, like judging eyes as dark as moonless night. "The Eadhadh. The Aspen."

"Like your mother's oak?"

"Yeah, exactly. Like the Derryth. These trees are the power centers of the Deep Woods, lucky for us. If there's yarrow within ten miles of here, the Eadhadh knows exactly where it grows and now

Phoebe does, too. It also makes a kind of anti-violence bubble, which is how Phoebe and I both know the balaur won't follow us. And it's a pretty good landmark, so Mabonnyn will probably come looking for us here once he realizes we left the holloway."

"Yeah but you said we had to keep moving," Juvie pointed out as he handed me the detached sleeve.

"Well, we'll leave Mabonnyn a note," I said, wrapping the sleeve around my upper thigh. I tied it tight and added, "Glad to see you and Phoebe didn't kill each other when you were alone together for five minutes."

Juvie nodded but didn't even crack a smile. "I think something's up with her."

"How do you mean?"

"She fell out of a tree."

I blinked. "No she didn't."

"I know, that should be impossible, right?" Juvie asked. "I mean, I didn't know, I just had a feeling."

"What happened exactly?"

"I don't know," Juvie admitted. "We were climbing through the trees and she said it was safe to climb down. I was skeptical, so she told me she'd keep a lookout while I climbed down first. I did, and then it was her turn, and I was looking around to make sure the balaur didn't sneak up on us. I heard her cry out and she was falling."

"And she just hit the ground?"

"Nah, I caught her," Juvie said. "By which I mean I got myself underneath her and gave her something collapsible to land on."

"Still counts," I said. "Pretty heroic."

"Yeah," Juvie laughed. "Big damn hero, that's me. She said thank you, and I got the feeling she wasn't quite as pissed about the cow thing anymore."

"Here's hoping."

Juvie gave another long look at the Eadhadh. "So does this tree have its own druid, like your mom? So-and-so of the Aspen? Somebody who could maybe help us out, from professional courtesy?"

"I'm sure there was a so-and-so at one point," I said. "Maybe a thousand years ago. There aren't as many druids around these days."

"Bummer," Juvie said. "On a lot of levels."

Phoebe returned with the yarrow. She set to work immediately, kneeling beside me as I untied my sleeve-tourniquet. She stripped the slender, feathery leaves off the stems and laid them into the wound, packing in layer after layer. The astringent oils hit my flesh like an electric shock, but I gritted my teeth until she had applied every green bit. I bound the wound up again.

"Can you walk?" Phoebe asked.

I stood up and tested my weight on my leg. It already hurt less, which I took as a good sign. "Think so," I said. "You?"

Phoebe cocked her head, "Why wouldn't I?"

"Maybe the better question is, should you?" Juvie cut in. "We were discussing it while you were gone, should we go and assume we'll meet up with Mabonnyn at some point, or should we wait here until Mabonnyn comes to us?"

Phoebe looked up into the green vault of aspen

leaves above us, considering the question seriously. She dropped her gaze and arched an eyebrow. "Moot point."

Juvie and I turned and saw Gern coming out of the woods. I raised a hand in greeting, which Mabonnyn did not return. "Did you find anything?" I asked.

"On the contrary," Mabonnyn replied. "I was found."

"Ugh, no, no," Juvie protested. "The last thing we need right now is riddles."

"Can't say I disagree with that," Phoebe said.

"No riddle," Mabonnyn said. It occurred to me that the spear I had envied when facing the balaur was no longer at the harrier's side. It also occurred to me that Mabonnyn looked miserable. "The remainder of our journey will be guided along a different path."

Branches rustled all around us. Phoebe and I froze, only letting our eyes rove the scene, while Juvie did one full-body doubletake after another. A puffy bird as large as Gern appeared next to the bullfrog, with a rider as diminutive as Mabonnyn; the bird was a firecrest, gray-bellied, brownish-green winged, with yellow and black facial markings and a bright orange stripe between its beady eyes, and the rider was pointing a halberd spike at our erstwhile guide. A few yards away, a wild boar emerged with a rider of its own. On the opposite side, a mounted al-mi'raj appeared, a golden-furred rabbit as large as the wild boar with a single spiral horn of ebony jutting from its forehead. A bobcat and rider came around one side of the Eadhadh, while a giant salamander bore another rider from the other side. The riders, I noticed, were garbed in what looked like livery, matching red tunics and black breeches and red boots.

Finally, after all of our guides had taken up position around us, riders brandishing their swords and flails and mounts pawing impatiently at the ground, a stag made its way into the Eadhadh's clearing. Its fur was pearl white, its antlers silver, and its wings a pale shining blue, as if each feather were a mirror capturing the clearest sky. The woodlander astride the magnificent steed did not appear to be armed, but projected such an aura of authority that any weapon would have been superfluous. "Son of Foltchain," the stag's rider said, "you are summoned before the Council of Ruis."

CHAPTER SIX: RED COUNCIL

T**HE WINGED STAG** led the procession, followed by the salamander, Gern and Mabonnyn, the firecrest and the al-mi'raj, Juvie, Phoebe and me, and finally the bobcat and the boar. None of us were bound in any way, no ropes or chains or other restraints. Mabonnyn's spear had been confiscated, but Juvie was allowed to keep his hazel staff. The riders kept their own weapons at the ready, but in a casual way, with none of the pointy bits aimed at us or poking our backs. Yet I had no doubts they could have those blades halfway through any number of our internal organs in the blink of an eye. Like Mabonnyn, the other mounted woodlanders were lean and ropy beneath their livery, not a trace of softness in their limbs or faces, like wild animals capable of either fight or flight as circumstances dictated. It was that feral, rawboned anatomy that made the woodlanders seem mostly androgynous; even the ones with whiskers grew only narrow, bristling slashes more like natural animal growth than the result of human facial grooming.

As we trekked along a circuitous path through the Deep Woods, we almost could have passed for a singular cohesive group, everybody on the same team, one for all and all for whatever. But there was an unspoken understanding that Phoebe, Juvie, Mabonnyn, Gern and I were not fellow travelers coincidentally heading the same way as the others, nor were they guardians or guides, despite what Mabonnyn had said just before they appeared. They were our captors, and we were their prisoners, and we risked being reminded of that at our own peril.

The forced march wasn't perfectly orderly, since we were cutting crosswise through the Deep Woods surrounding the Eadhadh. We wove through brush and around immense tree trunks, with our escorts subtly shifting their positions to outflank us and maintain lines of sight wherever we roamed. When Juvie went left around a shaggy cedar while Phoebe veered right, the boar and bobcat similarly separated to either side and guided them back together; when I stopped to tighten the binding around the gash in my leg, the al-mi'raj broke formation and retreated by several hops to allow the rider to watch me until I rejoined the group.

Above and beyond the watchfulness of our escorts, I felt other gazes tracking our progress through the Deep Woods. I couldn't see anything obvious, but didn't expect to. The denizens of the Deep Woods were more than capable of preventing themselves from being spotted, and only my lifetime of familiarity allowed me to perceive the eddies of interested consciousness in the air. Actually, it was two lifetimes, my upbringing at the heel of an ancient druid priestess plus my workaday interactions in the modern world. The expectant energy riding the currents of the fascicles of leaves and spikelets of grasses was reminiscent of the vibe in the gallery of a courtroom, full of rubbernecking onlookers hoping to catch the inevitable sparks thrown when some deviant force met the immovable object of state-sanctioned approbation.

Our route climbed uphill for a ways, causing Juvie to lean heavily on his staff, but he didn't complain. None of us did, not that Gern was equipped to do so, and not that Mabonnyn had any reason to, riding on the bullfrog's back. Phoebe seemed to struggle a little, but she suffered in silence. I felt the burn myself, but I wasn't going to be the only one grousing about it.

I maneuvered myself next to Phoebe and said, low enough that only she could hear me, "Juvie said you fell out of a tree."

"Stupid," she answered, as if the word tasted bitter.

"How?" I asked.

"I closed my eyes," she said. It wasn't an explanation. Phoebe could climb up and down a dozen trees blindfolded and never slip once, her hamadryad instincts guiding her hands and feet from bough to bough unerringly. I knew it, she knew it, and she knew I knew it, so I waited for her to continue. "I reached for a branch and my hand punched through a bird's nest. It startled me and I lost my balance. Like I said, stupid."

That was a little more plausible, Phoebe's innate sense of a tree's living tissue omitting the random dead twigs and fibers of a nest from her mental map. "Are you… you know, all right?" I asked.

"None of us are, right now, are we?" she shot back. I couldn't argue with that.

A moment came when the rider on the winged stag turned to look back over his shoulder, and some signal passed between the leader and the rider on the firecrest. The bird flapped its wings, rose into the air, and flitted ahead. I figured we must be nearing our destination, and once we wove through a few more trees, I knew without a doubt we had arrived.

A wall of redbud trees stood before us, different from most of the others all around us in a couple of crucial ways. These trees were only about twenty or thirty feet high, still tall enough to be reminiscent of a three-storey building but dwarfed by the towering giants that formed the canopy of the Deep Woods. And while those gigantic trees were relatively upright with stolid, straight trunks, the trees ahead had crooked boles, and branches which intertwined with one another like a finely woven tapestry, boughs that dipped close to the ground and formed a dense dome, covered in overlapping leaves, heart-shaped and deep reddish-purple, an angry contrast against the greens, yellows and browns of the backdrop. The firecrest was perched near the crown of the redbud grove, rider and mount watching as we approached. The winged stag drew near the trees, then made a stately quarter-turn, allowing the rider to point at a narrow gap through which we could enter.

Phoebe, Juvie and I had to crouch to enter the pavillion of interlaced redbuds, and when we were able to rise again we found ourselves in a grand crepuscular rotunda, the light muted by the carmine leaves to nothing more than a violet suggestion. Within, the perimeter was lined with dozens and dozens of creatures and humanoid denizens of the Deep Woods, quietly observing as we entered. Presumably they had all taken up positions around the outer edges when the rider of the firecrest had announced our imminent arrival. On the far side of the interior, something like a dais had been coaxed out of living redbud wood, treelimbs contorting even more than the exterior structure to form steps leading up to a broad platform with a fanned curving wall at the rear. On either side of the curved wall, lanterns had been hung, banishing some of the gloom. Individual branches rose up in zigzag configurations that formed seats, occupied by seven woodlander representatives. I knew one of them by sight immediately, another one I thought I could guess by reputation. The remaining five were unknown quantities, which didn't thrill me. I glanced at Phoebe as we approached, trying to pick up on any hints of recognition as she scanned the platform, but her head was down and her eyes were closed. No help there. I shifted my eyeline over to Mabonnyn, but the harrier of the Floret folk was inscrutable as ever. I had to rely on what I could piece together for myself.

The Floret folk were not the most powerful denizens of the Deep Woods, small in both population numbers and influence. The seven seated above us were representatives of more important factions, or more self-important at any rate. The one I recognized was Lurria, a pixie with mahogany skin and ringlets of burnished copper hair. She was as radiant as the last time I had seen her, in my childhood, twenty-five years ago or more. I had asked my mother once what had ever happened to her, and she had told me that Lurria was besotted with me when I was born, because she had a deep and abiding fascination with human babies. So long as it made sense to count my age in months, Lurria was a frequent visitor to our house, cooing over me constantly. But as I got older, her enthrallment waned, and by the time I was nine years old Lurria stopped coming around. I remembered getting very sick that winter before I turned nine, bed-ridden with something wretched that rendered me a pale, sweaty, oozing and wheezing little casualty. If Lurria had been losing interest before that, surely my lack of resemblance to anything flourishing during that bout had broken the spell forever. Which was kind of ironic, because once my mother had nursed me through that particular infirmity, my immune system had been outstanding.

I didn't have many specific memories of things Lurria had done or said during those early years when she still found me captivating, but her appearance had been burned into my memory, and of course she hadn't aged a day or changed at all as the decades had passed. I wasn't sure if she'd recognize me or not, or if it would matter either way. I still had no idea why the Council of Ruis had summoned us, since our captors had been less than forthcoming about it.

The other denizen I felt confident about putting a name to, despite never having been formally introduced, was Ffirk Halfhorned. Five feet tall, rail thin, with thick ginger body hair and a face like a devil: pointed chin, pointed ears, a dagger-sized horn rising from the crown of the skull above the left eye, and a broken stump on the right side. My mother had told me about Ffirk, in the form of dire admonitions to avoid him at all costs.

The rest were a diverse bunch. A sylph hovered above one seat, her wings fluttering so quickly they seemed insubstantial, a blurred halo surrounding her long, straight white hair. Like Lurria, the sylph was only a foot and a half tall and delicately proportioned. A knacker occupied the next branch, slightly taller than the sylph but almost two feet broad as well. He was covered in brown stains and some clods of dirt clung to his hair, beard and clothes. His oversized hands flexed of their own accord, as if it were impossible to keep them stilled, and if not for that repetitive motion the knacker would have looked like something carved of stone and recently disinterred. Ffirk was next, followed by a fat, verdigris-skinned goblin with a bulbous nose and drooping ears, wearing a long, black doublet and an assortment of gold bracelets, necklaces and earrings. Beside the goblin sat a sonney with alabaster skin, human shaped from the neck down but with the head of a young white pig. The sonney's eyes were red and intelligent, a world of morality and understanding away from the limpid brown eyes of the stout boar ridden by our pixie captor. Then came Lurria herself, and finally a spriggan, only a sapling, really, with a bushy head of leaves and smooth bark skin.

When Juvie, Phoebe and I reached the area directly in front of the dais, I half-expected Gern and Mabonnyn to veer off and join their fellow denizens in the gallery, as the other riders and mounts did. But the giant bullfrog squatted beside Juvie and Mabonnyn stared up at the council, resolute as ever. That made me feel a little better.

The sonney stepped forward to the edge of the dais. "Son of Foltchain," he said, his voice like a choirboy, "you honor the Council of Ruis with your presence."

"The honor is mine," I responded automatically. Mom's etiquette lessons again, overriding the fact that I felt no such sentiment. I thought about adding something about how the scale of pomp on display was unnecessary, but held my tongue.

"It has been many a season since you essayed our verdant paths," the sonney said.

Was he trying to shame me? My own mother, ancient druidess who literally gave me life and thus would be hard pressed to say whether she loved me or the Deep Woods more, had long since given up trying to guilt trip me into visiting her turf more regularly and reverently. I wasn't about to cower at the scolding of a puffed-up pigboy I'd never met before. "It has," I agreed in an unbothered tone. "So long that I have never before made the acquaintance of the current speaker of the Council of Ruis."

The sylph smiled at that, and the goblin let out a single yip of an aborted cackle. The sonney's tufted triangular ears flicked reflexively, his scarlet eyes narrowing slightly. "Indeed not," he said. "Forgive me. Your reputation far outstrips my own, but does not render introductions irrelevant. I am Tuscu of the Nutpine Sounder." He bowed his head slightly.

"My fellow travelers," I said, "are Mabonnyn of the Floret folk, Phoebiratopys daughter of Tithorea, and Juvenal Braga."

"Grandson of Altamira," Juvie added. I couldn't quite tell if he was trying to put himself on equal footing with all the genealogical honorifics, or if he was making fun of it. Knowing him, probably a bit of both.

"You are all well-met," Tuscu said, a touch hurriedly, trying to reassert control. "It is the will of the Council, in light of the abiding good will of your beneficent mother, that we hold this parley with you in peaceable fellowship."

"With all due respect," I countered, "we don't really have time for an extended parley. My mother is missing. If you know anything about where she is, tell me. If you want to help us look for her, we gratefully accept. If not, then let us be on our way."

"We know that Foltchain is missing," Tuscu said, "but do not know her whereabouts. And we cannot allow your search through the Deep Woods to proceed. The only aid we offer is to lead you out of our domain swiftly and safely."

"An offer which I must decline," I said. "You don't care what's happened to my mother? Fine. Tend to your own affairs. But stay out of my way." I took a step back and turned to walk away, immediately finding myself face to face with the al-mi'raj. The saffron fur of its hackles was raised, its mouth was opened to reveal a carnivore's fangs, and the jet spiral horn was aimed at my heart. The rider on its back brandished an axe which seemed redundant at best. I scowled at rider and mount alike, but reversed myself to face the Council again.

"The Council wishes to hold this parley in peaceable fellowship," the knacker said in a weary, gravelly voice. "But you must abide by our terms or face consequence."

"You can't expect to talk me into abandoning my mother," I said.

"It is what Foltchain of the Oak would want," the sylph sighed.

"Excuse me?" I said.

"Modita speaks true," the spriggan said. "If you remain in the Deep Woods, you will not find your mother. Yet the longer you remain in the Deep Woods, the more harm you may cause."

"I'm sorry you think my mere presence is so offensive," I said.

"Your presence has consequences," Tuscu snapped. "Bring them forth!"

I had thought that the liveried woodlanders, with their mounts and their weapons, were the Council's primary enforcers, but I had underestimated them. Three oosers marched out from behind the dais, each one the size of a champion bodybuilder, covered in curly fur except for their leathery hands and faces. Those faces were brutish, lantern-jawed with sharp teeth, broad noses, bulging eyes, and crowned with huge curved horns like water buffalo. Each of the oosers carried a weight across their shoulders, and as they reached the front of the dais they laid them out on the grass. The first one was the balaur that had chased Juvie, Phoebe and me off the path. It was dead now, its shaggy gray fur stiff with blood from a dozen wounds. The next was the remains of a cat sidhe, as big as a tiger, black except for a white spot on its chest. The cat sidhe's rear right leg had been hacked off. Finally was a boagane, a youngish one judging by the size, slightly smaller than the ooser carrying it. The yellow-skinned boagane had short legs, a bearish torso, long arms, and a head like a crocodile with tusks. Like the two corpses beside it, the boagane looked like it had met its demise in bloody battle.

The dead creatures had two other features in common: all three were leaking raw pink ooze from their lifeless eyes, and all three bore jagged growths cutting up and out of their hides, the faceted white thorns piercing the flesh of the balaur's heads, the cat sidhe's spine and tip of its tail, and the boagane's shoulders and chest.

I took a moment to grieve for all three creatures. None of them had deserved to suffer and die as they clearly had. I looked up at Tuscu and said, "What exactly are we accused of?"

"You are accused of drawing a great calamity into the Deep Woods," Tuscu said.

"And not even a particularly amusing kind," Ffirk added, with a smile that chilled me so deeply it was a wonder I didn't physically shiver. The oosers grunted in affirmation, telling me that Ffirk was the one responsible for their presence. That tracked.

"Something afflicted these beasts," Tuscu hurried on. "Something the likes of which has never been seen in the Deep Woods, something which was only seen once you crossed over into the Deep Woods, Son of Foltchain. Do you deny that this… this blight followed you here?"

"I don't know," I said. It was the theory that made the most sense, but I didn't know anything for certain, and I was damned if I was going to give the pig-faced boy and his court the satisfaction of a confession.

"Do you expect us to believe it to be mere coincidence?" Lurria finally spoke, soft and sweet. She looked penetratingly into my eyes. I had all but forgotten how utterly alien they were. Beautiful, mesmerizing, and not different from a human woman's eyes in any definable physical way. But there was depth and power to them which marked her apart. I couldn't tell if she was challenging me, rhetorically rejecting the idea out of hand, or if she was throwing me a lifeline, something which might sway the Council. I couldn't read her at all.

"You can believe whatever you want to believe," I said. "I need to reach the Derryth, for my mother's sake. Once I do, I promise you I will leave, but until I do, I will not let anything stop me." I kind of surprised myself with the outpouring. It was the kind of cut and dry plain talk that the denizens of the Deep Woods respected, but I wasn't just framing things for their benefit. I meant every word.

"You may not wish to let anything stop you," Ffirk said, leaning forward. "But your wishes count for very little here."

"Councilfolk, please, hear me," Phoebe said, stepping closer to the dais. "I have known Foltchain of the Oak since I was a seedling. Many of you may have known her longer, far longer, but all of you know of her, by her deeds and doings. You know that the Deep Woods has no greater champion."

"No greater champion living," the goblin sneered.

"None living," Phoebe said, bowing her head respectfully. "Which is all the more reason to be concerned when Foltchain has gone missing. If she is truly lost to us, the consequences to the Deep Woods would be devastating. She may not be yet, but time is not on our side. I beseech you, aid us, not for our sake but for your own, for all the woodlanders for whom you speak. And if you cannot bring yourself to do so, at the very least, do not hinder us."

"Every moment you and the Son of Foltchain remain here, more of these blighted creatures will run amok," the knacker said, scratching his filthy beard. "If they come in greater numbers, at closer intervals, we will not long be able to contain them. We were not able to contain these," he gestured at the corpses of the balaur, cat sidhe and boagane, "without great cost."

"Oh is this the part where you're going to bring out the bodies of the warriors who sacrificed themselves, too?" Juvie asked.

"Have a care, human," Tuscu warned.

"Why? This is already bullshit!" Juvie spat. "She's trying to tell you we're all on the same side, and she's absolutely right! How can you not see that? Kick us out or kill us, it's gonna bite you in the ass, and once Foltchain is gone then what? You think you can hide from this forever? You think they won't be back?"

The Council stared at Juvie in the wake of the outburst. Tuscu looked somewhere between annoyed and outraged, Ffirk looked amused, and the rest were maddeningly serene as ever. I gave Juvie a lot of credit for trying, but it was a tough crowd.

"Grytainne, I beseech you," Phoebe tried again, as if Juvie hadn't said a word. "In my mother's name, I beseech you most of all. Let Council and company part from one another as peaceably as we have kept time together."

The spriggan, Grytainne apparently, rose upon rootlike feet, leaves and twigs unfurling. "Shoot of the tree of Tithorea," Grytainne said, "I honor you as I honor your mother. I am sorry to see you upon this weg which puts us at odds. I cannot walk your weg with you, but I honor your right to follow it as far as you may. However, I am but one branch of the Council of Ruis. Each must speak by turn."

Phoebe bowed her head again. She looked defeated and exhausted. I stepped up next to her. "Will any of you change your mind, and allow us to proceed on our own accord?"

"No," the sylph Modita shook her head.

"No," the knacker harrumphed.

"I have seen nothing here to cause me to doubt the judgment of the Council," Ffirk said.

"Course you haven't," the goblin said. "The judgment should stand."

Lurria looked meaningfully at me. "I regretfully must agree with Ffirk and Weegth," she said. "The interlopers must be quarantined, both for their own good, and the good of the Woods."

And that was that. Tuscu looked satisfied. "Guards, return these interlopers to the realm where they belong," the sonney said.

The three oosers lumbered forward, each one eyeing a different target. Juvie took a reflexive step towards me. Phoebe didn't even bother to look up. She and Juvie and I at our best would have been hard pressed to tackle one ooser, and stood no chance against the trio in a direct confrontation. We were going to have to run, and I tried to determine which of the oosers looked like the slowest, dumbest, weakest link. Probably the one on the right. I'd bolt around that one, dragging Juvie and Phoebe with me. Then I'd immediately need to assess where the best point to charge the cordon of pixies was, but one reckless and ill-advised leap at a time.

There was a blur of mottled green in front of me as Gern jumped across the advancing line of oosers. As Mabonnyn was carried past the ooser in the middle of the triad, the harrier pulled a small knife from its boot sheath and slashed the brute's face, tossing a fan of dark blood through the air. Then all of the bullfrog's weight crashed into the ooser on the left, causing it to stumble momentarily. Sure enough, the ooser on the right was dumbfounded, looking to its two brothers with a furrowed brow and mouth agape. I grabbed Juvie's wrist in one hand, Phoebe's in the other, and broke into a run around the end of the line of oosers.

We crashed into the redbud wall as the dais and everything around it erupted into chaos. While Phoebe, Juvie and I forced our way through what gaps we could find, snapping brittle branches and scattering heartsblood leaves in our wake, all the while enduring the scraping, cutting points of limbs and twigs savaging our flesh. I heard the goblin's gurgling war cry, Ffirk commanding the oosers to ignore the harrier and the frog to run us down, the oosers growling and roaring obeisance, the woodlanders-at-arms urging their mounts into pursuit, but I paid it all very little attention because none of it mattered. I concentrated instead on smashing out of the redbud dome and then putting as much distance between us and it as I could as rapidly as I could. Juvie had gotten the hint fairly readily, jerking his wrist out of my grip so that he could find his own way through the barrier. Phoebe had been slower to come around but was at least plowing ahead under her own power when I was forced to drop her forearm as well.

The emerald gleam of the Deep Woods seemed almost dazzlingly bright compared to the ruddy pavilion of the Council of Ruis. We zigzagged through a hyper verdant landscape, where fronds and branches whipped our arms and legs and a veil of green and gray like a mossy fogbank prevented us from seeing more than a couple feet ahead at any moment.

So it seemed like the bobcat and its rider came out of nowhere, but really they had just overtaken us by sheer speed, blocked from our sight by the trees and duff while they looped around and doubled back to intercept us. The bobcat pounced at me, its forepaws brandishing shiny black claws that hit my chest like knives. I went down hard on my back, my eyes closing for a split second before I forced them open, in time to see the pixie leaning forward between the bobcat's tawny tufted ears, swinging the thorny head of its two-handed flail in a circle while taking aim at my skull.

The flail-head came whistling down toward me, and at the last possible instant I rolled to the side beyond its arc of approach. At the same time I reached up and grabbed the long handle of the weapon. While the pixie was off balance, I yanked the flail from his grasp. Much like Mabonnyn's spear, what was a large war weapon in the pixie's hands was a modest implement in mine, but you work with what's given to you. The bobcat still had me pinned, so I shoved the handle of the flail crosswise between the cat's teeth, barely able to bridge its mouth by putting one hand up against the corner of its lips. The bobcat yowled displeasure, but I forced it off me.

I jumped to my feet, looking around frantically for Juvie and Phoebe. Neither of them had stopped when the bobcat launched itself at me, and I was oddly grateful for that. Phoebe was fleet as a deer, darting through the brush and between the trees.

Juvie was more of a wrecking ball, smashing and trampling to clear a path through the heavy growth. I had to admit his style was closer to my own, especially when time was of the essence. I ran after him to make use of the trail he was stomping clear.

Unfortunately, his human bulldozer routine made it just as easy for the Council of Ruis to follow him as it was for me. I had closed the gap between us to a little less than ten yards when the earth exploded in front of Juvie, showering him and me both with clods of dirt and a smattering of pebbles and roots and worms. The knacker emerged from underground, now completely coated in a layer of dark brown glistening humus from head to toe except for his eyes. He held a rock over his head, an irregular stone a couple of feet in diameter. The knacker hurled the rock at Juvie, who threw himself flat on the forest floor. The projectile sailed over him and struck a tree, gouging the trunk in a spray of splinters like an enormous cannonball hitting the side of a ship. The wood groaned and the old bole swayed, as the remainder of the treetrunk cracked under the weight of its upper limbs. The tree fell with a tremendous crash, sending me racing out of its way. Once it had met the forest floor, I vaulted over it to make my way back to Juvie.

Juvie was already back on his feet when I reached him, and the knacker was gone. Presumably he'd be digging up another rock to sling at us, but he'd have to catch us first. I made sure Juvie was all right and got us both moving again.

"Should we climb?" Juvie panted as we stomp-sprinted.

"Wouldn't do much good," I said. "They can climb, too, most of them better than you or me. Not to mention…"

I had been about to say that some of them could fly, when I saw the firecrest. It had its claws in Phoebe's shoulders and was trying to lift her off her feet, wings flapping furiously. Phoebe, to her credit, was making that as difficult as possible, thrashing and twisting and kicking with all her might. She got one arm free and reached across her body, clenching a fist around the bird's leg still gripping her other shoulder. The pixie on the bird's back, meanwhile, was leaning far over the side of the mount, halberd in hand, ready to take advantage of Phoebe's otherwise occupied attention to take some of the fight out of her with one swift stab.

Juvie and I both poured on the speed, and Juvie made the first move, launching himself into the air and tackling the firecrest bird by the tail feathers. It may have been more of a shock than anything, but the bird was startled enough to release Phoebe and send itself skyward with a few flaps of its wings. The rider nearly lost her balance, recovering awkwardly as the firecrest rose in the air.

The pixie regained control of the bird and urged it into a dive, holding the halberd like a jousting lance as it zoomed toward us. The relative size of the weapon actually worked in its favor, since it would be hard for me to try to parry something so small moving so fast. I thought about throwing myself across Phoebe and taking whatever blow would fall across my shoulders or back, and then a slash of pink whipped through the air and snagged the pixie from its perch. I spied Gern with Mabonnyn on her back and the firecrest's rider in her mouth. The big bullfrog was making no effort to eat the woodlander, merely holding it in her powerful jaws effectively stifling all the flailing attempts to gain freedom.

I got Phoebe to her feet and Juvie jogged over to us, casting black firecrest tail feathers to the wind. Gern spat out the liveried rider and slapped a large webbed foot atop the woodlander's head. "Follow us! Hyah!" Mabonnyn called, and Gern leaped into the air, driving the rider down into the earth as she pushed off. Phoebe, Juvie and I ran after the harrier.

I had gotten a bit turned around and very much hoped that Mabonnyn and Gern knew where they were going. They seemed to, following a more or less straight path through the forest, until the guttural huffing of an ooser ahead and to the left sent them bounding to the right. A few moments later the goblin from the Council dropped from a tree branch overhead into our path. Gern changed direction again.

A heavy trotting noise behind us made me throw a glance back over my shoulder. The boar was running pell mell after us, snorting furiously, rider practically standing astride his back. There was nothing for it except to keep running.

Gern angled toward a deep furrow in the greenery, fifteen feet wide and spanned by a fallen tree. But instead of bounding across the log bridge, the bullfrog leapt straight up in front of a young, slender spruce at the edge of the crease. Bullfrogs are not tree frogs, as a rule, and the spruce bowed under the awkward weight of Gern and Mabonnyn, arcing over the furrow. On the far side, Gern held down the upper branches as Mabonnyn yelled, "This way!"

Phoebe swung out along the spruce trunk first, moving hand over hand as naturally as a gymnastics prodigy, at least at first. She started to flag at about the halfway point, and by the time she reached the far side she was obviously exhausted, dropping to her knees. Juvie arrived at the base of the spruce and looked at the hazel staff in his hand questioningly for a moment. I took the staff from him and shoved his shoulder to get him moving again. He wasn't as fast and graceful as Phoebe but he got himself across. Once he was standing on the far side I tossed the hazel over to him.

I lowered myself, dangling from the spruce. A stream ran through the furrow, turbid water swirling and splashing over rocks. I hand-walked rapidly and was a little more than halfway across when Gern started to back up. The spruce bobbed in time with my pendulous advances. I pulled my hips back, kicked forward and let go of the tree trunk, falling toward the far embankment as branches whooshed upward past my head. I landed awkwardly on my knees, but Phoebe and Juvie helped me up before I could slide down into the stream.

The boar and his rider reached the furrow and the beast alighted on the far end of the fallen tree. The dead wood was black, stippled with orange warts all along its upper surface. The boar charged ahead a few steps and then skewed wildly, slipping on the slimemold that blanketed the log. The boar squealed as its hooves went out from under it, and mount and rider pitched off the fallen tree and tumbled into the rushing waters below.

"That was lucky," I said.

"I know that one," Mabonnyn said. "Not one to carefully think things through, especially on the hunt. Hyah!" The harrier spurred Gern onward, and our little band of fugitives was on the run again.

The forest was intractable, but we kept moving forward, with Gern and Mabonnyn always able to skirt around the utterly impassable obstacles. Finally we came to a sheer rock wall with an opening in its face about the size of the front end of a city bus. Moss grew around the cavern mouth, hanging down in ragged strands, and it was impossible to see deeply into the space. "This is where you've been leading us?" Juvie asked. "A cave?"

"It is the only way which affords us any chance of eluding the Council," Mabonnyn said.

"Won't they just follow us through?" I asked.

"The path does not lead through," Mabonnyn said. "It leads down."

"Downhill?" Juvie probed, sounding skeptical.

"Downward," Mabonnyn corrected, making the word sound ominous.

"No, no, no," Phoebe shook her head. "Not the Undergrowth. There has to be another way."

"Must there be?" a sly voice asked behind us. We turned to see Ffirk Halfhorned standing less than ten yards away, his oosers lined up behind him.

"All right, look," Juvie said, holding his arms out to his sides and raising and lowering his open hands, as if he were trying to get a raucous middle school auditorium to settle down. But the Deep Woods were quiet around us except for the occasional phlegmy snort of an ooser. Birds chirped, and insects buzzed, but only in the distance. Juvie went on, "What are you going to do, drag us out of here in chains? Put a small army of guards on us for the trip, since we're determined to fight you and try to get away from you every step of the way? You gonna fight us and the… the what did you call it, the calamity, the blight, whatever's gotten into the animals? At the same time? Wouldn't it make more sense to just let us do what we came here to do, and keep a lookout for the blight? Give us one day, just one more day. Go back and tell the Council we got away."

Ffirk smiled sourly. I knew Juvie meant well, but he was grasping at straws. It would take us more than a day to get to the Derryth, and Ffirk knew it. He also knew that the Council could in fact raise a small army on short notice if necessary. None of Juvie's arguments were particularly compelling, and the way the old gant-y-tan's lips were twisting made it look like he was trying to decide if Juvie were deliberately insulting his intelligence, in which case he would gut him where he stood, or if Juvie were merely spectacularly ignorant himself, in which case Ffirk would have a good laugh at the mortal's expense first, then gut him where he stood.

Ultimately Ffirk Halfhorned did neither. "You know what lies beyond yon cavern, Son of Foltchain," he said. "Beyond… and below. You have exhausted the Council's patience, and should not expect gentle treatment from us. But to descend into the dim of the Undergrowth would be worse. Still, make your choice. Now." With a flick of his clawed hand, Ffirk sent his oosers to collect us.

I knew Ffirk was probably right about which option was more miserable, but only one option would allow us to keep looking for my mother. It barely qualified as a choice. "Down the hatch," I said, stepping backwards.

"Kellan…" Phoebe said, her voice breaking.

A slash of silvery lightning and blue flame hurtled down from the canopy overhead, and in the blink of an eye the great winged stag was interposed between us and the three oosers. The hulking brutes froze in their tracks, startled by the unexpected arrival and held at bay by the crown of razor sharp antlers pointed at them. The stag's rider ignored them, and us, addressing Ffirk directly. "No harm is to come to them, by the devices of the Council."

"The Council," Ffirk seethed. "The Council's vanity will not admit that its devices are weak and worthless. The druid's son slipped those devices once. I would not give him leave to assay again."

"You are not the council," the rider said. As before the woodlander in scarlet livery was unarmed, but there was a prickle in the air as if a weapon had been drawn, or as if a greater force were being gathered in the rider's tiny, open hands.

"And the Council is not here. These wretches are no longer the charge of the Council. They belong to me," Ffirk growled. "To me!"

With that the trio of oosers broke their stupor, heeding the command and lunging forward with massive, hairy fingers splayed. The stag reared back and drove its front hooves into the chest of the nearest ooser, a blow that lifted the brawny servant off its feet and sent it crashing into a tree twenty yards distant. That left two oosers intent on collecting us for their master while the Halfhorned dealt with the stag's rider.

"Go. Go!" I yelled. Gern was already hopping into the darkness. Juvie grabbed Phoebe's hand and dragged her with him into the opening in the rock face. I two-stepped backwards, squatted on my haunches, and grabbed a handful of dirt from the cavern floor. It was dry, gray grit and I cast it in an arc at the oosers' eyes. They snarled displeasure and clawed dumbly at their faces. I spun and ran after my friends.

Within just a few steps the darkness was so complete that I couldn't see a thing. A few steps after that the floor of the cavern pitched from a gentle downhill to a steep tumbling slope covered in loose debris, which could have been rocks or dead insect shells or bone fragments or all of the above. I lost my footing, skidded a few feet, then flopped on my belly and plunged the rest of the way down in a dizzying jumble of scraping, scouring pain. It was a long way down.

My fall was broken at the bottom of the stony chute by a couple feet of water atop a substrate of mud, which I hit face first. I pushed myself out of the muck and stood up wiping furiously at my eyes. It took me a few seconds to realize that I had gotten the sludge cleared away, and the reason I still couldn't see was because I was in a dark place. Gradually my vision adjusted enough for me to take stock of the surroundings.

Phoebe, Juvie, Mabonnyn and Gern were nearby, standing in water that reached my friends' knees, and half submerged the squat body of the bullfrog. Unbidden, my brain summoned up a memory of my mother from when I was only five or six years old. We were out behind the cottage on a summer evening, listening to frogs croaking contentedly in the woods. My mother asked me how deep frogs like the water they sit in to be. I told her I didn't know. She answered, "Knee-deep," but she said it in a way to imitate the ribbit of a frog. My mother wasn't really one for making jokes, and I was delighted. I ran around like a loon repeating the punchline and giggling every time.

Echoes of wordplay aside, present circumstances were nothing like that long-ago night. The cottage had been surrounded by lush greens, firm grassy ground beneath my young feet and clear air above. Now I was wading through cold, oily water, with a miasma floating around us that was too warm and clammy and smelled of death and rot. No colors stood out in the darkness, everything shadow-smeared as a faded charcoal drawing. The massive stone wall we had passed through blotted out landscape and sky alike to one side, and on the other the drab marsh extended uninterrupted until it was swallowed by fog.

I looked around at my companions. Juvie was scanning the area, trying to get his bearings.

Phoebe's head hung down, her arms wrapped around her chest. Mabonnyn stared at me expectantly, though I supposed all of them were waiting for me to say something, anything, to indicate what we should do next.

"We need to find a place to rest," I said. "The sooner the better."

"Makes sense," Juvie seized on my suggestion. "Catch our breath, gather our wits, and plan out how we stay ahead of the Council?"

I didn't answer him. I turned to Mabonnyn and said, "Can you find us a dry spit of land anywhere around here?"

Mabonnyn nodded and turned Gern around. The bullfrog splashed towards a small promontory, an arrowhead of stone jutting up out of the swamp. Gern climbed to the top and Mabonnyn surveyed the expanse of sickly stunted trees, brittle reeds and grasses, and dark stagnant water. After a minute or so Mabonnyn looked back at us and pointed ahead to the right. Gern leapt off the promontory in the direction Mabonnyn had indicated, and Juvie, Phoebe and I sloshed after them.

The bare hillock rising out of the marsh wasn't very big, but we didn't have many other choices. I collapsed onto the ripe-smelling loam, ignoring the sharp rocks poking into the muscles up and down the length of me. Juvie and Phoebe similarly laid themselves down, while Gern took up a position at the narrow end of the hillock. "We will keep the watch," the harrier said, "but we will want to return to the paths above as soon as possible, if we hope to remain ahead of the Council and their scouts."

"Do we, though?" I asked, throwing an arm over my eyes. Even to my own ears I sounded punchdrunk, which to be fair was how I felt. I lowered the crook of my elbow over my nostrils to block out some of the fetid stink of the air.

"Well, we don't want that whole mad dash to be for nothing, do we?' Juvie asked. "We got away because we've got things to do, right?"

"Kellan, we can't give up now," Phoebe added.

"I'm not talking about giving up," I said. "I'm talking about playing the hand we've been dealt. We could rest the absolute bare minimum our bodies need, hell we could skip the rest altogether, climb back up above, and no matter how hard and fast we pushed or how well we hid, the Council would run us down."

"You said you weren't talking about giving up, but that sounds an awful lot like giving up," Juvie said.

I sat up a little, propped on my elbows. "Giving up on safe passage through the Deep Woods, maybe. Which means we go the rest of the way through the Undergrowth."

"There's no such thing as safe passage through the Undergrowth," Phoebe muttered darkly.

"Then we might as well head for home," I said. "It really comes down to you, Mabonnyn. You're our guide. Can you get us all or at least most of the way to the Derryth down here?"

Mabonnyn said nothing for a brief span, then explained, "It would not be easy, and certainly, as Phoebe says, it would not be safe. But it could be done."

"Then that's our play," I said. "And maybe that's for the best. You heard what the Council said. The thing that took my mother followed us here and innocent creatures are getting caught up in all of it, getting killed. Maybe we'll dodge it better down here. And if not, at least we've lured it out of the heart of the Deep Woods."

Phoebe rolled over, away from me. "I'm too tired to argue any more," she said. She sounded angry, angrier than I'd ever known her to get, and if it hadn't been muted by exhaustion I'd have flinched from it. I let it go.

"At least things can't get any worse, right?" Juvie asked.

I slid back to my prone position. "You've really gotta stop saying things like that."

CHAPTER SEVEN: THE GREAT SLOG

I WOKE UP on my back, not having moved a muscle while I was blissfully unconscious. I felt slightly better than I had when I'd hit the dirt, which was really the only indicator I had of the passage of time. The light, or lack thereof, hadn't changed, which was unsurprising. Neither had the temperature, the humidity, or the smell.

I turned my head slightly, saw Juvie stretched out on his stomach with his head cradled on his folded arms. Beyond him was Mabonnyn, still dutifully guarding our position from atop Gern's neck. A few feet from the bullfrog, standing on the edge of the hillock, was a twisted Y-shaped tree.

That was new.

I scrambled to my feet and over to Mabonnyn. "When did that happen?" I demanded, pointing at the tree.

Gern opened the bulbous eye nearer to me, blinked slowly, and lowered her eyelid, unruffled. Mabonnyn shrugged and said, "While you slept."

"And you didn't think that merited waking us all up?" I asked.

The harrier of the Floret folk gave me a moment of head-cocked silence before replying, "Why would it?"

"A tree that springs up seven or eight feet in a few hours is alarming even in the Deep Woods," I said, feeling as unbalanced as if I were still asleep and dreaming, not least because I was telling Mabonnyn something we both already knew. "And nothing is supposed to grow like that down here."

"Grow?" Mabonnyn echoed, not a gasp of shock exactly, the harrier remained stiff-backed as ever, but the merest suggestion of being taken aback. "You don't see her. She didn't want you to see her," Mabonnyn said quietly.

I turned away from frog and rider and looked to the tree again. I stepped closer to it. The trunk was tapered toward the roots, only about a foot in circumference near the base, and maybe three feet around at its widest in the middle. It narrowed some toward the two rabbit-ear boughs, with a large round knot at the branch junction. A scattering of dark, limp leaves grew directly out of the knot, along with a few more from the handful of small branches forking at the ends of Dhe limbs.

I cupped my hand under the knot and gently lifted it. The knot yielded, not without resistance, like something barely movable to begin with. It had the rough scratchy feel of treebark beneath my fingers, but something malleable at its core. I tilted the knot up, and on its surface I could just barely make out two closed eyes, a wide nose, and a pair of lips. I let go, and the knot very slowly lowered itself again.

I went back to Mabonnyn and Gern and sat down beside a fore-flipper. "She's been reverting to a tree every night, hasn't she?" I asked.

"I have only been with you one other night," Mabonnyn reminded me. That was true, as strange as it seemed. Just two nights ago we had been hiding out at the hotel. "But yes, last night she transfigured as well."

"She said… she said she had been expecting tea from my mother. Medicinal tea. I didn't ask what for. It must be something that lets her stay in her human form indefinitely. So without it…"

Mabonnyn didn't respond, and didn't really have to.

"How long does she need to stay rooted?" I asked.

"It is hard to say," the harrier admitted. "Last night she was able to wait until you were asleep and had transfigured again before you awakened. But drawing sustenance from the Deep Woods is a hamadryad's essence. Drawing on the Undergrowth must be more difficult."

"She'll find a way," I said, and believed it. Phoebe was tough as anything. "We'll wait until she does."

Mabonnyn, Gern and I sat there in silence. There was no breeze, no foliage to rustle in it even if there had been, no songbirds or scurrying animals. Twice I heard a plaintive, screeching caw, like the blended voice of a hyena and a buzzard. The first time it came from somewhere back towards the rock wall we had emerged from after our downward sliding escape, and the second it was ahead of us, and sounded more choked than before. It could have been two different creatures, or it could have been the same one, prowling around, scavenging for carrion and eventually finding it, yipping through a mouthful of rotten flesh. In the long interval between the squawks, I watched a huge serpentine hump crest through the brackish water ten or fifteen yards away from the hillock and disappear into the murk again. Otherwise, the Undergrowth was shrouded in stillness.

"You've been very loyal, sticking with us," I said after a while.

"I have done that which I was charged to do," Mabonnyn said. "Either one is faithful to duty, or not. I do not think such things are measured in degrees."

"Nah," I said. "You could have abandoned us at the fairy ring. That was a pretty obvious sign that forces were lining up against us. You could have abided by the Council of Ruis's wishes, left us to be escorted away. I'm sure the other Floret folk would have understood."

"Duty is not exonerated by difficulty," Mabonnyn said.

"And now you're stuck down here with us," I pointed out. "You were charged with escorting us through the Deep Woods. That could very well be considered null and void once we wound up in the

Undergrowth."

"Escaping into the Undergrowth was my idea," Mabonnyn replied.

"Fair point," I nodded. "And it was a good idea. Well, it was the only idea any of us had, at that point. But still. All this trouble, and everything that still lies ahead… all because you feel obligated to see through the errand?"

"Do you doubt my resolve, Son of Foltchain?" Mabonnyn asked without looking at me.

"Not at all," I said. "I just wonder about the why of it."

For a few heartbeats, long enough for a fat greenbottle fly the size of a football to buzz around us and then apparently decide we weren't worth the trouble and whir off into the shadows, I thought Mabonnyn was going to leave the question unanswered. Maybe there was no why of it, maybe it was cut and dry in the harrier's mind, pure and functional engagement with the commission. Then Mabonnyn said, "I met your mother, once."

I didn't say anything, out of old private eye habit. When someone who usually plays things close to the vest finally starts telling a personal story, it's best not to interrupt. Let them pause as long as they like, stop and start whenever they need to, as many times as it takes to get it all told. The opening up is like a kind of magic spell, too easily broken. I kept my peace.

Mabonnyn went on, "I was young. I was no harrier then, just barely out of the nursery. There was a season in which our usual food sources were ravaged by pestilence. Arguments fomented without end, whether or not we should burn out the corruption, and risk the fires growing out of control and consuming our homes, whether or not we should flee to a place beyond the reach of the pestilence, if such a place even existed or would for long, Foltchain of the Oak came to us, unsummoned. She simply knew the Floret folk were in need. She spoke with the elders and offered her aid, asking nothing in return. And over the next few moons, she came and went, never arriving empty-handed, never accepting any recompense. She brought food, although the Floret folk had their own stores to compensate for such inevitabilities. Sure enough, when the pestilence continued unabated it even spread to the harvests in the larders, finding its way past all defenses. The food Foltchain brought us was different than our usual fare, and not of interest to the plague of vermin."

Mabonnyn continued, "She also brought rare substances, which she claimed were components of a cure for the pestilence. She could have amassed them at her own home, and brought us the final result, but she wanted the Floret folk to know that they were not forgotten, that their patience would ultimately be rewarded. And every delivery of the cure's ingredients brought more food supplies, more consultations with the elders for enduring the difficulties.

"I realized none of this at the time, of course. Much later, reminiscing with others, I realized how deep her commitment and compassion ran. I learned how many responsibilities she took on throughout the Deep Woods, how we were only one small sliver of her dominion, and yet to a youth it could seem as if all the priestess ever did was bring our folk what we needed most, then set off to find the next necessity.

"Near the end of the ordeal, when Foltchain of the Oak was due to return yet again, I took to walking out along the paths to catch a glimpse of her approach. And I was rewarded one morning as she emerged from the trees, a leaf-wrapped bundle in her arms. I was too young to be properly reverent, and I ran to meet her.

"When I drew near to her, I could see the angry welts on her forearms, and on her neck and face. I could see the redness of her eyes. I could see the price she had paid in obtaining whatever new ingredient she was delivering that day. And yet, she smiled at me and greeted me without a trace of rancor or resentment. We walked back to my home together.

"It was not long after that the pestilence abated. The priestess's cure had worked, without need for purifying flames, without destroying the food source or even the vermin themselves. We saw the creatures now and then but it was as if they had been urged to madness for a time and then coaxed to reason again."

I'd never heard the story before, which wasn't surprising. It could have happened long before I was born, given the longevity of some woodlanders and my mother's effective immortality. As Mabonnyn related the details I tried to figure out what exactly my mother had done. It sounded like there had been some kind of Deep Woods parasitic explosion, some microbe or fungus that turned hosts into zombies that overworked the food supply, and my mother had employed some kind of herbal remedy to disrupt the vicious cycle and restore the natural balance. That was her whole deal.

"I learned of duty from my people," Mabonnyn went on. "I was taught the importance of steadfastness, especially once I took up the mantle of harrier. But my true understanding of devotion," and here the harrier pressed fist to breastbone, "came from the druid priestess who saved us, not without suffering, but without complaint or hesitation."

I had to admit, with no small amount of shame, that that part of the story had surprised me in its own way. Not that I expected any less of my mother, but because I was just as guilty as a child of the Floret folk of never really thinking about the toll the druidic calling took on my mother. Performing her duties was as inexorable for her as the rising of the sun or the passage of the seasons, never in question or doubt, never requiring rationale. But that wasn't the same thing as being some unthinking, unfeeling machine. Often it meant performing her duties despite what she might think or feel, or what might be inflicted upon her along the way.

"So you want to see this through to the end for my mother, for her sake, as a way of paying back what you owe her?" I asked.

Mabonnyn said nothing for a time, long enough for a splash in the distance to echo across the water. Then the harrier turned my question around on me: "Is that why you carry on? A debt that must be paid?"

"It's not just that. It's a little more complicated than that," I said. "She's my mother. It doesn't even feel like I have a choice. It's just something I have to do. I'd be lying if I said it didn't feel like I owe it to her, on some level, in the mix with everything else."

Mabonnyn nodded. "For me, it is not that at all. Do you believe that Foltchain of the Oak would say that either of us owes her this?"

I took a deep breath, not that I need to stall for time since I knew the answer instantly. "No, she wouldn't."

"Which is why I will not forsake my charge," Mabonnyn said.

I was trying to formulate an appropriate follow up question when the arm-branches Phoebe was holding aloft began to bend and droop. The bottom half of the treetrunk folded as well, and in a matter of moments there was no tree any more, only Phoebe lying on her side atop the hillock. I moved over to her and put a hand on her shoulder. "Phoebe? You okay?"

She raised her head and squinted at me through bleary eyes. She looked utterly wrung out, like someone who had been awake for a day and a half, had managed to fall asleep for five minutes, and then had been startled awake again. "I'm… fine," she lied.

I turned to Mabonnyn and asked, "Is there any way Gern could carry her? Maybe you could ride on my shoulder?"

"I said I'm fine," Phoebe insisted, pushing herself up to her feet. "I'm not going to separate a harrier and mount. They'll need to work together to give us any kind of chance of finding our way through here."

"Phoebe…" I tried again.

"And I don't need to be carried in any case," she said, closing the subject to further discussion. "Wake Juvie up. We should keep moving." She moved to the edge of the hillock and stepped into the bracken, and Gern waddled out beside her, while I roused Juvie.

Our group covered a fair amount of distance, or at least it felt that way to my aching muscles. There were too few landmarks to properly gauge any distances, just unremarkable clumps of scraggly reeds poking through the all-encompassing murk. The passage of time in the dimness remained difficult to track, as well. Sometimes we waded through water that only reached our shins, with beds of rocks below our feet, other times our boots sunk into sucking mire beneath water that came halfway up our thighs, every step a supreme effort that made traversing fifty yards feel like sprinting half a mile.

Gern, Mabonnyn and Phoebe led the way throughout, with Juvie and I bringing up the rear. Eventually Juvie said to me, "So, I feel like I'm the only one who doesn't really understand where we are."

"The Undergrowth," I said.

"Yeah, right, got that," he agreed. "But the way you and Phoebe and Mabonnyn throw that word around, there's clearly a lot of baggage. Like there's more to it than just the fact that it looks like we're in the swamp now instead of the forest. Are we even in the Deep Woods anymore?"

"Yes, a part of it," I said.

"Okay," Juvie said. "The darker, worse-smelling part of it, where the water is unpleasantly cold and the air is even less pleasantly warm. Is that all? Is this just, like, real estate snobbery for you people who grew up here?"

"Not exactly," I said. "It's… look, I'm going to have to give you a bunch of analogies, none of which is exactly perfect, so don't interrupt poking holes in each one, okay?"

"Sure, fine, whatever," Juvie agreed. "I'm all ears."

"It's kind of like a wildlife preserve," I explained, "except only in the sense of ceding certain territory to certain species. When humans do that in the real world it's usually because we think certain species have value and should be given their own space to thrive, kind of a win-win. So we develop industrialized cities over here, and we let the bison roam free over there, and it's all good."

"With you so far," Juvie said.

"So it's just a combination of innate human attitudes and some socialized norms that we find bison or elephants or humpback whales majestic, but we don't want to have to share our neighborhoods and workspaces with them. We also don't want to share our neighborhoods and workspaces with cockroaches and rats, but we don't create designated refuges for them, either. We just try to kill them because they skeeve us out."

"Right."

"So for most of the denizens of the Deep Woods, the whole point of existence is coexistence. In theory, that's absolute and without exception. In practice, there are no absolutes. Coexistence with certain creatures is undesirable or even untenable."

"Yeah, that makes sense, I guess."

"And there's an overall ethos that life is better than death, which is even more pervasive than the coexistence imperative. So if it proves impossible to live side-by-side with something, the answer is never to exterminate. It's to live slightly farther apart."

"So it is real estate snobbery," Juvie concluded. "So what, do they vote on who has to live down here in the dark? Does it take a supermajority to banish creatures to the forest ghetto, or just half plus one?"

"Yeah, no. No voting. Just like a bunch of fish didn't have an election millions of years ago to decide if they should try walking on land and breathing air. Just like a bunch of rocks didn't campaign for and against the formation of the Grand Canyon. It's the way things happened over time."

"Well, then, your wildlife preserve analogy kind of sucks," Juvie said, "because that would be man-made, as opposed to, like, there's fish in the Marianas Trench that could only have evolved there, but nobody relocated them there and told everyone else to keep out."

"I said the analogies were imperfect," I admitted. "Okay, imagine if there just happened to be one valley where all the bison naturally lived, and which was inhospitable to people anyway. Just the way things happened on their own. Sooner or later somebody would say they needed some or all of the valley and screw the bison, right? Unless it was designated off-limits officially, right?"

"Right."

"And imagine if every once in a while a bison busted out of the valley and rampaged through some populated area, you'd have some people screaming to bomb the valley and kill all the bison so it never happens again, right?"

"Sadly I cannot argue against that."

"But, again, where the analogy falls apart is that this isn't about voting on laws or royalty issuing proclamations. It's just… the ethos. Dangerous things anathema to coexistence wound up here. And, just for the record, that's not just animals and sentient beings, that's plants and soil and miasma, the whole geography, everything."

"Down to the last little evil pebble, sure, why not."

"And the denizens of the Deep Woods avoid it on principle. Except for the ones who gravitate to it for their own reasons. Nobody's forced in or out, nobody has to be. And no matter how bad it is, no one would ever even countenance the thought of trying to wipe it out or anything like that."

"So it's the bad neighborhood, only with nobody trying to gentrify it."

"That's not far off. But here's the other thing. The Undergrowth is to the Deep Woods what the Deep Woods is to the world you and I live in."

"Meaning?"

"Meaning it's another abstracted layer of reality away. Remember the black hole analogy? Now imagine if the interior of each black hole had black holes of its own."

"Uhhh…"

"So it's not like we're in a different section of the Deep Woods. It's not like we walk a mile down here and it's like walking a mile up there. It's not even necessarily the same direction. Or the same dimension."

"But that was your plan, right?" Juvie asked. "To get to your mother's tree from here rather than there? How's that even going to be possible?"

"I didn't say it was going to be easy," I said. "And to be honest, I'm really putting a lot of blind faith in Mabonnyn and Gern. They can't use the same mental maps or landmarks as in the Deep Woods. But it can be done, because as different as they are, there's points of connection between the Deep Woods and the Undergrowth, including the name trees."

"Like your mother's oak."

"Exactly. The Derryth touches the Undergrowth… somewhere," I gestured sweepingly at the dark, dismal landscape. "We'll find it."

"Sure," Juvie nodded. His tone was right on the edge of encouraging solidarity and skeptical mockery, so I turned to look at him. I caught him wincing, putting weight on his hazel staff as he trudged forward.

"Are you okay?" I asked.

"Fine," Juvie said.

"You hurt your leg?"

"Just my ankle," Juvie shrugged.

"When?"

"On the slide down from the cave," Juvie said. "It's not a big deal."

"I'm sorry, man," I said. "I'd offer to hunt up some remedy plants but the pickings are slim down here."

"I get it," Juvie said. He gestured in the vague direction of my gashed leg. "We've all gotta suck it up about something."

That put an end to our back and forth for a while. I focused on keeping my own footsteps cautious and stable, heel-to-toe, while contemplating just how right Juvie was. Phoebe was sick, Juvie and I were both injured, Mabonnyn had lost his spear and I had lost my gun. Liabilities mounting, assets dwindling, and speed of progress hobbled when we couldn't afford any more delays or setbacks. I repeated it over and over in my head and it became my mantra as we plodded along. Left foot forward, no more delays, right foot forward, no more setbacks, left foot forward, no more delays, right foot forward, no more setbacks.

Mabonnyn brought our undersized Undergrowth caravan to a halt where a pair of gnarled dwarf cypresses rose out of the murky water. Phoebe leaned heavily against one of the trees, her breathing labored, and Juvie propped himself against the other straightaway. Neither of them could go much further without rest, so the stop wasn't so much a delay as a necessity, and I accepted it as such.

I looked around in the gloom, and saw a shape like a modest house a little ways off. It was hard to judge distances in the shadows, but it seemed to be someplace I could reach and return from within the span of a reasonable break from walking. "I'll be right back," I said. Juvie gave me a half-hearted thumbs up of acknowledgement, and no one else responded.

I waded toward the structure, really nothing more than a wattle and daub hut, the wattle consisting of spare, twisted sticks and the daub a dark brown slicked with slimy green. The whole thing sat atop a flat boulder that held it just above the waterline. A few stones breaking the surface of the water made a kind of walkway leading to the front door, which hung open. The single window on the side of the hut was dark, and the stump of a chimney rising at the rear was dormant.

I climbed up the side of the boulder and crossed the threshold of the hut, then paused to give my eyes a moment to adjust. As dark as it was in the Undergrowth, the interior of the hovel was even darker, with only traces of illumination admitted through the window and the doorway. Once I got acclimated, I could make out that there wasn't much to see anyway. A bare table against one wall, an empty bedframe against another, a bit of debris in the corners. And in the middle of the stone floor, lying face down, was a desiccated corpse.

A few patches of long, tangled hair still clung to the skull, just as shreds of soiled clothing draped the upper arms and back and legs. The feet, hands and forearms were skeletal, fleshless. The body had been there for a long time, long enough that it was impossible to tell what had happened. There might have been a struggle, or not. The deceased could have pitched over after a fatal heart attack, or been murdered, or committed suicide. Any weapon or note or sign that everything had been normal up to the fatal moment was long gone. The hut had been ransacked, or fallen to natural depredations, or simply been swept clean by time and the elements in service of entropy.

Actually, I was inclined to rule out the second possibility. The corpse's position was undisturbed, and I guessed it had been stripped of its meat by microbial rot rather than large scavengers. Animals of a certain size would give the hut a wide berth, whether its inhabitants were alive or dead, and even weeks after the death there would still be a strong aversion against eating the remains of a witch.

Lest you think me guilty of some kind of unfair profiling for leaping to the conclusion that anyone who chose to live in the bleak isolation of the dismal Undergrowth must be a witch, I point out that as soon as I registered the presence of relatively unmolested human remains I turned around and ran my fingers along the lintel above the doorway. It was a rough zigzag of crooked wood, but soon I found a carving on its face, the double-linked closed loops of a Solomon's Knot. The oblong grooves were deep, and the area around the carving was worn smooth. The witch would have pressed her fingertips to the seal every time she left her hut, casting a protective spell around her home and belongings in her absence. Dead giveaway, that.

I crossed the floor, stepping around the witch, and approached the hearth, where a pocked copper pot sat cockeyed in the drift of ashes. It was an enormous vessel, so large it was fair to call it a cauldron, darkened by years of heat exposure to exactly the kind of pitch black bowl one would expect a witch to own. I ran my fingers along the inside of the cauldron but felt only cold metal. I'd had some hope that I might find something in the hut to help Juvie with his ankle, or maybe even give Phoebe some relief. It hadn't been much hope, and it was all but faded to nothing now. If the witch had been on walkabout and I'd only had the shield of Solomon to deal with, or if she'd died recently, I might have been able to locate something useful. But others had beaten me there by a good margin, and taken anything and everything of value, and probably a good amount that was essentially worthless but deemed potentially useful simply because it happened to be in the home of a witch.

Still, since I was already there, I checked the corners of the hut. One held nothing but dead leaves and a few brittle scraps of cockatrice skin. Not that they had been collected or cured or anything like that. More likely the cockatrice had made a temporary nest for itself while it molted and then moved on, long after the witch had died and all others lost interest in the domicile. The opposite corner had more decaying organic matter heaped around a rusty iron cage, a cube about a foot and a half on each side. I picked up the cage and gave it a shake. It was empty, at least after I shook loose something which I heard clatter against the flat crossed bars of its bottom face. I set the cage aside and felt in the debris for the dislodged object.

It was small and round, about the size of a golf ball, made out of something that felt papery like a wasp's nest. A pair of crude Xs had been stitched in place for eyes, and a grimacing mouth formed from real, mismatched fangs underlined them. A poppet head. There were any number of reasons a witch might fashion a poppet, and once again I really had no way of knowing the events that had unfolded long before my arrival. Had the poppet been unfinished before the witch's death, or had it once been whole but fallen to neglected pieces? Had it been a plaything for whatever had once been trapped in the iron cage, or had it been magically animated and caged itself, or had the two things simply ended up in the same trash heap in the corner?

I stood up and put the poppet head in my pocket. It wouldn't help either Juvie or Phoebe, but I didn't feel right about leaving it behind. While I was at it, I plucked a couple of the hagwick leaves out of my pocket, tore them into fuzzy strips, and scattered them over the cage and in the corner where it had sat. If anything else weird and malign was hiding amongst the garbage, the hagwick would discourage it from rising up and following us or causing any trouble. Otherwise my excursion had been a bust, although I had known at the outset there was a good chance it might be, which was why I hadn't told any of the others where I was going or why.

I stepped out of the hut, hopped down into the water surrounding the boulder, and waded back to the cypresses. Juvie saw me coming and pushed himself back to a standing position. He continued to put a good bit of weight on his hazel staff, but not quite as exhaustedly as before. He held his free hand out to Phoebe. Her head still hung low, but she couldn't help but see Juvie's beckoning fingers mere inches away. I held my breath, but she slid her hand into his and rose from her perch on the cypress branch. She stumbled on her first proper step, but Juvie stayed close to her and caught her. She let him.

Mabonnyn turned Gern and the bullfrog hopped forward. Juvie followed, leaning on his staff, and Phoebe leaned on Juvie. I looked around reflexively to ask if anyone else had seen it, but of course there was no one else but me to bring up the rear.

We trudged through the Undergrowth with no idle conversation. At one point we skirted around a grouping of bleached white skulls on pikes, dozens and dozens arrayed in rows, all with the blunt beaks and large eyesockets of giant snapping turtles. The smallest of them was the size of a human cranium, and the largest could have swallowed a human body whole. No one in our party found them worth remarking on as we passed by without slowing and the decapitated remains silently gaped at us.

A little while later, we passed a laptop nestled in a clump of cockspur grass, opened like a butterfly filet of black meat. The screen was dark, of course, the surface splintered with circular cracks radiating from an impact point in the lower right quadrant. A few of the keys were missing, and mud was smeared across both halves, but it was otherwise intact enough to be recognizable. Someone or something had brought it here not long ago, and we would never know who that was or what they'd intended to accomplish. We walked on.

What finally did cause us to halt was the sight of a living creature, walking upright ahead of us. It wasn't walking particularly fast, so even after we stopped to watch it advance we still would have had no trouble overtaking it. The figure was man-shaped, terribly emaciated, and carrying a heavily laden sack over one shoulder. We all waited to see if it would notice us, but it never glanced backwards. It seemed single-minded as it shuffled through the mire.

A bright dot of color bobbed along in the muddied water, moving toward Juvie. It looked like a perfect ripe apple, its skin the rich hues of a tropical sunset, bright yellow orange melting into lush pinkish-purple. Juvie, to his credit, did not reach out for it. He didn't even assume it was an apple. "What is that?" he asked, pointing with the far end of his hazel staff at the floating fruit.

"Manzana muerta," Phoebe answered softly.

"A death apple?" he asked. "Seriously?"

Phoebe mutely nodded her head, and I took over the explanation. "Seriously and literally," I said. "You know how pepper spray is literally derived from peppers? Imagine pepper spray that didn't just hurt like it was melting your flesh, but was acidic enough to melt your flesh for real. That's what you could make from that fruit."

"Okay, no touchy, got it," Juvie nodded. "Those things grow down here?"

"They do," I said, "but they're fairly rare. And I don't see any of those trees around here," I added, scanning the vicinity.

"So maybe it came out of the bag the guy up ahead is carrying?"

"Maybe," I said. "But even harvesting them is dangerous. The trees are rough to even get near."

"We could ask the guy," Juvie suggested.

"Let's see if we can get a little closer before we decide if that's a good idea," I said.

It didn't take long to catch up, and to see from a closer vantage point that the figure wasn't just emaciated, it looked like death warmed over in a convenience store microwave. It continued to ignore us. "Gortach," Mabonnyn said.

"Yes," I agreed.

"You both know this guy?" Juvie asked.

"It's not a proper name, it's what it is," I said. "Like zombie. It means man of famine."

"Jack not name, jack job," Juvie said, his tone indicating that he understood me, though I didn't catch whatever reference he was connecting it to. After another moment, Juvie went on, "Zombies usually travel in hordes. You think there could be more than one of them?"

"Right," I nodded.

"So that's probably what those are?" Juvie asked. He swept his staff from left to right, and sure enough, more gaunt figures were visible, one coming from our left, another from our right, all seemingly intent on converging on the same point.

Like the gortach we had noticed first and been following, the others also had bulging sacks on their backs.

"Using a labor force of gortaches to gather manzana muertas," I said. "Clever."

"You sound impressed," Juvie said.

"Horrified," I said. "For the effort involved to be worth it, whoever was behind it would have to expect some specific, highly valuable outcome. Valuable to them, I mean. For whoever and whatever they'd use that many death apples against…"

"So what are we gonna do?" Juvie asked.

"We can continue to follow the gortach until we see where it is bound," Mabonnyn offered. "With luck, Gern and I will find a way around the gathering place that does not prolong our journey overmuch."

"No, I mean, what are we gonna do about whoever's stockpiling biological weapons?" Juvie clarified. "How are we going to stop them?"

"How can we stop them?" Mabonnyn asked in disbelief. "You are injured, she is unwell, Kellan has lost his only weapon and I have lost the more formidable of mine."

"I know, that's why I asked instead of just assuming we'd go charging in," Juvie said. "In this state, we're gonna need a pretty brilliant plan."

Mabonnyn and Juvie both looked to me. I groaned inwardly. "Well, either way, Mabonnyn's right about one thing. We need to see where the gortaches are going. There's no brilliant plan without having all the information. Maybe once we see what's going on we'll be able to figure out something to do about it, maybe not. One step at a time."

Mabonnyn spurred Gern onward, and as we followed the gortach the water level slowly fell. It was imperceptible at first, but as time passed, step by step, the surface of the dank swamp went from above our knees to below. Mabonnyn motioned to us to stay low, so Juvie, Phoebe and I stretched out on our bellies and crawled through water that was soon only a couple of inches deep. We stopped at the edge of a slope of churned mud exposed to the air, and from there we could see the structure the gortaches were converging on.

It was crude, mostly uncut stones and timber, rough but strong and straight, no doubt brought from the Deep Woods to the Undergrowth. The foundation was nothing more than four braces of large rocks placed at the corners of a square fifty feet on each side, with massive wooden poles rising up from them to a height of about fifteen feet. A wooden platform stood atop the pilings, and suspended from the underside of the platform by chains was a huge iron bowl. The center of the platform supported some wooden apparatus that was slowly grinding and revolving, housed within a ten-foot tall frame that supported another, smaller platform. Ladders were secured to the four sides of the larger platform, and the gortaches made their way to those and climbed up them with the sacks still awkwardly slung over their backs.

There were three figures which were not gortaches on the upper platform, ostensibly keeping watch over the enterprise, scanning the marshland in all directions. Others of the same ilk were scattered around the island, checking the iron bowl below and the grinding apparatus above, or brandishing spiky clubs at any gortach that wandered off course. The creatures in charge wore vests and breeches made of stained patchwork leather, and roved around constantly like industrious insects in their hive. They stood only three or four feet tall, stout with thick limbs. Their skin was scaly, the cinereal color of oyster shells. Their bestial faces were dominated by snoutlike mouths filled with sharp teeth. Atop their heads rose spiny crests of red flesh, the color so intense it stood out even in the gloom of the Undergrowth.

"Those are redcombs," I said in a low voice, mostly for Juvie's benefit, but also because I was having a hard time believing how adept the Undergrowth was at taking a miserable situation and making it so much worse.

"Five-second explanation?" Juvie asked.

"Nasty little blood-eaters," Phoebe said, her disgust palpable even through the crackle of her weak, exhausted voice.

"Like, vampires?" Juvie asked.

"Not exactly," I said. "They're not unholy undead or anything. They murder for fun. They make blood a major part of their diet because they like the taste." I stopped myself from saying anything about their beetleblack eyes, which held more loathing grievance against other living things than a hundred huulders. "More like mosquitoes if they were inherently malicious."

"You should see the mosquitoes in Batangas, but point taken," Juvie said. "And just to be clear, these murderous blood-enthusiasts are the ones stockpiling the death apples for some reason?"

We watched a gortach open its sack and dump the manzana muertes into the slowly rotating grinder, which reduced the deadly fruits to pulp. The caustic juices drained down through the bottom of the apparatus and into the iron bowl. Two redcombs, one holding an animal in hand, approached the underside of the bowl, where a bent nozzle projected from the curved surface. The animal, something like a spiny crayfish the size of a housecat, flailed its segmented legs uselessly in the air as the redcomb placed its head under the nozzle. The other redcomb pulled up on a bar on top of the nozzle. Juice of manzana muerte dribbled out, smelling so toxically acidic it stung my eyes at a distance. The crayfish melted like butter in a frying pan, the exoskeleton reduced to sludgy reddish-brown drippings and wisps of greasy steam. The redcombs both laughed, and the one holding the bar lifted it further, increasing the flow of juice. It splashed freely, dissolving the rest of the crayfish and splattering up the arm of the redcomb. The redcomb shrieked, jerking its arm back and dropping the twitching, liquefying remains of the crayfish. The redcomb holding the bar laughed even harder, until the unfortunate victim backhanded his companion, knocking him to the ground. The bar fell against the nozzle and the flow of juice finally stopped.

"We should leave them to their own hateful

devices," Mabonnyn said. "I daresay there is a level chance they succumb to traitorous self-sabotage before long. Redcombs do not suffer one another's company as a rule."

"Even money they kill each other means even money they don't," Juvie pointed out. "I don't like that action. If they don't, what are they going to do with all that death sauce?"

"Nothing good," I ventured. "But if we try doing anything about it, it's a sucker bet we don't all wind up as blood slicks across the surface of the marsh. We're outnumbered and it's not like we can call in reinforcements."

"Maybe we can," Phoebe said. We all turned to look at her and she pointed back at the redcombs' structure. We finally had a clear view of the creature providing the power to the grinding apparatus, trudging in a circle, yoked to a crossbar attached to the central shaft. It was neither a redcomb nor a gortach, but an amber colored giant, ten feet tall and built like a two-legged elephant. It plodded silently around and around, a redcomb at its heels wielding a smoldering brand.

"Dammit," I exhaled, something between a sigh and a growl.

"What?" Juvie asked.

"If we walk away right now, find our way to the Derryth, get some idea of how to help my mother, and actually pull off a rescue or whatever it is she needs… and she finds out we abandoned an arbutus doing forced labor for redcombs in the Undergrowth? She will kill me," I predicted, no longer placing odds. Truthfully, I wouldn't have been able to live with myself, either. It was the courthouse hallway all over again. See a white power freak making a break for it, tripping him up is a no-brainer. See a gang of slaver redcombs juicing death apples...

"We gotta do what we gotta do, then," Juvie said. "So what's the plan?"

"Distract the redcombs," Phoebe suggested. "Leave the arbutus to me."

"Phoebe..." I said.

"Just do what I say," Phoebe said. "You go that way, I'll go this way." She crawled off before I could protest any more, heading counterclockwise around the edge of the island. I squirmed through the shallow water with Gern and Mabonnyn on one side and Juvie on the other, moving clockwise up the curving waterline.

We had made it about a quarter of the way around the island when I spotted a gortach shuffling up the slope out of the marsh. I reached into one of my pockets and pulled out a protein bar, unwrapping it and lobbing it over the gortach's head. The gortach followed the bar's arc, maybe smelling it as it flew through the air, maybe just intuiting the presence of dense, calorie-rich foodstuff. The gortach lurched towards the bar as it struck the murky surface of the water, dropping its sack of manzana muertes.

A redcomb atop the watchtower screamed, guttural gibberish that nevertheless conveyed the idea that there was a malfunction in the system. Another redcomb jumped down from the middle platform and strode toward the wayward gortach, spiked club upraised.

We waited until the redcomb had turned its back on us in pursuit of the gortach and then moved in unison. Mabonnyn spurred Gern to leap past the redcomb, allowing the harrier to lean over the bullfrog's side and rake his knife blade across the nape of the redcomb's neck. The redcomb spun with its sharp teeth bared in a savage snarl and its club high, but Juvie and I hit it before it had finished turning around. Juvie tackled the redcomb around the knees while I slammed into its shoulder and wrested the club from its fingers. The redcomb howled, and every instinct in me recoiled, partly because the sound was hideous and partly because in my line of work I always tried to do things quietly. I had to consciously remind myself that the task at hand was to create a raucous commotion to draw the other redcombs to us. I hammered the spikes of the club into the redcomb's shoulder, eliciting more agonized wailing. Juvie had positioned himself across the redcomb's shins and ankles, so I took another shot with the club, this one aimed at the redcomb's stomach. The redcomb thrashed and yowled as I pondered my next target, but before I could take a swing Mabonnyn appeared and drove his knife into the redcomb's left eye. The creature spasmed as the tip of the blade punctured what passed for its brain, then went still.

I looked at Mabonnyn questioningly as the harrier drew out the knife and wiped it on the redcomb's vest. Mabonnyn jerked a thumb toward the structure, indicating three more redcombs coming at us at a run. So far so good, the trio of bloodthirsty monsters bearing down on us notwithstanding.

Juvie got to his feet beside me, pulling himself up on his walking stick. I shoved the spiked club into his hand and he dropped the hazel. He and I spread out, and the redcombs mirrored us, each one choosing a target. I glanced over to Mabonnyn, looking for any sign of a strategy to share. Juvie opted instead to charge at the nearest redcomb, giving his own battlecry which was probably at least in part to mask the pain of galloping up the rocky slope on his injury. The redcomb screeched, a ragged ululation that conveyed both wrath and giddy excitement, and swept its club up at Juvie's head. Juvie pirouetted out of the way on his good foot and brought his own club around, directly into the redcomb's wrist. The redcomb dropped its weapon and yowled, while Juvie spun again and smashed the redcomb's mouth to a bloody ruin, just before losing his own balance, betrayed by his lamed ankle.

All of that happened in the span of a few heartbeats, and then the redcomb attacking me was within arm's reach. Like Juvie, I gave the redcomb a tempting target, crouching down and crossing my forearms in front of my face to ward off the expected blow. The redcomb hooted with cruel delight as it bore down on me, swinging the club like an executioner's axe. At the last possible moment, I twisted to the right and stuck out my left leg. The redcomb tripped and stumbled wildly, splashing into the water at the island's edge.

I chased after him and was on top of him before

he regained his bearings. I pulled the redcomb into the filthy water and wrestled him down into the submerged mire. The redcomb flailed, swinging the spiked club blindly but only managing a couple of glancing blows. I willed myself to stay calm even with foul, stagnant water splashing me in the face and a ferocious killer writhing in my grasp. I kept my head above the surface and held the redcomb under, until the foam of bubbles from its mouth slowed to a trickle and finally stopped. I stood up, taking the spiked club as I rose, and kicked the redcomb over. It floated off into the muddy marsh facedown and unmoving.

I turned around and waded back up onto the island. Juvie had dispatched his initial opponent and now had a spiked club in each hand, wielding both to fend off the next redcomb that had seized on him. Mabonnyn was locked in a deadly dance with another redcomb, nimbly dodging blows from the club and darting in and out of reach to score hits up and down the redcomb's legs in return. Another redcomb approached from Mabonnyn's blindside, and I was about to run to the harrier's aid, but Gern was already there. The bullfrog interposed herself between her rider and the arriving redcomb, and kicked out with one back leg. The flippered foot slapped the redcomb's jaw so hard it twisted the ugly head around and snapped the redcomb's neck, killing him instantly. Without hesitation Gern then leapt forward and bowled over the wounded redcomb dueling with Mabonnyn, and Mabonnyn rushed forward to thrust the knife into the hollow of the redcomb's exposed throat.

I glanced toward the structure looming over our skirmish and saw Phoebe creeping up the farthest ladder. Three redcombs still remained, two on the observation platform above the grinding apparatus, and the one with the brand keeping the arbutus in motion. The brand-bearer was distracted, his attention divided between our fight and the laboring giant, but they were on the opposite side of their slow circuit from Phoebe. The two redcomb lookouts were completely absorbed in the fighting below them, whooping encouragement at their fellows, but they seemed content to stay where they were. If Phoebe reached the middle platform, and the three redcombs were still on the structure, I didn't want to think about the lopsided carnage that would ensue.

I ran towards Juvie and teed off on the lower back of his redcomb. The redcomb wailed and reared back to deal retribution to me, and Juvie caved in the side of its head with a double blow from both of his clubs. I pointed toward the tower and said, "We need to lure the last few holdouts away from Phoebe."

Juvie nodded. He raked his forearms with the spiked clubs, first the left and then the right, from elbow to knuckles, then threw down the weapons. Bright red blood welled from the lacerations, running down his arms as he raised them over his head. "Hey, assholes! You hungry?" Juvie bellowed, waving his hands back and forth in the air. He snapped his arms forward, sending ruby sprays to the rocky ground. "Come get some!"

It was not the tack I would have suggested, but I

had to admit it was effective. The two redcomb lookouts clambered down from the perch as fast as they could, shoving and jostling each other to be the first to the ground. The redcomb overseeing the arbutus looked conflicted, even as his compatriots went sliding down past him, but ultimately gave in to his baser instincts, dropping the brand and vaulting over the rail to the ground below. The three redcombs gamboled toward us, voices raised in a ravenous clamor.

Mabonnyn and Gern and Juvie and I instinctively drew together. The redcombs we had already dispatched had fallen for feints and tricks, all while the lookouts had been watching us fight; now that those sentries were joining the skirmish, they did so with forewarning of our tactics. We needed to present a unified defense. The redcombs drew closer and closer, until an impossibly loud crack split the air, and the redcombs froze in their tracks. Three more rapid cracks in succession caused them all to look back at their structure.

The arbutus was free. The yoke that had kept it in captive submission was gone from its shoulders, and its thick arms were upraised, holding up the top platform of the structure. The sounds that had demanded everyone's attention had been the snapping of the support posts, now splintered fragments of their former selves. The arbutus heaved and sent the lookout platform sailing through the air, over the redcombs' heads, over my and Juvie's and Mabonnyn's and Gern's heads, and into the water beyond.

The redcombs forgot about us and retreated to

their damaged structure. The arbutus shifted to the corner of the platform in one long stride and threw its weight into the support post there, obliterating the upper portion and knocking it out at an angle away from the platform. The entire corner of the platform dropped suddenly, as did the iron bowl attached to its underside. Juice of the manzana muertes sloshed over the lip of the bowl and sent a wave down the island to meet the onrushing redcombs.

"Get to the lookout!" I yelled, as the deadly extract dissolved the lower legs of the redcombs on contact. They screamed for a moment as they pitched forward and their hands melted while trying to arrest their falls, then were silenced as their faces dissolved in the flood of caustic enzymes.

"Where the hell is Phoebe?" Juvie demanded, but I dragged him with me towards the water, pausing only to retrieve his hazel staff. As usual Gern outpaced us all and had already made it to the former lookout platform which now floated upside-down in the marsh water as a makeshift raft. I hauled Juvie to the raft and up onto its surface, tossed the hazel at him, then climbed aboard myself. He stood at the edge looking back to the island.

Through the vaporous curtain of sublimated redcomb flesh rising from the spreading pool of manzana muerte juice, we could see the structure was burning. The brand had been dislodged when the corner of the central platform had collapsed, and the nearby wood had caught fire. The flames were small and growing slowly, but the arbutus was already abandoning the structure, jumping over the side to the exposed rock below.

"We have to go back for her!" Juvie said, tensing himself to dive into the water. I grabbed his arm hard, and he swiveled his head to shoot daggers at me from his eyes.

"Look," I said, pointing at the water. Fingers of corrosive juice were creeping out across the surface, like a shimmering oil slick, cutting down reeds and grasses and turning them to gray-green smears of pulp. "You jump into that, you're going to lose your legs. Our best bet is to stay on this raft, hope that the juice gets diluted enough that it only partially dissolves the underside."

"Then move the raft," Juvie said, a seething edge to his words. "The juice all spilled down one side of the island, right? Let's steer over to the opposite side and go up that way. We can't just leave Phoebe there!"

"Unfortunately, when the arbutus thoughtfully tossed us this lifesaver he didn't think to include any oars," I said. "You want to second guess him on it, here he comes."

The arbutus sloshed through the water towards us, having skirted the mordant fluids and come down the side of the island, giving a wide berth to the spill into the marsh as well. His long, powerful legs had closed the distance quickly. He approached the edge of the makeshift raft, grabbing hold of one of the fractured support posts with a thick-fingered hand. The arbutus's other arm was folded across his chest, as if holding something close, and the arbutus leaned forward to reveal Phoebe's unconscious body, lowering her gently to the floating platform. Juvie jerked free of my grip and knelt by Phoebe's side, while the arbutus began to pull the raft away from the island, the burning structure at its apex and the deadly mixture in the surrounding water.

"Phoebe? Phoebe?" Juvie prodded, shaking her shoulder. "Phoebe, are you all right?"

"She sleeps," the arbutus said, in a voice that was preternaturally deep as well as clotted with stickiness. "Spent."

"Spent?" Juvie repeated. "What the hell does that mean?"

"Woke sleeping wood," the arbutus said. "Gave of herself. No more to give."

Juvie looked to me, eyebrows raised, beseeching an explanation. I said, "When you cut down a flower or a tree, most of the cells are still alive, right? The whole thing doesn't die at once, it's more gradual. If any part of a plant is still alive, even one cell, Phoebe can communicate with it, and sometimes convince it to do things."

"What kind of things?" Juvie asked.

"Well, based on everything that just happened, I imagine Phoebe got up into the redcombs' structure and then coaxed some of the still living wood in the restraints on the arbutus to expand and split and crack. The restraints fell apart, and the arbutus did the rest."

"And Phoebe?" Juvie pressed.

"She was already…" I almost said 'dead on her feet', but caught myself and went on, "… pretty drained. It's not easy getting dying plant matter to do what you want. Sometimes it means lending some energy to the process. Phoebe did what she felt she had to do, and it took a toll."

"Is she going to be okay?" Juvie asked, too deflated to argue any more.

"She should be," I said, although all I really meant by that was that life should be fair and none of us should have had to go through what we'd already endured, no closer to finding my mother and no end in sight. It seemed kinder to say that than to admit out loud that I had no idea what to do other than allow the arbutus to barge on through the fen.

It took a little while longer for me to convince Juvie that the arbutus was not merely on our side as a matter of temporary convenience, but genuinely trustworthy. It's usually easier for people to accept that a whole race of weird-looking creatures, like redcombs, are inherently evil, than that a whole race of weird-looking creatures, like arbutuses, are inherently good. Juvie's introduction to the arbutus had been as a titanic humanoid wrecking machine, which further fueled his skepticism; from his point of view, the arbutus had recklessly endangered Phoebe while she was in an extremely vulnerable state, and had only brought her back to us as an afterthought. I pointed out that arbutuses and dryads were closely related, making the one pulling our raft and Phoebe something like second cousins in a clan that took familial relations and responsibilities extremely seriously. Not to mention that Phoebe had freed the arbutus from the redcombs, and that was a debt not lightly repaid.

Phoebe had never been in any danger while the arbutus was nearby, and never would be so long as he stayed with us.

The entire conversation took place at the aft end of the raft, where Juvie and I sat with Phoebe laid out between us. Gern and Mabonnyn had assumed a position near the bow, where the harrier gave direction through the marsh which the arbutus was happy to follow. Juvie shook his head and said, "I promised to trust you while we were on your turf, so I guess I will as far as that thing is concerned, too."

"Maybe it would be easier if you didn't think of it as 'that thing'," I suggested.

"Does it have a name?" Juvie countered.

That was a fair question. I duckwalked toward Gern and Mabonnyn, leaned out a bit and asked, "What are you called, tree-brother?"

The arbutus turned and looked at me. His facial expression didn't change, but I felt a challenge in his gaze all the same, as if he wondered by what right a human could call him brother.

Mabonnyn spoke up, "This is the Son of the druid priestess Foltchain. It is both for her sake and for his that we make our way to the Derryth."

"Called Corb," the arbutus said. "Know of Foltchain."

"You don't happen to know where she is right now, I suppose," I ventured.

"No," Corb said, and nothing more, which was pretty much what I expected.

"Thank you," I said. "For your name, and for your help." Corb made a throaty, gurgling sound of assent, and I made my way back to Juvie and

Phoebe. "His name's Corb," I said as I settled back against a post.

"Corb," Juvie repeated. "Okay."

"Anything else?"

"Nah, I'm good," Juvie shrugged. "And I'll give him this, he's the best-smelling thing we've run into down here in the muck. Kind of envy the little guy and the frog riding up there next to him. What exactly is it… I mean, he… made of?"

"Pitch," I said. "Tree resin. Living sap."

"Oh, of course," Juvie said. I waited for him to ask another question, or change the subject altogether, but he only stared out at the fetid gloom surrounding us. We were making much better time, with Corb advancing tirelessly through the marsh, drafting us in his wake. Whatever wild creatures inhabited the stretch of the Undergrowth we were crossing gave the arbutus and the floating platform a wide berth. The dank air was still and quiet.

After a while an enormous shadow loomed before us, a tangled grove of black-bark trees which all seemed to be competing to reach their outstretched branches toward the same point. The trees at the periphery of the stand contorted themselves the most, bending and corkscrewing toward the center, while the trees near the heart of the grove craned straight upward, their extremities lost in a dense, clinging mist. Mabonnyn indicated that we should enter the grove, and Corb pushed through a hanging curtain of graybeard moss.

We slowed somewhat as Corb picked his way among the gnarled boles in the grove, until finally the spaces between the trees were too narrow for the raft to proceed. I started to slide my arms under Phoebe's supine form, until Juvie said, "I got her."

"Juvie, seriously, it's fine," I said.

"Yeah, it is," he agreed, while moving to pick her up himself.

"Gern can bear her forward," Mabonnyn interjected. "It is not much farther."

"What's not much farther?" Juvie asked.

"The Derryth," Mabonnyn answered. "The way that remains is short, but difficult. You may wish to be free of burden."

Juvie lifted Phoebe from the platform, but walked straight to Gern and laid her gently on the bullfrog's back. Gern slid smoothly into the water covering the trees' roots. Juvie splashed down behind her. A moment later I was beside him, handing him his hazel staff, which he took with a muttered "Thanks."

Corb continued to lead the way, while Gern swam slowly, Mabonnyn flitted from canted trunk to low-hanging bough lightly as a squirrel, and Juvie and I waded through stagnant slime and tried to keep our footing amongst the sprawl of submerged radicles.. It was even darker within the confines of the grove than it had been in the open marshland, but eventually I noticed a faint light color reflecting on the rippling surface of the murky water lapping at our legs. I looked up and saw a ropy tendril snaking through the branches overhead. Everything else around us was cold and dark, but the runner was suffused with a warmth that was shocking in contrast to its surroundings. We followed it as it grew thicker, golden flesh covered in hairy umber filaments. Finally it swept up perpendicular to the water, rising and rising until it disappeared into the crowded press of ebon limbs chasing after it, and we all came to a halt beneath it.

"One of these things is not like the other," Juvie said, eyeing the massive tendril. "What's that branch belong to?"

"Root," Corb rumbled.

"Pardon?" Juvie asked.

"It's a root, not a branch," I clarified.

"There's something growing up above us?" Juvie asked.

"Sort of," I said. "It's one of the roots of the Derryth, which is growing above us in the sense that the Deep Woods is above the Undergrowth."

"Which you said wasn't literally true," Juvie reminded me.

"Yeah, well," I shrugged. "The name trees are powerful enough that they kind of transcend distinctions like that. So the Derryth has roots that extend all the way into the Undergrowth."

"So, we made it?" Juvie asked. "I mean, this is it, right? This is what we've been looking for?"

"Nearly so," Mabonnyn said. "The heart of the Derryth is above. But via the same puissance that allows the Derryth to enter the Undergrowth here, we should be able to pass through to the Deep Woods. And there, in the true presence of the heart of the Derryth, we may seek aid for Foltchain."

"And Phoebe?" Juvie asked hopefully.

I was going to answer him with something vaguely affirmative that would also keep him focused on tackling one step at a time, when I heard a hissing noise like the world's angriest cat. It was echoed and amplified into a chorus of aggressive whispers, all coming from overhead. A sleek furred creature crawled along the oak root. Its body was six feet long, with short legs and long bushy tail, covered in yellow fur that darkened to green at its paws, the tip of its tail and the tufts of its ears. It stopped just above us, fixed us with its glowing white eyes and bared its sharp teeth menacingly. Another creature, identical except that its darker fur color was orange, emerged nearby, as did another with white paws and ears, and two more with reddish-brown markings. All of the creatures regarded us unblinking with growls emanating more or less constantly from their throats.

"Parasites?" Juvie guessed.

"No," I said. "Those are martens. They're guardians of the Oak."

"Right," Juvie agreed. "So what we do, give them the password? Solve some kind of riddle?" I gave Juvie a skeptical look but he only half-shrugged. "There's always a riddle."

"Not this time. That's not what the martens do. If they're down here, that only means one thing."

"The Derryth does not welcome us in its presence," Mabonnyn spared me from having to admit it myself.

Chapter Eight: Deeper Roots

I STARED INTO the eyes of the guardian marten overhead. Along with the other furry sentinels, it was coiled, tense, and ready to strike at any moment. Even in the Deep Woods, even amongst the breed devoted to protecting my mother's name tree, the martens' lifespan was only a dozen years or so, and it had been much longer since I had ventured this far. I couldn't count on any of the animals recognizing me, and wouldn't have been able to reason with them anyway. They were operating on territorial instinct, augmented by the influence of the Derryth.

"I kind of wish we had grabbed some of those redcombs' clubs before we shoved off," Juvie said.

"Not me," I replied. "They wouldn't scare off the martens, they'd only make us look like more of a threat."

"Maybe we should be more of a threat," Juvie said.

"If you think the outcome of violence against the guardians would tend to our favor," Mabonnyn said, "you vastly underestimate the Derryth."

"He's right," I said.

"Fine, fine," Juvie shook his head. "The tree's little pets won't let us through without a fight, and it's a fight we'd lose. So now what?" He snapped to me suddenly. "Hey, wait. Do we even need to go through? I mean the whole point was to see if something bad had happened to the tree, which would mean something bad had happened to your mom. But the tree's fine, right? The root looks healthy, the defenses are working, everything as it should be?"

"I take your point," I said. "And yeah, on some level, I feel better just being here and seeing this. I feel like the task at hand is still to find my mother, not just find whoever…" I trailed off, took a breath. "But making sure that the tree is all right, and presumably so is she by extension, that was just part of the point. The other part was to see if we could get some kind of lead on where my mother is, what's happening with her. And for that, we need the whole tree, not just marten sightings along the root in the Undergrowth."

Juvie returned his attention to the guardians. The lead marten made another show of its long canine teeth. "All right, a brawl would mean getting clawed and chewed to death," Juvie mused. "What about the Mabster there? Little sneaky-sneaky, ninja style?"

"Doubtful," I said.

"What about with a head start?" Juvie asked.

"How?"

"You know, just..." Juvie pantomimed an overhand toss. "Yeet!"

"No," Mabonnyn declined.

"He's kidding," I said, pointedly ignoring the look on Juvie's face that said he wasn't.

"What about Gern and Phoebe?" Juvie asked. "One's an animal, the other's unconscious, they can't be perceived as threats, right?"

"I don't think the martens make distinctions like that," I said, "and even if they did, what good would that do? Neither of them could tell us what was going on up there."

"Can't they see that Phoebe needs help, though?" Juvie demanded, furious. "We're not here to cause trouble!" he shouted at the martens. "We're on the same damn side!"

"No side but Derryth," Corb said, accurately if unhelpfully.

"No, wrong," Juvie said. He stepped closer to the root and raised his empty right hand toward the lead marten. "Come on, you look like a semi-intelligent critter." He wiggled his fingers. "We come in peace, you feel me?"

The marten stared at Juvie's extended hand. It gripped the root with its rear paws and partially unfurled its sinuous body, slowly stretching a foreleg toward Juvic. The stubby digits of the marten's paw splayed, mimicking Juvie's spread fingers. Then the retractable claws popped from their sheaths like scalpel blades, and the hissing marten lunged for

Juvie.

I threw myself toward Juvie, even as he was already stumbling backwards in alarm. The marten swiped viciously at empty air once, twice, three times, and then was engulfed by a huge shape that exploded out of the dark water. It moved so fast that at first I couldn't make sense of it, my mind trying to parse too many connected parts moving independently, all while I was reaching for Juvie, who had fallen onto his back. I braced Juvie's shoulders to get his head out of the water and got a better look at the new arrival that had shattered the tableau.

It stood about six feet tall, on two legs that looked too skinny to support the bulk of it and zigzagged from joint to joint like a bug's. Four more legs emerged from its hunchbacked body, the middle pair held out from its sides to brandish chitinous hooked claws, the upper pair wrapped around the marten screaming and writhing furiously in its grip. The central mass was furry, but so mud-slicked it was hard to tell if it was a pelt of hair or a layer of vegetation adhered to its carapace. Its head was rounded with disturbingly humanlike features, small eyes, flat nose, large mouth, but still more like a person than any kind of animal. Small horns grew along the jawline and two massive plates extended from the sides of the head, like wings or the heads of battle axes, chipped and nicked along their sharp curving edges.

"What the everliving fuck?" Juvie asked.

"Pretty sure that's a bukavac," I said, hoisting him to his feet. "I've never seen one in person but…"

I was cut off by a roar from the bukavac, a noise so loud it would have drowned my words out completely if it hadn't struck with enough force to knock the breath from my lungs. I staggered, my ears ringing, feeling Juvie wincing in my arms as well. After the bukavac stopped roaring, all I could hear was a throbbing echo of the thunderous outburst. Gradually I realized that the martens still on the root above were all squealing in frustration, torn between their duty to remain with the Derryth and their desire to protect one of their own.

The lead marten was raking all of its claws against the bukavac's belly, jaws snapping at its arms, with no visible effect on the swamp monster. The bukavac opened its maw, revealing rows of jagged fangs, and attacked the marten with its teeth. There was nothing the marten could do to defend itself as one of its forelegs disappeared between the gnashing teeth and was torn away, leaving a stump covered in bloodstained fur. The marten howled.

Mabonnyn, who had to have been up among the branches of the twisted black trees, leapt down onto the back of the bukavac and stabbed at the crown of the monster's head. The harrier's knife was as ineffective as the marten's claws and teeth had been. The bukavac reached up with its middle pair of arms to swat Mabonnyn away, and Mabonnyn parried the shiny hooks until one blow from behind knocked the woodlander down to the water.

Gern remained a safe distance away, Phoebe still balanced across her back, but the bullfrog's tongue shot out and snared one of the bukavac's arms holding the marten. It dislodged the monster's chokehold just enough for the marten to slither down into the water and limp away as fast as it could. The bukavac snapped its arm to shake off Gern's tongue, and roared again, rattling the trees, vibrating the surface of the water, and making my back teeth hurt.

"That thing could have attacked any of us any time," Juvie said, laboring to catch his breath. "Why'd it wait?"

"Maybe the martens taste better," I said. "Seriously. They're infused with the Derryth's essence, so it's like…"

"Beer-battered wagyu beef?" Juvie volunteered.

"Sure, if the cows had also been fed psychotropic mushrooms that make you feel like you're cruising through the happiest parts of Oz," I answered. I wished I had some mushrooms like that, or anything from my mother's herbarium, that might level the playing field between us and the bukavac. But I was low on supplies and short on options. I looked to Juvie and eyed his hazel staff. "Give me your walking stick," I said.

It had come out as more of a direct order than a request, and Juvie obliged, handing it over. I passed the staff behind the nearest black tree and pulled both ends toward me. The hazel bowed in the middle but held together. I tried again, throwing all my weight back, but the result was the same.

I felt a warm, slightly sticky pressure on the back of my neck. Corb reached over me to grasp the staff, and I stepped aside to let him take it. The arbutus held the ends of the staff and broke it like a toothpick. He offered me both halves, but I only took one. Then he pressed his massive hands to the sides of my head like a silent benediction.

I marched toward the bukavac, and for a split-second the monster actually froze, startled to realize that one of us was approaching it so brazenly. But the respite was short-lived and the bukavac spread its four upper limbs wide, claws clacking, and unleashed yet another strident blast of noise. I felt the reverberations across my skin but didn't break stride, jamming the splintered end of the broken hazel staff into the gaping mouth.

The bukavac's roar sputtered out as it choked on the wood. I pressed forward, driving the monster back on its spindly legs. Juvie and Mabonnyn intercepted it mid-retreat, each grabbing an opposite leg and lifting the bukavac up and out of the standing water. The bukavac thrashed and flailed, jerking its head from side to side, until Corb grabbed it by the hump of its shoulders and pushed it down. I pushed up at the same time, the sharp scraggles of hazel penetrating deeper and deeper until a torrent of black ichor gushed from the bukavac's mouth.

Mabonnyn, Juvie, Corb and I all stepped back as the bukavac pitched forward into the water, unmoving. Juvie and I stared at the lifeless monster for several seconds, too steeped in western horror movie tropes to turn our backs on a fallen foe. But Corb waded over to the wounded marten, gently scooping the animal out of the water. Corb carried the marten to the Derryth root, lifting the sentinel up to be set delicately on the golden coil. Two of the other martens escorted their leader on either side as it shuffled haltingly up the length of the root, while the last pair followed them.

I noticed Juvie staring at me, lips moving and eyebrows raised expectantly. I scraped my ears with my index finger, removing the pitch that Corb had deposited there to shield me from the bukavac's sonic assault. "Sorry, what?" I asked.

"What do we do now?" Juvie asked.

I looked to the root again, just in time to see the marten with the white tufts on its ears poke its face out. It transfixed us with its shining eyes, which no longer held the same violent challenge as before. "Permission to enter territory?" I asked, except not really, because I didn't so much use words as bestial vocalizations in High Arboreal. Or an approximation of High Arboreal, since mine was admittedly rusty. But the marten barked back at me in a way that seemed affirmative, then disappeared into the shadows again. As it departed the Derryth root expanded and lowered closer to the stagnant water.

I gestured for Juvie to climb onto the root. "We go up," I said.

Juvie in turn gestured at Gern to go up first, and the bullfrog hopped onto the root and waddled along its twisting length, carrying Phoebe. Mabonnyn followed, and then Juvie climbed up after them. I fell in behind Juvie, and Corb brought up the rear. As we all ascended I could feel the root gradually contracting beneath us, as the branches of dozens of the black trees on every side scratched at us in a way that felt almost deliberate.

The gloom of the Undergrowth became impenetrably lightless as we followed the course of the Derryth root. The dark, fetid miasma that permeated the air of the brackish marsh gave way to a brighter, cleaner mineral smell, the loamy tang of freshly turned earth, which in the blinding blackness was the only indication we had that our surroundings were changing. Eventually that odor also changed, as our heads were filled with the strong scent of oak, as if somehow we had gone from clinging to the outside of the root to rising up through enormous vessels within the structure. Then, ahead of us, there was light.

I poked my head out of a knothole that was just wide enough to let me wriggle out by pulling through one arm and then the other. Phoebe was lying propped against a root nearby, with Gern squatting attentively beside her. Mabonnyn had remounted the bullfrog. Juvie was lying on his back a few paces away, his hands swishing the soft tips of the blades of grass appreciatively. I finished crawling through the gap, stood up and turned around to see Corb oozing upward from the knothole, his body of pitch squeezing out and reconstituting itself into shape as he emerged.

I looked around and saw a few martens sitting around the edge of the clearing, with no sign of the leader who had lost a limb to the bukavac. I assumed the unfortunate creature had gone somewhere more secluded to convalesce, accompanied by the same martens that had been escorting him earlier. The number of remaining martens had been augmented by more of their kin, with their own unique markings, fiery orange on yellow, bright green and brown on yellow, and one which was a strange inverse of the others, most of its sleek fur inky black, with saffron colored ear tufts, paws and tip of its tail. The martens were watching us attentively, but seemed serene about our presence, or at least content to keep their distance.

Like the Eadhadh, like all the name trees, the Derryth dwarfed everything in the nearby surroundings, and nothing grew beneath its massive overhanging boughs except the lush carpet of green grass. The boughs closest to the ground were thirty feet above our heads, dense with foot-long leaves whose shapes I could have drawn with my eyes closed: the tripartite crown at the apex and the three lobes marching down either side of the midvein smaller and smaller. The tops of the leaves were vibrant green but the undersides were pale and glaucous, making the entire canopy above into a towering fountain of emerald and silver. A single leaf detached from its stem and twirled dreamily down toward me. I reached out to catch the leaf from the air, and slid it into my pocket.

It was impossible to see the top of the tree, of course, but the trunk was fifty feet wide, bigger than the Eadhadh, one of the biggest and oldest living things in the Deep Woods. The nearest branches were fifteen feet overhead, and I knew the crown of the tree was nearly a thousand feet up. A rustle from above heralded yet another marten descending, carrying a bundle of yellow-green shoots in its teeth, the broken ends glistening with sap. The marten approached Phoebe and dropped the shoots on her chest, then tried to nudge one of the strands up Phoebe's neck, toward her face. Juvie drew closer to the pair, slowly and non-threateningly. He pinched the shoot and lifted it toward Phoebe's face, pausing to look to the marten for approval, then to look to me once he remembered he couldn't talk to the guardians or even read much from their facial expressions.

I nodded. "Touch the wet end to her tongue. It's good for what ails."

Juvie proceeded, passing the shoot delicately between Phoebe's parted lips. He dabbed the fluid on her tongue and drew back a bit to watch her reaction. For a few moments there was nothing, then Phoebe's eyelids fluttered open. She looked around, only moving her eyes as she took in the scene and got her bearings. Ultimately her line of sight settled on Juvie's face. Her right hand rose, very slowly. Juvie reached out, taking her hand in his. Phoebe weakly but unmistakably swatted his hand away, her fingertips continuing to drift up to her chest where she plucked a shoot and brought it to her lips. She sucked on it like a straw, sighing once she had drained the sap. She rearranged herself, sitting more upright.

Juvie regarded her. "Feel better?"

Phoebe nodded once. "How's your ankle?" she asked in return.

"Still attached," Juvie said.

She offered him one of the oak shoots. "This'll help."

Juvie's brow furrowed. "I thought it was only good for… your…"

"My kind?" Phoebe challenged.

"I was going to say, your particular exhausted condition," Juvie said.

"What's so particular about it?"

"Well, you're the only one who passed out, so…"

"Amusing and adorable as the banter between you two is," I interjected, "you need to stop before the shoots dry out. They're most effective when they're fresh."

Juvie took the oak shoot from Phoebe and sucked on the end. He stood up and experimented with putting weight on his leg. "Not bad," he said.

"Good thing," I said. "Sorry about your walking stick."

Juvie tilted his head philosophically. "No apology needed, under the circumstances."

"What circumstances? What happened to the hazel…?" She cut herself off, shaking her head. "No, doesn't really matter, does it? We made it to the Oak. We're here. Though I take it your mother is not."

"I didn't really expect her to be, but no, she's not," I confirmed.

"But the tree itself looks good," Phoebe said.

"True enough," I said.

"Yeah, your mom's okay, wherever she is," Juvie said. "So can the tree tell us where that is?"

"I don't know," I admitted. My eyes sought Phoebe's.

"I don't know either," she said. She rolled to her hip and worked to get to her feet. Juvie moved to assist her, and I half expected her to swat at him again, but she allowed it. He helped her upright, mostly holding her arms and allowing her to lean on him, and then stepped back once she was stable. Phoebe walked to the Derryth and placed her hands on the broad, rough surface of gray bark.

A quiet reverence settled over the glade beneath the boughs of the name tree. There were sounds all around us, the whisper of wind in the leaves overhead, the intermittent calls of birds and buzz of insects, the rustling of small animals among the shrubs and other ground cover just beyond the clearing. But all the same, the very air in our vicinity felt tranquil, like the atmosphere of a temple, which I suppose is exactly what the space belonging to the Derryth was. Phoebe stood very still, at one point tilting her face forward until her forehead touched the bark as well.

A minute or so passed, and Corb silently strode to Phoebe's right side. The arbutus mirrored her posture, laying hands on the gigantic bole. They stood together, two supplicants before the Derryth, and then they were joined by Mabonnyn and Gern. The harrier stood on Phoebe's left, hands laid on the trunk, and Gern squatted on Mabonnyn's other side. The bullfrog put its forelimbs up like the others, webbed toes splayed against the rugged bark.

I watched them all, Juvie standing nearby, waiting to hear what they could glean from my mother's anchor in the Deep Woods. I wasn't inclined to join them, for reasons which I assumed Juvie had managed to intuit as well. Mabonnyn and Gern and Corb all inhabited the Deep Woods, and

Phoebe had a strong claim to belonging there as well, but Juvie and I were interlopers from the outside world, the deforested, asphalt-paved, brick and metal and glass stretches that had forsaken the greenery. Whatever I might know and understand about the teachings of the druids, I didn't exactly live by those tenets. My presence was being tolerated at arm's length at best.

"Kellan," Phoebe said. "Come."

I almost laughed, given that I had just been reflecting on exactly why coming closer to the Derryth would be the exact wrong thing to do. "Why?" I asked. "I don't want to mess up the whole xylem and phloem communion you guys have going."

"Don't be an ass," Phoebe snapped.

"Phoebe, I'm serious," I said. "All kidding aside, I'm not operating on the same level as you, not even close. I'm barely…"

"That's the point," Phoebe cut in.

"Come again?"

"The Derryth, it… it doesn't know where your mother is. Or, it doesn't grasp where she is. Because she's so far from the Deep Woods. Understand? Your separation from the weg of root and branch isn't as important here as your connection to the outside world. So come. Juvie, you too," Phoebe said.

I suppose it was Phoebe's use of the word 'weg', that archaic, druid-only term, that got through to me. I nodded to myself, nudged Juvie encouragingly, and approached the vast bole of the Derryth.

Juvie whispered out of the corner of his mouth,

"What am I supposed to do, exactly?"

"Exactly, I'm not sure," I said. "But approximately, just relax, make yourself mentally open." I remembered a mantra my mother had taught me long ago. "Picture yourself inside a flower, budding at the end of a twig growing from a small branch growing from larger and larger branches all the way back to the three, and capable of making a seed that can grow into a new tree that grows and branches and flowers again and again."

"Visualize the entire eternal cycle of plant life, no problem," Juvie said.

"Just a suggestion to get you started," I said as we laid our hands on the tree trunk. "If Phoebe's right, just let your mind go wherever it leads you."

"I'm right," Phoebe said. "Now shut up and do it."

I closed my eyes and deepened my breathing. I started the visualization as I had described it to Juvie, which made me think of my mother's voice. That made me think of my mother's house, back when it was my house, too. I remembered sneaking a walkman in one day at the bottom of my school backpack. It was a gift from a friend at school, though really it was a castoff, embarrassingly outdated by that point, lo-fi analog technology at a time where almost everyone had gone to digital recordings and the early adopters were going to online file sharing. But magnetic tapes run and read with the power of AA batteries were something that could work even in my mother's unwired, off the grid cottage. And the melodies and lyrics that the tinny earphones carried to my brain were a window into a larger world I was desperate to learn more about. Lying in my bed, covers pulled up over my head, headphones upside down with the brace under my chin, where it could be yanked down and shoved under the pillow where the walkman already waited if my mother entered my room unannounced, I listened to bands from another planet and started to form my earliest plans to journey there myself…

I sensed Corb stepping backwards and opened my eyes. I glanced at Phoebe, who was also retreating from the Derryth. Mabonnyn and Gern soon followed, and Juvie did as well. I pushed off and looked up and down the ancient oak. "What did we get?" I asked.

"What did you get?" Juvie asked.

"Nothing new," I said. "Old memories." Belatedly I felt a pang of guilt that my reminisces had mostly been about avoiding my mother and deliberately breaking her house rules. If my goal had been to communicate to the Derryth how keenly I wanted to be reunited with Foltchain of the Oak, I had telepathically faceplanted. But I didn't think that was the case. I was certain the Derryth knew why I was there, why we were all there. According to Phoebe, I had only been enlisted to act as a translator between the arboreal world of the Deep Woods and the rest of the hiding places on the planet where my mother might be held. "Phoebe? Did the tree have anything else to say once Juvie and I joined in?"

"Not… exactly," Phoebe said, frowning. "I got the sense that the Derryth had finished interacting with us. The transmission, both ways, ended. But I still don't know where your mother is. I'm sorry."

"Don't be," I said reflexively. "I mean, this was a long shot anyway. So it didn't work. I never had a clear idea how it was supposed to work to begin with." A dragonfly floated past me, wings beating an iridescent blur in the air.

"So are you giving up?" Juvie asked.

"No, of course not," I said. I suddenly felt very tired. "At the very least we know that my mother isn't anywhere in the Deep Woods. Next step is to go back home, work the streets, do my job."

"Do you think Phoebe has that kind of time?" Juvie pressed. The dragonfly did a lazy loop around him at shoulder height. No, I corrected myself, it wasn't the same dragonfly I had seen a moment earlier. That one had landed on the trunk of the Derryth, and the newcomer circling Juvie alighted near it.

"Phoebe, maybe you should stay here?" I offered. "At least you'll have a steady supply of…"

Phoebe shook her head. "Not happening."

I rubbed my eyes, thoroughly exhausted. I also couldn't bear to look at any of them, not Phoebe, not Juvie, not Mabonnyn or Corb. They all wanted to know what came next, what our little collective should do to make it all turn out all right, and I had no easy answers for them. I didn't even have hard answers. When I lowered my hand and opened my eyes, I aimed my gaze at the Derryth.

There were more than two dragonflies on the trunk of the ancient name tree now. There were more than two dozen, and new arrivals were settling onto the rugged bark with every passing moment. The dragonflies came in all sizes, from tiny ones with matchstick bodies, bright red compound eyes like double phosphorus heads, to giants with eighteen inch long abdomens and two foot wingspans, tails segmented like brigandine armor and black veins wrought through each wing. Hundreds streamed into the clearing around the Derryth to take their positions among the fluttering sheath: darners with their black and white snakeskin thoraxes, earthy brown and green hawkers, distinguished gray emperors, yellow-winged darters, meadowhawks with their dusky midsections and bright tails the color of ripe fruit, clubtails with their lengthwise striations of charcoal and chartreuse that looked like bamboo stands, demoiselles shimmering like deep green ink, downy straw-colored chasers and skimmers, groundlings and dropwings and dashers. Soon it was all but impossible to see any of the bark of the Derryth at all from the roots to a height of twenty feet above the grass.

"What's happening?" Juvie asked, without a trace of fear in his voice. He wasn't even really posing the question to me, or to anyone in particular, merely voicing acknowledgment of his own lack of any explanation or point of reference, even just a name for the phenomenon. I assumed his mind was trying to process the carefully orchestrated movements of a thousand thousand insects, forming into orderly ranks, vertical lines running up and down the trunk, dragonflies perched in eerie, expectant stillness except for the occasional twitch of a tail or flex of a wing. I likewise had no name for it, because I had never seen anything like it, either.

The entire aggregation was a motley patchwork of insect bodies the colors of earth and leaf and wood and glassy wings, but as the last dragonflies entered the clearing and took up their positions in the formation, a concentrated patch of color formed in the center. Metallic, iridescent blue spread across the trunk, a brilliant sapphire dazzle amidst the swarm. The other dragonflies became even more subdued, not stirring, wings flattened, six legs locked, while the blues beat their wings in an overwhelming, buzzing frenzy.

I glanced around at the others. Juvie was still agog, adding to the overall surreality of the scene since I had never seen him anywhere close to agog before. Phoebe was staring intently at the dragonflies, not as bewildered as Juvie but not really understanding what was happening any better than I did. Mabonnyn stood impassive, one hand atop Gern's nose, as if holding the bullfrog's mouth closed, refusing to allow any disruption of the proceedings via an errant flick of a hungry tongue. Gern looked relaxed enough, occasionally blinking her huge amber and black eyes. Corb was even harder to read than Mabonnyn, but the arbutus seemed if not awed at least humbly respectful, like a traveler who wanders into a church ceremony, knowing nothing of its significance or the language in which the rites are performed.

Juvie noticed me and blinked. "I told you, man."

"Told me what?"

"There's always a riddle."

"I'm not sure that's what this is, either," I said.

"Well whatever it is, it's pretty wild."

"Can't argue with that," I said.

"Does it mean something?"

"Not to me," I admitted. "You?"

"Not remotely. But I'm not the one steeped in this stuff." His line of sight was drawn inexorably back to the dragonflies. "I guess no matter how deep you are on the big picture there's always going to be details you've never seen before."

I was inclined to agree once again, but my train of thought latched onto the idea of the big picture. The quivering, rippling tableau of insects was so vast that my head had to swivel to take it all in. I backed up, all the way to the edge of the clearing, so that I could see the whole enormity of the Derryth's trunk and the dragonflies' display as one. From that distance I could see how the blues had formed an oblong rectangle, straight on its two tall sides but somewhat irregular along the top. The longer I looked, the more I realized that those irregularities were still well-formed shapes, a canted crescent moon, a pair of lines, and a perfect square from left to right. I saw that while all the blues were beating their wings, they did so in different patterns, some in tight oscillations that remained perpendicular to their bodies at all times, others in wider arcs above their compound eyes, down to their tails and back up again, still others sticking straight up and away from the Derryth. The differences in the wing positions gave textures to the middle of the big blue rectangle, creating lines that felt architectural. They resolved in my consciousness as columns and ledges as it occurred to me that was exactly what they were supposed to be. The dragonflies, responding to profound signals from the Derryth which only they could perceive, had made a picture of a building. Not some abstract representation of modern urban construction, but a very specific building, one with a wide windowless band around the fourth floor and a satellite dish and egress on the roof. A building I had driven past many times, one of the myriad architectural monuments lining the streets of the place I called home.

"It knows… I know where my mother is," I said.

INTERLUDE II

FOLTCHAIN OF THE Oak visualized the sunset, as it would appear above the enclosure of her own cottage. In her mind's eye she saw the striated bands of pink and orange and purple clouds softening to darker and darker blue, all while the crowns of the surrounding trees became inky silhouettes. She saw the stars spark into existence above the leafy black proscenium, and heard the last mournful soliloquies of the evening songbirds give way to the querulous cries of owls and the chitter of nocturnal insects.

She could not say for sure if the sun was at that very moment setting behind her cottage. She could not say for sure if the sun was at that very moment setting in the area where she was presently being held. She could not in fact say with any certainty at all if the area where she found herself was a space which experienced rising or setting or any light of the sun in any meaningful sense of the word. She could be at the bottom of the ocean or at the center of the moon or orbiting the event horizon of the black hole at the center of the galaxy or somewhere beyond the physical boundaries of the so-called known universe. She had no way to tell, as no sensory evidence was allowed to penetrate her pale, asymmetrical prison cell. Whenever an aperture to the cell opened, all she could see was a continuation of the same surface of jagged, irregular planes and vertices, with no windows or gaps. All that Foltchain could say for sure was that she was separated from the forest, cut off by the alien barrier at least and, in all likelihood, by vast distance as well.

She had no idea how long she had been unconscious between the time she had been abducted and the time she had awakened to her strange new surroundings. Her sleep had been brutally silent and dreamless. But since then, she had kept to a diurnal schedule according to her body's reliable sense of the passage of time. Visualizing the sunset and the sunrise was part of that internal reckoning. The discipline was an old ingrained habit for her, which had always allowed her to live without clocks even beneath the heaviest of winter clouds.

The far wall of the cell parted and Foltchain opened her eyes to regard one of her captors, entering and bearing a flat shingle covered in food. Foltchain had been expecting the delivery of the daily meal, which always coincided with her sunset meditation. Yet she pointedly remained seated in her lotus pose, breathing in through her nose and imagining she could smell the nightblooms of home, with the entity standing before her expectantly.

"You will ingest," the uncanny being said. Its voice was incapable of conveying impatience, annoyance or any other emotion.

"I will not," Foltchain said serenely, closing her eyes again.

"If you do not ingest," the entity said, "we will force nourishment upon you. We will not allow you to escape us into death. Not until you teach us what we require."

"You have no idea what you can or cannot force upon me, or what you can or cannot allow me to do," Foltchain said.

"You have no idea what we are capable of," the entity said.

"Nor do you," Foltchain said. "Is that not what you wish me to teach you?"

"Even now, without your tutelage, we are capable of more than you can know," the entity said.

"But we do not wish to test our mettle against yours."

"You leave me little choice," Foltchain said.

"Choice," the entity echoed, still devoid of feeling but with some disdain conveyed by drawing out the word with deliberate slowness. "Would the choice you make for yourself be different than the choice you make for another?"

"That question seems moot," Foltchain answered.

"Sooner or later we will find your offspring. And those who have aided him. Are you truly indifferent to all of their fates?"

Foltchain opened her eyes. The being's approximation of a face was literally expressionless, as always. She took the question as a genuine inquiry, and not a rhetorical challenge. The entity genuinely could neither predict nor truly comprehend how she might answer. Her reaction was immediate and irrefutable, but she inhaled and exhaled several times with slow control before answering. Finally she said, "I will begin to eat. But the fare you have been offering is not to my liking. If you wish me to take my own sustenance, without testing my mettle, then I would suggest you bring me something more palatable."

"Tell us what you will ingest," the being said. Eating was as abstract and unknowable to its kind as compassion; the fact of its necessity was acknowledged, but no frame of reference for it existed.

Foltchain considered carefully and said, "Sesame seeds. Red turnips. Milk thistle. Bladder wrack and mustard leaves. Bilberries and hornbeam nuts."

"These will be given to you," the being said. "And you will ingest them. And then you will teach us what we require."

Foltchain tilted her head in acquiescence. The entity turned to leave through an opening in the wall which sealed itself after the entity had passed through. Foltchain continued to meditate, mentally transporting herself to sit amidst the semi-tamed grasses and wildflowers of her home.

The entity, or another one identical to the first, returned sooner than she expected, though she controlled herself thoroughly enough to give no outward sign of surprise. Her captor set the white shingle, which looked as though it could have been peeled from the very walls of the prison, on the floor beside her. Foltchain glanced down at it, quickly ascertaining that it contained every item she had requested. "Thank you," she said.

The nicety was wasted on the entity, already leaving her to consume her meal in solitude. She did so, with great deliberation, stripping the stems from the mustard leaves and chewing them thoroughly, peeling the skins off the bilberries and swallowing those skins whole. All the while, the tiniest smile played on the corners of her lips.

Chapter Nine:
Ascension

"Where?" Phoebe asked. "Where is she?"

No sooner had she posed the question than the dragonflies began to let go of the Derryth's bark, zooming away to all corners of the clearing and disappearing among the surrounding trees. Juvie turned to me with eyes widened in theatrical disbelief.

"The dragonflies made a picture of a building, one I vaguely recognize. I don't know it by name, I've never had reason to go there, but it's a background detail in my mental map of the city," I explained.

"Well, what are we supposed to do, go back to the real world and drive around until you happen to spot it?" Juvie demanded. "They had to play Pictionary with you, they couldn't have just formed into letters and numbers in a street address?"

"Doesn't matter," I said. "I'll find it."

"How?"

"Research. Old-fashioned detective work," I said. "It's kind of my thing."

"So what are we waiting for?" Phoebe asked.

"We're still fighting against the clock, and the last thing we need is to get slowed down again," I said. "If we go straight through the Deep Woods and back to the city, we might run across the Council of Ruis again. If we dodge them by going through the Undergrowth, it'll take longer, even if we don't run into something worse down there. Mabonnyn, what do you think?"

The harrier considered before answering. "Is it your desire to find the nearest egress from the Deep Woods, or to return from whence you came?"

I mentally weighed our options. We could increase the odds of avoiding the servants of the Council by heading straight to the closest exit, but I didn't know where in the real world that would drop us, and I doubted Mabonnyn would be able to tell us either. I had no desire to see another ooser for as long as I lived, but I didn't love the idea of walking out of the forest only to discover that we were on the outskirts of a small town in the northern reaches of the Masurian Lake District. Which was in Poland.

"We have to get back to my mother's cottage as fast as possible," I clarified. "We..."

A shrill scream sounded overhead, its source obscured by the vault of dense green leaves. It was answered by the yowl of a marten, followed by thrashing among the tree limbs punctuated by hisses and squeals. The single initial scream doubled, tripled, became a hellish chorus that echoed menacingly all around us. Nearby boughs of the Derryth rattled and shook and then two bodies crashed down to the grass in a shower of broken branches and fluttering leaves. A marten was locked in mortal grapple with a giant bat, both animals attacking each other with bloodthirsty ferocity. No sooner did the marten and the bat hit the ground than a storm of leather wings and glistening fangs burst upon us in a shrieking cacophony. A few martens were falling among them, thrashing and clawing at the invaders, but the bats vastly outnumbered them.

I didn't yell for everyone to run, because I didn't have to. Few things inspire the flight response quite like a swarm of shrieking bats. Gern took off even as Mabonnyn was mounting her, and Phoebe and Juvie were close behind the bullfrog. Corb only hesitated long enough to make sure everyone else was getting out of the Derryth's clearing before bringing up the rear, shielding our escape somewhat with his bulk. Gern rammed through the wall of membranous wings and furred bodies and the rest of us had no choice but to batter our own way out, clubbed and slashed by the bats in return with every step. Then all of us were racing through the bushes and brush and ferns, weaving among the smaller trees surrounding the Derryth, before we really had time to fully register just how many bats were after us. Too many to count, well beyond the number necessary to inspire terror.

And beyond the sheer numbers, there was

everything wrong with the bats, the pale, jagged spikes bursting through their skin in irregular clusters from backs, bellies and arm bones, and the pink slime cataracting their tiny eyes. That, more than anything else, made my skin crawl and my stomach contract into a frozen gnarl of fear. Whatever the blight was, it was getting stronger, powerful enough to compel the afflicted bats to violate the sanctity of the Derryth's grove. The prohibition against violence within the locus of the Derryth should have been absolute, or so I had always been taught. But the blighted bats had put the lie to that.

A bat as big as an eagle with two crystalline spikes sticking out of either side of its neck overtook us and dove for Phoebe, its mouth wide and its grooved tongue unfurled between rows of needlelike teeth. Phoebe threw up an arm defensively as the bat wrapped its wings around her. She reached up with her free hand and sunk her fingers into the rubbery upturned nose. The bat thrashed to escape, until Mabonnyn fell on its back and drove a knife into base of the bat's skull. One down and what felt like a hundred more still beating their wings in pursuing thunder. We ran on.

Two bats attacked Corb, latching onto the arbutus's neck with claws and teeth. Corb charged into the nearest tree without breaking stride, lowering a shoulder and crushing the bat against the trunk. The tree splintered with a loud crack and toppled to the side as the stunned bat tumbled to the forest floor. Corb reached back to grab the other bat and snapped its wingbones, eliciting a wild wail from the creature, which nonetheless refused to let go. Corb yanked the bat from its perch, dislodging gobbets of pitch that arced through the air, and slammed it to the ground, where it lay insensate. "Come!" Corb yawped, veering off to one side.

For lack of any better ideas, we all followed the arbutus as he tore through the forest, grunting and straining to keep up with Corb's long, loping stride. The ground beneath our feet began to slope upwards, but Corb never flagged, climbing the hill with the same single-minded speed. The mound rose some twenty-five or thirty feet and then flattened out at the top in a triangular area about twenty feet across at its widest. A line of trees ran down the hill, and two boulders sat near the narrowing point of the triangle, but otherwise it seemed that Corb had led us all to a dead end. Corb positioned himself between the pair of identical rocks, large and moss-covered, and I half expected him to lift one of the boulders and hurl it into the nearest bat wheeling around the hilltop. Instead the arbutus dropped to his knees and plunged his hands into the earth.

And the boulders blinked.

Not that the rocks opened and closed previously unseen eyes on their faces, but each boulder split along a horizontal line and revealed the huge, dark orb within. The ground beneath our feet, which was overgrown flesh and bone, pitched and shifted as the colossus responded to Corb's touch. The hilltop rose, rearing up and shedding clods of soil and a few small ferns. I grabbed hold of one of the young trees growing out of the spine to keep myself upright as the surface undulated, and watched Juvie, Phoebe and Mabonnyn do the same, while Gern flattened herself and braced all four legs.

The hilltop snapped forward, like the tip of a cracking whip, and three bats disappeared from the sky in front of us. The momentum carried us forward, the gargantuan creature surging ahead through the forest along a serpentine path. The bats furiously beat their wings and their baleful shrieks chased us, but they were left behind as we were carried along on a rumbling green wave.

Eventually I felt steady enough to let go of the tree bracing me and cross over to Corb's side. As always his sludgy features were hard to read, but it seemed to me that he was concentrating without expending too strenuous an effort. I didn't think talking to him posed too great a risk of calamitous distraction. "Did you know that this sachamama was nearby, or did we just get incredibly lucky?"

"Forest provides," Corb answered. It was something my mother would have said, something she had said countless times when I was growing up, the closest thing to a creed of druidic philosophy that could be distilled into a few words. Living in harmony with nature, understanding that the green backdrop to everything was worthy of both protection and deep understanding, led in turn to reaping its bountiful abundance. The difference between my mother and me was that I knew the forest provided a lot but I also knew there would always be gaps I'd need to fill for myself. My mother had unshakable faith that the forest would provide everything, always. If it wasn't provided, she didn't need it. Corb apparently lived by the same tenets.

"You saved us," I told him. "We're all in your debt. Or, if you thought you were in ours, I'd say the scales are more than balanced."

"No," Corb said.

"Yes, really," I insisted. "I'm pretty sure the others would agree with me, but believe me, I owe you one."

"Have not saved you," Corb said. "Have not saved anything. Bats follow still."

"You bought us some time," I said. "That's all we've been doing all along. Trying to stay one step ahead. That's all we can do."

Corb considered this, then asked, "Know you of banniks and moon of rot?"

"I know banniks," I said. They were denizens of the Deep Woods who tended to congregate around natural hot springs, with occasional sightings around the saunas or hot houses of farms and rural villages. About the size of dwarfs or goblins, they were basically benign and mostly kept to themselves. "Not sure about the moon of rot."

"Rot came to the eyes of banniks, long long ago," Corb said. "Morning after the full moon a bannik woke blind. The next, two woke blind. The next, ten. Banniks left pool, fled from rotting eyes. Night passed and day dawned and the rot was gone. But next morning after the full moon, one bannik woke blind. The next two. Banniks fled again. Over and over from one full moon to the next."

"All right, I get it," I said. "Running away doesn't solve anything. But we're not just running away, we're..."

"Banniks realized they should never have left their warm waters," Corb went on as if I hadn't said anything. "By then, all banniks were blind. Tried to find pool by smell, by sound. Could not."

"I said, I get it," I repeated.

"Warm waters had changed to mud pot while banniks were gone," Corb continued. "No tending of banks, no warding of springs. Pool was no more. Banniks home was no more."

I decided that saying for a third time that I got it wouldn't accomplish much, so I kept quiet. If there was a twist in the story about how the banniks could have handled the crisis which would apply brilliantly to the situation we were currently in, I'd be happy to hear it.

Instead Corb asked, "How long will you seek Foltchain?"

"As long as it takes," I answered automatically.

"While the Deep Woods ails without cease," Corb said.

"Well that's the point, isn't it?" I asked, trying in my frustration not to blow up at a giant lump of pitch. My mother was missing, and I had to find her, no matter what. Because she had left Phoebe in the lurch, we all assumed she was being held somewhere against her will, in some building the Derryth and the dragonflies had been able to sketch the outlines of. Once we found her, and by implication rescued her, that would be that. "It's certainly not going to cease if we don't find her."

"Or if all is lost by the time she is found," Corb said.

"We still have to try," I said, but even to my own

ears I sounded like a stubborn child.

Corb allowed a few moments of wordless quiet to spin out, as the sachamama's movement made the wind rush past us and created a crackling whisper of breaking brush and branches below. "Foltchain may restore wholeness to the Deep Woods. Or may be found too late. Or…"

"Or?"

"Son of Foltchain may restore. Now," Corb said.

It had been a long time since anyone had brought up the fact that, on the day I was born, I had been deemed my mother's inheritor, her bloodline successor in the druidic priesthood. And even though I had cast off those expectations long ago, they still had the power to stun me silent whenever someone brought them up. Being deep in the heart of my mother's domain no doubt added to the weight of Corb's words, too. There was a certain compelling logic in the notion that, in my mother's absence, I should step up and assume her role, defending the Deep Woods on her behalf rather than looking for her so that she could do it. The problem with that logic was that it was entirely hypothetical and assumed as a given that I was the equal of my mother in all ways, an indistinguishable replacement-in-waiting. Which I emphatically wasn't. "I wouldn't even know where to start," I said.

"Make peace with Marra," Corb suggested.

"Marra?" I repeated the name. "Marra Troda? What does she have to do with anything?"

"Make peace," Corb insisted. "Lift the ailment upon the forest."

"No, these… there's no ailment." I was with the arbutus when he said that the Deep Woods was ailing, thanks to the weird things that were wreaking havoc and destruction. But it was sickness only in the metaphorical sense, a fair comparison to the effects of whatever had openly attacked me back in the real world and had been taking control of fauna here. Marra Troda was associated with true sickness, literal plagues and illnesses. "Look, someone, something, has taken my mother and is sending things to stop us from finding her and getting her back. Once my mother is safe, these attacks will stop on their own." Or they should, at any rate, I told myself. There might be some implicit threatening of the abducting party or parties first. Or explicit threatening. Or beating to a pulp to deter and dissuade any future retaliation. Finding my mother was the main objective, and settling accounts with her captors would work itself out in due course.

Corb was looking at me skeptically. "Not simple to stop now," he said. "Harder to stop with each passing hour."

"We'll stop it," I said.

Our pace slowed noticeably, the gusts tugging at my hair becoming a gentle breeze, which I thought was fair since the bats were far behind us. "Would it be asking too much for the sachamama to carry us all the way to the selvage between the Deep Woods and my mother's house?" I asked. "I can ask Mabonnyn to come up here, to show the way."

"Cannot go much further," Corb replied.

I started to ask why, not to argue so much as to just assess the situation, when I noticed the sachamama's head was lowering. The hill-sized skull hit the forest floor as the crawling body came to a halt. Corb leapt down beside the sachamama's head, with me just behind him, followed by Juvie, Phoebe, Mabonnyn and Gern.

The sachamama's head lolled awkwardly to one side. Its eyes were closed again, but its scaly lips were slightly parted. The pointed tip of a bat's wing emerged from the broad aperture. I approached the sachamama with one arm extended and rested my hand on its nose, which elicited no reaction. I braced myself and tried to pry the mouth open farther. Corb and Juvie lent me their arms and in a moment we had the jaws propped apart by several feet.

The remains of the bat tumbled to the grass, no more than the wing to the shoulder and some bloodied fur trailing strings of shredded muscle and sinew. I looked deeper into the sachamama's oral cavity until movement caught my eye. On the roof of the mouth, a pale crystalline cyst was squirming and reshaping itself, spreading tendrils through the pink and red flesh.

"Damn," Juvie breathed out. "I didn't know those things could jump from host to host."

"And yet here we are," I said.

"Poor thing," Phoebe said, appearing beside us. "It was only trying to help us. It had no idea what these things were. We have to help it."

"I get where you're coming from," Juvie said, "but what can we do? We're pressed for time and we don't even know what would help. Do we?"

"Marra knows," Corb said.

"Who?" Juvie asked.

I stepped back, as did Juvie and Corb, and the sachamama's mouth fell shut. I decided that if Corb wasn't going to let it go, we might as well have it all out as a group. "Marra Troda is one of the eminences of the Deep Woods."

"Like royalty?" Juvie asked.

"More like a pagan goddess," Phoebe said. "Immortal sentient beings in charge of different spheres. Marra Troda is the eminence of disease."

"That doesn't sound very fairy tale forest," Juvie said.

"She's more subtext than text in the folklore," Phoebe said. "But think about how many times the fairy tale is about how the king's child falls mysteriously ill and the hero has to go venturing off for the cure. Marra Troda is the might behind the mystery illness."

Unbidden, I thought of the ineffable glamor of Lurria's face, how she had cast her vote at the Council of Ruis for us to be quarantined, just like I had been quarantined to my room the winter I had been so deathly ill, the winter after which the pixie never returned. I shook my head. "Anyway, Corb thinks there's a connection between my mother disappearing and these things chasing us and Marra's sphere, because these things are like a plague on the Deep Woods," I explained.

"This cannot be the work of Marra Troda," Mabonnyn said.

"I agree," I said. "We didn't find my mother in some fevered swoon. Diseases don't generally abduct people."

"If Marra were behind all this, then it's not like we could go to her for help," Phoebe said. "And if she's not, then she's not any more likely to know what's going on than any of us, or anyone else in the Deep Woods."

"But if she's not the one behind it," Juvie countered, "then maybe she's got some skin in the game, because someone is messing with what's supposed to be her area, right?"

I snorted. "It's like a plague. Like. Superficially similar. Marra doesn't care about some parallel analogy…"

"Kellan," Juvie interrupted. "Dude. It's not an analogy. It's a legit sickness. All the creatures with the spikes growing out of them are infected hosts with physical and behavioral symptoms. Right?" He looked around at Phoebe and Mabonnyn for support; both of them nodded agreement.

He made a reasonable point, I had to admit it. I had been thinking of everything in terms of the mythical nature of the Deep Woods, seeing the creatures as vessels of something like demonic possession, but it fit the profile of biological disease just as well. Maybe better.

"All right," I said. "The plague is literal, but still not… it's just not Marra Troda's style. Where does that leave us?"

"You said she's like something out of a fairy tale," Juvie said. "When there's more than one villain, they get played against each other, right? So we go to this Marra and tell her what we know, and she tells us what she knows, and maybe we sic her on whatever's controlling these things, or maybe she sics us on them. Doesn't really matter either way, does it? And maybe she helps out the turf snake here, too, while she's at it, just out of sheer spite because nothing is supposed to sicken the Deep Woods critters except her, right?. If it's not too late by the time we get to her, that is."

"Sheer size is a pretty good defense right now," Phoebe said. "It's gonna be a while before the infection spreads through the sachamama enough to take it over. And it won't take us long to get to Marra Troda."

"She just happens to live right around here?" Juvie asked. "Or are we banking on our girl Gern here knowing a shortcut?"

"Marra lives everywhere," Corb said. "Only need be found."

Juvie raised a skeptical eyebrow and I interceded. "Eminences aren't really tied to a specific place like the name trees," I said. "If we're meant to find her, we'll just come across her before too long."

In the interest of hedging our bets, Mabonnyn began to lead us out of the Deep Woods, which was less a matter of retracing the steps of our journey so far and more finding a liminal area where the mycelial dreams of the trees verged on the space we thought of as the real world, specifically on the stretch of green where my mother's cottage stood. I knew from experience that the woods behind my mother's house contained multitudes of entrances to the Deep Woods, each connecting to the primordial forest at far-flung locations completely unrelated to earthly geography. The harrier astride his bullfrog was tasked with locating the nearest of those points, which was slightly trickier than navigating toward a fixed point like the Derryth, but still well within Mabonnyn's capabilities.

We left the sachamama where it lay, having no other viable options since we lacked a lowboy hitched to a tractor trailer and the sachamama was incapable of moving on its own. Corb, Juvie, Phoebe and I followed our woodlander guide through the Deep Woods, each of us quiet. Juvie's limp was gone, Phoebe's strength was at least partially renewed, and we were surrounded by lustrous greenery dotted with colorful blooms, a murmur of animal contentment sounding on all sides. All the same there was a pall over us, a sense that we had already traveled far and been pushed to our limits with the hardest, most dangerous of tasks, with the least certainty to succeed, still ahead of us.

"Something is watching us," Juvie said quietly.

"Yeah that's pretty much always the vibe around here," I answered.

"Not just the vibe," Juvie said, staring at the ground and barely moving his lips. "Eyes in the trees, man."

I stared at Gern's backside, but paid more attention to my peripheral vision, and soon found Juvie was right. Yellow eyes set in mottled green faces peered through the leaves at us as we passed through the woods.

"Goblins," Phoebe said.

"Looking for a fight?" Juvie asked.

"If they were, they would have started one already," Phoebe answered. Like Juvie, she kept her voice low and her head down.

"She's right," I said. "Probably dispatched by Weegth to keep an eye on us."

"I thought we got away from those guys when they decided not to follow us into the Undergrowth," Juvie said. "How did they know we were back?"

"News travels fast," Phoebe said. "Especially when you rouse a sachamama. But Weegth wouldn't send her goblins just to keep an eye on us. They haven't attacked, they're probably not going to… but why?"

"Because they think they don't have to," I said. I scanned a bit farther ahead of us and saw what looked like a drop-off of the forest floor. Gern stopped when she reached it, and the rest of us soon drew even with the harrier and the bullfrog at the top of a long, gradual downward incline. The bottom of the small valley was covered in low, sprawling shrubs, which even from atop the slope we could see had prickly star-shaped leaves, with stems and branches covered in yellow thorns. In the midst of the spiny shrubbery was a well with low stone walls, its interior an impenetrable black.

"Marra Troda," Mabonnyn announced.

"A hole?" Juvie asked. "She literally lives in a hole?"

"When it suits her," Phoebe said. I knew Phoebe was just being honest, and not deliberately cryptic, but I imagined how crazy it might sound to Juvie. He held his tongue, though.

"All right, let's go then," I said. We set off down the hillside. I looked back over my shoulder once, about halfway down, and saw a dozen bulbous, bow-legged goblins lined up where we had been standing before. None of them were as large as Weegth, but like her they wore black rags and assorted golden decorations. They held crude weapons, too, mostly long knives and hatchets with worn, nicked blades, and two holding short bows. One of the goblins nocked an arrow and trained it on me, but another goblin raised a clawed green hand. The second goblin wore more gold than the others and presumably stood in command, and the first goblin lowered the bow. The leader of the goblins stared down at me and gave me a leering grin, seemingly perfectly content to watch us march down to the abode of Marra Troda, eminence of disease, killer of an untold million million living things in the Deep Woods. No need to waste an arrow on the doomed.

Corb cleared a path for us through the pricking leaves and branches, which did little to the gelatinous pitch that made up the arbutus's body. Up close, the fruits of the shrubs were visible, red and white swirled spheres that resembled nothing so much as swollen boils. An unpleasant smell hung in the air at the bottom of the valley, the rancid tang of sepsis. At first it seemed to be coming from the plants, like some kind of defense mechanism warding away predatory insects and birds with a foul, death-mimicking miasma. But the closer we drew to the shaft sunk into the earth, the stronger the stink became, and by the time we were able to peer down into the depths the stench was eye-watering.

"I didn't think there could be a worse smell than that Undergrowth swamp," Juvie said, as we carefully picked our way through the narrow passage Corb opened before us . "But I didn't say anything, because I figured, why tempt fate?"

"You think this is bad, wait until we get all the way down the hole," Phoebe said.

"I have to imagine at some point in our encounter with the death goddess, the smell is going to be the least of my worries," Juvie said.

"Not a death goddess," I said.

"Eminence, whatever," Juvie said. "My comparative religion class started at 8:00 a.m., usually without me, sorry I misidentified a non-goddess."

"Not death, either," I said. "Disease."

"What's the difference?" Juvie asked.

By then we had reached the well, which the star-leaf shrubs naturally gave a wide enough berth for all of us to stand around it. The bare earth encircling the bleak aperture was gray and dusty, a mingling of black rot and white salt. The low perimeter of stones were actually, on closer examination, irregular chunks of gray scum that seemed to have flaked off of something in the early stages of decomposing. "Take a look," I said.

Juvie stared at the boundary wall, bent at the waist to inspect it, and jerked backwards violently. "Maggots. Gross," he said, then turned to me.

"What's your point? Don't maggots feed on dead things?"

"They do," I said. "But they're living things, themselves. Just like a lot of diseases are living things. Some are just systems breaking down from age or something toxic in the environment, but your classic plagues are really microorganisms doing their own thing."

"All right, fine, point taken," Juvie said, adding with an involuntary shudder, "We have to go through maggots to get down there, don't we?"

"Fraid so."

"Be not afraid," Mabonnyn said, urging Gern forward. The bullfrog sprang up over the well and dove into its depths. A couple of seconds later, Mabonnyn's voice floated up from below ground. "It is not so long a drop, perhaps two hundred feet or less. The inner surface is uneven, with many handholds."

Corb followed the harrier and his mount into the gaping maw, his loose limbs allowing him to smoothly lower himself out of sight. Juvie sighed, "All right, good thing I'm up to date on all my shots," and made his own way into the shaft. I gestured to Phoebe, watched her disappear down the well, and then started my own descent.

As the circle of sky above my head shrank, the thick odor of putrescence had me breathing through my mouth while my glottis tried to plug up my nose from the inside. I concentrated on finding the small shelves of decaying plant and animal matter that could support my feet without crumbling, the rocks that I could grip despite the layer of slime adhering to them. I thought about my mother all the while, and her relationship with Marra Troda. They weren't exactly enemies, though they did sometimes find themselves at cross purposes. I hadn't been lying when I had explained to Juvie that disease was not just an obstacle to life but life itself. The druidic tradition has always been the stewardship of life in harmonious balance, predator and prey and parasite, from humans and faeries to trees and flowers, megafauna to microbes. And everything dies, a truth without which life would never be able to properly thrive. Living diseases might be a cause of death, but almost every other living thing encompasses the potential to end life as well. The biggest distinction between Marra Troda and Foltchain of the Oak was never death versus life, but excess versus restraint. A plague that wipes out an entire population doesn't perpetuate the cycle of life, it terminates it. And once that whole mass of people or pixies or pine trees or whatever is wiped out, the disease dies off as well. Unchecked epidemics are ultimately self-defeating.

Not that pathogens are able to listen to reason, from either a priestess or an eminence, which was why Marra Troda was the steward of nostrums as well as diseases. She was capricious, and indifferent to suffering, but not a death goddess working towards extinction. That was why I had been willing to seek her out, for whatever good it might do one sachamama, or my mother. In the end, there's no arguing with death. There's almost no arguing with the incarnate manifestation of diseases and their redress, either, but the difference between almost none and none was crucial.

The bottom of the well was blessedly dry. It shouldn't have been a surprise, since I supposed Mabonnyn would have warned us if Gern had landed in a deep pool of infectious yellow pus, but I felt a grateful relief all the same. I kept breathing shallowly through my mouth, but I could still feel how mephitic the air was. The subterranean space was dark, and I drew the Derryth leaf out of my pocket. The silvery underside glowed with pale light, not much more than a cellphone screen but more than enough to reveal our immediate surroundings and allow us to move forward without stumbling blindly. I moved in a circle around the bottom of the wall and found a gap in the earthen wall.

I turned back to the others. "Looks like I go this way. Anybody wants to wait here, I'll understand."

"Why do you even keep asking that?" Phoebe said as she moved to join me, with Juvie on her heels and Corb, Mabonnyn and Gern following them.

I led the group into the tunnel. I kept my eyes down, watching every step I took, only occasionally stealing glances at the walls to make sure nothing caught me by surprise. The tunnel was like a hollowed out tumor, uneven with excessive and abnormal outgrowths. I wove around blood-red craters and tried not to brush against purple lesions pushing through the surface surrounding us. There were more maggots, and fleas, and rats, and clusters of black scab fungus, and incomplete sets of disarticulated bones. We pushed through it all.

The tunnel widened into a cavern, where in the

far corners low peat fires smoldered with dull orange light that cast sharp black shadows on the walls. The cavern was a wider and taller version of the tunnel we had followed and barren except for a stone the size of a bed, or a coffin, in the middle of the floor. Tapestries of spiderwebs fluttered in the upper corners. A buzzing sound echoed all around us, growing steadily louder, and then an insect alighted directly before us. Its gray exoskeleton was dusted with ivory bristles, its clear wings marked with dark horizontal bisecting bands, horn-like orange and black antennae mounted between compound eyes with rorschach patterns of red, gold and blue. It was unmistakably a deer fly, the only reason to doubt it the fact that it was monstrously gigantic, the size of an industrial dump truck. It separated its mouth parts, opening them like the wicked blades of a titanic pair of scissors.

"I've been meaning to cut back on sleep," Juvie said, "this nightmare fuel should definitely help."

The deer fly's mouth snapped shut, opened again for a second or two longer, closed again. It skittered backwards, gnashed its mandibles as fruitlessly as before, and took flight, swooping through the darkness overhead and disappearing into some unseen recess.

"That was… confusing," Phoebe said.

"For us, or for it?" Juvie asked.

"Both," I said. I stepped forward, walking to the upraised stone in the middle of the cavern. In the barely illuminated space, the formation appeared to be a solid low-domed mass of black shadow and dull red reflection, as if a low, wide boulder had been only partially fashioned into a squared off plinth. But as I drew closer I could see that the upper half of the shape was not a continuation of the stone at all. It was the back of Marra Troda, recumbent and unmoving.

The behemoth deer fly landed in front of me, as gracefully as a distressed helicopter, blocking my progress toward Marra Troda. I stopped, and held up my hands, while the deer fly twitched its mandibles. This was without question the deer fly's turf, and I was the intruder. I didn't want to hurt the sentinel, which was only acting out of instinctive fidelity to its eminent mistress, and even if I had wanted to, I wasn't terribly confident that I could. But more than that, I didn't think I needed to, because I didn't believe the deer fly wanted to hurt me. I knew it was a bit of misguided anthropomorphizing to think in terms of the deer fly wanting anything, but it felt true nonetheless.

The deer fly jabbed one of its front legs at me. I stepped back out of the way as the curved tarsal claws and spiny spurs hissed through the corrupt air between us. The deer fly jerked its leg back, and gnashed its mouthparts uselessly once more. The creature was confused, because its demesne was unbalanced, because something was wrong with the eminence of that demesne. The deer fly was torn between its proclivity to defend Marra Troda and an equal desire to see things set back to rights.

I took a tentative step forward. The deer fly buzzed angrily, but took a stuttering step backwards with each of its six legs. I took another step. The deer fly lurched forward so quickly I jumped back, lost my footing on the slimy chamber floor, and fell on my back. The deer fly straddled me. I gritted my teeth and sat up. The deer fly retreated slightly. I got to my feet and stepped close enough to the deer fly that I could have plucked a bristle from its proboscis. It backed up. I advanced, and the deer fly bobbed its head, like a bull readying to charge, but I continued slowly, step by step, as the creature warred with itself.

And then I was even with the stone, and Marra Troda, and the deer fly could not forestall me any longer. It flew off, leaving me alone with its mistress.

Marra Troda had always been described to me as an imposing gargoyle, gray-pallored and large-boned with sagging folds of cracked, scabrous skin. Her feet and hands were slightly oversized, the fingers short and thick. Her head was bald, her face broad and flat with full lips twisted into a permanent pained grimace, her eyes bulbous and jaundiced. The very picture of unwellness, in other words, without in any way resembling frailty herself. Lying on the plinth of stone in her cavern, she still did not appear frail, but her stillness was disquieting. I had heard tell of her restlessness, her constant state of perturbation, scratching at her pitted hide while stomping in agitated circles or rocking queasily back and forth.

I walked around the flat rock formation to look her in the face. Her lips were parted slightly and her eyes were wide but sightless, not with the dull opacity of true death but the burnished glassiness of catatonia. She smelled like an open plague pit, a noxious cloud of ruination clinging to her, but as far as I knew that was her usual noisome aura. I wasn't entirely sure that Marra Troda could die, or what it would mean for the Deep Woods or the nature of reality as we know it if she did, but this depth of reverie didn't strike me as great news, either.

"What's the word, Kellan?" Juvie called out. He and the others had remained close to the mouth of the tunnel, no doubt ready to retreat into its relative safety if the colossal deer fly had ripped me limb from limb and then turned on the rest of them.

"I don't think we're in any danger here," I answered. "Marra's servants will let us be because they don't know what else to do. She's not telling them what she wants them to do. She's not telling anybody anything." That drew the others from the tunnel toward the plinth. They gathered around me, all of us looking down into Marra Troda's immobile mien. Juvie moved as if he meant to reach out and shake Marra's shoulder, but I barred him with one arm. "I wouldn't do that," I advised.

"So then what do we do now?" Juvie asked.

"Well, we don't make peace with the mother of malady," I said. "Sorry, Corb. It was a reasonable thought, but it doesn't look like Marra is pulling the strings on any of this. Unless she was betrayed by her co-conspirators, but how dumb and self-serving would you have to…" I trailed off.

"Peace still must be made," Corb insisted. "Now on Marra's behalf, not with her accord."

"Easier said than done," Phoebe said.

"Gah," I said. "Gah gah gah gah gah. I know what's going on. I get it. Well, some of it. I think. Come on, we have to go." I was already circling around the plinth toward the tunnel.

"What about the sachamama?" Phoebe asked.

I halted in my tracks and clapped my hands together. "Right. Sorry." My mind was racing as I surveyed the room and quickly crossed to one of the peat fires. A beaten iron bowl sat in the center of the banked embers, smoke rising from its contents. On the floor around the fire were scattered pieces of debris, brittle plant stems and the headless, desiccated bodies of centipedes and hairy spiders. "This might help," I said.

"How can you be sure?" Mabonnyn asked.

"I can't be, not a hundred percent," I admitted. "But it tracks. If this is all connected, whatever's been hunting us through the Deep Woods because we're looking for my mom, and whatever put Marra Troda into that swoon, then maybe Marra was trying to make something that would counteract the effect, which means it would work on the sachamama too. It's the only thing really cooking around here, and it's almost burned down to nothing, so it's all we've got."

"All right, antidote away," Juvie said, "and fingers crossed it works on our... dote? Prodote? What the hell is 'antidote' supposed to be the opposite of anyway?" Juvie said.

"Idiot," Phoebe muttered, although weirdly I thought she sounded more amused than annoyed.

"We just have to figure out how to get it out of here," I said, eyeing the hazy nimbus of superheated air around the iron vessel.

Corb came to me in a couple of long strides, reached down and lifted the bowl out of the fire.

The pitch of the arbutus's hands sizzled against the heat of the iron, but Corb made no complaint. "You seek Foltchain now?"

"That's right," I nodded. "I think I've got a better idea of where to look and what might be waiting for us there."

"Go, then," Corb said. He hefted the smudge pot meaningfully. "Sachamama will receive ministration from me."

"Thanks," I said. We left the cavern, the sounds of stridulation echoing after us in the tunnel still sounding forlorn and lost.

True to his word, Corb parted ways with us once we had all climbed back up the shaft to the valley floor. The arbutus quickly made an egress through the choke of thorny, star-leafed plants and climbed up the valley wall to return to the place where we had left the ailing sachamama. The rest of us followed the trail he had flattened before the spiny branches could spring back up like razorwire in our path, until we reached the clear grass of the valley floor.

Phoebe scanned the sides of the valley. "Looks like the goblins gave up on us."

"Just as well," I said. "Mabonnyn, how quickly can you get us out of here?"

"Gern is as fleet as any mount in the Deep Woods," the harrier assured me. "Can you keep the pace she sets?"

I looked at Juvie and Phoebe. They looked as tired as I felt, but they both gave resolute nods. I turned back to Mabonnyn and said, "Just lead the way."

Gern was off like a shot and Juvie, Phoebe and I ran after the bullfrog and rider. We scaled the sides of the valley and dashed through the forest, heedless of the attention our crashing might draw. I suspected I would probably have to explain myself a bit more to Phoebe and Juvie, but that could wait until we were back at my mother's house, where we could catch our breath in every sense of the word and plan our next steps. On and on we ran to reach that destination, sometimes following nothing more than flashes of Gern's bright green hide through the staggered boles.

At one point, the bullfrog paused, and Mabonnyn look back to make sure we were still within sight. The ground was becoming more and more uneven and rocky, and through the trees ahead could just barely be seen a vertical plane of basalt. Gern had stopped at what looked like the mouth of a tunnel, in truth one end of an enormous, hollowed-out fallen treetrunk. The timber pipe was canted upward, and I realized the far end must come out at the top of the elevated section of the forest. Once Mabonnyn confirmed that we were following, rider and mount disappeared into the bole.

The path through the toppled tree's empty heart was steep, yet somewhat easier than the floor of the Deep Woods, straight and relatively smooth compared to zigzagging through riots of long grass and turbulent sprays of creepers and natural speed bumps of old roots kinking up through the earth. The enclosed space was dark, as well, although near the top of the incline a crack in the bark allowed some light to enter, along with other small pieces of Deep Woods detritus. A sapling, no more than six inches tall, had managed to grow up there in the patch of light inside the hollow tree. I almost stepped past it, but stopped myself. I dropped to one knee and gently worked the sapling loose, breaking and scraping away some of the periderm with my fingers. I carried the sapling up out of the tunnel, and looked for a place to transplant it on the elevated surface we had reached.

Eventually, the tree tunnel would have rotted enough to collapse. The sapling would have been buried under its remains and died. Moving the sapling now didn't guarantee its survival, but it gave it a better chance. Moving the sapling was something my mother would have done without even thinking about it, if she had chanced upon it like I had. It was something I did because my mother was all I had been thinking about for days.

Eventually Gern slowed her relentless bounding to more measured hops, and described the arc of a half-circle, back and forth, as we closed the distance. I could sense the subtle difference in the air, the rustling of the surrounding leaves and the yielding of the ground beneath my feet. We were close to the edge of the Deep Woods, a space where the worlds were close enough to bridge from one to the other. Mabonnyn pointed toward a nearby black walnut tree, not a name tree but still old and stately enough to command respect. The soil around it was dry and bare, with a scattering of broken black shells. "Make your way round yonder tree, keep your backs to it, and you should find the weg to Foltchain's abode."

"So this is goodbye?" Juvie asked. "You're not coming with us?"

"My place is in the Deep Woods," Mabonnyn said. "My task was to guide the son of Foltchain through my home, to find the druid priestess, or find what he could of her whereabouts. If the search now leads you out of this forest, I wish you every boon. But I can guide you no further."

"We may not need a guide any longer," Phoebe said, "but we could use all the help we can get."

Mabonnyn inclined his head to her deferentially. "My prowess within the Deep Woods is far greater than outside of it. I might prove to be not at all the help you need."

"Still," Phoebe said, and the entreaty hung in the air. I thought there was something in her voice like longing, a hunger for some familiar comfort of home. I couldn't blame her, but I didn't think awkwardly dragging out the farewells would help any of us.

"You have fulfilled your task with honor, and you have our thanks," I said. "My mother's, as well."

"I am sure I will see Foltchain of the Oak again soon," Mabonnyn said. "I look forward to it, knowing I have acquitted myself well in your eyes."

Gern gave a loud croak to send us on our way, and Juvie, Phoebe and I turned toward the black walnut. An immense brake fern, a riot of narrow green leaves spraying up and cascading down, stood at the edge of the bare ground surrounding the tree. Juvie pushed aside part of the wall of fronds to walk past it, and nearly tripped to the forest floor. He recovered in a half-lunge and looked back at his left leg. "Caught on something," he told us. He tried to disentangle the limb, which remained stubbornly snagged.

Phoebe sighed and squatted down beside his left foot. "All right, hold still," she admonished, pushing aside more of the brake to see how he had been trapped. She suddenly let go and cried out in equal parts pain and alarm as her body jerked forward, as if something had yanked on her arm.

I grabbed Phoebe from behind, under her arms, and pulled her up and away from the base of the brake. A slender, pale green strand was wrapped around her right wrist, anchoring her to the ground, and over her shoulder I could see a similar whiplike tendril snaking around the lower part of Juvie's left leg, creeping higher and higher and wrapping itself more and more tightly with every passing second. The ribbons of green were covered in hairs like teeth, already raising red welts on Phoebe's skin and trying to tear through Juvie's cargo pants.

I shoved my fingers between the tendril and Phoebe's arm. The grasping coil was sticky and the hairs stung like needles, and the surface was feverishly warm, but the green part was clearly a leaf, and I tried to rip it apart to free Phoebe's arm. It tore up my palm like hell, and unfortunately it didn't affect the hungering plant at all. It was like trying to tear a rawhide thong one-handed. I was a heartbeat away from trying again with both hands when Gern bounded to my side and Mabonnyn sliced the tendril in half with one swift knife blow. Phoebe spun and staggered away.

Half a dozen more hairy tendrils burst out from under the brake as the severed leaf retracted. One wrapped around Phoebe's waist, two snared me by my left forearm and right upper arm, two more clutched at Gern's back legs and the last one hooked around Mabonnyn's neck and snatched the harrier off the bullfrog's back. Mabonnyn stabbed at the fanged shoot but the stalk thrashed so wildly that the woodlander could scarcely tell up from down.

I stomped on the tendril holding my right arm, pinning it to the ground and then raising my arm to rip the shoot apart. My skin burned where the keen teeth bit into my biceps, drawing trickles of blood, but I managed to get a tear started through the heart of the serpentine leaf. The grip on my arm lost a good bit of its strength, and I slid the coil off my arm, then repeated the process on the other tendril shackling me.

Phoebe was rolling on the ground, trying to extricate herself from the lash around her midsection and looking like she was close. Juvie, on the other hand, had gotten his own green garotte and was struggling to breathe. Mabonnyn was still being scourged in midair and striking blindly back at the ravening plant, and Gern was straining against her bonds to reach her rider. I decided to help Juvie.

I tackled Juvie to the ground and wriggled my fingers under the leaf noose constricting his windpipe. With my other hand I felt around for anything hard and heavy. My fingers brushed a mossy rock and I clawed it out of the dirt, then smashed it down on the choking tendril again and again until there was nothing but a chlorophyll stain. I gave the same treatment to the tendril cinched around Juvie's leg, then rolled him away from the brake as fast as I could.

It wasn't fast enough. More tendrils rose up, more than a dozen, lashing themselves around ankles, knees, elbows, wrists and shoulders to completely immobilize Juvie and Phoebe and me. A single biting leaf stole around both of Mabonnyn's legs, binding them together, and pulled the lower half of the harrier's body in one direction while the leaf around Mabonnyn's neck wrenched the opposite way, threatening to tear our erstwhile guide in half.

Gern gave a throaty, bellowing squawk and exerted herself against the leaves enmeshed in her mottled skin. With abrupt swiftness, Gern pulled loose and leapt for Mabonnyn. Gern's back right leg was torn off, and gouts of amphibian blood poured like dark rain from the ragged socket as the bullfrog soared through the air. An instant later Mabonnyn was on the ground, nestled below Gern's puffed out chest like a baby chick beneath a brooding hen. Gern's front flippers mashed the tendrils flat to the earth, and Mabonnyn's knife made short work of the two carnivorous stipules. I was as happy as I could be for the woodlander, given that I was still bedeviled by my own handful of slashing leaves.

A thunderous impact shook the forest floor, announcing Corb's arrival. The arbutus was immediately assailed by spiny stalks, but ignored them as they oozed deep into the viscous pitch of his frame. Corb reached the brake fern and uprooted it in one uninterrupted motion, tossing the plant aside. The plant that had hidden beneath it was revealed, a gorgon roridula. All of the tooth-edged leaf blades radiated from a central root, the shoots shading from pale green to deep crimson where they met the main stem. Sepulchral white cysts, jagged and crystalline, breached the base of the leaves.

Corb heaved on the roridula, which held fast to the ground more tenaciously than the brake. Mabonnyn moved in a slicing, gashing flurry, carving a path through the toothy leaves to separate Juvie, Phoebe and me from the plant's clutches. Finally the harrier arrived beside Corb and stabbed the center of the roridula's starburst of leaves. The entire green mass convulsed, and Corb unmoored it from the soil. He lobbed the roridula to the middle of the arid expanse around the black walnut, where it twitched and writhed. Corb sank an arm into the shallow pit left behind and drew out an anvil-sized boulder. He walked to the gorgon roridula and dropped the stone weight on the midsection of the plant.

Juvie, Phoebe and I extricated the bisected leaves from our savaged flesh, but none of us made a sound of protest. We were looking at Mabonnyn and Gern, as the rider knelt beside the bullfrog. Gern was lying flat, her wide chin resting on the grass, her large eyes almost completely shut. The bloody stump where her leg had been was surrounded by raging blisters and welts, impressions of the roridula's teeth. The wound itself was no longer spurting blood, but the pool of crimson staining the ground had already spread wide. Mabonnyn rested one hand gently atop Gern's head. The bullfrog's sides hitched and quivered with shallow, rapid breaths as the woodlander stroked her skin. Then the movements stopped, and the eyelids lowered fully, and Gern was still.

Mabonnyn's back arched and a howl of exquisite outrage and wretched grief burst from the woodlander's lips, echoing through the Deep Woods until it became hoarse and strangled and then silent.

We built two separate fires, because it seemed wrong to combine the two necessities. First Juvie and I burned the gorgon roridula, with a small fire using walnut shells and twigs and dry grass for kindling. Once it was started, Corb lifted the boulder off the wounded plant and relocated it to the flames, where it burned and shriveled. Then the arbutus joined Phoebe and Mabonnyn, who were gathering larger pieces of wood for a proper funeral pyre, while Juvie and I stood watch over the roridula.

"I don't think it's going anywhere," Juvie said once most of the tendrils had been reduced to blackened char. "Should we go help Mabonnyn?"

"I don't think so," I said. "This feels more right. Gern was a creature of the Deep Woods, just like the rest of them. You and I are the outsiders. They have their job, this is ours."

"If you say so," Juvie said.

The others didn't really need our help anyway, as they quickly had the bier laid in, running east to west, and Corb placed Gern's lifeless body in the center with her head facing to the west. The harrier had gathered some votive offerings to lay beside Gern in the pyre; I saw a snail shell, a pair of beetle's wings, and a bundle of meadow saffron, flowers emblematic of reluctant separation. After nestling those grave goods beside Gern, Mabonnyn untied the knife sheath from its place in the woodlander's boot and laid the sheath beside the bullfrog. Phoebe got the fire started, aided by the traces of flammable sap that Corb had left behind on several of the branches, and the orange tongues soon leapt up through the structure to consume the deceased and the grave goods.

The fire for the roridula burned out first, and Juvie and I kicked it apart, scattering the ashes. We drifted over to Phoebe and stood as part of the silent vigil watching Gern's cremation. I put my hands in my pockets, and felt the single leaf of the Derryth that I had been carrying. I pulled it out, spinning the stem between my fingers, swirling the deep green and pale silver. Oak leaves symbolize many things, one of which was saving a life in battle. I took a step closer to the pyre and tossed the leaf into the flames. The leaf fluttered through the convection currents as if of its own accord and landed perfectly on the crown of Gern's head.

When the larger blaze had burned down to embers, Mabonnyn moved in front of me, holding my gaze with a look of pure flint. "Son of Foltchain," the woodlander intoned, "I shall remain by your side for as long as it takes, until those who abducted the revered druid priestess and killed my faithful mount are no more." The last three words were as heavy as the tolling of mourning bells.

"We'll avenge Gern, I promise," I said. "You don't have to…"

Mabonnyn held up a silencing hand. The harrier turned to the ashes of the pyre and thrust a hand into the ash. Mabonnyn held up a palm smeared with dark cinders, and clapped the hand over lips, chin and cheeks, leaving the lower face branded with a black imprint. There would be no further argument.

"Would join you, too," Corb said.

"The sachamama is going to be all right?" Phoebe asked.

Corb grunted assent. "The preparation from Marra Troda did as you hoped."

"You didn't happen to keep any extra for us, just in case?" Juvie asked.

"No extra," Corb said, which none of us doubted.

"All right," I said, looking back at the black walnut tree. "If we're all in, then let's go."

Chapter Ten: Preparations

The five of us walked out of the Deep Woods and into the backyard of my mother's cottage just as the sun was setting. Her humble house still stood, as if nothing were amiss and Foltchain's imminent return were assumed without qualification. I noted the subtle shift in the air as we passed from the hidden arboreal world into the environs I called home, and felt something akin to relief, if only because I knew we were one giant leap closer to rescuing my mom. Corb looked around wonderingly, experiencing for the first time what I had taken for granted long ago. Mabonnyn might have been feeling something similar, but the harrier's steely carriage and expression gave absolutely no indication.

I stopped in the middle of the grass. "There's a

couple of things I need to do," I explained, "and they'll be a lot easier to accomplish quickly and unobtrusively if I do them on my own. Can I leave you all here until I'm ready to proceed?"

Phoebe nodded. "I'm going to have a look in your mother's herbarium. I doubt I'll be so lucky as to find the batch of medicine she was going to give me all ready and waiting, but maybe I can scrounge together something to help me get through whatever comes next."

"Sounds good," I said. "Corb, stick with her. Juvie, you take Mabonnyn inside and see if you can find anything that might make a good weapon for either of you. Whoever finishes up first, go huddle up with the others. I don't want any of us to be isolated for any longer than necessary."

"Except you," Juvie said.

"Like I said, not any longer than necessary," I said. Phoebe and Corb cut across the yard to the herbarium, and I led Juvie and Mabonnyn into the cottage. I went to my mother's room and retrieved my phone and both Juvie's keys and my own, then left the others to ransack mom's kitchen wares and gardening implements at will. In less than a minute I was behind the wheel and speeding back to the city.

I drove very irresponsibly, especially considering it was Juvie's car, going over the speed limit with one eye on the road and one eye on my phone's browser as I looked up some likely candidates for the building the dragonflies had shown us. Fortunately it didn't take long to zero in on what I thought was the right address. I tossed the phone to the passenger seat and accelerated, making a beeline for my apartment.

I ran upstairs and into my place, back to my bedroom where I pulled down a small gun safe from the shelf of my closet. I spun the combination and took out my backup SIG Pro, shoving the gun in my holster with a deeply satisfying slap of leather. The feeling of relief, of having found something missing and having filled some important absence, was short-lived, though. As I gathered up some extra magazines of ammunition I realized that I had both more time to kill and an imperative to keep moving. I couldn't give the creatures stalking us a chance to notice I was home, someplace they had already proven they could access at will, or to zero in on my location if I stood still for too long. Driving around aimlessly making random turns to run out the clock seemed risky as well. What I needed was a fixed destination that was unpredictable.

As I shoved magazines into various pockets of my expedition pants, I felt something already resting against my leg and had a flash of inspiration which sent me sprinting back out of the apartment. I didn't even bother locking the front door, because either I'd be back soon or it truly wouldn't matter that I'd left it unsecured.

I got across town quickly enough, considering that I only committed three or four moving violations, and parked my car in front of a fire hydrant, telling myself I would only be five minutes. I bounded up the front steps of an old brownstone to a front door flanked by huge marble planters overflowing with yellow and orange flowering trefoils and rang the bell.

I was starting to cycle through backup ideas which might come into play if no one was home when the door opened. Ajax Masterson regarded me with a fair amount of suspicion. "Son of Foltchain," he said, "I was not expecting you."

"I know," I said. "Sorry to drop by unannounced. I've got two pieces of urgent business and didn't have time to call ahead."

Masterson blinked, trying extremely hard not to look as caught off guard as he no doubt felt. "I also have pressing matters of my own to attend to," he said, unconvincingly, crossing his arms over his puffed out chest.

"This won't take long," I promised. I reached into my pocket and pulled out the poppet head I had taken from the abandoned witch's hut. I offered it to Masterson. "Will you take this?"

Masterson's hands remained braced on his biceps. "You urgently needed to render an early tribute to me?" he asked.

"Not a tribute," I said. "It's way outside of all that. Just take it. Please."

Still unmoved, Masterson asked, "What is it?"

I had been mentally rehearsing an introduction on my frantic drive over, and I launched into it. "It's a powerful artifact, the head of a sympathetic magic doll. I took it from a very old and very malignant witch in the Otherworld. Every handiwork of her craft is imbued with power undreamt of, and this is the most potent element of one of her most sinister spellworkings. I beseech you, Ajax Masterson, will you receive this fell artifact into your keeping?"

Masterson reached for the poppet head, but his fingertips froze an inch from the rough surface. He regarded me with narrowed eyes as he lowered his hand. "The temptation is great. Your silver tongue does you credit."

"Masterson…"

"But I am not so easily duped!" he raised his voice to drown out my protests. "You seek an escape from the covenant which binds us together, and you see this witch's remnants as the key. You think I will unleash the power within the artifact and it will prove my undoing, and you will then be free. I am not sure which disappoints me more, Son of Foltchain, that you seek my demise through such ungallant trickery and deception, or that you think me such a fool that I would willingly traipse down the primrose path and into your snare."

"Wrong," I said, and I admit I was gratified to see Masterson flinch at the force of my denial. I softened my tone a bit. "You've got it all wrong, Masterson. I'm not trying to slip you a magical timebomb. I'm not out to do you any harm."

"Then the trinket is weak and worthless, and all your admonitions of its potency are lies?" Masterson challenged me.

"You know that's not true," I said. "You can feel how powerful this thing is even without touching it. You know I'm telling the truth about that."

"I know," he said in a husky whisper full of the bittersweet pain of wanting something unattainable. He stared at the poppet head for a moment longer, then returned his gaze to mine. "My own power grows ever stronger with each passing day, but I am not capable of controlling a conduit such as this. Not yet."

"That doesn't matter," I said. Masterson's brow furrowed in confusion again, so I hurried on, "This thing is powerful. And dangerous. Which is exactly why I want you to have it. To keep it safe. To keep it out of the wrong hands. I don't want you to use it. I don't want anyone to use it, and I don't have time right now to take the appropriate precautions against that. So I ask you again, will you receive this fell artifact into your keeping?"

"Why?" Masterson asked. "Why me?"

"Because I trust you." And in a weird way it was true, as true as all the rest. Masterson was a pretentious dilettante and had the potential to become a true threat not only to me but to the world as a whole. But I never thought that he was rotten-to-the-core evil, just a dangerous combination of arrogant and ignorant. Left to his own devices, he'd probably give in to his worst impulses just like any other human being. But if I offered him a little faith and conviction, he might just live up to it. One of us had to start somewhere to break the cycle of mistrust.

"I am unworthy," he said shakily.

"I disagree," I said. "You're the best protection against the calamity inherent in this artifact I can think of. Please, help me. Take it." I stretched my hand toward him.

Masterson finally took the poppet head, rolling it in his palm as if it were a hot coal he needed to keep from burning the flesh of his hand. "I will guard it with every resource at my disposal. I have a warded coffer which shall serve. It was crafted from the wood of an ancient bito tree, planted to honor a powerful pharaoh, and inscribed... "

"Great," I said, cutting off Masterson's recitation of provenance which was probably ninety percent wishful thinking anyway. "And if the temptation gets too great, maybe we can work out another arrangement when I get back…"

"I will not fail you," he broke in.

"Well, good," I said, "because there's also a chance I might not be back. Like, ever. Nothing personal, it's just this other thing I gotta do…"

"Wait!" Masterson said as I tried to leave. "You must allow me to offer you one of my own artifacts in return."

"That's really not necessary," I protested, then pointed to Juvie's car. "And look, I'm kind of parked illegally, so I should really get going."

"I insist," Masterson said. "I have nothing so grandiose as this, of course, but if only as a symbol of my acceptance of the charge, I will not allow you to leave empty-handed to face whatever peril awaits you. I bid you enter my home, with my boon."

I really hadn't been expecting any quid pro quo, unless you counted the possibility of maybe getting Masterson off my back in the future because I had treated him with the respect of an equal. I could have told him that I didn't have time, and he wouldn't have been able to do much to prevent me from leaving, but since we were still establishing our initial level of mutual trust, I went along. I stepped into the brownstone, and Masterson shut the front door. "Wait here," he said.

I was left standing in the foyer, which had wainscoting on the lower halves of the walls and wallpaper above, dark stained wood surmounted by deep green with gray pinstripes that looked like velvet. The wallpaper was only visible in small patches between the various frames and objects mounted on the walls, scraps of scrolls and fractional pages of illuminated manuscripts under glass and ceremonial masks from around the globe. A chandelier of blood red crystals hung overhead, and a plush oriental rug in browns and golds was beneath my feet.

Masterson returned quickly, proffering a small pendant of white stone on a silver chain. The stone was an irregular, fragmentary shape, flecked with green and yellow mineral deposits, and contained most of a bas relief carving of a fanciful creature blending aspects of a lizard and a snake. "I offer you this lare medallion. It invokes a Roman guardian spirit of the home and hearth, and may it guide your safe return," he said gravely. "Will you accept this into your keeping?"

"Sure, totally," I said, taking it. I started to stuff it into my pocket but caught the look of disappointment on Masterson's face. I slipped the chain over my head and turned the pendant so that it laid against my chest with the serpent facing out. "Thank you."

"Blessings be with you, Son of Foltchain," Masterson said, opening the front door for me. I nodded and slipped past him into the night.

As I drove back out of town, I took a slightly circuitous route in order to roll past a specific address. I confirmed my earlier hunch without having to stop the car, and continued on past the city limits out to my mother's property. I arrived just after the full dark of night had fallen.

I found everyone in the living room of my mother's cottage. My mother's interior design aesthetic was spartan and functional in most areas of her house, but she had always valued the ability to offer guests a plush and inviting place to unburden themselves, physically, mentally or otherwise. So while the other rooms in the cottage were somewhat uniform in their oiled wood palette, the living room was a patchwork rumpus of color. The couch had been upholstered in a black, brown and gold plaid, originally, but patched over the years with whatever scraps were handy. Two of the seat cushions had been replaced altogether, so that none of the three were the same height. One of the replacements was burgundy velvet, the other swathed in fabric with a red and orange paisley pattern against a dark blue background. A motley assortment of other pillows reclined against the sagging arms. The two easy chairs opposite the couch did not match it at all, nor did they match each other, except that both were overstuffed, one faded gray and one covered in hot pink faux cowskin. Frayed quilts draped the backs of the chairs and the couch, and a yellow and green rag rug covered the floor, extending beyond the legs of a low coffee table with one fat candle in the center. Battered old stands stood in the corners of the room holding small plants in humble clay pots, specifically chosen for their decorative looks, the way most non-druidic people would. Aside from those green, flowering touches, almost everything in the room had been either bartered goods or a gift to my mother, all of which she had gladly and uncritically accepted in order to make this one corner of the cottage a perfect nest of comfort.

Juvie and Phoebe sprawled at opposite ends of the couch. Mabonnyn stood at attention past the far end of the coffee table, with a hatchet braced head-down before the woodlander. It was a simple hand tool, but my mother kept the steel blade sharp, and compared to the diminutive woodlander it looked like a massive battle axe. Corb sat on the floor between the easy chairs, presumably to avoid getting any pitch stains on the fabric, though he needn't have bothered. My mother might never have noticed and definitely would not have cared. Around the candle were four teacups with damp leaves clinging to their bottoms. I had to assume Phoebe had brewed some for everyone. They all looked to me when I walked in, but no one spoke. I sat in the pink cow seat and took a deep breath, letting it out slowly.

"All done with your secret prelude to the mission?" Phoebe asked.

"Done," I nodded. "Not that it had anything to do with the mission." She had used the word sarcastically, but I repeated it without a trace of irony. "Except in the sense of artificially manipulating the timeline."

"Dude, it's been a long, trippy, constantly-on-the-verge-of-death-and-disaster few days," Juvie said. "Can you skip the cryptic mumbo-jumbo? Because I'm too tired to wade through it right now."

"I went… it doesn't matter where I went. It's not important," I said. "I mean, it was important, but it didn't have anything to do with finding my mother. I chose to do it now to give all of you a little bit of time, to rest and to think. Things got pretty heated there at the edge of the Deep Woods. We were all fired up and freaked out and everybody was ready to charge right past the verge and on into actual death and disaster. I wanted to tap the brakes. Does that make sense?"

Nobody answered me, which I took as silent assent. I went on, "Everyone's caught their breath and had a cup of tea and that's all to the good. So now I can ask everyone to make a decision, when you're all fully capable of doing so. I'm going after my mother, and I can go alone. I wouldn't ask any of you to do it with me, any more than I'd ask you to do it for me. This is the real point of no return, and there's no harm in anyone saying this is as far as they'll go and no further. At the same time, I'm not going to argue with anyone or forbid anyone from coming. I'm tired, too, Juvie. That's why I had to force everyone to cool their heels, so that I could trust everyone to make the right decision for themselves. I don't have the energy to fight, especially not with you guys, since I feel like there's one more fight to come."

"You do know the old saw - no offense, Phoebe - about the definition of insanity, right?" Juvie asked. Phoebe picked up a pillow and whomped Juvie on the top of his head, but she was smiling as she did it.

"Trying the same thing over and over again and expecting different results?" I asked. "Sure."

"So after all the times since this whole thing started that you asked us if we wanted to turn back, and none of us ever did, what makes you think we're suddenly going to change our minds this time?" Juvie pressed.

"Because this time, I think I'm going to have to go… I don't know where I'm going," I admitted.

"I thought you understood what the dragonflies were trying to tell us," Phoebe said.

"I did," I said. "I found the building. That's the easy part. But once I get there…"

"Once we get there," Phoebe corrected me.

"It's not like going into the Deep Woods, it's a total unknown," I explained. "Between you and me, and Mabonnyn and Corb, whether we were in the Council of Ruis's custody or down in the Undergrowth or looking for Marra Troda, at least we all had some familiarity with the ground rules and the lay of the land. Whatever's inside the building, it's outside our frame of reference."

"But it's just a building," Juvie said, brows knitting in confusion.

"That's still way outside the norm, for a harrier and an arbutus from the Deep Woods," I said. "And maybe we can assume that whatever's inside the building will be as normcore as the outside. But my gut tells me that it won't be. The building's just the threshold."

"To what?" Juvie asked.

"That's what I'm telling you," I said. "I. Don't.

Know. We are officially on the outskirts of blind-leading-the-blind territory. So that's the difference, between letting you follow me someplace I know and letting you stumble into some nameless secret space."

No one said anything for a few seconds, until finally Corb rumbled, "Even blind cave fish school together."

"Tall, dark and sticky has a point," Juvie said. "We're taking a leap into uncharted territory. Duly noted. But it makes more sense to do it together than for you to do it alone."

Phoebe and Corb nodded their agreement. Mabonnyn remained stoic and silent, but didn't leave, which I had to take as a sign that the harrier still intended to see things through to the bitter end. "All right," I said. I looked at my phone and said "It's 9:30. Let's try to get three hours of sleep, at least. I'll set my alarm."

"Why?" Phoebe asked.

"Because we all need it, for one thing," I said. "And because if we're going to break into a building downtown, and bring a harrier of the Floret folk and a pitch giant with us, we're going to do it in the dead of night when there's as few witnesses around as possible."

My phone chirruped at half past one in the morning and I uncurled myself from the ball I had folded into on the pink easy chair, letting the quilt fall to the floor in a shapeless pile. Juvie rolled onto his side on the couch, threw aside his quilt and pushed himself upright. We blinked at each other and looked to the front door, where Mabonnyn stood sentinel, occupying the same spot in the same pose as when we fell asleep. Juvie and I simultaneously rose to cross to the back door of the cottage.

I opened the door and we stepped into the back yard. Corb was seated on the ground near a small tree. We came closer and I could see the contours of Phoebe's face. Her tree appearance was healthier looking than it had been in the Undergrowth, but still seemed infirm, somehow. Corb looked up at me and asked, "Time?"

I nodded. Corb placed a hand on Phoebe's trunk, about where her heart would be. Some kind of communication passed between them, and Phoebe roused from her slumber, metamorphosing rapidly from tree back to woman. Her eyes fluttered open and she looked past me to Juvie. "Weird, I know."

"Doesn't even crack the top twenty of weird things I've seen since I got here," Juvie said.

"You ready to go?" I asked Phoebe.

"Ready as I'm going to get," she acknowledged.

We walked around the exterior of the cottage to Juvie's car, where Mabonnyn was already waiting for us. I got into the front passenger seat while Phoebe, Corb and Mabonnyn piled into the back. Even with a space-saving configuration of the arbutus's pliant body, Corb took up more than half of the rear seats, leaving just enough room for Phoebe to sit with Mabonnyn standing on her knees.

Juvie backed the car down the rutted hill and onto the road, then drove back toward the city. As the car glided through the night, I shared my theory about my mother's abductors with the others. "I did a drive-by of the building earlier, just to confirm what I had found online. It belongs to a company called Chirax Bioengineering, or it did. The company lost funding, went bankrupt, and the building isn't being used anymore. Lock and chain across the front doors, no doubt because the creditors are still sorting out who gets what before they gut it and sell it."

"Abandoned building, pretty classic bad guy hideout, right?" Juvie asked.

"Yeah," I said. "But from what I could gather, Chirax was into some extremely cutting edge research with DNA and RNA replication and nanomachines. Honestly a lot of it was jargon I couldn't penetrate."

"Okay," Phoebe said. "But you don't think a bunch of laid-off researchers kidnapped your mother, do you? Just because she's being held there doesn't mean what the building was formerly used for matters much. It could have just as easily been an internet startup or a vacuum cleaner factory or anything else. And now it's just another foreclosure."

"Maybe," I said. I was staring out the passenger window up at the night sky, the deep dark immensity and the amplitude of stars, so much more remote and unknowable than the canopy of the Deep Woods. I was happy to see it. "But I feel like there's more to it than that. The dragonflies made an image of the building, as opposed to any other clue or piece of information they could have conveyed."

"Like what?" Juvie asked.

"I don't know, a likeness of whoever kidnapped my mom?" I asked. "They didn't focus on the who, they focused on the where. Maybe it matters. Maybe it doesn't. I just thought it was noteworthy because it's so different from what we were expecting. It's not rogue pixies, or an angry witch, or anything to do with the Deep Woods at all. It's here in our world, and not only that, it's the former site of a bioengineering research enterprise specializing in molecular microtechnology. It's about as far from the druid sphere as anything I can think of."

"Well, at the very least, I promise not to touch anything once we get inside," Juvie said. "Even if I see a miniature bioengineered cow. Pissing off a huulder was bad enough. I don't want to accidentally unleash the nanobot apocalypse."

I wanted to laugh, if only to recognize Juvie's effort to lighten the mood with a joke. But at that point, I couldn't rule out the nanobot apocalypse. I couldn't rule out anything.

With me directing Juvie as he drove, we arrived at the Chirax building and Juvie coasted slowly past the darkened front entrance. Up near the roofline, the company logo projected out from the wall in glass-fronted steel, a blue hexagon standing on point with small red circles at each corner and a triad of larger red circles in the center. The dragonflies had likely approximated the geometric logo in their representation of the building, though it hadn't really registered at the time. But other elements were easily recognizable, even from our street level vantage. Everyone in the car could see the satellite dish and egress on the roof, as well as the spacing of the windows and the wide band of marble on the facade. Overall the image formed by the dragonflies had been remarkably accurate, if lacking somewhat in human-scale details, such as the heavy chain and lock looped through the handles of the front doors. In the overall architecture of the building as a whole, they were too small to have been represented by the insects' wings and bodies, but there was no doubt they were substantial enough in the real world to prevent us from simply walking through the front door. Juvie continued down the block, turning at the next corner.

A fence topped with razor wire surrounded the empty parking lot behind the Chirax building, and an empty security guardhouse stood just inside a gate in the fence, also padlocked and chained. Juvie brought the car to a stop against the curb. "Back up and hit the gate at ramming speed?" he asked.

"We're still trying to be inconspicuous," I reminded him. I took a magazine out of my pocket and loaded my gun. "Let's get out and see how sturdy that lock is."

The lock was more than adequate to prevent any of us from forcing it open, either with a bullet or with Corb's considerable strength, but standing there at the gate I realized that the arbutus, finally unfolded from the confines of the backseat of Juvie's car, was nearly as tall as the fence. "Corb, I almost hate to ask, but do you think you could throw an arm over this gate to protect us while we climb over?"

Corb said nothing, merely complying with my request. I hoisted myself up his side, onto his shoulder, walked along his extended arm covering the razorwire, and jumped down to the other side. Phoebe and Juvie followed, as Mabonnyn simply squirmed through one of the diamond-shaped gaps in the chainlink pattern of the fence, pulling the hatchet under the fence after. Finally Corb flattened himself into a wide but shallow puddle of pitch and slid beneath the fence, reforming beside us.

There was an access ladder bolted to the side of the building, a simple set of struts with safety rings encircling it at intervals all the way up to the roof. I grabbed the bottom rung and started the ascent, the metal chiming with every step I climbed. The others came up after me, Corb bringing up the rear. Everything was going according to plan until, somewhere around halfway up, fifty feet above the ground, the ladder jerked suddenly. It only fell a couple of inches, but the downward lurch turned my stomach to ice. I looked at the wall of the Chirax building, searching for the nearest anchors for the ladder. I spotted them and saw the massive industrial bolts poking out askew, barely hanging by their threads. "Down!" I shouted. "Get back down!" But before any of us could descend more than a rung or two, the ladder came away from the building and we were freefalling in an iron cage toward the unforgiving concrete below.

"Hold fast!" Corb thundered, louder than the rushing wind in our ears. It was hard to take stock of what everyone else was doing while gravity hurtled us spitefully down, though I had a feeling we were all gripping the ladder tightly already, out of sheer reflex alone. I gritted my teeth in anticipation of the inevitable, but the ladder slowed and, with a great clang and scrape against the Chirax building, stopped.

My eyes made a sweep of the wall to the roofline above, where I saw Corb's elongated arms rising up from below and grasping the edge of the roof with both hands. I didn't need any urging to continue climbing, and I could hear the others resuming their ascents as well, feeling their footfalls reverberating through the iron.

I reached the roof, threw myself over the top of the wall, and turned around to help Phoebe and then Juvie off the ladder. Mabonnyn bounded up unassisted, and Corb oozed up out of the ladder's rings and onto the roof. The ladder, free of the pitch tethers, finally fell to the ground with a discordant peal like a broken bell.

The egress in the middle of the roof had a heavy fire door, not chained and padlocked like the front entrance or the rear gate had been, but secured with an electronic keypad, with a single red LED flashing on the upper right corner. I tried the handle of the door anyway, but the lock was engaged and I could only rattle it in its solid frame.

"Please don't tell me this is one of those unpickable locks," Phoebe said.

"I mean, it's not impossible," I said. "But it's not easy, either."

"Maybe it is," Juvie said. He stepped forward, bending slightly to peer closely at the keypad. "Oh, man. Unreal."

"What?" I asked.

Juvie laughed. "Maybe I'm not so useless on this dream team after all," he said. He laughed again, a sound like a person on the verge of losing their mind. He turned to me and said, "A little while back I was trying to make time with this girl at work, Elisha. She took smoke breaks twice a day, and she'd go up on the roof for them, and I'd go with her, you know, couple minutes of conversation, try to make her laugh, figure out what she was into so I could ask her somewhere she'd be inclined to say yes to. The roof access was just like this, same punchcode lock, same manufacturer."

"Okay," Phoebe said, sounding skeptical, though I wasn't sure if she was merely wondering how this helped in our present situation, or if she didn't much care for the way Juvie was reminiscing about Elisha.

"Anyway, one Monday morning we went up, she smoked her cigarette, we went to go back down and the code didn't unlock the door. They must have changed it over the weekend. We really weren't supposed to be up there, not officially, so whoever had changed it hadn't told Elisha. I thought we were screwed, but she told me that she knew about a failsafe. A master code that would always work no matter what, in case someone ever got accidentally locked out. It's the year the company was founded, and an extra one at the end."

Juvie turned back to the keypad and pressed 1-9-7-5-1. The LED went from red to green. Juvie took the door handle and opened the door, bowing theatrically and gesturing us all inside.

The egress contained only the landing at the top of a narrow stairwell, eight steps down to another landing with blank white walls. I had reached that level by the time Corb entered the egress and the door slammed shut behind him, plunging us into absolute darkness. I pulled out my pen light and shone it down the next set of steps, where the landing faced a beige door. I leaned on the pushbar, which thankfully hadn't been secured in any way, and entered the middle of a long corridor.

The hallway was ominously dim, the only illumination coming weakly from emergency lights powered by batteries that were dying by the day, like something out of a cheap horror movie. I kept my pen light on and bobbed it back and forth, up and down, sweeping the carpet ahead of my path to make sure it was clear and swinging up doors as we passed them, checking for any indications that someone else had been through recently. I chose to walk down to my left at first, and while every door was somewhat different, some with papers or photos taped to them, some with official warning signs mounted on them, none gave itself away as a likely hiding place for my mother or whoever had abducted her. I shone my pen light through a few windows, but saw nothing but unoccupied rooms, empty except for debris in the corners and pale silhouettes where equipment had stood a while but since been removed. I looped down to the end of the corridor, doubled back and explored the side to the right of the stairwell door, but again, found nothing out of the ordinary.

At the end of the full, narrow, elongated circle I huddled with the others. "Any suggestions?" I asked. "Anyone picking up on anything?"

"Don't look at me, I already performed my one miracle for the day," Juvie said.

I looked to Phoebe and Corb, both of whom shook their heads. Mabonnyn pointed mutely at the door to the stairwell.

"Nowhere to go but down," I agreed.

"Deeper into the belly of the beast," Juvie added.

As soon as we emerged from the next landing down, into another shadowy corridor, we could feel a difference in the air. I could, at any rate, and judging by the tiny hissing sounds of sharp intakes of breath behind me, I thought the vibe was manifesting for everyone else as well. Physically the hallway was identical to the one above, dark and disused and lined with doors. But the temperature was noticeably warmer, and the smell was off. Undercutting the pervasive background odor of ingrained industrial cleaners were more piquant notes of decay and sepsis. It made the hairs on the back of my neck stand up. Mabonnyn was instantly at my side, battle-hatchet at the ready, and then striding ahead of me down the right side of the corridor.

For just a moment, out of sheer habit, I accepted this as the right and natural order of things. Mabonnyn was the closest thing our little band of would-be rescuers had to a warrior, and here we were, about to confront whatever dragons were laired within the grim, foreboding fortress. The quest was almost done except for the final, fateful battle, and the woodlander with the improvised axe would lead the charge.

Mabonnyn lightly sidestepped a crumpled knot of foil, the long-ago discarded wrapper of an energy bar, and suddenly I remembered that we weren't in the Deep Woods, we weren't reenacting any fairy tale, we were in an abandoned biotech research facility with no good idea of what would be waiting behind any doors, potentially walking into deadly danger none of us could be prepared for. This was a shadowy corner of my world, one I at least had some passing familiarity with. For a hot minute at the beginning of my time in college I had entertained the thought of majoring in electrical engineering, of immersing and losing myself in the sphere of technological progress, the artificial, the synthetic, the fabricated, the ultimate teenage rebellion rejecting the old family ways. Plastic shells and unnatural dyes and stamped circuits of rare earth metals and the buzz and hiss of unliving mechanical systems never set my teeth on edge, because I had the benefit of enough exposure to become accustomed and develop a tolerance for them.

But Mabonnyn and Corb, our secret weapons, were now every bit as out of their natural element here in a laboratory building, all latex painted sheetrock and polyethylene carpeting, as Juvie had been in the Deep Woods. And nobody had explicitly coached the arbutus or the woodlander to exercise caution and take nothing for granted, to be aware of or deferential to their own lack of knowledge and reference points. On top of all of which, Mabonnyn was still half-mad with grief over Gern and not predisposed to caution or prudence, a preoccupied mind with no thoughts to spare for trying to comprehend the utterly alien purlieu.

"Mabonnyn, wait!" I called out just as the harrier leapt for a door knob, pulling down on the brushed-chrome lever with all the weight of a foot-tall pixie.

The door swung inward and Mabonnyn disappeared into the shadows beyond it. I rushed ahead, vaguely aware that the carpet around the doorway looked to have been leached of its original dyed hue somehow. I shone my penlight into the room and at first I could barely make sense of what the small circle of light revealed: an uneven composite of myriad odd angles and planes, some glittering with reflected light and others spectrally pale, with nothing remotely recognizable as a floor or wall, a piece of furniture or equipment. By the time I recognized the white sheen and the jagged shapes were fundamentally the same as the protrusions afflicting the flora and fauna of the Deep Woods, the same as the surface of the creatures that had attacked me at my apartment and my office, one of those very same creatures was leaping out of room and tackling me.

The force drove me backwards into the opposite wall. I just barely managed to tuck my head down and avoid having the base of my skull collide with the wall. My shoulders took the brunt of the impact, and I drew my SIG Pro from its holster and jammed it under the colorless creature's approximation of a chin. I pulled the trigger, and though the bullet tore through the top of the creature's head, it continued to manhandle me against the wall, like some kind of automaton with no real need for a brain to command its moving parts.

I looked around the corridor for some kind of miraculous solution but saw only that everyone else was faring just as poorly. Juvie and Phoebe were each wrestling with spiky, facet-skinned creatures of their own, while Corb was beset by three of them at once. I couldn't see Mabonnyn, who had probably been ambushed inside the shadow-filled room. Trying to spot the harrier through the doorway, I saw that the substrate that covered the inside of the room was spreading out past the doorframe. It entered the hallway, a growing, living thing, expanding in slim tendrils at first and then in terrible, irresistible waves. It came on like something out of a film they would show in biology class, video recordings of an electron microscope depicting single-celled organisms, their locomotion and feeding. But it was a billion trillion times bigger than something seen at that undetectable scale, immense enough to nearly fill the corridor, and still probing and groping and swelling. The creature grappling with me ignored it, even as the mass rose up around both our legs, merging with the creature, or possibly reuniting with it. The mass rose halfway up my thighs and then began to draw back, pulling me with it.

I fought it, of course. I squirmed and kicked, thrashed and beat at it and even in final desperation emptied most of the SIG Pro's magazine into it. But nothing had any effect or created even the slightest amount of space around my legs, which felt like they were being swallowed by a giant snake with a raging fire in its belly. My eyes swept the area for something, anything attached to the building itself I could grab onto in an effort to anchor myself and resist the drag, but there was nothing. Everything looked far away, the doorway to the room was already impossibly distant, not as if we had crossed more distance than the room contained, but as if we were shrinking, the corridor now a mile away because you could lay a thousand of me end to end and not reach it. The ceiling was stratospherically high, the walls looming, and they looked like regular walls and ceiling again. Everything belonging to the strange amorphous whiteness was diminishing, collapsing in on itself, and pulling all of us inward with it, abandoning the space that had contained it before we had breached the door. Soon there would be nothing left, I realized. Even if the Chirax building still merited some kind of security surveillance, even if our break-in had not gone unnoticed and prompted some kind of investigation, no one would ever find a thing. The alien matter was inverting itself out of sight, out of existence, leaving nothing behind. We would never be noticed. We would never be seen again. That was the last thing I thought before my entire field of vision became a broken kaleidoscope of random achromatic facets, as if I had entered the compound eye of a ghostly insect, and I gave up trying to think any more.

Chapter Eleven: Reunions

I DREAMED I was very young, six years old at most. Except I was also myself, the current adult version, mid-thirties both mentally and physically, though sometimes I felt older in either dimension, or both at once. But by the paradoxical logic of the dream itself, I was inhabiting one of my own memories, so I was the boy and the so-called man at once. I was in my backyard, when I still thought of it as mine, before it became the place I outgrew and the home I left behind, ceding it entirely to my mother. I was beyond the grass and the wildflowers and into the woods, because at age six there wasn't any distinction, all the great green outdoors were part of my backyard. The whole wide world was my backyard, because my home was my whole world. I was in the woods, and I was in the Deep Woods, alone, even though when I had been four years old I never ventured into the Deep Woods alone. I didn't know how. My mother had brought me there a handful of times, I doubt that I could remember the very first time even in my dreams, but this wasn't a memory of any of the times I had been in the Deep Woods with or without Foltchain of the Oak to guide or protect me. It was a memory of climbing a tree, except in the dream the tree was in the Deep Woods. In the dream I was climbing a name tree, none of them in particular and all of them united, Beithe and Eadhadh and Aball and Draighin and Sial. As I made my way higher and higher from branch to branch, my adult mind kept trying to latch onto the tree's one true name, to spy a whole and unspoiled leaf that would speak the sacred epithet, but the leaves were a shifting multitude, heart-shaped and sickle-shaped and palm-shaped, spiny and smooth, lobed and pleated, rushing past me like green froth on a wind-whipped ocean. My child mind didn't care what kind of tree it was, of course, only that it was tall, and that every bough was a rung in a ladder inviting me further and further up. I knew what was waiting at the end of the climb, I wanted to spare myself that end, especially wanted to spare my younger self that end, but the dream carried itself forward with irresistible momentum. In the throes of reverie it felt as though unlocking the hidden name of the tree would somehow break the cycle, somehow interrupt the impetus of motion of the dreamchild whose eyes I was looking through. I reached out to pluck a leaf as I rose, but the stem crumbled in my fingers and the blade disintegrated into a scattering of motes. Every leaf in the vast host all around me yellowed and whitened and fell to pieces. The limbs and trunk of the tree became dark and gnarled, the tips of branches sharp as thorns. Suddenly I was too high, the ground too far below, my perch too precarious on a brittle black twig that could not support me and did not care to try. Before the little branch could snap, before the tree could hurl me to the earth of its own volition, I tried to climb back down, to safety, to solid ground, and that was when I lost my footing and my grip and fell.

The wind howled in my ears as my small body plummeted, and I did not wake up. The ground below, which should have been uneven but grassy, was spikes of bare upthrust rock, the sullen blue-violet of deep bruises, the prongs growing larger and seeming to leap toward me with hungry anticipation as I dropped, and still I did not wake up. The anticipation of striking the stony knuckles at terminal velocity sent a deathly chill shudder down my spine, and even still I did not wake up. That much, at least, was true to the past, and true to my memory. As a child, when I had fallen from a tree, I had half-expected to suddenly discover it was all a dream, just before the thud of impact knocked the wind from my lungs and filled my eyes with shooting stars. I had a vivid memory of the fall subjectively taking forever, and instead of my mere four years of life passing before my eyes I had only marveled at the languid way the canopy of the woods had swirled above me, and awaited the inevitable realization that I was safe in my own bed, coming out of a vivid dream. I knew, with hindsight, that when I had fallen from a tree in sight of my house, I had only been a dozen feet off the ground, the fall could only have taken a second or two. But at the time, it had felt like forever, just as the fall felt endless now. And despite believing I would awaken, I hadn't, just as I stayed in the dream now.

I crashed to earth and absorbed the scraping, biting embrace of the agonizingly broken terrain. I survived, because I was four years old with bones that bent before breaking, but I also suffered every injury, because now I was getting old. I didn't bounce and I wouldn't heal overnight. My skull rang like an anvil and my muscles cringed at the bite of deeply driven nails and my skin screamed in the red wake of burning hot razor blades. My eyes were clamped shut and I assumed that even if I opened them they would reveal nothing but darkness and pain.

When I had fallen as a child, I had lain on the ground, unable to draw enough breath to call for my mother, wondering how long I would have to spend rocking weakly on my back before I was found, how many days and nights. But my mother had come to me right away, somehow knowing when I needed her, appearing and gathering me into her arms and carrying me straight to the herbarium. She put a poultice on a cut on my elbow and gave me a few seeds to swallow for the pain, and then she simply sat down and held me, stroking my hair, my cheek, my neck, and telling me I was going to be all right. In the dream, I felt that old fear again, the certainty of abandonment, the understanding that death was near at hand and I could not fight it off by myself. I felt a gentle caress on the side of my face, so reminiscent of my mother's touch that it hurt in its own unbearably sweet way. I was dreaming that I had survived an impossible fall that would kill anything, so that I could dream that I was slowly fading into nostalgic madness while I bled to death internally. Not such a bad way to go, really, listening to my mother softly singing the pain away.

That... wasn't right. The singing hadn't been present in settling me down when I had fallen out of the tree. The singing had been instrumental in my convalescence from illness, the winter I had been bedridden and ill, when my mother had resorted to far more than kind words and soothing touch, when intercessions had been required to stave off the darkest specters, and a song recalling the oldest myths had bound the ritual in time and place around me. My mother's voice had woven the descant of the first fire that consumed everything before it, the ashes left behind, and the waters that coaxed forth from those ashes the first green shoots. Her lilting words had evoked the countless cycles of lowering, seed sowing, and decay, and the embers of fire still hiding in the ashes, in the newborn earth, that had caused some seeds to arise with a spark of brilliance, becoming animals, eventually becoming men, eventually becoming all life in the great green cradle. The words and their story, the canticle and its melody, had praised life and rebuffed death. I hadn't heard the myth or music since.

Until now.

I wasn't remembering the ancient evensong, I

was hearing it, a wordless humming rather than the recitation of the elemental lore, but the unspoken paean was the same. Finally I did wake up. My body still hurt, not quite as badly as if I had been dropped from the crown of a mile-high tree onto fractured bedrock, and my mind still reeled trying to reconcile whether I was a child or an adult, but at least I felt free to act of my own volition rather than being trapped in a memory. At the moment, the only volition I had was to remain supine, even though most of the length of my body was resting on an uncomfortably warm, unyielding surface. My head and shoulders were cradled more softly. I opened my eyes, to look up into the face of my mother.

"I would offer you something for your head," she said, "if I had anything here to offer."

"Mom, are you…" I started to ask, sitting up at the same time. I took her in, sitting beside her on the uneven ledge, her face serene as always, her hair and skin and homespun clothing showing no signs of physical harm or even uncleanliness. "You're all right. Of course you're all right."

"Yes, I'm fine," my mother said. "As are you, a few bumps and bruises aside. You always did find the most ingenious ways to record your adventures."

And there it was, as usual, less than a minute in the same room with my mother and the vast differences between us, the enormity of the gulf you couldn't see the far side of, were the only things that merited commenting on. Foltchain of the Oak, druid priestess, protector of the Derryth, legendary figure of renown not for her actions and effects left in her wake, but for their lack. She was harmonious coexistence incarnate, able to pass effortlessly between the worlds and make her way through them without so much as snapping the smallest branch or bending the lowliest blade of grass. She was effectively immortal because she was untouchable. As opposed to her would-be legacy, me, the harbinger of unintended consequences, a one-seven-billionth sized sliver of the undifferentiated human mob, an unremarkable brute of a boy who had tripped and stumbled and crashed against the grain of his surroundings so many times that he was lucky to still be alive. I stood up and took a few steps away from my mother. Without turning around I said, "We looked all over the Deep Woods for you, and the Undergrowth, too. Even wound up at Marra Troda's cave at one point."

"I wasn't there," my mother said.

"Obviously," I said. "Once we figured that out, we came back, near an old black walnut tree."

"I think I know the one."

"I'm sure you do. Took us a little bit to actually get across from the Deep Woods to your house. Attacked by a possessed carnivorous plant, had to burn a slain bullfrog that had been a harrier's companion, the harrier had to swear an oath of vengeance, you know, standard Deep Woods stuff. The longer we spent there, in the shadow of the black walnut, the more I felt like that tree and I had a lot in common. Maybe that should have been the name I took. Kellan Walnuts. Would have made me sound like more of a tough guy, at least with the big

Sopranos fans."

"Kellan…"

"I mean, that's beside the point, really," I went on. I was still facing away from her, staring at the strange irregular wall of the cell my mother and I were enclosed by. It was the same pale chaotic mosaic as the creatures that had first attacked me, as the growths that had erupted from the balaur and the bats and the roridula, as the surface of everything inside the Chirax laboratory. There were no breaks or openings, no way I could see how either of us had been brought here. "The payoff symbolism of a black walnut is the allelopathy. You know, the chemicals the roots release that won't let anything else grow anywhere near the tree?" I paused, but my mother didn't answer, so I went on, "I mean, that's what's always worked out best for me, standing on my own, keeping everything else at a safe distance. I could have done a whole family crest, a big black silhouette of a solitary tree, and like a Latin translation of 'My shadow is doom to all within its compass' for a motto."

"That's a bit of a garble of Pliny the Elder's quote," my mother said, which was also typical of her, none too subtly reminding me that she might not know chapter and verse of prestige cable dramas but she had read Naturalis Historia, and had lived long enough that there were more obscure facts she had randomly run across over the years than everything I'd managed to retain from three years of college put together.

I took the humbling in stride, still didn't turn to face her. "I should be a tree with boundaries, that minds its own business and doesn't get caught up in anyone else's. I am that tree. And I wish we had come into the Deep Woods through that bare patch around the black walnut, instead."

"Why?"

Finally I brought myself around, fixing my gaze on my mother's curious expression. "Because," I answered, "maybe it would have reminded me to mind my own business. To not go traipsing back and forth looking for you when you're nowhere to be found, because wherever you are you're going to be fine. You're always fine. And I'm always one step away from just making everything worse."

"That's not true," my mother said. "Oh, you wanting to define your self-reliance, that's always been a fundamental part of who you are, but so has wanting to help people. And you do help people, Kellan, you always have. No one could look at everything you've achieved in your life and say you only make things worse."

"Yet here we are," I said, gesturing helplessly at the cell. "You're no better off now than when I started looking for you. I shouldn't have come here. I shouldn't have bothered."

"But you did," my mother pointed out. "Despite your fierce independent streak, and despite definitely knowing what a black walnut tree was beforehand, you came. Why?"

I was about to snap at her, to tell her I had no clue what had come over me and no earthly idea what malfunction in my brain had made it all seem like the best plan at the time, but I realized immediately that wasn't true. And just like that the tension went out of me, I wasn't a petulant pre-adolescent desperate to prove that my mother didn't know everything. "I did it for Phoebe. She needed you, and neither of us knew where you were. I had to help her."

"You didn't have to," my mother said, "You chose to. And that's who you are, Kellan."

"Not that it does Phoebe or you or me any good," I said. I sat down next to my mother, feeling exhausted. "I don't even know where we are. I didn't help Phoebe find you, I managed to get all of us captured with you. Do you know anything about where this place is, who these people are or what they want from you?"

"Yes and no to each of those," my mother said. "You should eat something." She pointed past me, and I noticed for the first time a rough-hewn platter with a good amount of food on it.

"So should you," I said.

"I've taken what I need," my mother said. She saw the unswayed skepticism on my face and added, "Indulge me. Eat. At least have some of the nuts, they will help with your pain."

I popped a small brown nut into my mouth and chewed, waiting for my mother to resume her explanations.

"Let's dispense with who these people are, since they simply aren't people."

"Right," I nodded. "Creatures. Entities. I don't know what to call them because they're not like anything else I've ever encountered or even heard about. And I know there's tons of mysteries out there among the unknown unknowns, but I'm pretty sure they're not magical, supernatural manifestations, which leaves… what? Aliens?"

"Your instincts are on the right track, as usual," my mother said. "Not supernatural. But not from another world, if that's what you mean by alien."

"What else might I mean?"

"What you said at first," my mother said. "Anything extrinsic to your prior experience."

I closed my eyes and took a deep breath. "Mom. I've been camping out in the Deep Woods for days, over the course of which I almost got thrown off a bridge by an enraged huulder, barely outran Ffirk Halfhorned and his oosers, threw down with a gang of redcombs, all bookended by these aliens, but not galaxy far far away aliens, showing up out of nowhere to beat me up. Do you think maybe you could skip the teachable moments approach and just tell me the deal. Please?"

"I'm sorry, Kellan," my mother said, and sounded like she actually meant it. "These things are viruses."

"Yeah, okay, that's one way of putting it," I said.

"I'm not being poetic, Kellan," my mother said. "They are large, ingenious viruses. What is that verbal modifier you use to put things in a class of their own? Mega? They are mega-viruses."

I had assumed something along those lines already, back in the underground chambers of Marra Troda. The blight on the Deep Woods, the physical wrongness that had followed me there, was a literal infection, a particularly savage and unstoppable plague, a doomsday biological weapon which might at one point have had a specific target but had spread along vectors so far and so fast it had become a pandemic. It had hunted me while I looked for my mother, but had also afflicted the beasts that the Council of Ruis had needed to cull, and had devastated the mother of malady, and who knew what else in the far-flung selvage. And it was still running wild. "Yeah, fine, mega-viruses, but who's behind them? Who kidnapped you to keep you out of the way while the pox bomb went off? Who's pulling the strings?"

"No one," my mother answered. "They are acting of their own accord. They are cognizant. They have… awakened."

"What? How? How is that even possible?" I asked. I knew there was no small debate over the question of whether or not viruses were even technically alive, or just some kind of naturally-occurring self-replicating bundle of chemical processes, a precursor to life at best. Nothing, not even my upbringing among pixies and sentient plants and dragonflies capable of groupthink, would have prepared me to hear that microscopic balls of amino acids and lipids had developed independent consciousness.

"I don't know," my mother said. I stared at her, my brow furrowing deeply enough that I could feel the skin pinching above the bridge of my nose, and she gave me a slight shrug. "I don't know everything, Kellan, and I don't think I've ever claimed otherwise."

But of course the answer wasn't going to come from druid tradition or Deep Woods lore; this kind of anomaly could only arise from the exponentially complicated cunning of technology, the world I chose to live in. "It must have something to do with the research Chirax was doing," I said. "Maybe somewhere between whatever onboard artificial intelligence their nanotechnology carried, and whatever viral group they were experimenting on, something impossible became real."

"Perhaps," my mother nodded. "I did sense something... machinelike about my captors, when I was in contact with them. But I didn't know if it was truly man-made artifice, or simply an anima so different, so far removed from the weg I know, that I can hardly relate to it."

"What kind of contact have you had?" I asked. "What have they...?"

My mother put a hand on my arm. "Nothing. They've done nothing to me except keep me isolated here." She glanced down at the platter meaningfully. "You stopped eating."

"Those nuts are hard to choke down," I said.

She picked up one of the dark green leaves, put two nuts in the center, and folded the leaf edges in. She handed it to me and I popped it in my mouth and chewed. The leaf helped, a little bit at first, but as the mashed nut and the green fibers mixed in my mouth the whole became much more palatable. "You might want to mix in some of the seeds, too," she said.

"All right, so they haven't tried to inject DNA into you or anything," I said. "Which is the whole point of existence for viruses, so that's weird, but then again maybe that's been overwritten by some nano-programming or something. But why would that new mandate be to just keep you imprisoned?"

"Imprisoning me is only a means to an end," my mother said. "This place… not just this cell, but whatever surrounds it, the answer to the question of where we are now… this is the viruses' equivalent of the Deep Woods. I don't think they have a name for it, they don't have their own names for much of anything, but I've been calling it the Oblate. It's their point of origination, primal, primitive, literally so from our perspective, just waxy protein enveloping everything."

I knew that there were other reality-adjacent realms like the Deep Woods, yet another lesson from my childhood, albeit a brief one. It was something my mother had felt obliged to mention, to acknowledge the existence of other traditions with other beginnings that manifested as physically accessible locations. The Deep Woods was one among many, but it was the only one that mattered to the druid priest or priestess. "So what is the Oblate's equivalent of you?" I asked.

My mother spread her hands and smiled sadly. "That's just it. They don't have one. They never have, in all of the time of their self-awareness."

"Which, if I'm right about this being a biotech experiment gone off the rails, might be all of about three or four years, tops," I said.

"Even so," my mother said. "They feel the lack, and feel it desperately. Perhaps they even experience time differently than we do."

"So, they kidnapped you? To force you into the role of the priestess they never had?" I asked.

"No, not quite," my mother said. "They

kidnapped me so that I would teach them how to discover their own weg."

"I don't think that's quite how it works," I said.

"No, of course not," my mother said.

"So have you made any headway in convincing them to let you go?" I asked.

"No," my mother said. "To be fair, I haven't tried."

"Why not?"

"Because I may be able to help them," my mother said.

I squeezed my eyelids with my thumb and forefinger. "What were we just saying about how you really can't?"

"I don't know that for certain, Kellan," my mother said. "I know scarcely anything about this place or about the creatures in it. I could learn more if I chose. I don't know what would constitute meaningful harmony for these creatures, because I am not one of them. I could guide them toward those self-discoveries, given enough time."

"How much longer is that going to take?"

"I imagine it would take quite a long while," she said. "If I decided to do it."

"You haven't decided yet?"

"No, I haven't. All the time I've been here, I've been trying to intuit whether or not the viruses are truly alive, truly conscious in a way that could be capable of something like druidic enlightenment. If they are, I think I would be obligated to help them, however I could, however long it might take."

"And if they aren't?"

"Then I would be equally obligated to do

everything in my power to stop them from wreaking destruction across my world."

"So, just to sum up, I absolutely should not have come looking for you, because there's a chance you might want to stay here indefinitely, and on the other hand if you decided to leave, you'd just up and do it, right?"

"You couldn't have known what I was thinking," she said. "I'm sorry I wasn't able to let you know. And as far as leaving this place, I hadn't gotten that far. I don't know if I could do it under my own power. I might need help."

"You might," I said, skeptical.

"It's good that you came," my mother said. "Because they would have brought you here anyway. The viruses are even less understanding about my inner deliberations than you are."

"I never said I didn't understand," I protested. Then I reflected on what my mother had just said. "They came after me… to put pressure on you to make up your mind?"

"And to make up my mind in a particular way," she said.

"Is that seriously going to work?" I asked.

Before my mother could answer, a portion of the cell wall irised open, and a pair of the virus creatures stepped in. One of them pointed at the two of us and beckoned us toward the aperture. My mother rose and made her way toward them, and I followed. A moment later we were in a corridor, distinguishable from the cell only due to its long, narrow configuration. The floor, walls and ceiling flowed seamlessly into one another, the same membrane of white irregular shapes. One of the virus creatures led us down the winding passageway, and the other followed behind my mother and I, walking side by side. Both of our escorts remained perfectly silent.

"They've already made a good start on the whole wreaking destruction thing, you know," I said, just as if we were still in the cell and the virus creatures couldn't hear what I was saying. For all I knew, they had been listening in on the whole conversation in there, anyway. "Serious damage in the Deep Woods."

"Anything permanent?" my mother asked.

"Maybe?" I said. "Nothing that I saw over the course of the past couple days, exactly, but that's the thing about disease vectors. Who knows how far the viruses have spread their influence, under the surface of things, in ways that might not manifest right away, until it's too widespread and too late to do anything about it. I mean, the Deep Woods is literally the environmental manifestation of physical resilience, I get that, but it's never had to deal with anything like this before, has it? What if this— Oblate—is an environmental manifestation of infectious pathology? What happens when the immovable object comes down with a bad case of the irresistible force?"

My mother stopped walking, and put her hand on my arm to stop me as well. She looked me in the eye with a strange mixture of pride and concern. "That's truly the heart of the matter, Kellan. How very well-observed of you."

The virus creature behind us prodded me

between the shoulder blades with its stiff, sharp fingertips, and I started walking again, spared having to answer my mother directly. "But for what it's worth," I said, as my mother fell into step beside me, "I don't see why you should care either way. The Deep Woods didn't care about you going missing, and the Deep Woods didn't care about facing the virus creatures headlong, either. If the Oblate colonizes the Deep Woods, burns it down, leaves it an empty ravaged husk of its former self, fine. It gets what it deserves."

My mother made no response for several paces down the twisting corridor, as we crested a rise and then began a spiraling descent, the jangly walls narrowing and widening in stochastic patterns around us. Finally she said, "And when you say the Deep Woods didn't care, are you speaking of the entirety of it? Not a single tree, not one creature through the height and breadth of that domain was willing to offer you aid?"

I didn't answer.

"My captors said you and your friends would be coming. Was it only you and Phoebe, after all?" she pressed.

"Do you remember my college roommate?" I asked.

"Juvenal? Of course," my mother smiled, genuinely charmed to be reminded of him. "So only friends from the so-called civilized world?"

"All right, fine," I sighed. "There's a harrier of the Floret Folk, and an arbutus. Mabonnyn and Corb. They hung with us to the bitter end, to the Chirax building, and they're probably locked up in here somewhere, too."

"What of the harrier's steed?" my mother asked.

I shook my head. "Gern sacrificed herself to save Mabonnyn when a virus-infected roridula attacked us."

My mother was respectfully silent for a few paces. "The Floret Folk, and their companions, aspire to *plukustede*," she offered at last. "Did I ever teach you the term?"

"Something like a battlefield that's also close to home. Like fighting the enemy at the gates."

"It is that," my mother said, "but also a resting place, a final dwelling, because of duty fulfilled."

"Yeah, well, I take your point that not every denizen of the Deep Woods abnegated their duty, but the vast majority of them did, including the Council of Ruis," I snapped. "And if they hadn't, maybe Gern wouldn't have… have had to…"

"Maybe," my mother agreed quietly. She reached into a pocket of her dress and took out a pinch of seeds, placing them delicately on her tongue. We walked on, looping through the capricious turns of the corridor, until the corridor ended. The arched walls fell away, and the rudimentary agglomeration of protein surfaces beneath our feet continued, becoming a bridge that stretched away and forked out in eskers and flumes and yaws as far as we could see. The open space we had entered was astronomical, especially compared to the cramped confines of the cell I had awakened in and the passageway we had been escorted through. The branching helical walkways met up in nodes at outlying locations above us and below us and to either side, huge semi-flattened orbs and elongated trapezoid footballs and other globular masses, each one at least as big as a good-sized barn, some the size of battleships. Almost every surface was white, not bright or gleaming but flatly devoid of coloration. Yet every so often an unexpected patch of blue or red or green stood out, with no pattern or reasoning that made itself apparent to me. The helices and spheroids extended and multiplied until their shapes and edges became indistinct and merged into a pallid firmament, dotted with blue, red and green stars.

The two virus creatures continued to march my mother and me along the tributary spans, until we came to a colossal structure with a footprint as big as a pro football stadium. The face of it was hexagonal, and a circlet with a serrated outward edge floated around it like a demonic planetary ring. The only feature in the vast six-sided edifice was an aperture, a beveled teardrop-shaped portal, absurdly small compared to the looming mass of the structure. Still, it was large enough to allow the four of us to pass through and enter the stronghold of the viruses.

Chapter Twelve: Ultimatum

Mᴏʀᴇ ᴏꜰ ᴛʜᴇ virus creatures awaited us within the stronghold, ranging all around its inner surface. The interior was hollow, the vaulting planes of its architecture featureless except for occasional bulges and other irregularities. The virus creatures observed us from vantage points on outcroppings and ridges just barely large enough to stand upon. I was watching one of the creatures, trying to discern anything at all useful, whether the creature was bored or bloodthirsty, attending whatever was about to unfold out of communal obligation or any deeper self-interest. But the anthropomorphic virus was as inscrutable as carved stone, like a statue that had only been granted a crude and primitive human likeness to begin with, and then had been abraded over millennia to mere suggestion. I stared nonetheless, unable to even imagine how my mother had intended to go about determining if these approximations of life had souls capable of enlightenment. And as I stared, a second virus creature appeared beside the object of my gaze. The creature extruded itself out of the very surface of the angled wall, or pitched roof, depending on how you interpreted the oblique geometry of the stronghold. The building and the creature were, after all, made of the same colorless, variegated lipid sheath. It was as if the stronghold were choosing to manifest in part as individual entities. For all I knew, that was objectively the case. Maybe the virus creatures were all that existed within their own realm, and the topography of paths and buildings was a reconfiguration of those creatures into scenery that could accommodate forms like my mother and me. Maybe the Oblate was all that existed, a self-aware expanse, and the creatures it had spawned were a reconfiguration of the place into beings that could interact with my mother and me.

The walkway that had conveyed us through the door continued, seemingly unsupported, to a white disc-shaped platform in the center of the cavernous space. The virus creature ahead of us guided us onward, pausing when we reached the center of the disc and looking back over its shoulder, as if to indicate that we should remain there. The creature then took up a station on the perimeter of the disc. I looked back at our other guard, and was unsurprised to see that there were now three virus creatures where there had been one, all identical, and similarly fanning out around the edge of the platform.

I also saw, beyond the virus creatures positioned on the disc, yet another pair proceeding up the walkway, with Mabonnyn between them. The virus creature duo had manifested at the same scale as the woodlander, standing only a foot and a half tall. The harrier was brought to the middle of the disc with us; Mabonnyn greeted my mother by silently dropping to one knee, head bowed. She bent at the waist to touch the back of Mabonnyn's head. Soon a new pair of virus creatures was escorting Phoebe into the stronghold and up the walkway to the central disc. She and my mother embraced, and I thought I heard my mother whispering into Phoebe's ear, but couldn't make out the words. Juvie was brought in next, with only a single virus creature escort. I wondered if Juvie would on some level be insulted that he merited half as much guarding as Mabonnyn or Phoebe, and I also wondered if the virus creatures weren't seriously underestimating him. Juvie saw my mother and smiled in obvious relief. Throughout our whole bizarre quest, trekking in and out of the Deep Woods, breaking and entering at Chirax and getting abducted into the Oblate ourselves, Juvie had never expressed any doubt, but clearly he hadn't known deep down if we would ever see my mother again, until that very moment. Finally, Corb was ushered up the walkway by more virus creatures, and we were all together again.

The virus creatures positioned themselves shoulder to shoulder all around the outer edge of the disc, forming a kind of living balustrade, or a giant set of white spikes lining the open jaws of a bear trap. It did feel more than a little bit like we were about to be eaten, consumed and subsumed by the fractal facets of the Oblate. And sure enough, without warning or any outward sign of communication, the teeth snapped closed on us. Corb, Juvie, Phoebe, Mabonnyn and I were grabbed by the arms, a pair of virus creatures for each of us, two pairs in Corb's case. Their grips were not painful, at least not intentionally, but they were as unyielding as steel shackles. The virus creatures dragged us all backwards, so that we were arrayed along one half of the disc's perimeter, leaving my mother isolated in the center.

One of the virus creatures broke the circle by stepping forward. "You see we now have your offspring," the creature said. "You will teach us what we require, or they will all face the consequences of your refusal. Their suffering will belong to you, and will be enacted here, for you to witness."

I wondered for a moment if the virus creatures had managed to take the measure of Foltchain of the Oak after all. They could have been trying to get leverage on my mother by threatening to hunt me down and kill me all along, but my mother was always sanguine about death, since to her it was a natural part of life. Still, there was a difference between accepting the inevitability of mortality, as an abstract concept, and being forced to watch torture conducted in such a way as to maximize the excruciating pain inflicted. My mother wasn't made of stone.

She took a step toward the virus creature, a small movement which didn't do much to change their relative positions, yet nonetheless interposed her between us and the virus creature, really between us and all of them. I knew that wasn't physically possible, given that the creatures had us surrounded, but that was one of my mother's many gifts, her ability to stand taller than her bodily stature, to be heard louder than the volume of her voice, to exert influence so profound that it felt like a fundamental force of the universe. For a long time, as a child, I had taken this as a foundational reality of existence. Then for a time after that I had concluded it must have been purely subjective in my eyes and ears, some variation on the way all children hold their parents in awe. Eventually I came around again; it wasn't just me, it wasn't just our relationship, it was a virtue of every element of the historic enlightenment that Foltchain lived with and embodied. Even here, in a micro-universe that knew nothing of the druidic tradition from the Deep Woods, her absolute mastery was as undeniable as if she had a shining diadem on her head. "You offer me only the two choices, then?" my mother asked. She held out her hands, palms up, one higher than the other. "On the one scale, revelation of the great secrets and mysteries entrusted to my bloodline. On the other," she raised one hand and lowered the other, "death?"

"Yes," the virus creature said.

"Only two, and no other?" my mother asked.

"Yes," the virus creature repeated in an impatient hiss. "Make your choice. Now."

"I choose death," my mother said, "but ask that you make it my own."

No one said a word. Mabonnyn's vow of silence held, and everyone else was too stunned to react, including me, and including the virus creatures, who apparently hadn't completely decoded my mother after all. The imposing inner space of the stronghold was eerily quiet for a few moments, until finally the lone virus creature separate from the ring said, "This is a trick. You cannot be killed."

"Not without my consent," my mother conceded. "That is my choice to make."

"Answer what we ask!" the virus creature said. "Spare yourself and your offspring! Give us the knowledge we require!"

"I cannot," my mother shook her head. "It is not that I choose not to impart my knowledge, not that I will not or believe I should not. It cannot be done. It is beyond me. And since I am incapable of giving the one thing that would ransom those who sought me out, I may only offer an alternative. I may offer myself to fulfill your demands."

"Your death fulfills nothing," the virus creature said.

"There is a meta-substance of life," my mother said, "which is a physical part of me. It flows through my veins and abides in every fiber of my being. That is the birthright of my lineage. It transcends knowledge, transcends questions and answers and teaching and understanding, and yet makes them all possible. And you lack that essential fuel of enlightenment. When I offer you my death, I offer you that which animates my life. I bequeath it to you. Take it and make it your own, if you can. Then you may be able to find your answers."

The virus creature considered her words, probably looking for the hidden ploy, the dagger that would stab them in the back. But it wasn't subterfuge, I was sure of it. My mother meant every word she said.

"We accept," the virus creature said.

"No!" Juvie roared, throwing himself forward against the grips of the two virus creatures restraining him. He flailed and twisted and got one of his arms free, then leaned toward the creature still holding him and braced himself to deliver a ferocious kick at the midsection of the creature he had slipped away from. His boot connected and the virus creature staggered back, but only a single step. I was straining against the pale, febrile fingers encircling my arms, and I could see Phoebe and Corb and Mabonnyn making similar attempts to escape, but Juvie's outburst had put the rest of the virus creatures on high alert and none of them were likely to be caught off guard. The twin cinctures at my elbows were unyielding, and steadily increasing their pressure. My joints would fracture before I came close to breaking away. The virus creature Juvie had kicked swiped at Juvie's head, connecting a punishing backhand that made Juvie's knees buckle.

"Stop," my mother said, not particularly forcefully, but once again her influence was undeniable. I felt the grips of the virus creatures loosen just a little, even as I relaxed back off the balls of my feet. Juvie was spared any further physical punishment, with his attendant creature simply resuming its station beside him. My mother turned back to the virus creature with whom she had negotiated her choice. "What comes next may be easier if you were to release the five of them now."

The virus creature made a scoffing noise. "They will be released, but not until after you have fulfilled your promise."

"Then at least allow me to say goodbye to each of them," my mother said, and the virus creature offered no objection. My mother crossed the distance between herself and Juvie and laid her hands on his shoulders. "Juvenal," she said. "For as long as you and Kellan have known each other, you have been a brother to him. And for that, you have been like a son to me. Don't stop looking out for him." Juvie blinked back tears, and my mother leaned in and kissed him on the mouth, lingering for a poignant moment with their lips pressed together. When she drew back, Juvie looked calmer.

She went to Phoebe next, and once again rested hands upon shoulders. "My sweet Phoebe," my mother said. "Watching you flourish so vibrantly and so quickly has been my delight. I cannot express in the time I have now how proud of you I am. I hope I have given you some idea through all the moments before this one."

Phoebe nodded. "You have," she said, her whispered voice breaking.

My mother smiled wistfully. "Give my love to Tithorea," she said, and kissed Phoebe, exactly as gently yet adamantly as she had kissed Juvie.

Then my mother approached Mabonnyn and knelt before the harrier. "The Floret Folk have no shortage of courage," she said. "And none need look any further than their champion. I am so sorry for the losses you suffered in coming here, Mabonnyn. They were not in vain." She kissed two of her fingertips and pressed them to Mabonnyn's tiny mouth, smearing a bit of the black ashes on the harrier's face.

Corb's benediction came next. My mother couldn't reach his shoulders, but Corb stretched and curved his pliant body so that he and my mother were eye to eye, and she laid her hands on the sides of his face. "Corb, mighty arbutus," my mother said. "You joined willingly a cause which you knew nothing of before it crossed your path. Your deeds will stand tall and proud in the songs of the Deep Woods forevermore." She kissed him.

Finally she came to me. "Kellan," she said. And then she paused, holding her breath with the slightest hint of uncertainty in her eyes. "All of the things I said to each of your companions, I could say to you, and mean every word from the very roots of my heart."

"I know," I said, also meaning it from the roots of my heart.

"Be open," my mother said, "to all things that come to you." She gave me a kiss that tasted of bitter fruit and the piquant aroma of scorched wood exposed when lightning strikes a tree. She hesitated again before leaning over my shoulder to whisper in my ear, "You are no black walnut tree."

She backed away and turned toward the virus

creature. She bowed her head in submission. The virus creature stared at her, but to be fair, we were all staring at her, wondering if she would speak any final words, if she would just lay down and expire, if she was waiting for the virus creature to strike some sacrificial blow.

Mabonnyn jumped straight up in the air. The sudden burst of motion surprised everyone, none more than the two small virus creatures still holding the harrier's arms. The creatures were lifted off the platform as Mabonnyn was propelled ten, twenty, thirty feet over our heads in one bound. At the apex of the ascent, Mabonnyn kicked out with both legs, the double blows striking each of attendant creatures in the elbow hard enough to blow the joints apart. The virus creatures fell away, beyond the edge of the platform down into the lower reaches of the stronghold, while Mabonnyn managed a midair jackknife followed by a dive, landing in a battle-ready crouch beside my mother's feet.

The platform erupted into utter bedlam, as several of the virus creatures rushed in from the perimeter and charged at Mabonnyn. In the same instant, Corb rapidly expanded, easily throwing off the virus creatures holding his tacky arms. The arbutus didn't simply stretch taller and longer-limbed with every inch of length gained offset by attenuation. Corb swelled into an even more gargantuan version of himself, adding mass in every dimension. More of the virus creatures piled onto him, but Corb's swinging fists, now enormous boulders of semi-solid pitch, scattered his attackers in all directions. The virus creatures that came at him from behind found that their fiercest blows did nothing more than indent puckered grooves in Corb's substance, marks which filled themselves in after a moment or two.

Phoebe wasn't enlarging on the same scale as Corb, but she was generating new matter as well, in the form of shoots and tendrils sprouting from her flesh and quickly growing into branches and vines. A wreath of foliage and blossoms crowned her and covered her hair as she lashed at the virus creatures nearest to her. One of the creatures was ensnared in a tight coil of green wood and leaves, then whipped aside with such force that the creature spun like a top off the edge of the platform.

Juvie still looked exactly the same, but jerked both of his arms free from the virus creatures on either side of him. The one that had struck him earlier reared back and delivered a thrust of its razor-sharp fingers that should have opened Juvie's throat in a tumult of gore. The jagged digits rebounded off Juvie's skin instead. Juvie grinned maniacally and tackled the virus creature to the platform. The creature flailed at Juvie, and its counterpart hacked and chopped at Juvie's back from above, but Juvie ignored both assaults, neither of which had any visible effect. He wrestled the virus creature to the edge of the platform and threw it over, then rolled onto his back, swept the legs out from under the other virus creature, and knocked it down to follow.

Mabonnyn caromed from foe to foe like a tiny ninja, Corb bulldozed across the platform, Phoebe stormed through knots of virus creatures like the wrath of the Deep Woods incarnate, and Juvie picked off unwary opponents at will, while my mother stood calmly in the heart of chaos, and I waited on the periphery. I would have been happy to wade into the fray with my newly acquired superpowers like photosynthetic laser vision and dragonfly speed. I wouldn't even have minded if my head had transformed into an oversized Venus flytrap. But nothing about me, inside or out, had changed, not that I could detect, not even the slightest tingle in my fingertips, let alone the metamorphoses the others had demonstrated.

Which was no excuse not to join in, I belatedly realized. Juvie was making good use of the fact that the virus creatures tended to ignore him in favor of the flashier displays of brawn and potency Phoebe, Corb and Mabonnyn were using to cut a swathe through their ranks, and I decided to exploit the same blind spot. I rushed at the closest virus creature as it began to climb up the back of Corb's mammoth leg. Maybe the virus creature was going to try to find a more vulnerable spot to attack around Corb's head, or maybe it had no particular strategy in mind other than weighing down the titanic arbutus if enough other virus creatures joined it hanging off Corb's shoulders, but it never had a chance to follow through either way. I locked the virus creature in a full nelson and yanked it off Corb's lower leg. The virus creature's body squirmed against mine, heat radiating through the jagged planes of its skin. I twisted around, let go of the virus creature's neck and kicked it away. It clawed at me, drawing blood from a gash on the inner part of my forearm.

My arm stung like it had been bitten by a dozen poisonous snakes, but I returned my attention to the mass of virus creatures behind me. Too many to count had been knocked off the platform, yet the disc still swarmed with them. In fact, the disc was shrinking like melting wax, with new virus creatures rising up out of the mosaic surface, almost all of them focused on rushing the titanic arbutus wreaking havoc in their midst. It still seemed improbable that the creatures could do any real damage to Corb in his current state, but at the same time his ability to mete out physical punishment with his newly acquired stature and massive strength was dependent on little things like a stable surface to stand on. If the platform continued to reconfigure into virus creatures until there was no platform left, Corb would simply tumble down to the lower reaches of the stronghold.

I glanced down and realized that the situation was even more precarious. The lower reaches of the stronghold were disintegrating even more rapidly than the platform, reconstituting the pale lipid planes into hundreds of virus creatures scrambling insect-like up the sides of the structure, a color-leached version of a nature film showing leafcutter ants at work. If Corb fell, he would keep falling through that endless void of space for who knew how long.

All well and good that my friends were putting up a good fight but there was no endpoint, no exit strategy. For the moment the virus creatures were confused by the unexpected turn of events, but the element of surprise had already been expended. The virus creatures outnumbered us and had us surrounded, this physical manifestation of reality was their home turf and was literally composed of them, and they of it, and we couldn't get away. We could only die trying.

A virus creature grabbed me from behind, with an arm across the front of my throat that felt like a monstrous jagged claw poised to decapitate me in a single snap. I tucked my chin against my chest, growling at the scraping pain of the edges of the creature's arm along my face, and stepped back while bending at the waist to throw my attacker over my shoulder. It didn't work, and the virus creature didn't so much as budge. With my head still lowered I could see behind me, where one of the virus creature's legs was effectively fused to the platform, making the surface I stood on and the creature grappling me one continuous entity.

The virus creature wrenched me upright again. The platform was no longer a disc but a zigzagging beam jutting out into empty space in defiance of physics. The narrow strip of whitish mosaic was barely wide enough for Corb to balance on, even with his sticky feet wrapped gelatinously around it. Several virus creatures had merged into one another to form a giant with equivalent mass to Corb, and traded blows with the arbutus like the weirdest kaiju movie ever, but that tactical adaptation was an isolated development. Phoebe and Juvie and Mabonnyn continued brawling around the monstrous legs with human-sized and pixie-sized virus creatures, none of whom seemed able or willing to adjust to the sudden emergence of their captives' new abilities. I had thought the virus creatures must be connected in some kind of hivemind, but the disparity in their reactions to the unexpected put the lie to that. Unless the hivemind was so primitive that it could only focus on and solve one problem at a time.

I might have found out eventually whether the virus creatures could solve the Dryad Dilemma or the Floret Folk Flummox, if not for one misstep, as Juvie tried to shift his weight onto his back foot and instead found only empty space at his heel. Mabonnyn was small enough, not to mention still bouncing around like a jumping jack so much, that the dissolving of the platform was no hazard at all. Phoebe was maintaining her footing and balance much like Corb was, with sinuous green tendrils unfurling from her feet and ankles and vining around the beam. But Juvie was not so lucky, and he fell backwards, flailing. Corb reached out to catch Juvie before he plummeted out of the stronghold and into the endless expanse of the Oblate, but in doing so diverted his attention from the oversized virus creature for a moment, long enough for the creature to delivering a punishing hammerfall of jagged fists that sent the arbutus reeling. In the blink of an eye Corb was hanging by his feet, upside down below the beam, with Juvie cradled in one enormous hand.

And the next thing I knew my mother was being thrown off the beam as well. Corb caught her in mid-fall, easily, but Phoebe was already lurching defensively towards the edge of the beam as well, and before her shoots could find purchase again she, too, was knocked out into open space. Everything was happening too fast for me to tell if the virus creatures were learning and exploiting or simply benefiting from random chance, and all the while I was trying desperately but futilely to escape the grip of the virus creature whose arm remained clamped painfully around my neck. One second it felt like a doomed yet valiant last stand, and the next Mabonnyn finally came to rest just in front of Corb's elongated toes, looking utterly exhausted and surrounded by virus creatures ahead and behind, and the only thing that stopped the pale horde from finishing the harrier off then and there was the bellow of *STOP!* from the virus creature that had me in a headlock.

The tableau froze. The virus creature released my neck and pushed me forward. I caught myself after an awkward step and turned around to face the creature. I looked into its eyes and tried to make the determination I had made so many times before when encountering the denizens of the Deep Woods, to ascertain if there was any spark of a sentient soul or the affectless instinct of an animal or the totally unthinking manifestation of a force of nature. The problem was that the virus creature didn't truly have sight organs, only eye-shaped approximations. It was the same problem that had dogged me this entire time: I didn't know what I was dealing with, because it was so different from everything I had ever run into before, everything I thought I knew about life and reality and the hidden things just off the beaten path. Even now, face to face with the things that had kidnapped my mother and scourged along after me ever since, I didn't understand them or know anything about them beyond some superficial observations, could barely comprehend what they were all about.

And to make matters worse, I didn't know what I was supposed to do. My mother had taken the lead while my head was spinning, and I had let her, but now she and everyone else was at the mercy of the viral collective while I faced off with the closest thing the creatures had to a leader. I was the last one standing, and I was the worst possible choice for that position. I couldn't make sense of how we had even gotten to this point, from my mother brokering some kind of deal that the virus creatures didn't seem to fully understand but were inclined to accept because from the beginning they had assumed the druid priestess knew more than they did, to a violent clash in which everyone but me exceeded their usual capabilities and yet ultimately amounted to no more than a brief scuffle we couldn't possibly help but lose. Somewhere in the course of my mother accepting her own fate and saying goodbye to each of us and seeking our acceptance, everything had gone crazy…

Unless everything had gone exactly according to plan.

"Do you accept our surrender?" I asked the virus creature.

"You are in no position to offer anything," the virus creature said.

"Wrong," I shook my head. "I am everything

that Foltchain of the Oak offered you, and more. I am her legate. The last in line of the children of the druids, and so their birthright is my birthright. I offer you Kellan of the Derryth." I held my arms out, low and with palms upturned.

For a moment I wasn't sure if the virus creatures could reconcile the seeming contradiction. Ever since they had abducted my mother, she had been as imperturbable as only a nigh-immortal being could be. And also since that moment, I had been volatile in equal and opposite measure. She had offered her life but the virus creatures hadn't known how to kill her. They'd come close to killing me half a dozen times over. And yet our common bloodline was a given, and everything I'd said about my inheritance was rooted in truth. If my death could provide them everything hers could, if the only difference between my mother and me was that she had elevated herself beyond vulnerability in a way that I had not, then I must be the key the virus creatures were looking for.

The creature opposite me reached out with a ghastly hand that distorted into something more like a mouth, an orifice surrounded by spikes. It met my outstretched palm and I felt the barbs bite into my flesh like thorns. Then from the opening in the virus creature's appendage a wiry filament extended, snaking under my skin and into my arm, piercing muscle and scratching along bone but ultimately probing for some more subtle channel within me. It made me want to scream, both in horror and in pain, but I ground my teeth together and scowled into the nothingness of the virus creature's face.

It quickly became as hard to breathe as if I were trying to run up the side of a mountain with a refrigerator strapped to my back. I flashed hot and cold. I don't know how much time passed. It might have been a scant handful of seconds that felt like hours, or hours that flew by between the thunderclap beats of my racing heart. All I knew was that, even with dark spots blossoming larger and larger around the edges of my vision, I was locked in a mortal staring contest with an invasive machine and, finally, the machine blinked. The virus creature let go of my hand, which was painted scarlet with blood. I wiped my palm down my leg and looked again, but couldn't see any wounds at all.

The virus creature reconfigured into something more spherical, its head flattening and midsection expanding while the arms melted into the central mass and the legs retracted. It looked more like something that was happening to the virus creature, directed by some outsized external force, than something the creature was accomplishing of its own volition, particularly once it became an orb-shaped inanimate object.

I looked back over my shoulder and saw the rest of the virus creatures without exception undergoing similar transformations. That was the good news. The bad news was that the architecture of the stronghold was undergoing similar alterations, slowly separating into floating lipid balloons. I ran to the pile of globs that had been virus creatures and pushed them off the beam, uncovering Mabonnyn buried below. I scooped the harrier up in one arm and leaned over the edge of the beam, calling out to Corb, "Can you make your way back to the entrance?"

Corb said nothing but answered by moving down the length of the beam, still upside down and suspended beneath the precarious structure by his feet. I matched the inverted arbutus's pace as best I could and met him at the stronghold's portal. Corb reached up with my mother in hand and deposited her next to me. Juvie and Phoebe followed, both looking completely wrung out, but my mother was there to help usher them out of the stronghold. Corb pulled himself up to the portal, looking significantly smaller than he had been during the pitched battle with the virus creatures, and as his feet let go of the beam the beam let go of the portal, fragmenting into a string of beveled beads. Corb and I hustled out together.

The six of us barreled down the mosaic pathway as fast as we could, which given the pervasive injuries and fatigue affecting us all to one extent or another, was on pace with a vigorous geriatric power walk. The arching walkway swayed ominously and a loud crack sounded behind us, as the entire stronghold came unmoored and spun away like a ringed planet. I urged the others forward but a moment later a broad span of the walkway similarly fell to pieces, leaving us stranded.

We all looked around desperately for another more continuous path we might try to jump to. Juvie and I glanced at each other and I had the distinct sense that we both realized the same thing: none of us knew where we were supposed to be running to. The entire Oblate was crumbling around us, and we needed to find the exit. Not only did we not know where said exit was, we didn't even know if said exit existed in any form that would be recognizable or physically useful to us. And the only creatures who might have that knowledge had all turned into inert white buckyballs.

"Well this sucks," Juvie said.

I felt a tug at my neck. Mabonnyn's eyes were open, but didn't meet mine. The harrier was looking at my chest while pulling down on the front of my shirt. I moved my hand there and felt the outline of the lare medallion that Ajax Masterson had insisted on giving me. I had forgotten I was wearing it. I pulled out the medallion and squeezed it tight, feeling the outline of the reptilian hearth spirit on its face. I knew that the chances of the medallion actually being an authentic object of power were slim, but a slim chance was better than none. Maybe Ajax was the proverbial broken clock, and maybe every once in a long, long while he'd be right about something. Maybe he was due. I thought about getting out of the Oblate, but quickly realized that was a little abstract. The walkway buckled beneath my feet. A fissure opened up right in front of me, with Juvie and Mabonnyn and me on one side, my mother and Phoebe and Corb on the other. The tether to the latticework of paths snapped and we all plunged downward. I thought about falling out of a tree behind my mother's cottage. I thought about her gathering me up and taking care of me after I fell. And once more everything went black.

I never quite lost consciousness that time. I almost thought that I had, because for a few disorienting seconds there was a dreamlike quality to what little my brain was able to process happening all around me. But it was dreamlike in more of a poetic sense than in resembling anything that unfolded in my mind during REM sleep: my vision filled with darkly inverted colors like negative fluorescents blooming one out of the other out of another, a sense of dislocation as if gravity and air pressure and ambient temperature all ceased to exist between one instant the next, then reasserted themselves. But through it all I never felt confused or forgot how I had gotten myself into a vortex nullifying every bit of matter and energy around me. I knew there were two possibilities, that either this was what the final passage of life into death felt like, or the lare medallion was working its magic to bring me home.

I skidded back into reality in the entryway to my mother's cottage, with my back against the solid surface of her front door, with a high-pitched ringing in my ears and some residual floaters in my eyes that I tried furiously to blink away. It was all a bit on the nose, but magic is like that sometimes. Everyone else was sprawled across the scuffed hardwood floor, too. My mother was rubbing her eyes, but Juvie, Phoebe, Mabonnyn and Corb all looked unconscious. My mother lowered her hand, caught my line of sight, and said, "Come and help me move them."

I got to my feet and assisted my mother in carrying Juvie over to her couch. He remained a couple hundred pounds of dead weight throughout the transfer. We picked up Phoebe and carried her to my mother's bed, then I went back for Mabonnyn and laid him next to Phoebe. When I returned to the entryway I found my mother looking down at Corb; she glanced at me and said, "I think he's fine where he is, for now. Don't you?"

"Sure," I shrugged. "Is he… are they all going to be okay?"

"No doubt," my mother nodded. "They need a good amount of rest to recover their strength, but that's already underway."

"Should I be expecting to crash soon?" I asked.

"Not like this," my mother said.

"So, what exactly happened back there?" I asked.

"Let's sit and talk and have something to eat," she said. I followed her to the kitchen and sat at her table. She went to a cupboard, pulled out a small basket and set it on the table. It was filled with dried jujube fruits, red and wrinkly. My mother took a bite of one of the fruits, and I followed suit. "I think it's going to be some time before we know exactly what happened in the Oblate," my mother said. "But I suspect it was something quite unprecedented."

"You think?" I asked, raising an eyebrow.

My mother smiled. "Not just for us," she said. "I think the consequences will be much more far-reaching than our lifetimes."

I considered that for a moment. "Before today I would have said there wasn't much that reaches farther than your lifetime, mom," I said. "Were you really going to die for those creatures?"

"If it had come to that, yes," my mother said.

Then she smiled slyly. "I didn't believe it would come to that. Or so I hoped, at least."

"But you said you would," I said. "And the viruses believed you. So you got them to let their guard down, and then they let you get close to each of us."

My mother nodded.

"After you had already somehow gotten them to give you the ingredients for concoctions?"

Another nod. "It never occurred to them that that was what I was doing. They thought I was merely eating for sustenance. The entire concept of transformation is alien to them. They understand replication, and they understand destruction. Taking disparate elements, combining them, producing something new… it's all quite beyond their ken."

"But that's one of the tenets of druidism," I said. "Which is what they wanted you to teach them."

"And which is why it was such a conundrum," my mother said.

"So they brought you a bunch of reactive plant stuff, because you said you would eat it."

"I did eat it."

"Right but you didn't fully digest it," I said. My mother had such a harmonious relationship with living things, the mutualism extended all the way to her personal microbiota. If need be her stomach could serve as an alchemist's flask. It was one of those things I understood an insignificant sliver of, something I might have learned to do for myself if I had kept with the devoted druid lifestyle for another two or three hundred years. "You made concoctions and coughed them up and passed them into everyone else's mouths when you kissed them goodbye. So they all got superpowers just in time to pre-empt your ritual self-sacrifice and confuse the hell out of the viruses."

"Everyone else?" my mother asked.

"Yeah, you were pretty much tapped out by the time you got to me, right?"

"Why do you think that?"

"Because I wasn't suddenly hypercharged or bullet-proof or giant-sized," I pointed out.

My mother sighed. "No, not giant-sized."

"But that was all part of the plan, right?" I asked. "I mean, after you, they thought I was the next biggest threat, and they thought the others were just tagging along after me. That was the best way to catch them off-guard, wasn't it?"

"Was it?" my mother turned the question around.

"I don't know," I admitted. "What would you have done if the viruses hadn't agreed to let you say goodbye to everyone? If they had just immediately…"

"Killed me?" my mother asked. "I would have allowed it to happen, for all of your sakes."

"You really trusted them to let us all go after you made your sacrifice?"

"Not at all," my mother said. "The virus creatures would have penetrated my body…"

"Mom," I groaned.

"At a cellular level," my mother chided me. "They would have dissolved inside me, spliced their genetic material into mine, gleaned from it what they could, reassembled themselves, and started the whole cycle over again, as many times as they could until they were enough like me that they could find their own paths of harmony, become a new breed of druid priests and priestesses."

"That sounds like something you could have let them do as soon as they kidnapped you," I pointed out. "Without having to die, either."

My mother shook her head. "My body would never allow it so long as I was alive," she said. "The only opportunity the virus creatures could possibly have had was literally over my dead body."

"And you thought they'd be enlightened enough after that to set us free and send us home?" I asked.

"No," my mother said. "What I just described was a combination of what they would have tried and the outcome they would have wanted. What really would have happened was a lethal genetic catastrophe. The virus creatures would not have been able to handle the slightest reassortment of my makeup into their own. The Oblate would have self-destructed."

"The Oblate pretty much did self-destruct," I said, "and we barely made it out of there at all. The only difference between the two scenarios is that in one you die and the other you live. Even with the concoctions introducing some unknowns and leveling the field a bit, you still risked everybody's life to save your own. That... doesn't seem like you."

"That wasn't the only difference," my mother said. "Kellan, you asked me why I continue to live out my calling as I do, without reciprocity, without appreciation or even acknowledgement."

"I asked you why you bother helping those who can't be bothered to help you," I corrected her.

"I think you already know the answer."

"Other than being stuck in a centuries-old rut?" I asked. My mother only stared back at me mildly, and I relented. "It's the right thing to do, whether anybody else recognizes that or not. You do good and you make the world a better place, I know, I know."

"Not everything I do makes the world a better place," my mother said. "And truly, I don't always know whether any given action will make a difference or not. All I can do is try, and do what I hope is best, and clear a little more of the path for others whenever I can."

"So you homebrewed your gut concoctions, revved everybody up, and pulled the rug out from under the viruses before destroying them… what, to teach me something?"

"No."

"What other good could it have…?" I trailed off as the answer occurred to me. "You did it for the viruses. They're not destroyed?"

"They're dormant," my mother said. "I don't know for how long, and I don't know what they will be like when they come out of it, if they ever do. But there's a chance that they may have evolved by then into something more receptive to learning a path."

"Because they tried to synthesize something out of me rather than you," I said.

"It had to be you, Kellan," my mother said.

"Only you were strong enough to not only survive the attachment but push back on it, and all without overwhelming and annihilating the virus creatures."

"Why not just tell them that?"

"They wouldn't have believed me, would have thought it was a trick," my mother said. "They were single-mindedly focused on me, and they only saw you as a means of leverage to get what they wanted from me. I am sorry that I put all of you at risk, I would have avoided that, but it was a resort of desperation, the only way to reframe things in terms of survival, which the virus creatures would understand. Or so I hoped."

"Just like you hoped you were right about me being strong enough?"

"I never had any doubt about that," my mother said. "I hypercharged you, too, Kellan. I made you bulletproof. Your kiss didn't transform you into someone who could fight tooth and claw with the virus creatures, but it elevated your cellular resistance. Again."

"What is that supposed to mean?"

"Do you remember when you woke up in the Oblate, that I was singing to you?" my mother asked.

"Yeah," I said. "It was the same song you sang that winter I was sick, when I was little."

Foltchain of the Oak nodded. "That was the druid creation hymn. Do you know where it comes from?"

Weirdly, in all the time my mother had indoctrinated me in the ways of druidism, this particular tenet had never come up. "I'm gonna go out on a limb and say, from the dawn of time?"

"An understandable assumption," my mother chuckled. "But it is vital that you understand how wrong it is."

"Do tell."

"Our creation hymn, all myths of biogenesis, human lore of any kind, doesn't come from the beginning itself. It's all invention. It's a way for humans to understand that which they do not remember, cannot remember because they did not witness it themselves."

"Right."

"By the same token, druidism or any other path of harmony is an act of creation that comes from trying to retrace old patterns that cannot be seen any more, trying to remember that which was never really known. Over time the repetition of the patterns imbues them with power, profound power, such that even an imagined version of the creation can have a tangible and lasting impact in differentiating sickness from health, life from death."

"Tangible and lasting," I repeated. "So when you reached for that power, when I was little and sick, you didn't just cure me, you immunized me?"

My mother nodded. "You have been safeguarded against all manner of sickness ever since. And it took only a drop or two of concoction to elevate that even further, at the proper moment, to counteract anything the viruses might do to you."

"Well I appreciate the backstory," I said, "but I don't really get what's so important about it."

"The importance is more to the viruses than to you," my mother said. "I could not teach them druidism, not mine and not a new version of their own. Every way along the path of harmony must be discovered, beginning with the reconstruction of the creation story."

"Which the viruses are incapable of," I said, finally grasping it. "They're so new, they jumped up so fast into sentience that they actually do remember their own creation, the emergence of the Oblate, everything. It's not a mystery to them so there's no power in seeking the pattern."

My mother inclined her head, and I saw the barest hint of a proud gleam in her eyes. "They were incapable of it," my mother agreed, "but now they are dormant, and when they awaken, perhaps they will have forgotten. Perhaps they will have questions thrown into relief by their lack of answers, and they will take their first steps toward enlightenment. Only you could have made that possible, Kellan."

I held a dried jujube between my thumb and forefinger, and drummed it on the tabletop. "Because I'm not a full druid," I said. "I'm not a full anything. I'm not a denizen of the Deep Woods but I can't get completely clear of them, and I live in the modern world but I can't shut out the ancient ways. I don't fully belong to the past, I don't fully belong to right now, I don't belong anywhere. Don't get me wrong, I'm glad the fact that I'm a shiftless neither-nor helped us save the worlds from becoming virus fodder, but it feels like I've more or less peaked."

"Kellan," my mother said, lullaby soft. "None of that is true. Belonging isn't a function of the purity of your ancestry or any other token of exclusivity. Belonging need not be singular. That has always been your greatest gift, your ability to acclimate wherever you go. You belong in the shade of the trees, and you belong in the glare of noonday sun, and you belong in the halo of electric lights. You are sitting there trying to tell me that because you are at ease in more than one place you must be cast out from all places, but I know better. I didn't always. It took time for me to understand that your path, your weg, wound from sphere to sphere intersecting points unknown, and yet you would always make things right wherever your footsteps fell, near or far. You showed me that. See it yourself, for your own sake."

"I'll... try," I offered. It was a lot to take in.

"Above all, no matter which environment you inhabit, you are Kellan of the Oak. You are my son, and you have always been stronger and more capable than you know," my mother said. She nudged the basket of jujubes toward me. "Eat, eat."

"Why?" I asked, even as I popped a fruit in my mouth and chewed. "Is this some phytochemical follow up to fight off an elevated cellular resistance hangover? Or some pattern-tracing ritual to ensure all is right with the world?"

"Every once in a while, Kellan," my mother said with a smile, "we eat food simply because it tastes good."

Epilogue

WE ALL SPENT the night in my mother's cottage. In the morning everybody woke up and, just like my mother had said, we were all none the worse for wear. I made breakfast for everyone, a huge skillet of eggs scrambled with exotic, unidentifiable root vegetables and meat. Mom hauled out more fruit and bread from her seemingly bottomless cupboards, and made tea, of course. We ate like we hadn't seen food in a month, which was definitely how we felt.

Shortly after breakfast, Mabonnyn stood on a chair and spoke for the first time since we had collectively mourned Gern. "My duties are done, to my companion, to you Foltchain of the Derryth, and to you Kellan of the Derryth. I return now to the glades of my people."

I smiled at the honorific, but I was dead serious

as I answered, "I'm eternally in your debt, Mabonnyn of the Floret Folk, and eternally will be. I can never fully repay you, but if I can ever do anything for you or your people, you know where to find me."

Mabonnyn nodded at that. The harrier swept keen eyes around the table and added, "Should any of you ever find yourselves in the glades of the Floret Folk, know that you would be honored guests. Speak my name and you will be well-received."

"Appreciate it," Juvie said. "And I'm telling you right now I appreciate it because, if I have any say in it, I am pretty much never going to take you up on it."

We all walked out my mother's back door and across the grass to the edge of the woods. My mother approached the oak tree and broke a small forked twig off a low branch. She pressed it between her palms for a few seconds, then handed it to Mabonnyn and said, "There are hidden paths in and out and around the Deep Woods which even the most renowned of the Floret Folk harriers may not be able to mark. Some of those are mine, and this will allow you to pluck them from among the leaf-shaded storey, and speed your way home."

Mabonnyn bowed deeply, then pivoted to Corb and said, "Will you join me for as long as our steps lead down the same path?"

Corb rumbled, "When redcombs captured me, they destroyed my home. No place left for my steps to lead."

"You may always find haven among my people," Mabonnyn said.

"Haven is not home," Corb replied.

Phoebe laid a hand on Corb's arm. "Homes can be made over in new places. Even in places others already call home. Sometimes especially there."

Corb said, "The Floret Folk surely have good home." He looked meaningfully at my mother. "This is good home, too. Much could be learned here, while learning to make new home."

"You flatter me," my mother said, though her tone sounded as though she were about to very gently and politely demur.

"I, for one, would sleep better at night knowing that you had a nine-foot arbutus for a roommate, mom," I said. "I don't think I can handle another rescue mission like that any time soon. Or ever."

"Perhaps I have lived alone too long, at that," my mother said. "I would be honored to open my home to you, Corb. Much could be learned from you, too, I am sure."

Satisfied at the conclusion reached, Mabonnyn turned and entered the woods with the twig held out like a dowsing rod. We watched the small form disappear behind the trunk of a beech, and fail to reappear, gone already into the selvage of the Deep Woods.

We went back inside, and Phoebe and Juvie insisted on clearing the breakfast table and scrubbing the dishes and pans. As they worked I tried to point out to my mother all of the things we had borrowed and subsequently lost when we had raided her home for supplies. She took it all in with an air of unbothered acquiescence, which under the circumstances of our unlikely escape made a certain amount of sense. In her room, she picked up a small porcelain jar, and when we returned to the kitchen, she handed it to Phoebe, who accepted it gratefully.

Juvie called an Uber and when the driver arrived, Phoebe, Juvie and I said our goodbyes to Corb and my mother and piled into the car. The driver was chatty but the three of us were fairly quiet for most of the ride, responding to the driver's questions with pleasantries and letting him do most of the talking. Once we arrived in the city, Juvie directed the driver to the side street where we had left his car. Juvie paid as we got out and switched cars.

It wasn't until I was walking through the front door of my apartment building that it occurred to me that there had been no discussion as to what order Juvie would drop us off. Juvie had simply started driving to my address and when we arrived I had said something vague about calling one or both of them later, and then Juvie had driven off with Phoebe.

I wasn't sure what to make of that but I was sure that I lacked the mental capacity to make anything of anything at the moment. I had slept soundly under my mother's roof, I had eaten well in her kitchen, and it was only midday, but my body still felt as if I owed it a crushing debt of sleep. I wasn't about to argue. I let myself into my apartment and headed straight to my bed, barely sparing a thought to whether or not any strange person or creature was lying in wait to welcome me home with unimaginable violence. No one was, or at least no one initiated any assault before I flopped onto my mattress and quickly sank into sleep. If any entity had attacked me afterwards, I wouldn't necessarily have noticed.

I did not call Juvie later. He called me, the following afternoon, after I had spent the bulk of the previous twenty-four hours sleeping with a brief interruption to stagger a circuit around my apartment from the bathroom, then to the kitchen where I gobbled down a block of cheese, a handful of wheat crackers and a takeout container of lo mein, then back to bed. When my ringing cellphone woke me up I was pleasantly surprised to feel more human and well-rested than I had in months if not years.

"Good afternoon, sunshine," Juvie crooned into my ear. "Where you at?"

"Home," I said.

"Not for long," Juvie said. "Come meet me at that diner."

"What day is it?" I asked.

"It's the day I gotta take off, brother," Juvie said, "so come and grab a bite with me so I can say goodbye in person."

Fifteen minutes later Juvie and I were right where we had been when his ill-fated visit had begun, in the same greasy spoon, sitting in the exact same seats and the exact same table, no less. "Sorry for being such a crap host," I offered.

Juvie waved it away. "Totally not your fault. If you came to visit me, and you absolutely need to do that sometime soon, you know."

"I know. I will."

"Just saying, you come and visit me and some family emergency comes up on my end, I'd deal with that, too. And I know you'd understand, and help out any way you could," Juvie said, before stuffing another forkful into his mouth.

"Fair enough. So, without me to show you around, what'd you get up to last night?" I asked.

"Went out with Phoebe."

"Get out of here."

"Cannot tell a lie," Juvie shrugged.

"Well, but… how did that… happen?"

"You do remember how asking out a woman works, don't you?" Juvie waggled his fork at me.

"Theoretically."

"We dropped you off and then I drove her home," Juvie explained. "And I just asked her what she was doing later, and she said she didn't know, and I suggested we get dinner or something."

"And Phoebe agreed to this?"

"You ever know her to do something she wasn't agreeable to?" Juvie asked.

"Point taken. How did it go?"

"Good."

"How good?"

"Is there some objective measurement you're looking for? A number on a scale?"

"No."

"Surely you are not asking me to be indiscreet with a lady's affairs?" Juvie smirked.

"No, just… is there going to be a second date? Is this a thing now?"

Juvie shrugged. "We'll see. That's exactly what she and I said to each other, we'll see. Right now I gotta head home. Next time…" He left the possibilities unspoken. "Anything else?"

I had more questions, but I had a feeling I had already extracted as much concrete detail as Juvie was willing to part with, which wasn't much. "Say her name," I said.

"Why?"

"Humor me."

"Phoebe," Juvie said. He smiled as he said it, his eyes lighting up for a moment. It's an old trick, getting a read on one person's attitude towards another by having them say the person's name, just irrepressible human nature. I might try the same thing on Phoebe the next time I saw her, but if her reaction was anything like Juvie's, I was pretty sure a second date was inevitable.

We finished our meal and Juvie insisted on picking up the tab, and then we headed outside to his car. "All right, don't be a stranger," he said to me as we clapped our arms around each other's shoulders.

"I won't," I promised. He climbed into the driver's seat and I leaned down to the open window. "I'll try to get out to your neck of the woods before you come back to see Phoebe."

"That might not give you a very big window," he said.

"Well, either way, next time you're visiting I'll make sure that I really do clear my calendar. Things will be much more chill."

Juvie laughed. "Somehow I doubt that's in the cards. Later."

He pulled away and I watched him drive down

the street. I pulled out my phone to check the time, and realized I had time to pick up a latte for Irina down at the courthouse. My week off was over and it was time to get back to reality. Or one of my personal versions of it, at any rate.

ABOUT THE AUTHOR

DALE W GLASER is a lifelong collector, re-teller and occasional inventor of fantasy tales. He grew up right on the line between suburban cul-de-sacs and unspoiled wilderness, and has been known to get up to mischief in the woods late at night from time to time. He is a small town boy made good, the small town in question being one built entirely out of Tinker Toys and Lincoln Logs and populated by off-brand sword and sorcery action figures, alien finger puppets, and wind-up robots. He needs air, food, water and stories in order to survive, not necessarily in that order. His lifelong love of written words has manifested as a devotion to the English language almost exclusively, which is probably just as well because if he were to master any of the dead tongues that conceal ancient mysteries and invoke malevolent forces, we'd all be in trouble. He currently lives in Virginia with his wife, their three children, and a small menagerie of rescued pets. Follow his blog and find links to all his published works at https://dalewglaser.wordpress.com/